MIDLANDS

James Harris

Illustrated by Ke Zuo

CONTENTS

AUTHOR'S PREFACE

My youth was not a miserable one. Indeed, I was acutely aware even at the time that I should try and maximize the amount of revelry and pleasure while I was still in my best physical shape. And so, in the mid-2000s, I went to Berlin.

The other thing I was aware of early – and still am, to be fair – is that I wanted to write for a living. I have certainly been able to write. Yet this fully-formed desire, this clear sense of vocation and purpose, served to slightly isolate me as a young man, as I wanted to both have my experience and attempt to record it. From the age of 17, I would say I was seriously committed to the business of refracting my experiences through fiction, and perhaps that always put me at a slight remove from events, meaning I was both engaged in passing my most passionate and volatile years, while also trying to catch them via a developing fictional voice.

Then in my late-20s, a very strange thing began to happen: I began to have success in another artistic form. From the age of 17, I had been performing stand-up comedy, and in Germany ten years later my act began to unexpectedly blossom. I had about seventy minutes of comedy on expatriate life, a couple of wonky songs, and a secret weapon: I spoke fluent, idiomatic, and apparently Russian-accented German. It was a weapon my generally German audiences were not expecting, and hilarity often ensured. Over several years, I bounced all around Germany and Europe with my 'international act', often to enthused crowds – a fate I share with the protagonist of much of this novel, Stuart, although his life is different from mine in crucial respects.

Living the life of a performer while also being engaged in the project of writing realist fiction seemed to me, and still seems, a unique and productive combination. Developing this book, I wanted to give a reader a realistic experience of what it is like to be a working comedian – not, as is usual, 'a comedian who gets involved with a crime syndicate', or 'a comedian who finds a portal to another world', but a comedian who writes material and goes and does comedy gigs. That might mean passages of this novel seem lacking in incident, or are overly repetitive, but that's what the life of a road comic is like. And the reader should by no means feel that, for the people depicted in the story, it's an unhappy life. I don't look down for an instant on the showbusiness dreams of Stuart and Dougie, the main characters here; I share their excitement in getting to share their comedy, and I don't think performances have to be happening on a grand scale to be exciting and worthwhile. Dougie and Stuart are out there doing it, exactly where they should be and, to the extent they're doing it in a foreign country, they're serving as pioneers.

But the crucial difference between Stuart and I is that

younger one and they sat together and drank Club Maté like it was old times when they had sat together before shows eating pickles.

But the younger comedian became jealous. Jealousy is a poisonous thing for a comedian, because there are so many opportunities to put it into use. For the young man now came many nights of humiliation and rejection, came many nights of watching others - less talented, his heart cried - succeed. And eventually, finding himself not as successful as he wished in his island home, he began to travel again: to small new countries in the east, to small old countries in the west, to bars in mountains and theatres near the sea. He brought his smart shoes with him and did his little show, and after every performance he took off his smart shoes and put them back in his bag, and shook hands with his hosts and headed off again.

But all the time the older comedian did the same. Sometimes it seemed like that in every little town the younger comedian visited the older one had been there already. 'Yes,' his promoter would say, 'we had him here last month. That guy is so funny.' Or: 'We gave him four rounds of applause', and the younger comedian would bristle at this, never mind that he had got four too. It seemed that the older comedian had been everywhere first, and that every European town had a bollard of that face, that smirking little face of his old friend grown biggest rival.

You might ask at this point why the younger comedian got so jealous, why he wasn't satisfied at the evident acclaim he was himself receiving. That would show, however, your complete lack of understanding of the natures of comedians, who grow anxious if nobody laughs at the way they say 'Hello.'

One day in a restaurant eating dim sum in an industrial town in Europe's east, he saw a documentary about the coldest part of the world, the North Pole, where seals and Eskimos congregate, and a scheme was born within him. He would go there, or as near as he could! He would go there and do a show and would be for once in his life indisputably *first*! With that kind of publicity he would surely settle the rivalry once and for all.

It wasn't too hard to arrange – in the big city on the little island somebody always knew someone, even so far away. And soon he was booked, for two days at a trading settlement a few hundred miles from the most northerly point of the world. He even tried to learn a few phrases of the local Inuit dialect, North Baffin, in case some of the First Peoples of the area came to see him. He planned for the show for months, documenting his physical and comedic preparation in an increasingly popular blog, called, if you must know, 'Snow Jokes'.

It was summer when the younger comedian flew north. When he landed he took another flight and then finally sailed in a red-hulled boat to the edge of the world. This, he thought, will surely help me with my future plans. This will give me inner peace and anecdotes to tell the beautiful woman who will surely one day come into my life.

The ship dropped him off at the settlement and for its part continued on north. When he disembarked, the locals were waiting beneath a banner for him, for him, so deeply honoured were they apparently to have him there. The Mayor of the settlement, Brian, self-proclaimed promoter of 'The World's Most Northerly Comedy Night', greeted and embraced him warmly, almost in tears that he had come. The first show would be tomorrow night; for now, they took him to a wooden hut, where, under the clear freezing sky in a vast darkness, he slept like a newly-minted child.

In the morning he walked on the ice, and met the ice fisherman, who showed him how they did it, and took him out to see the walruses and whales.

Then after his dining on tinned fish and condensed milk it was show time already. He took out his sound recorder and his shoes and a bottle of Club Maté, with which he took a selfie. He stood in the frost and felt himself growing up at last. Mayor Brian came in, asking: 'Are you ready?' and walked with him to the venue. It was amazing – they had built a giant igloo and from all around people had come and were waiting seated there. Mayor Brian warmed up the audience with some local material, about why sea lions were funny and what he thought of his now ex-wife.

So here he was at the Arctic. While he waited to go on he looked over the rows of locals, thin-haired researchers and fur-pelted hunters who had come to see this, his most adventurous show to date. Would he do his Obama joke? What about his song about having kids? And as he contemplated this he noticed one of the igloo's central pillars, on which a photograph had been stuck, and which he almost couldn't bear to see.

The photo showed a man stood with Brian, his arm around him and a date – just one month previously. The man was drinking a beer and smiling, and behind him the massed ranks of an audience – a very big audience

– were sitting filling this same fake igloo. His rival wore the smile of a comedian who was big enough to play a secret show at the Arctic.

Brian was finishing the material about his now ex-wife. Having done so, he placed the microphone gently back in the stand, and gestured to the younger comedian. 'We're ready for you now!'

The younger man held frozen a moment before, after a brief moment of sadness, going on stage to perform with great brilliance for the next two hours.

Later, both comedians died.

PART ONE

I.

'If you had to give yerself a nickname as a comedian, what do you think that would it be?'

'Maybe the scalpel. The scalpel, you know – cutting out all the bad stuff until the wound is clean, like a forensic procedure. What about you?'

'Dunno. The French tickler mebbe. The housewife's choice. Sex moose.'

'Ha ha ha, you do look like a mouse.'

'I know man. I've been told. And you are kind of like a wee pug dog, you know, when you look for your glasses like you are doing – I think they're in your pocket, man, there you go - anyway you've got a little pug nose and everything.'

'Actually I always felt I resembled a rat.'

'Aye aye, that too, a rat. But even more a pug dog. You do alright though 'ey? You do alright.'

'I've never had problems getting women, no. Particularly Canadians for some reason.'

'What do you put that down to?'

'Maybe they like my sense of humour. It's a Canadian sense of humour, very cold, very Northern.'

'Get away. It reminds me, right, once I was up in

the Shetlands – did I tell you about this? no? - and I was looking through their tourist information and I found an advert for a Chinese restaurant. Under the picture was a caption, and it said, get this: Everything a man like you has come to expect. Now I'm not sure exactly *what* a man should be expecting from a Chinese restaurant in Shetland. But nonetheless: Everything a man like you expects!'

'I like that. What were you doing in Shetland?'

'Me? I ran away from my University.'

Stuart could hear the voices as if they were talking now. He sat in the green dining room in Hamburg and listened to their words. Sure, it had not been all that long ago; three years if that, but it seemed longer with so much having changed. They would not be making any more trips like that one. The Lone Star, the small expatriate pub they had performed in that night, had closed, and Dougie was gone, tempted back to the island by the chance of lucrative television contacts. That weekend they had swaggered across Germany, from Berlin to the west and then south, 'performing in some of the prettiest cities in Europe, and Mannheim,' as he had improvised on stage the final night. They had seen the beginnings of spring in fields and trees worn by Germany's hardest winter in many years, and their conversation had been unceasing from the moment they had met that Saturday morning at Berlin's gleefully unfashionable central bus station.

For the record Stuart had got there first. It was just

before eight; the time of meeting had been discussed through text messages the evening before, and Stuart had arrived slightly early. Waiting he had sat at a bench inside the waiting area, a small series of brown plastic chairs within the seedy, worn station, unchanged since its construction in the 1960s. He was eating a couple of bread rolls from a brown bakery bag and looking out the window at the bus bay. He looked across the concrete bay with its brutalist architecture, its unsheltered bus stops, and large white and green buses heading to Belarus, to Sofia, to Tallinn.

When he looked up a small man was sitting opposite him. He had a dirty face and greasy hair in a small, absurdly isolated clump and wore a shabby moleskin jacket. In his hand was a small paper tray with a sausage on it.

'I want a *Brötchen*,' the man said.

Stuart had half a bread roll left, which he had already partly chewed. 'But I've already bitten into it,' he said.

'Doesn't matter,' said the man.

Stuart handed him the remainder of the roll. Receiving it, the man bent forward and began using it to mop up the remaining mustard. As he did he made quiet scoffing noises. Stuart looked away and, rooting deeper in his bag, found and began eating the slightly-damaged banana he had brought. The man finished the bread roll and spoke, still looking down.

'I need a euro.'

Stuart looked back. 'I don't have one,' he said.

The man made an apparently acquiescent grunt and returned to the tray, where he finished his sausage. Stuart watched him, his little face chewing; he noticed the dirt on the man's cracked fingernails.

The man finished eating. He set down the tray and let out a satisfied gasp. 'But I need an euro *unbedingt.*' I *absolutely* need a Euro.

Stuart repeated, 'I don't have one.'

'Why not?'

'Because I don't. It's my choice,' said Stuart.

There was a slightly longer pause. The man appeared to be giving great thought to Stuart's response as he chewed up the very last of his sausage. Then after a pause he said, '*Du bist dumm.*'

You're stupid.

'What?'

'Du. You're stupid. *Dumm. Dummgans,*' silly goose. The

man was staring at him quite clearly now. '*Du bist ein Arschloch.*' You're an arsehole, and then, like some tiny little bird, like the preening display of a hibernator disturbed, stuck out his tongue exposing his throat to emit a little hostile beep of displeasure – 'Nerrr!'

Stuart sat looking at him. He was smiling already thinking of telling Dougie about it, about how he had wanted to say 'You'll have to try harder mate – I'm from the Midlands' when, through the window, he saw his friend at the bus bay. 'Excuse me,' he said, standing and leaving the tramp behind.

Dougie was waiting at their stop, wind-ruffled, bare-headed, leather jacket buttoned high. 'Alright pal!'

'Alright mate,' said Stuart.

'Is this our bus aye?'

They were in front of their ride, a huge single-decker chariot of a striking pale green.

'I think so.'

'Nice, nice. I'm telling you man it was hard to get up this morning – when you've got a beautiful lady lying next to you. You know how it is.'

'At the moment I do.'

'Ah you dirty dog you! You'll have to tell me about that later. Shall we get on? Looks like he's ready for us.'

The driver had turned the engine on and his assistant was gesturing to people around the bus to begin loading their suitcases. Dougie and Stuart had just tote bags with them so they joined the queue at the bus' front entrance. As they waited Stuart told him about the tramp.

'Really?' said Dougie laughing. 'You've got a bit there man.'

Stuart said, 'Yeah, I wanted to say to him; you know I'm from the Midlands right?' He repeated the man's little 'Nerrr' sound a few times, trying to get it right, knowing that only if he reproduced it exactly as it had occurred would it be funny.

They were now at the front of the queue, and Stuart handed over a printout of their tickets; the driver, in a white shirt and enormous sand-rimmed glasses, authorized their entrance with a simple performative 'Ja.' Dougie went first, ascending the step into the large, plush bus. There were few people around and they found two free spaces two-thirds of the way down, with Dougie, after they got comfy saying, 'This is nice man hey? How much were the tickets?'

They were cheap. And despite this there would be time, during the journey, to spread out, to occasionally move to separate pairs of seats, to retreat into their own little worlds of writing text messages and preparing sets.

Now the bus was pulling out of Berlin.

'So tell me about this girl. You seeing her, aye?'

'Yeah; she's nice. I'm happy about it.'

Who had that been at that time?

'Debbie, aye?'

Oh, Deborah, of course. That had not lasted long. He

remembered little about her; just her pale, mascara-ringed eyes.

'You don't sound so sure about it mate, if you don't mind me saying.'

'It's just –' Stuart paused. 'Well, I sent her a text last night and she didn't reply.'

'Ah, do yourself a favour man and don't worry about that shit. 'Cos she's not worrying about you.'

'You think I shouldn't worry? Because I always worry.'

'Aye, I tell you man. She'll be in touch,' Dougie said. 'I tell ye though man, my bird's amazing. I have honestly never been so in love. Really. I'm telling you man – I would be the biggest bloody fool on the planet if I ever cheated on her.'

'But you are a bloody fool.'

'Aye, I'm a wee gobshite, but not that much man. Not that much.'

As Stuart remembered all this talk his beer was gradually going flat. Next to that was his notebook, evidencing thin pickings for that day, just the idea to do 'something about hamburgers.' There had been a vogue for American-style hamburger joints in Berlin; not British ones presumably in a country where anybody who had lived in the UK for more than six months was banned from giving blood due to fear of BSE. But where was the humour in that? Something about you should be glad of my blue English blood, you German peasants? As if; Stuart was a middle-class bloke from Nottingham.

So he was struggling to write jokes and would do no new ones that night, just repeat his best fifteen, all remunerated at a rate he could have only dreamed of on that spring weekend. He would entertain the usual raft of Anglophile businessmen before returning to his hotel. There he would write a Facebook message to Kamila, or Angela, or Cristina, if he had not given up on them and their damn mysteries, before sleeping for a few hours and taking the early train to Berlin. There he would shower, pay bills, and plan the week ahead. Unlikely as it might seem, Stuart was a pioneer, one of the founders of the new wave of English-language comedians breaking over Europe in the early years of the 21st century.

They had worn their pioneer status lightly that weekend as they headed down to Essen for the first show. They had been travelling for several hours and had not stopped talking. They didn't often get to hang out.

'I didn't know you ran away from university.'

'Oh aye. I was having a right shite time of it. And to be honest with you I was doing a lot of coke as well.'

'Really? How did you afford it?'

'I had a mate who was a dealer. Well, he was a dope dealer actually but I guess he was diversifying.'

'What Uni did you go to?'

'Glasgow. I lived with my dad the whole time. Anyway, I was directing a production of the musical 'Calamity Jane' – don't laugh, you wee bollocks...'

'I'm sorry. But did you sing?'

'Too fucking right I did! Oh the deadwood stage is a-rollin' on over the plains... Whip-crack-away man, whip-crack-away!'

Dougie was slapping his thighs and their mutual laughter showered the bus. The passenger behind them, a young man with glasses and earphones plugged in, communicated displeasure via extreme silence.

'I had a couple of birds on the go and I was taking too much cocaine. This came to a head when I had my Czech exam and I realized I didn't know any Czech. So I went to the pub and sat down there with a beginner's guide to Czech. In fact I ended up just reading a history of the language. It was quite fascinating actually – did you know until the 19th century it was known as *bohemian*?'

'That's what we speak.'

'Well I didn't then. I just sat there with my pint and thought, naw, this isn't going to work at all. I'm going to have to get out of here. So I packed up a wee bag and got on the bus to Aberdeen.'

'How long's that take?'

'Three hours. Beautiful journey up there, staring out the window on the Highlands. I gave up on the Czech about halfway and started reading Dickens. D'you like Dickens?'

'He's not my favourite writer to be honest.'

'I love him man. I fucking love him. You get plenty of value out of his books. I love his characters, his language. Anyway, from Aberdeen you get the ferry.

That's a good fourteen hours. You stop at the Orkneys. They're beautiful, the Orkneys, though I've never been there, only seen them from the boat that one time – beautiful and all shimmering in the light, people dismounting, families and kids. Like, as soon as I saw them, man, I knew I'd be going on.'

'To Shetland?'

'In *life*.'

'Was it in doubt?'

'I felt like a right bumhole, to be honest with you. I'm the first person in mae family to have gone to University and I really felt like I'd disappointed everyone; I felt like a failure.'

'Saved by the Orkneys.'

'Aye, and then I got to the Shetlands. You know, they say the Orkneys are really different from Shetlands. The Orkneys are very agrarian, right, it's bullocks and all that, whereas the Shetlands, you know, they're more like a little piece of the Highlands blasted out to sea. It's a long way to get there and when you do get there it looks *exactly* like Scotland. I mean, it is Scotland, but you know, even more so. The Shetlands are Scotland for people for whom Scotland is not Scottish enough.'

'What did you do there then?'

'First of all I stayed in a youth hostel. And you have to remember this is like totally out of season, so there's no fucker there. It's just me in a room watching the rain on the window. And I'm taking Prozac right, the antidepressant.'

'Yeah, I know it.'

'Burns your throat man. Feels like molten silver in your throat. I mean – you ever taken them?'

Stuart was silent, then said, 'No.'

'It's weird man, I don't know how to describe it. I'm not intelligent enough you know? It's like... you don't feel what you supposed to be feeling. It's an inauthentic state of being. They were dark times for me man. Still,' Dougie went on. 'A few months ago I took DMT and it felt like the world went into my eyeball. Like woosh - Wow! And since then I have literally no concept of unhappiness. I mean just don't feel it any more.'

Had Dougie taken a sip of beer then? A beer he had likely purchased on board, German buses being relaxed enough to sell alcohol to their passengers and cheaply.

'And they're all so friendly around there man. They're all saying 'hello', 'how are you?' and what have you and asking you what you're doing there in Lerwick,' Dougie went on. 'They burn a Viking ship in the harbour every year and jump in the water. Fucking nutters. I wasnae there for that, though.

'What I did was – I have this thing about the North man. I mean, I'm Scottish obviously, and really Scottish, everybody in my whole family is Scottish: Even my Uncle Archie, who was actually born in Pakistan right, is insanely fucking Scottish. In fact more so – he's a hardcore Nat. He calls England the Raj. But more than, I wanted to get as far North as possible. And the thing is I didnae have a passport at that time, so Shetland was as far as I could go. And on Shetland the farthest I could go was the island of Unst. That's the most northerly of Shetland's islands, right. Was actually the inspiration

20

for 'Treasure Island' in Robert Louis Stevenson's book of that name.'

'Now Stevenson I do like.'

'Aye, he's alright man. So I wanted to get up Unst, but there's only one bus a week right, and as you know, I don't have a driving license; I mean I can drive, but I don't have a license. So I waited three days, just biding my time you know, laying the foundations, and then I got on the bus. And it takes me right all the way to the ferry to Unst, but no further. So I have no way of continuing north. And there's these two South African lads right, and they're on the ferry with me too. It's pissing it down, and we're all standing there trying to work out how we're going to get up Unst, right, because there's a youth hostel there we can stay at. Must be the most northerly youth hostel in the United Kingdom in fact. But there's also a truck and it's going that way too, aye, so we ask the driver and he says, sure, pal, just hang on to the back of my wee truck and I'll drop you off. And the rain is coming down and striking us and the wind and we're hanging on to this fucking huge truck and I'm like I'm alive, man! I'm really fucking alive! After that I stopped taking the Prozac.'

'The other thing I remember,' Dougie continued, the beer can in his hand, 'is that there were no cash machines on Unst. What would happen is that a truck with a cash machine would come by once a week. And as it happens I ran out of money while I was there so I had to chase after the cash machine with my card. And I remember, it just drove on over the hill. In many respects, I've been chasing after cash machines ever since.' Dougie slowly finished: 'The North man, I'm telling ye.'

Now he was sipping again at his beer while Ludwig and Otto, his promoters for the evening, talked next to him. Apparently Ludwig booked the acts, in this case him, while Otto was responsible for catering.

The bar was located in the Hamburg Anglo-American Club, a mocked-up version of a 19th century gentleman's establishment, though itself too orderly a structure to date any earlier than the 1950s; Germany had rebuilt itself thoroughly. Well done, Germany. Hamburg had for its part been located in the British-controlled sector of the country and centres like this blocked out its exceptionally dense cultural landscape, were relics of the love of Germany for and from its occupiers.

Next to him Otto was saying '*Das sind halt tolle Leute* –' it meant 'they're great people', but he wasn't really listening to them – as his promoters discussed football and specifically, the merits of the FC Bayern, who had recently completed another year of pan-European triumphs. 'Müller, Götze, Reus, Neuer – they are quite simply great people.'

'Great people,' said Ludwig. 'But Reus is weak.'

'Weak? Reus is weak? Weak?'

'He's weak,' said Ludwig. 'He is the weak link.'

'Bwoah!' How Otto objected to that, with the disapproving bray customary of the German contesting a point. 'Reus is not weak. He is far from weak.'

'And how is it in England?' asked Ludwig, tilting to him.

'Seems these days all the best Germans play in England.'

'Eh,' he said. He just wasn't interested.

'Or for Arsenal,' said Otto, also turning.

'Yes, that's right, Özil,' Ludwig went on. 'They call him *Oh*zil there, isn't that right? He lost his Umlaut somewhere over the English Channel.'

'Actually I was thinking more Mertesacker,' said Otto. 'For me, Özil, that's not a German.'

It took a few seconds for the comment to sink in but after it had done he instinctively asked, 'What is he then?'

They were talking, in Mesut Özil, about a football player born in Germany, who had lived in Germany until twenty-two years old, before being transferred to a club abroad where his manager had complained of his ability to only speak German, who possessed a German passport and a German passport only, having been compelled by his country's law to refuse any other – and they were seriously raising the question of whether he was German or not. It begged the question as to what magical level of Germanness Özil was somehow missing, and if it was likely if he, Stuart Holmes, an Englishman resident in Berlin for only a mere decade, a third of his life, would ever be able to attain it.

'What is he, then?' he asked again. 'He was born in Gelsenkirchen, for God's sake.'

Here and at such moments he doubted the wisdom of his choice to call Berlin his home, or at least faced the delusional aspect of it. Would he ever be accepted, if even Özil, hero to schoolchildren across the land, wasn't? Or was it worse than that, that, by dint of his pale skin, he would be forever, if behind the indigenous Tectonic mass, marginally ahead of Mesut Özil in the Germanness stakes? English people were not German, but they were more German than Turkish ones; how subtle and thoroughly differentiated German racism was.

Ludwig looked to Otto, who had opened his mouth just a touch, shrew-like and anxious, and then –

'Ah, Claudia,' said Ludwig.

A tall young woman approached. She brushed herself down and sat.

'Hello,' said Claudia. 'You're Stuart?'

'Yes, that's me.'

'The comedian.'

'For tonight.'

A waiter approached their table. 'Can I get you some drinks?'

'Drink, anybody?' asked Ludwig.

'Just tap water,' he said.

'No, that won't do – you must have a mineral water. Mineral water,' Ludwig ordered, then stood up and walked out the room.

'Gintonic,' said Otto, in the compressed German way, then nothing else.

The drinks came, and he found himself looking at her, this elegant German woman of considerable height. She was young – although Germans didn't seem to age at the same rate as other peoples, retaining their youthful demeanour until the termination of their student days at the onset of their 40s – and clearly, masculinely dressed in black trousers and a long-sleeved white shirt. She said nothing.

'About five minutes,' said Ludwig reentering. 'They're still eating up there.' He took up his drink and sighed out of affection for it.

'And are you also from Hamburg?' Stuart asked her.

'Yes,' said Claudia. There was a pause – she seemed to search her mind for what might come next. 'I did live in South Germany, but there's not enough sea there. Do you perform in German as well?'

'Sometimes,' he said. 'But there's a technical problem: I'm much funnier in English.'

'Do you know Chris Howland?' asked Ludwig suddenly. 'Mr. Pumpernickel?'

'Mr. Pumpernickel?' he couldn't help repeating, amused. 'No, I don't know him.'

'He was a compatriot of yours who DJ'd on German radio after the war. He was in Cologne for a long time; he also recorded some songs. He used to do something a little like you – you know, never losing his accent. There was another one too, an Ami, what was his name? Brian… Anyway, that was his thing too, ruining German for comic effect.'

Stuart smiled thinly.

'I'm talking about the 50s here though,' said Ludwig and drank.

'I saw a clip of you on YouTube,' said Claudia, 'You were talking about Germans. And you said – that we always smile after we tell jokes.'

'That's true, you do,' he said.

'Really?' Claudia smiled.

Her flirting was either delicate as banging a carpet out on a porch, or she was simply naïve and sweet, more likely the latter. But Stuart didn't have much time for naïve and sweet.

'That's what I do,' said Stuart. 'I tell jokes in English to the Germans. That's what I was put on this earth to do. It's a very – specific mission.'

'I thought the clip was very funny.'

'Thanks.'

'Bill Ramsey, that was it,' said Ludwig. 'But he was American – you know, it's not as good. Well! I'm going to go up and see if they're ready.'

'Sure.' He was looking at Claudia.

'And then I'll come down and get you. Will you be here?'

'I'll be in the other room,' he said, moving into action.

'The side room?'

'Yes – I'll be there, rehearsing. Just come and get me when you're ready.'

'Good luck!' said Claudia, in English.

'Thanks,' said Stuart, straightening himself.

Otto was still seated, hands angling up on the armrests. 'Make a nice show.'

'Thanks,' said Stuart, and with a final rush of blood, 'And just so you know – I think Mesut Özil is German. German, German, German.'

And he left to go and get ready.

They were on a bus going down to Essen and it was spring. They were two of the representatives of the fledgling Berlin English comedy scene, young comics pushed out of by the costs and competitiveness of their native lands and their failure to provide them with an adequate space to fail. In London you could be finished by 22, not even realizing some quiet stranger at your rocky gig was your big chance, that that after-show enquirer who you blanked in your disappointment was actually a comedy agent. In Berlin, groups of expatriates, allied with rogue Germans seduced by the international reputation of Anglophone comedy, worked for little money in the exhilaration of mutual support.

Dougie and Stuart were two of the best; Dougie, a scraggy-haired Scottish beanpole fond of wearing leather trousers and brown winklepicker shoes, and Stuart, bearded, intellectual, but alive and unworried on stage – more unworried, always, in company. Both of them wore leather jackets; neither of them smoked; each of them was obsessed with women. It was to these that their conversations turned as the bus moved on towards Niedersachsen.

'I saw you man, with that girl Deborah, leaving *Bananen* –' *Bananas* being Berlin's premier English comedy night, a crammed spectacular held in a shoe store basement, usually hosted by Dwight Kreutzer, a bony German-American perpetually weighing whether to leave the tiny comic potentate he had himself largely created or continue enjoying its dryadic riches, i.e. beer and sex – 'sneaking off together giggling. And I heard you laughing and I thought hello, that's a nice little scene!'

'Is that right?' Stuart smiled. 'She is very lovely. How's Anja, anyway?'

'Ah man, she's great. I have honestly never been so in love. Yeah, it's great.'

'And?' It was not a usual silence Dougie had fallen into.

'No mate, it's nothing. Honestly. So do you think it's going to be serious then with this lady?'

'Who knows?' Stuart of course deeply hoped so. But his hope was provisional; he had reached an age where he expected all his loves to fail, where the break-ups were getting easier and the hangovers worse. As he said on stage, the concept of not being able to live without someone became somewhat hollow after a certain amount of splits. Food, water; you couldn't live without them. But other human beings? Unfortunately they were mostly expendable.

Dougie talked about women in his stand-up too. He talked about being locked out of his apartment wearing 'nae trousers' and a story, apparently true, where he had been too pissed to get a bra off so had improvised the use of a Swiss Army knife. 'They're useful objects,' he'd say, holding up an example of said knife under the stage light, 'Don't rust or anything. And afterwards you can open up a post-coital tin of beans.'

'How long we doing tonight?' asked Dougie after another few moments surveying the flat German countryside.

'I don't know, ask Dwight.'

'You ask him.'

Dwight coordinated their appearances, sitting in Berlin scrolling over a map of the country, thinking where they could descend on next: Stuttgart, Gießen, Bayreuth, Mainz, shows in small handsome German towns which offered English-speaking comedians one great thrill, that of having got there first.

'I sent him a text.' Stuart looked up from his phone. 'But what is it about Anja?'

'What?' Dougie resumed with a sigh, 'Oh, right. It's just – I've never had my heart broken, that's all.'

'Well lucky for you.'

'Aye, aye. I mean I've broken up with people before; lots of people. But I was always the one who ended it.'

'Why did you break up with Laura again?'

'Lots of reasons, lots of reasons. There wasn't just one.'

'That's what my dad said.'

'Your Dad?'

'Yes when he left my Mum. There wasn't one reason, he said.' Stuart added, 'When my dad was my age he had three kids already.'

'Really?'

'From his first marriage.'

'Well the thing is I'm thinking – it's kind of inevitable isn't it.'

'What?'

'That I get mae heart broken. I mean I love Anja with all my heart and soul. I just know I'm never going to leave that lassie. I mean, there is literally more chance of me cutting of mae own penis than that happening. Honest tae god man. So given that I'm not going to leave her, and given that it's inevitable that I get my heart broken –'

'It's inevitable that Anja is going to break your heart.'

'Exactly man. Exactly.'

Dougie leaned forward a little, perhaps touched by the intentness with which Stuart had listened to him, to the stories inside. His skin was pale, eyes underlined by the late nights in the bar in which he worked, the talk with the customers, the sustaining alcohol. Sometimes Anja would come and sit there with him, she a blonde, pretty German, silent over a drink.

'Don't worry about it,' said Stuart then. 'I always feel that getting your heart broken is a bit like losing your virginity. It's a rite of passage; it's the other side of things. Through the looking glass.'

'Like having a kid,' said Dougie.

'Or having a kid,' Stuart, childless, said. 'I imagine… Does she want them?'

'Aye, but I've told her, there's no way I'm even thinking about that for at least ten years. First I'm going write myself the nicest little stand-up show man, an hour of absolute brilliant stuff, then do a run of it. You know, full houses, really fill it. I'm going get 20,000 bucks. I'm going to take that money – go away – and do it again.'

'Only hopefully for more money.'

'Hopefully!' Dougie grinned.

Stuart's phone chirruped; he looked to the screen. 'Ah right – Dwight says half-an-hour each both nights. I thought I'd go first tonight, if that's alright, then we can swap.'

'Aye that's nae bother man.' It was strategy on Stuart's part as the next night, Heidelberg, was the bigger gig. 'Nae bother at all. Now if you don't mind, I'm going to go through my notes for tonight.'

'Of course,' said Stuart, eyes secretly flipping over to Dougie's book, the drawings, the scrawl, another comedian's world.

II.

Why did people feel the need to be funny? he considered, alone in the club's side room now. Some people were just funny, of course, their face, their turn of phrase. Some people were funny and didn't want to be. Stuart had always wanted to be, a humour rooted in his own incompetence, an apology for and validation of it. At the age of four, he had performed a Christmas magic show for his parents, then still together, picking only the simplest tricks; the cup under balls, the doctored handkerchief. Unable to execute even the most basic of them he had grown increasingly furious and began a series of bewildered stompings over to root through the tricks box and, cheeks reddening, read the instruction sheet. His parents had been in hysterics and, though at the time he had not appreciated the humiliation, perhaps even then his course had been set.

The magic led to initial success in school variety plays which led to catastrophic failure at University, a failure which had wounded him in his very soul and precipitated his exile to Germany, though not before he moved to London after his finals and began working the comedy circuit. But London life was hard and stage-time scarce; he soon grew tired of the endless bus rides across the city, the cramped back rooms and the hurried after-show pints. And he was haunted by the events of the previous spring, events which had sapped his confidence and called his very concept of self into question. London was not the city in which to call your very concept of self into question. It was the city of hard realities, of girls in tight coats walking, heavily made up and cold. It was the city of self-promoters; it was a city that worked.

Then a chance meeting in a pub had earned him an invitation to Berlin. Laura, Danish and short, was staying there for the summer, rummaging around in the archives for information about a particular Jewish family who had gone on to achieve cultural success in post-war Denmark; Laura, a snub-nosed Danish girl with glasses who loved Israel and wheat beer. Stuart didn't care much about her interests but did enjoy spending the days reading on her balcony and socializing with university friends at night; by the end of the summer his hair had lengthened and his German increased fifty-fold, meaning he now knew about a hundred words. '*Hallo!*' he would say, then '*Weltschmerz*' and following a further pause '*Auf Wiedersehen*,' saying a final farewell to people he would see again the next day. He also hadn't yet learnt to ask whether something was sugar or salt, leading to an evening eating some very sweet chips. But even speechless he wasn't, at last, uneasy in Berlin – it seemed to him a gentle city, where the trains slid in and out and the open spaces pacified tourists drunker and rowdier elsewhere. It was like the Germans had become one of the peaceful races in Star Trek, the ones introduced by an insert screen of their orderly, verdant planet, Bajorans, say, or some other species permanently threatened by obliteration; and what a change after the tiny cubicles and traffic-jam living of the English, who could only ever be the Borg.

Surrounded by pacifists, Stuart revelled in the license of Englishness, his ability to voice the odd mildly aggressive opinion or wildly over-celebrate during that summer's football tournament, until England lost. He swam in lakes, and bought a bicycle, and gradually stopped thinking of England and the ashes it had fed him. In Oxford, where he had been President of the University sketch revue, people had printed gossip about him in the student newspapers, asked him to leave parties, dealt with him as the man who had committed that deepest and most unforgivable of Oxford crimes: failure. He had failed, as a comedian and a young man, and that publicly; his country had rejected him. He had been humiliated in front of an audience of his contemporaries and sent into internal exile. Afterwards, many of these young dilettantes, at the time apparently picturing future lives as bereft of unforeseen distress as possible, lives composed of simply an endless procession of success, successes occurring within a network of contacts which they had built up at University and which would continue to provide them with unstinting support throughout their adult lives, never violating the simple and essential principle that all was permissible as long as it did well – did not want his name on their social CV.

Years later he took out his stage trousers; he always brought a clean pair for shows. Polyester was best on the road because it dried quickly. He stopped with them at half mast, amused by his scrawny thigh hair in the elegant drawing room, then hoisted them all the way up.

Funnily enough, though, nobody cared about Oxford

drama in Berlin. The relative merits of his performance as director of the Oxford Revue meant very little in his new country; not only that, said country seemed to be dealing with specific and some might say more profound issues of its own. Not that he thought much about those, as Germany faced him with ample unique modern annoyances, chiefly the natives' insistence on speaking English with him. Even ten years after his arrival, he would still be battling with the Ottos of this world and their expectation of free English tuition from their Anglophone guests, in a society which had apparently come to assume that English was the *langage de choix* with any foreigner. Apart from the Turks – now they could and should speak German.

At the end of that first summer Laura was set to go back to London and, ending a relationship which had never in fact officially started, Stuart told her he would be staying on. He did not even go back to London to pick up the few pairs of shoes and books he owned, instead asking his dad to go along with a box and store the items for when he would eventually return, which ended up being never. Even back then he felt, and told people he felt, utterly done with England.

Then the years of struggle, or the early struggle as it might be called, with little money in his wallet and less in the bank; sharing flats with difficult people, freezing cold commutes on deep winter mornings to go and teach 7AM *'Breakfast Mit Englisch'* to people bleary-eyed at their desks. The flatmate who smoked dope all day and accused him of stealing his paint roller; the other one who got them all thrown out for owing thousands of euros in back rent. Berlin had greeted his decision to move there with the coldest winter in forty years, and the dreamy soundstage he had fallen in love with that summer seemed very far away as he descended, broke, to the six a.m. subway.

Gradually he began to heal. He started teaching English at a school, learning German at a night class where he had met a Swiss girl who wore cardigans and who he later surprised at the airport with a bunch of flowers. It didn't go anywhere – she blushed, her greatest expression of passion for him – but it was his first romantic gesture in the Fatherland and a sure sign that his strength, intimately bound up with his sex drive, was returning. And he began to shed things which had seemed necessary in London, like having a state-of-the-art mobile phone or wanting to drive a car. He grew increasingly remote from his old world, tucked up under trees in the canal-side district of Kreuzberg, safe in his little social-democratic heaven where no one hated him or indeed knew who he was.

Now he was standing before a mirror in Hamburg, talking through those few jokes for tonight he was uncertain about, seeking out those few moments not quite right, where the shape of the joke was not quite in place. A lot of the time when he wrote he knew how much space he had for the joke but not the content; knew only the moment it had to end in order to satisfy.

One day, comedy began again. It all started in his English classes, as early as the first one, where he had sat faced by a group of personable German engineers and asked them to tell him, as an icebreaker – he had written the word on the board, himself unsure whether it was one word or two – an interesting anecdote from their lives.

There was a pause. Christian, a middle-aged German with tanned skin and a pudding-bowl haircut, was to answer. He took a pause before saying solemnly, 'Nothing interesting has ever happened to me in my life.'

Was it a joke? It surely was.

'Surely at least something interesting must have happened to you by now?'

'No,' Christian repeated. 'Nothing interesting has ever happened to me.'

Either his student had so dry a sense of humour as to have almost evaporated or he was being serious. He saw it there as a glimmer, the chance to resurrect his comedy in this country, but only as a hint, and he could never have guessed, nor had he ever planned, the lengths to which he would take it; from early gigs in multicultural social clubs to appearances on German television, at comedy festivals, being voted 'Foreigner of the Year 2015' and all via a single joke; the joke he had seen that day when Christian spoke: that of being a funny person in a country with no sense for it. 'I'm writing a book about German comedy at the moment,' he would say in his set, 'It's called humour as a sign of moral weakness.' And the deeper he got into understanding the culture, though not of being accepted into it, the more he could exploit this deep-stretching comic seam. It was a joke which had come to rule his life.

He was sat, suited and booted, looking silently in the mirror when Ludwig opened the door. 'Ready? They're ready.'

'I'm ready,' said Stuart and followed Ludwig upstairs.

When they arrived in Essen they had to change, taking the city train, what the Germans called the *Stadtbahn*, out to Kettwig, the small suburb where their evening's performances would take place. For those arriving to them, most German cities introduced themselves like this; a large, newly-built train station, aside the inner city, hooked up to the - invariably good - local transportation network, where sleek modern trams coiled into pedestrianized old towns. The towns of West Germany didn't all feel the same but they did look it; the country had been destroyed sixty years earlier as the result of a series of bad decisions and rebuilt in a uniform and utilitarian way. Even the older-looking buildings were often in fact new, built out of quick-weathering sandstone to perhaps give an air of seniority.

The ticket machine was broken, and Dougie didn't want to pay for a ticket, so they decided to travel without or *black* as the Germans had it. This led to a tense journey for Stuart; ever the worrier, each time the train stopped at another suburban station he anxiously scanned the platform as to if any of the people entering might be ticket inspectors, usually plain-clothed in Germany. He had once been told that the people performing this service were unemployed, and bound to carry out their task under threat of benefit removal, and were as such likely to prosecute it with particular ferocity.

'Half an hour,' Dougie was saying. 'And you?'

'Half an hour.'

'New, old?'

'All old. Best of,' said Stuart. 'Always best on the road. None of them have ever seen it, after all. I'm just curious if there'll be anyone there, that's all.'

'Sure there'll be plenty of people. Dwight and Malcolm, right, when they did it they said there was forty people. I don't think it's a very big place.'

'We'll see.' He was too used to it, getting himself all internally pumped-up, the rehearsal, the rituals, to step out to an audience of ten people, few of whom spoke English.

The train slid on, a river visible now. 'What do you think of Malcolm anyway?'

'Aye, he's a funny guy, he's talented, but he needs to talk about something else other than being bent, you know?'

'Mmm. I tell you who I do like,' said Stuart, with all the seniority of his ten years doing comedy, 'Joe Onion.'

'Joe Onion? Aye, he's alright.'

'What, you don't like him?'

'No, no, I think he's funny, it's just that – There's too many dry guys, that's all. You know – just sitting there at the front of the stage, talking.'

'You don't like comedians who sit at the front of the stage talking? You're ruling out a fair few people there.'

'It's not that man, it's just, where's the show? You've gotta move man, you've gotta move around a bit! That's what I've been working on anyway.'

'Well, I don't move much.'

'No, but you do *move* man. I've seen you. When you get going man, you can be quite the little mover.'

'Yes.' Stuart considered it. 'Maybe I can.'

'I spend a lot of time practising mae moves in my bedroom. Getting the right turn, the right drop of the shoulder, like –'

Dougie had stood up and was demonstrating in the nearly empty train carriage. No one saw it; in the meantime, a sign for Kettwig had appeared outside the train window.

'This is us, come on,' said Stuart, and the pair of them bustled out onto the quiet platform. Through the square window of the next carriage a small child could be seen staring at Dougie, this wild-haired foreign extrovert.

They had to work out which way to walk and spent a few minutes in discussion before a sign; though Dougie had a smart phone but its Google Maps function wasn't working, and it was hard to tell exactly where to go. But soon they had it, moving down an incline to where they found that river, wide, still and grey. The air was perfectly quiet and the town peacefully benign.

'It's nice, isn't it?'

'Beautiful man, beautiful. I should bring Anja here.'

Stuart smiled. Somehow he felt a sense of pride in Germany, in its underratedness. It was a hidden gem, albeit a rather large one.

'I should bring Deborah here too.'

'Aye man – you don't sound very sure?'

'Oh I don't know.' They were sloping upwards now. 'I'm not sure it's going to work out.'

'No?'

The fact was that several hours ago he had sent her a new text message and she had failed to reply since and this fact burnt within him. At that time, before success and greater cynicism took hold, Stuart had still monitored every instance of romantic communication like a man searching for a gas leak.

'I've had a lot of girlfriends,' Stuart said at last.

They were on cobblestone streets, by thatched, colourful houses, awkwardly placed alongside each other in the clumpy street. Their walk took them past a Chinese restaurant placed in faux baroque housing and several shut tourist shops. Dougie took the occasional phone snap and Stuart walked on, head down and an eye on the numbers; they needed number 36.

'I tell you man – I was needing this after Berlin.'

'We're here.' In front of them was a tall red and brown thatched house, small from the front but rearing up behind to a garage and garden.

'Here?'

'That's right. The Lone Star Pub, Kettwig.'

Dougie frowned. 'Is it open?'

Stuart pushed at the door, which came open a tad. He stepped back immediately. 'Looks like it.'

'Do you have her number? It's a woman, right?'

'There's a buzzer here.'

Dougie peered. 'Ah hello –'

'Yes?' An American accent, sharp and high.

'Yeah, we're the comedians.'

'Be right down,' said the voice in a neutral tone.

Dougie looked at Stuart, who looked back with a smile. 'It's all happening,' he said.

In a way the comedians' presence was an effect of language. English's ascent into the world-language brought myriad stories along with it, love affairs which would never have had a shared language earlier and business deals which would never have blossomed previously. And this scene, of two young expatriates rocking up at a wealthy *Ruhrgebiet* suburb, offering imported entertainment to the locals, in the process gaining stage experience Anglophone lands would never have granted them without a stronger scent of money about them both, was really just another instance of globalization: the world's citizenry obtaining their evening's stand-up in its language of origin, English comedy now just another high-quality product like Scottish salmon or French red wine. But without the history of language – and as Vico had said there was no real difference between the study of language and that of history – it would not have happened; the question being was whether it was language that determined event or the other way round.

Meanwhile, ironies abounded. Stuart's act was exceptionally local; he juggled between English and German, referenced the country's politics, albeit in superficial fashion, i.e. what people looked like, and relied for some of his biggest laughs on exploitations of particular quirks of German grammar which only people who shared his own linguistic background, fluent speakers of German and English, could understand. And if this kind of comedy now became possible, or at least more frequent, the English-speaking world and Britain in particular grew ever more insular, ever more hostile to the linguistic other, to the extent to which speaking a foreign language became inherently pretentious and the nation indulged in pointless debates as to whether Britain should be 'in Europe' or not which begged the further question of, if Britain were not to be, where exactly was it? South America?

Dougie, meanwhile, sauntered through dick jokes and pretended he had soiled himself, a brand of humour which proved reliably universal in character and could make itself understood to even the most basic of English speakers. Stuart, an elder comic statesman in Berlin, was often asked what he thought of his frenetic friend. He'd indicate the crowd with an airy wave and say, 'They're laughing.'

This all came to mind as they looked around the space where they would be performing that night, Dougie's brown leather heels tapping the swept wooden floor. There was no stage.

'Nice, man, nice. How long you had this place?'

'About two years,' said Paulie, the big smiling Texan at

the bar.

Stuart was sat there looking at her, estimating her age, scrutinizing her looks. Meanwhile she made him tea.

'I was doing all kinds of things before,' she said. 'Working as a singer for example. You know how Germans get about country music.'

'Yes.' Stuart did indeed. Some years ago he had watched a documentary about the Third Reich and been struck by the fact that all the broad-speaking, tight-hatted former Nazi officials resembled nothing so much as Texan cowboys – at which point the comparisons ended, obviously.

'Played for everybody. Look, here's a picture.' She pointed to a frame of herself executing a dance step, standing in front of line of tall blonde German women in cowgirl boots, their faces locked in concentration. 'Say, do you guys know John Doyle?'

'We know of him,' said Stuart.

'Do you think he's funny?' she said.

'He's OK,' said Stuart. Doyle, Rachel Braithwaite and Frank Sanazi – these comedians were all native English speakers and representative of, for Germany, the zenith of what the Anglophone comedian might achieve. Stuart didn't like to be reminded of them; of Doyle, an American in a T-shirt talking about the similarity between the German *Verkehr* (traffic) and *Geschlechtsverkehr* (sexual intercourse); Braithwaite, a classically-trained pianist who sang Abba songs over Mozart tunes and Sanazi, whose name explained itself. Stuart had gigged with him once; he was a very nice man.

'And what kind of people will you have coming tonight?'

'Oh, we have a very tight community. Normally just about everybody comes; the whole village.'

'Nice, nice,' said Dougie, pacing around the stage. 'Is this working?' he said into the microphone he now held.

'Needs to be louder,' said Stuart; Paulie pressed something at the bar. Dougie's speech became louder.

'Now?'

'That's fine,' Stuart said.

'Dwight and Malcolm said they had a good crowd,' he said.

'Oh yes, they were great. I'll never forget when Malcolm showed up here. He looked like a hobo! Just came in from the street without knocking with his little suitcase. I thought he was, you know, a homeless person or something. He came in here – you know those big eyes he has and I said, "Yes, can I help you?" And he said "I'm the comedian." Well, I figured that made sense.' She smiled. 'Later he drank *Sekt* and all, I mean all, my whisky.'

'That sounds about right,' Stuart said, stirring his tea.

'Thanks for the pint, aye,' said Dougie, now turning his attention to the pint glass she had supplied him with. 'Veltins right?'

'That's right. And you're welcome. Anyway, he said he'd come by tonight.'

'What?' Stuart raised his head.

'Mmm – ahh!' Dougie swallowed a large gulp.

'What? He's coming?'

'Yes; apparently he's got a gig in Düsseldorf tomorrow so decided to stop over on the way through. I told him he could have the spare room. You guys are friends, right?'

'We –' began Stuart. But words failed him.

III.

Malcolm Deepak Brading was one of the most inimitable of the new crop of English-language acts at that time swarming Europe. He was also sexually voracious, morbidly obese, and Stuart had seen the worst of him.

A few years ago Malcolm had become something of a cause célèbre via a YouTube clip in which he campily lambasted his own hometown of Vancouver and its accents; the video, gone viral had made him a celebrity in the very town he professed to despise and ultimately expedited his exit from it. After the clip he had began to land parts in many of the mainstream comedy films being shot in the city at the time, including The X-Files and Catwoman, in which he had played a particularly brutally dispatched goon – it had something to do with a sluice pipe – while at the same time he had carved himself a niche as Canada's first openly gay pro-wrestling artist. His character, Big Gay Deepak, exploited his mixed-raced parentage to the full in an outlandish costume of flowing sackcloth tied with a belt bearing a maple-leaf imposed on a rainbow flag. In the peculiarities of the Canadian wrestling circuit, always keen to distinguish itself from its southern neighbours, his character became extremely popular with teenage boys, who became enamoured of bellowing his catchphrases 'You're so hot!' and, even more simply, 'Stop it!'

Unfortunately, due to exploitative labour contracts and bad financial decisions – read, his own decision to purchase, and then crash, an Aston Martin sports car – he saw little of the profits of his early 20's success, which was itself fairly transitory. As such he packed a bag and, without informing the Canadian Wrestling Federation, flew to Australia where, quite quickly and almost by accident, he wound up opening for Emily Harding, an outspoken Australian comic on the cusp of minor fame. He had met her on the night before her warm-up show and, over mojitos, basically charmed himself into a performing berth; he was an oleaginous, eel-tongued man. He walked out before a crowd of several hundred educated Australians and dazzled them with ten minutes of hilarious, entirely true stand-up about celebrity, car accidents and gay sex in the wrestling world.

Now Malcolm's itinerant odyssey began. He found he had a taste for travel; why, he didn't even go back to Canada but just added a few essentials to his little suitcase and began cruising the world in search of gigs, crossing stages from Auckland to Montreal, talking, cavorting and essentially refining the same thirty-minute set via constant injections of local colour. 'So,' he would say, 'hello you gorgeous *Hrvati*,' that kind of thing. He became in the process the first openly gay comedian to play Serbia and the first stand-up comedian to play Albania at all. He was one of the few *professional* comics who ended up in Berlin and as such all the local acts worshipped him.

'Why do you play all these shows?' Stuart asked him as they lay naked together.

'Well – it's my job,' said Malcolm, his eye wide. 'I mean, once you've made the decision to be gay, it really is a question of absolute freedom. That's why so many artists are gay, so they have the time for their work.'

One night Malcolm had walked into their mutual dive bar and by way of introduction squeezed the bottom of every straight man there – '"straight-acting" guys,' he called them – some men even getting a kiss. And Stuart had to admit that he had enjoyed and encouraged it when Malcolm's attentions for the evening settled finally on him. The Canadian had treated him with an almost embarrassing friendliness which Stuart had responded to, fairly or otherwise, in a manner calculated to be both gamely flirtatious and somehow unmistakeably 'straight.' His new friend offered compliments on Stuart's act – 'you've got a really interesting stage presence' – on the quality of his thought – 'you have a beautiful mind' – and propositions of mutual sex club visits, threesomes with friends, and his being apparently 'so open-minded.' There were compliments and confessions all night long, and the two men parted with Malcolm's invitation to dinner extended and accepted.

And so it was that just days after the invite Stuart found himself sat in Malcolm's kitchen telling him the story of his recent break-up. Malcolm for his part was sweating over a magnificent turkey dinner, an example of what he called 'good old Canadian home cooking.' For his part Stuart had eaten it, also in the process helping Malcolm consume two bottles of wine, at which point a third was located. Stuart played him his favourite Kate Bush clips. About now praise for his eyes began to be heard. A massage was offered and the room started to shake....

Well, Stuart could have said no. But there was curiosity; bi-curious they – who, actually? – called it. And what could it hurt?

The massage was, it had to be said, world-class, Malcolm's big splodge fingers working up and down his back like a first class cook who was kneading a huge cake out of his arse. As the fingers laboured, a deep singing began.

'Malcolm,' said Stuart.

'Yes Stuart?'

'Are you singing Kate Bush?'

'I thought you *liked* Kate Bush.'

'I do. And you?'

'Oh yes.'

'Mmm,' said Stuart. 'I'm surprised you like any bush whatsoever.'

Malcolm flipped him, and the fingers worked harder now.

Blind drunk, Stuart found himself lost in thought as Malcolm slipped a finger into his arse crack. He found himself thinking about comedy, and what a good joke this would make in his set – seeing Malcolm's brown puffer-fish face sniffing around near his genitals, and then returning up to give him a firm, moist kiss, before moving down to make a noise which could only be described as being like some kind of giant sexing donkey. 'Mweeaaaah!' This was made all the more tragicomic in that in contrast to Malcolm's apparent or simulated raptures Stuart was personally experiencing less an erotic epiphany than the strong sense he was being fiddled with. 'Gwuuuuuuuhhhaaa! Mer! Lwerr.'

In a further misfortune, following Malcolm's mouth fastening around his shaft and sucking him to a damp conclusion, Stuart committed the bi-curious *faux-pas* of contracting gonorrhoea, a disease surprisingly receptive to transfer by oral sex. A week later Malcolm had come round with pizza – Canadian pizza, whatever the fuck that was – and Stuart had mentioned that the tip of his penis appeared to be on fire. Malcolm had responded by weeping in his arms.

'There, there, Malcolm. It's alright.'

'I'm so embarrassed!'

'Don't be.'

'No, I am! Your one gay experience and you get a sexual disease! Oh my God! What you must think of us *filthy* homos!'

'I don't think anything. I stand by my actions.'

'Really?' said Malcolm, looking up at Stuart with an unfurling smile.

'Not like that,' Stuart replied.

Their relationship hadn't survived that short flourish. After a series of Facebook message exchanges Malcolm had ascertained that Stuart really was done with his excursion into bisexuality and, in response to Stuart's repeated rejoinders over the next months that he get his sexual health checked out, unleashed an avalanche of invective. There is no need to detail that here, its accusations of homophobia and moral failure, its repeated laments of Malcolm being too busy 'to deal with this right now'; suffice to say it was a magnificent collage of insults which soon worked its way into Malcolm's comedy. Since then the pair had not exchanged so much as a mail.

'What's wrong? You look so pale.'

'Oh.' Stuart looked up at Paulie. 'We haven't spoken in a while, that's all.'

'Malcolm gave Stuart a blow job and gave him the clap,' said Dougie with a helpful air. Paulie began to laugh out loud.

'Is that true?'

'How do you know about it?' Stuart turned to his friend.

'Everybody knows about it man. Malcolm did ten minutes about it on Greek television.'

After a long pause, Stuart said 'Appropriate. I think I'll have a beer now.'

*

Later that afternoon Stuart sat looking out the window of the upstairs room. The air outside looked damp, the night beginning to draw in, but it wasn't raining – it didn't rain enough in this country for him, although the rains which drowned his own birthplace a year later were excessive even to his taste. He could look out on the cobblestone street below to the green, tidy forest and just spy the beginnings of the lake beneath.

Somehow he was thinking about his former actress girlfriend, of someone he thought he had genuinely forgot. And he was thinking, of course, about his set, or rather revolving his thoughts around a simple question related to it, whether it would be good or not; whether this joke would work or that one, might that one be cut? Even his waiting was in some way all about the gig. He carried his set around with him like a basket on his head, rehearsing only those jokes recently altered or whose reception was unreliable; his set list consisted of fourteen key words ('Cloud', 'S-Bahn') on a piece of paper. The set was written on his heart; backstage quiet, one night, he was told by an old pro that 'I knew you'd be good because you didn't rehearse; you just went out there and did it.'

Life always tried to buy people off, turn radicals into academics, poets into statisticians. And in Stuart's era, one of the chief pacifying professions was comedy, an area in which men – and still at this time generally men – channelled enough intelligence to unravel the crises of finance and ecology into achieving the rather more limited goal of making crowds of strangers laugh. How could this not be a sign of cultural decadence? And the men did this because unlike politicking, protesting or writing poetry, people were prepared to pay them for their services, particularly if you were able to show up in Kettwig on a wet Saturday night.

But comedy had a great redeeming feature. It was a place, in a world saturated with bullshit, of great honesty, and one of the few professions of any kind where you could get paid for telling the truth. Onstage Stuart could talk about issues of race, history and sexuality more honestly than anywhere else in his life allowed him. And if such taboos were necessary for comedy than Germany had one hell of one, one giant elephant in the room sitting there with a target on its back. Stuart aimed for it. One of his favourite routines revolved around his theory as to why the Holocaust had not happened in Britain because, he'd say coolly, looking at his hand on the microphone, 'the public transportation system just wasn't good enough to transport that many Jews. You'd have a load of Jews waiting around for a replacement bus service to Leamington Spa.' Then the harassed bus driver returning, reading over a clipboard in the rain: 'Sorry folks, the train to the camp has been cancelled. I repeat, the train has been cancelled; there will be no service to the camp today.' (Where would the camp have been – an abandoned Butlins? Nazis in Redcoats?) 'Please write to this address to receive a coupon valid against future travel.'

Years later, briefly back in the UK, he had seen a British comedian doing much the same routine, demonstratively regarding their watch like a waiting Jew, and sighed. Later still a bald and bearded comedian called Abraham Shelvey upbraided him for stealing the routine from said UK comedian. Yet Stuart still went away thinking he was the braver, performing the routine to its subjects, daring the Germans to laugh at their inherited misdeeds.

In English, of course. To have done it in German would have been too close to the bone, for a country where large sections of vocabulary still stood fenced off nearly fifty years after the concepts they denoted; big shattered blocks of words like *Führer* or *Rasse*. These great movements of history had also, somewhere in their tiniest repercussions, also hewn out Stuart's niche; that little shelter where he could forget his Oxford demons and, safe from the disaster of his homeland, quietly ascend the comic ladder to – where exactly?

A voice came singing up the stairs. 'They're so wonderfully *pretty*...'

The door opened; Dougie entered, holding a plastic bag bulging with croissants. 'Alright mate, I bought some croissants.' He placed the bag on the windowsill; a croissant fell out of it. 'Help yourself.'

'I'm surprised you found some,' said Stuart. 'Anybody down there?'

'About five people.'

'Is Malcolm there?'

'Naw man; I'd have definitely noticed him. What's this obsession with Malcolm anyway?'

Stuart shook his head. 'No obsession. How Dwight finds these places I'll never know. Maybe there used to be a troop presence here or something.'

'Mebee. Doesn't look like there's much to guard here though. A few houses and a lake.' Dougie was lying on his bed in his boots, arms spread out. 'I wish my lady was here.'

'I know what you mean,' said Stuart, never much good at this kind of talk.

'Aye. Are you alright man? You look kind of gloomy.'

'I'm alright.' Stuart was, too, although it did rather depend on what your definition of alright was – perhaps no longer being surprised by disappointment. 'Just thinking about my career.'

'Yeah? '

'Yeah.'

'Do you think you'll go back to England?'

'I don't want to. Do you?'

'Oh yeah, definitely. I can hear the UK calling me. When I'm there I can smell the success. But at the moment I've got time, y'know? Somebody said to me the other day, you're 28, what do you know? And I was like, aye, you're right, I am 28; I'm young and I'm going to enjoy it for a bit.'

'Thing is, I'm a little older than you. And I get the feeling that it's too late for me. In the UK, at least.'

'Too late? Nah man, it's not too late. You'd do fine there; it's your home. It's a question of whether you want to do it or not.'

'I don't know. Myself and the UK – we don't have a very easy relationship. I had a – very bad experience there.'

'What happened? If you don't mind talking about it.'

'No, not at all. I directed at play while at University and it was booed off by an audience of my contemporaries. I was rejected.' Always this story, this story. Always the cat-calls, the walk outs by friends and the decision to flee. Always Pippa Dryslade laughing in the auditorium. Always the next day when his actress girlfriend had bought him a change of clothes and he had taken the train to Bournemouth. And then walking the pier, Goethe (in English) stuffed into his pocket, and wailing because he had failed in a culture which did not allow for that. He felt that not just an audience, but England itself, had rejected him. Though that was self-dramatizing bullshit. 'Anyway, I don't want to talk about it. We've got a show to do!'

'Aye man, we're going to rock it! We're going to destroy this town!'

'Literally destroy it.'

'This town right, this town,' said Dougie, sitting up on the bed now, 'Is literally going to have a new arsehole after we're finished with it. Gonna have a new arsehole as big as – as big as –'

'As Christmas!'

'Aye! As big as fucking Christmas.'

They loved to laugh together. They were comedians; they would do their job; would go out there night after night to flatter and knife the assumptions of the age. It was, for all its ego and cruelty, an honest profession; there were no shortcuts to success up there. And you could never kid someone who'd failed. It was like trying to talk someone down from a ledge after they'd jumped.

'If you don't mind man, I'm gonna have a wee read of my notes,' said Dougie.

'Knock yourself out mate.' Stuart, who didn't practice, tried to imagine his set as a compass within him, a needle which when straightened lent him balance and grace. He picked up his bag, including socks and shoes; ready. 'I'm just going downstairs,' he said.

Downstairs he found about ten people seated, Shania Twain playing and no Malcolm. Paulie, resplendent in a red dress and boots, came to him. 'You nervous?' she asked, and Stuart actually grinned.

Three years later, he had become the kind of comedian who could nail for every public a twenty-minute set, who, while far from famous, had been on German television in German, who was, on this particular occasion, receiving just under eight-hundred euros for fifteen minutes of humour and the odd improvised barb to a manufacturer of high-end industrial cleaning lacquer.

The gig was going well. He always felt walking out for a gig was somewhat like heading down a tunnel and today the tunnel had brought him out in a handsome boardroom, with low-ceilings and soft yellow light on the faces of adults; perfect for comedy. The tighter the room the easier it was to hold their attention, as a confined space gave them no room to hide. Them, the eternal, nightly-replenishing them.

For those fifteen minutes, he seemed himself; his heaviness, his gloom disappeared and the performing *him* emerged like a mouse which had slumbered all day but now put on a top hat and twirled. He hit the jokes, waited for breaks and, learning that the company's boss was British – so that was why they had booked him – improvised a while. He had noticed the boss' shirt was somewhat unnecessarily opened at the top and all it took was a remark on this situation and the resultant ease of spotting the Brit amongst them to get them all on his side; after all, who didn't love to see their boss being mocked?

And now he was almost done, closing tonight with

one of his gentler anecdotes, of the night when he had been busted for riding his bike over a red light and surrounded by six police officers.

'You know, guys,' he said, 'I'm not sure six police officers is really necessary. To be honest, I'm a little bit scared.'

'And the officer said' – he turning now to look at the audience, to slow the pace of the sentence, almost having to do this with the whole of his body, his gait shortening – 'something which sums up exactly why I live in Germany and why I love it here so much -' - this one of the rare lies in his set - 'And the officer said; 'Why – we're all really nice!'

A big laugh; he bowed. Even the few people who appeared to speak little English applauded, perhaps in relief at this unexpected linguistic challenge having come to an end. He headed back out through the double doors. Ludwig was standing there, and offered him an immediate clap on the shoulder; 'Well done.'

'Yeah, I think they enjoyed it.' This was the aim, always; entertain.

A figure emerged up the stairs; it was Otto. From behind him came the noise of the audience, a trisyllabic pounding every performer in Germany loved to hear; '*Zu-ga-be, Zu-ga-be*.' Encore, encore.

Ludwig arched an eyebrow and said, in English: 'You go?'

'I've nothing prepared...'

The loud call of the British boss resounded, 'You come back in here young man!' The mocked siding with the mocked; that'd help him shore up his support in the office.

He moved towards the door, hesitating as he realized he didn't actually know what he was going to do and then, realizing audience desire was peaking, walked back into the room again.

He retook the microphone. 'So, I have literally told all my jokes.' They all laughed. They'd laugh at anything he said now, so complete and decisive had his victory been.

'Do your bit about Hitler and Göring,' said a voice; he turned, it was Otto, stood at the side of the door giving a little smile. 'You know, the one on YouTube.'

'Oh no – I don't do that bit anymore.'

'You must. It's very funny.'

'No, seriously – that was the only time that bit ever worked. There just happened to be a camera there so I thought I'd –'

'Come on!' shouted a voice from the audience. 'You've already broken every taboo tonight.'

'Well I...'

At this point the audience had began a chant, again of three syllables but this time gradually ascending in volume, of the words 'Nazi joke!', 'Nazi joke!' The British boss was particularly into this, drumming the balls of his fists on the table and shouting the phrase with an almost fanatic intensity.

He surveyed the nut-brown boardroom, the tables of young, casually-dressed Germans with their piercings and dreadlocks, faces flushed by the wine and candlelight as they bellowed out the phrase. 'Gosh,' he said after a long moment, 'Germany's really changed.'

Having told it – a joke far too facetious to be worth detailing here, but postulating the Nazi appeal as being based on mass rubber fetishism, and Hitler's desire to create *Lederraum* for the Germans, extending over several minutes and ending with the *Führer* in San Francisco, gagged and bound and bellowing the safe word – to wild laughter, he bowed and removed himself more finally from the stage. This time Ludwig the promoter was nowhere to be found; he moved over to a windowsill and crouched there, trembling, exhausted after his brief performance as if it had run over an hour. Then a hand touched his shoulder.

'That was good.' Claudia stood before him.

'Thank you. They seemed to enjoy it.' At such moments, after these small moments of triumph which interspersed a comedian's life, he always felt licensed to talk about himself a little more. After all, he was paid to. 'A German audience chanting for Nazi jokes. I'd say that's a first, but exactly the same thing happened to me in Bayreuth.'

'How are you getting back to your hotel?'

'I don't know. Ludwig will give me a lift, I guess.'

'Oh.' Claudia seemed to consider the next part very deeply. 'Because I'm here with my car. I could drive you if you like.'

He saw another night of frustration; a German girl who was too well brought up and too vanilla in flirting to sleep with a man on the first date. Still, where was the harm in trying? And at least there would be the aesthetic pleasure of staring at her frame, her stiffly-combed hair, her slightly brown skin.

'Yeah, sounds good,' he said.

'Great! Are you staying long?'

'Just tonight. My train leaves at 08.06.'

At this point he saw before him Ludwig and that open-shirted boss. This latter was holding up a large tub. 'Great show mate, great mate. And on behalf of everyone at CleanGo I'd like to present you with this complimentary tin of cement cleaning fluid.'

'Thank you, really, thank you,' he said, taking the tin into his hands.

'Will you be joining us for a drink?' asked the boss.

'You know,' he said, 'I think Claudia and I are going to get off now.' He looked at her, and then Ludwig, and smiled.

'Sure,' said the boss. His shirt was still open. 'Great show! Keep flying the flag.'

Ludwig handed him an envelope and they shook hands. 'We see us again, I hope?' said the older man.

'I hope so.' Stuart nodded and headed down to the exit. He stood a moment in the cold autumn air, enjoying the feeling of a job well done, sober as so often; he enjoyed the cool empty space. Down by the road, car lights flashed.

He moved down to the roadside and pulled at the car door; Claudia looked up with a smirk. Even after nearly a decade he still had to think to enter cars on the right. He moved round the car and got in, embarrassed.

'Phew,' he said. 'What a night.'

Claudia looked over. She wore a coat now. 'Did you enjoy it?'

'I enjoyed it.'

'Does it get easier?'

He paused, though he knew his answer. 'It does, yes. The jokes become part of you. Or they become you. I'm not sure which yet.'

She started the car.

'Now what I want to know,' she said, 'is why you want to do comedy in Germany.'

He smiled. 'It just sort of worked out that way.'

'But why don't you do it in England?'

'I did. They didn't like me. Hated me in fact. Besides,' he said tensely, 'I speak German.'

'Yes, but with a very strong accent.'

'Thanks. And you work in hospitality? You know, I do comedy for a living here. Something has to be going right.' Then a pause. 'I think it would be difficult going back now.'

The streets were quiet as she steered the little pod through them, wide, almost American-sized streets, flanked by bike lanes where the occasional cyclist puttered home, often white-haired and slow. How old Germany seemed, like the world's largest and richest retirement home.

'I saw you on television,' she said. 'You were funny. But I thought – this man is a not a comedian. He's a poet, a writer. I don't understand why you'd want to be a comedian.'

'Well, a lot of writers have to work as comedians these days, because you can't get paid properly writing.'

'But still – a comedian!'

'What on earth's wrong with being a comedian? You say it like it's a paedophile or something.'

'It's not important. We're here.' They were indeed, parked across the corner from the hotel and the station from where he would depart in a few hours.

'Thanks for the lift.'

'You're welcome.'

'D'you fancy a drink?'

'Fancy?'

'Would you like a drink?'

'Now?'

'No, tomorrow, when I'm not here.'

There was a pause. A few years ago, she would have knocked him back, but it was amazing what an appearance on Germany's third biggest talk show did for you, particularly one where you had acquitted yourself so well, correcting the host's German grammar once to the delight of the crowd. Now Claudia smiled, and with a slight wave of her head said, 'Just let me park this – I'll meet you inside.'

'Sure. I'll be in the lobby,' he said, offering her some

German. That branch was always there.

'Nice,' she said.

Stuart got out and she drove off. He watched the car a moment and moved into the hotel behind.

IV.

In Essen, Stuart was sitting in the front room of the Lone Star, watching his friend parrot, mime and stroll, to a small appreciative crowd. Watching him nail every joke, raise the tempo expertly, and gather applause breaks. Stuart had never seen Dougie so good, and it was making him jealous.

Not that his own gig had been bad, at least to the external observer, who would have seen an audience sometimes laughing, sometimes focusing intently, trying to understand, to hold onto every word. English knowledge deteriorated rapidly outside of Berlin. But he had struggled; struggled to get his jokes in the right order, to put paid to the automatically lowered expectations the audience had of the performer who went on first. And now Dougie was killing it, killing it, killing it – killing it like he had never seen him kill it before. What had happened? When had Dougie become so good? This wasn't in the script – that other people got funnier too!

He sipped his beer, melancholy, as the audience erupted into applause again.

From across the tiny room, the door opened. A tall, overweight man entered, clad in a black raincoat and wearing a squat leather hat. He paused, observing the scene, face already wearing an inviting smile, the kind of man everyone had to look at when they entered, which was kind of the point of Malcolm. The new arrival gave a little wave across the room at Dougie and, this unnoticed, redirected it at Paulie, who indicated the beer tap; Malcolm gave a little flick of the wrist which, presumably, indicated acceptance. By the time he had crossed the room, squeezing those tree trunk legs past the big Germans in their tiny chair, there was a beer waiting for him at the bar.

'Hey you,' he said in a whisper to Paulie.

'Hey Malkie, how are you?'

'I'm so good.'

'Guys, shhh!' Stuart said, indicating the stage.

'Oh! Sorry!' said Malcolm exaggeratedly and, without making eye contact, plumped himself on a stool to watch.

'It's alright man,' said Dougie, taking a break to sip on his beer. 'My mate Malcolm everyone.' And for a last time all eyes turned to the latecomer, who gave a flirtatious wave.

Dougie was into his closer now, his chilli-con carne set piece. 'Now, have y'ever been having sex with your girlfriend, right, and she puts her finger up your bum? Aye? And what's she do man –' playing the crowd here – 'that's right! Eew! She squeals. And I'm like, what do you expect darling if you put your finger up mae backside? Do you expect it to come out smelling of roses with little chocolate sprinkles on the top?' Stuart nodded to the rhythms of the jokes. He knew the routine; he knew all their routines; Malcolm, Dwight, Dougie, nice

Carly Dobson, Joe Malone with his strip club bit, even old man Carey who did nothing but talk about his children and weight - and they knew his. There were no secrets between comedians. 'And anyway love –' this calling back an earlier joke about the logistics of buying multiple chilli con carne against one larger one, *großer Eintopf* the Germans called it, and buttressed by Dougie's actual production of a mini chilli con-carne tin; 'And anyway, I've had to eat five tins of chilli con-carne this week!'

Deafening applause. Dougie milked it, waved, but he was out of jokes – Stuart would have been too a few years earlier; for comedians, extra years meant above all time to develop more bits. Nothing was ever lost and the years afforded surprising opportunities to resurrect jokes thought definitively obsolete.

Dougie walked the ten paces to the bar to collect the waiting victory pint.

'Nice job,' said Paulie.

'You were so funny,' said Malcolm. He placed his hand on Dougie's sweat-soaked sleeve. 'Look at me.' Dougie did so. 'You did such a great job tonight.'

'Thanks man,' said Dougie, for all the world the homecoming king at the Glasgow barn dance.

A middle-aged man had approached, face smiling although for some reason in him that conveyed no affection or enjoyment. 'You were very funny,' the man said to Dougie.

'Thanks very much man, aye.'

'Do you do this for a job or is it just a hobby?'

'Trying to do it as a job, aye. Cheers!' Dougie raised a glass in congratulation; staring into each others' eyes, all present toasted each other.

'Yes – it was really quite good. I live just round the corner and Paulie invited me. I'm really glad I came. Tell me – are there many opportunities to perform English comedy in Germany?'

'This is your man to ask,' said Dougie. 'He's been doing it longer than anyone.'

'Hello there,' said Stuart.

'Arno. Yes.'

But no compliment came.

Unprompted, Stuart elaborated. 'There's an emergent English language comedy-scene in Berlin. When I first got there, there was one comedy night in English, and I ran it. Now there's the opportunity to perform in English every night of the week.' Stuart was talking too hard, getting pissed off; no texts, the bad set, Malcolm, who had briefly vanished to the bathroom and spared him for an instant his weird flirtatious hate.

'And do the Germans get your humour?'

'Oh aye. I'd say about half the audiences at these shows are German, right?'

'Right.'

'Because you English…'

'I'm not English, mate.'

'Oh yes, sorry.' The questioner popped his hand onto his mouth. 'Because you British say we Germans have no sense of humour.'

'That's bollocks,' said Dougie. 'Most Germans I know have a fantastic sense of humour.'

'Everyone has a sense of humour,' Stuart said.

'Really?' said the man, almost hopefully.

'I do a bit about it in my show, actually. One night after a gig a German guy came up to me and said, "You know you have this bit in your set about Germans not being funny? I don't think that's very amusing,"' Stuart said.

'No!' said their interrogator. 'Did he! Noooo! - You're joking, right?'

'Right,' said Stuart.

'Anyway – Dougie,' said Dougie, offering his hand. The man took it and shook warmly.

'I'm Arno. I live in Kettwig. Thank you guys – it was really very good,' Arno said, and then, with a little laugh as if at the absurdity of them having met, moved back to the bar.

Meanwhile Malcolm had come back from the toilet, his face dripping with water. 'Shots?'

The evening wore on, and the inhabitants of Kettwig came to pay tribute to the young out-of-town Billy Connolly and his warm up act, Stuart Holmes, earning coos from local women and the overbearing recounting of beloved jokes from greying middle-aged men. Alcohol was drunk, and Paulie chatted with each of the guests.

'How's David?' asked one.

'We broke up,' said Paulie.

'Oh I'm so sorry!'

'It's alright – it was a year ago.'

'My God!'

'News travels fast in Kettwig,' Stuart said to Dougie.

Finally, two hours later – people lingering unusually long after a comedy evening, there being presumably nowhere else to go – and with a final 'Amazing show guys! Thanks Paulie' – Arno, the last of the revellers, was gone. They were left alone in the after-hours glow; Dougie, Malcolm, Stuart and Paulie. Plus a silent young couple who did nothing but drink vodka and order more. In this country, even in a provincial town at a slow time of year, you at least got to decide when you went to bed.

'So you're Scottish,' said Paulie.

'Aye, I'm from Glasgow.'

'Is it nice?'

'It's a great town, yes.'

'And you?'

'Stuart is… Stuart is…' Malcolm was very drunk. He was big, so it had taken him some time to get there, but get there he undoubtedly had. His face was sweaty and he mumbled through wide slobbery gawps.

'I'm half-Welsh,' said Stuart. 'More Welsh than anything else, actually.'

'Really? I dated a Welsh guy – he was amazing. We were

together for four years.'

Paulie's expression had changed; something in the memory moved her. They were seeing a new side to her – if you stayed up late enough, these things came out. Perhaps this was why the British had acquired their reputation for reserve; with their truncated opening hours and frantic rushes home, such opportunities for late night conversations, when the drunken soul unfurled in full, rarely arose.

'I went to visit him in Wales. And on the train he told me: I want you to prepare yourself, they're going to fight. And I said, huh, I'm from Texas, I can deal with it. And we get there and we all meet each other and there they all are at the table, big guys in check shirts, sitting there saying 'And how are you Rhys?' 'And how are you Bryn?' So I think, hah, these guys are pussycats, and I get up and go to the ladies room and when I come back, they're all at the bar, one of them has his hands round Bryn's neck and is trying to kill him, and the other three brothers are all trying to pull him back. Would you believe it! I thought my family was bad but I've never seen anyone fight like those boys.'

'The Welsh are passionate people,' said Stuart. He actually believed that; believed that his fire, his drive, his wit, had come from the wet valleys and black soil. He believed it particularly when he was, as now, drunk.

'Here – that's a photo of him.' Paulie held over her iPhone, displaying a tall, lanky man in a red jumper looking away from the camera, eye cut through at the edge of the frame. 'He's got a restaurant in Berlin now.'

'His name's Bryn?' The name had rung something in

Stuart; not quite a bell, more a little chime of memory. 'I remember eating in a restaurant owned by a Welsh Bryn a few years ago. Can I use this?' he said, indicating the computer ahead of him.

'Of course,' said Paulie.

Dougie appeared. 'Alright man.'

'I'm debating whether to have a cigarette,' said Stuart.

'Aye do it man. And let's have a couple more shots shall we?'

'Absolutely,' said Malcolm. 'We shall.'

Paulie poured out four shots of tequila. 'No lemon, I'm afraid.' She looked at the silent couple; no, they were done.

'There we have it,' said Stuart, indicating the results of his Google search. 'The Llŷn, Berlin. I went and ate with my ex-girlfriend there. She was from Chicago.' He neglected to mention that the restaurant had been bloody awful. 'She was American and had a thing about the Welsh, you see.'

'Figures.' Paulie looked at him with a kind of friendly disinterest and then to Doug with a look which said, you're much sexier.

In response Dougie tapped a hand on the bar and flashed that mischievous smile. 'Are we doing these or not?'

'Totally.' Malcolm again. 'We're doing *these*.'

The four friends, all foreigners, gathered in Germany, took a moment to celebrate their being alive at the same moment of human history, and to be spending the tiniest portion of this minute time – or viewed in another way, a not inconsiderable chunk of it – in a bar in Kettwig, West Germany, a place undisturbed by human history, but nonetheless, at this moment, a site of happiness and conviviality on the human map. They drank.

Malcolm, however, took this latest libation even more badly. Almost as soon as the tequila hit his throat he made a huge swaying movement, like a flag blown on a masthead, and swayed back from his stool, his big hands flailing like shovels. Dougie propped him, saying, 'Whoa, whoa big man. Steady now, don't want to hurt yourself there.'

'Sorry. Sorry Dougie.' Malcolm had straightened himself. He looked to the mute couple. 'Sorry random people.'

The young couple looked over briefly and bemusedly and then decided, with quiet thanks to Paulie, to finally leave. Paulie glanced to Dougie, who had dealt with enough drunks in his time to know what to do. 'How's about we get you to bed, big man?'

'I –' Malcolm gave a little fishy gape. 'Will you tuck me up?' he said to Dougie.

Dougie looked to Paulie. She said, 'There's a spare room on the ground floor, just over from yours. Should I show you up?'

'No, no, I know where it is. Just set me up with a wee whiskey for when I come back, will you? None of this tequila shite.'

'Will do,' said Paulie.

And Dougie put his hand behind the big Canadian's back and steered him out the exit and up the stairs.

'He's really funny,' said Paulie after a moment.

'Yeah – and he's a great guy.'

'You seem to get on.'

'We're good friends, yes.' Stuart looked at his drink. He no longer particularly wanted it. 'Do you have a cigarette?'

Paulie opened her package – Lucky Strike, a brand Stuart had always loved – and he took one from within. Even before it was in his mouth he knew it was a bad idea; he lit.

After a while she spoke again in the friendly, smoking silence. 'You know I thought he was a homeless person the first time I met him.'

Stuart smiled. The smoke was in his mouth; 'You said,' he said releasing it. He liked Paulie, as he admired all women who tried to do something different with their life, who tried to go another route than the conformity, and willing themselves to love the conformity, of marriage and children. He adored her bar, her little piece of freedom, even if, as she explained, it cost her insane amounts to maintain.

'It doesn't really make sense to be honest,' she said. 'I'd need to be making twice as much as I am to make any profit. I mean, I'd need to be making twice as much as I am now, and you saw it tonight. So I think I'll keep it another six months and then I'll cancel the contract.'

'It's a shame,' said Stuart. 'It's a nice place.'

'Oh yeah, it's a shame. Ever since I was a little girl I wanted to have my own bar. *Really.* Well – at least I can say I did it now. On to the next ambition.'

'Any idea what that is?'

'Maybe I'll go back to school.'

'To study what?'

'I was thinking about speech therapy. Teach German children how to say *th*.' She smiled. 'What about you – do you think you'll go back to England?'

'No plans. I left under a cloud.'

'What happened?'

'I did a show. It didn't work out.'

'Isn't that a bit extreme?'

'What?'

'To leave because of a *bad show*.'

'It was a *really* bad show. I mean it was the kind of show you leave town after. And also I didn't think I'd be successful there. No prophet is accepted in his own country. I mean, I'm not actually a prophet - I am a comedian though; there are similarities. What similarities? They're both, er, talking professions. Anyway, what's your story? Why did you leave?'

'What? Oh, one thing led to another I guess.'

'No, tell me,' said Stuart, raising his rapidly-disappearing cigarette. 'I'm interested.'

'I fell in love.'

'With a German?'

'Yeah – he was. He was selling meat in Austin. He'd just been in the *Bundeswehr* and had this idea of becoming a German butcher in Texas. He sold cuts out of the back of his truck. A very handsome, tall, mixed race German-Moroccan man, called Heiner. Oh, he was gorgeous! He had these beautiful brown eyes. Anyway we spent a few years driving round Texas living in the truck. I tell you those were some of the best years of my life – living in the truck, camping out, making love under the stars. You can't do that in Cologne. One time – do you know the actor J.T. Walsh? One time we picked him up after he broke down and drove him all the way to Houston. I can tell you he was a very charming man and extremely elegantly dressed. But then my husband had visa issues, and U.S. immigration are such assholes, you know; well, if you don't, they're assholes. So he had to go home. I waited a while in Austin and I couldn't take it without him so I went too. I spent a few years learning German, and then I was in a line-dancing group. After that I just sort of stayed.'

'And your husband?'

'Oh, we split up a long time ago. But we're still friends – he's an *Elektriker* now.' An electrician; she spoke the German word completely without accent. 'We still see each other and talk about how fucking crazy we were.'

'Does he come here?'

'Oh God no. He barely even drinks. Anyway, have you always been doing comedy?'

'I was doing it before I came to Germany, yes.' Stuart stubbed the cigarette. 'But that's not why I came to Germany – I'm not sure many people move here for the humour.'

'That's what you said in your set,' Paulie said. 'So why did you come?'

'It's really a long story,' Stuart said.

'Go on.'

'Do you actually want to hear it? I hate talking about myself.'

'Sure. I'm not tired yet.'

Stuart looked around the bar; they were the last people left and only music could be heard softly playing, quiet, country music. 'Well I think you could say I broke up with my country. Or rather it broke up with me. And the whole thing was dramatic, really, in the purest sense of the word.'

Paulie looked at him and smiled. 'Do you want a drink?' she said.

'Thanks,' said Stuart. 'A vodka tonic.' And he began to talk.

'I came to Oxford from a medium-sized town in the Midlands, the most English part of England, grey, flat and well inland. When I think of my childhood the main memory I have is boredom. Maybe not so much boredom as a void. An existential absence. It was a consumerist society, but there was a kind of discomfort to everything. Once a friend came to stay with me in my childhood home and she said that something about the house I grew up in really inspired someone to start living. I suppose it was asking her too much to state what that something was.

'I've always been funny. Peculiar and ha-ha. I could make my parents laugh by giving them accounts of how hopeless I was at school sports. I'd tell my parents that we'd do an exercise and afterwards the teacher would say, and now, as an example of how not to do it, here's Stuart. They'd laugh and I liked it; never mind that no one in reality had ever said that. I remember once attempting to throw the javelin and it got stuck vertically in front of me like a pole.

'Are these memories even interesting to you? They are? Because it's a long story and there aren't many laughs. Next question. What do you think of when you think of Oxford? Dreaming spires and punting toffs? Libraries and Harry Potter? Do you know what I think of? I think of the taste of overpriced sandwiches. Eating endless overpriced sandwiches and talking with people about the meaning of being at Oxford, a little market town in the Midlands where bugger all has ever happened and bugger all ever will. And there we couldn't voice what we all knew; we were all, even those of us with exorbitant inherited means, getting ripped off.

But when I arrived at Oxford I was determined to conquer the place. And comedy was a big part of that; I wanted nothing less than rapid fame. In my first year I performed in the Oxford Revue – it's the University sketch group, the Oxford equivalent of the Cambridge Footlights but less good - and a little trio of trust-fund comedians decided *I* was its natural heir, despite the fact that my ambition had always been to be a writer.

'The Revue had never been as popular or professional as the Footlights, but had still delivered up a fair few famous comics; they had Peter Cook, we had Dudley Moore, you catch my drift. As such it still had prestige and I was determined to make something of it. In my first year I'd also been offered, stewardship of the Oxford Comedy society, started by award-winning comedian and second-year student Pippa Dryslade. A lovely, strong-headed girl, blessed with talent and ego, already victorious in a national comedy competition, and as such a hallowed figure.

'Anyway I accepted both the comedy society and the Revue into my hands. My first mistake, as it soon became clear that I couldn't do both roles. But worst of all I tried to and I took people's money off them for Comedy Society shows which I could not provide, something I deeply regret. And so we agreed that two other comedians, Teddy Woodthorpe and Arnold Thwaite, Dryslade's protégé, would take it over, and I set up a meeting with them to discuss this and their involvement in that year's Revue. But then, and this was my biggest mistake, I failed to attend. Who was it who said that a classic sign of drug addiction was not showing up? Well depression's the same.

'Why was I depressed? Looked at now, what depressed me was a mediocrity, a shoddiness to things. A sense of never having got the best of what life had to offer – I never felt that later, until Berlin. Imagine me, raised in the English provinces, a childhood which, apart from the divorce of my parents, was notable mainly for its complete absence of event, and then I get to Oxford - and things were just as bad; the place full of people who saw ideas, subjects, literature purely as lines on a CV.

'My direct peers were also neurotic, stressed-out

individuals. But my own mental health crisis was deeper than most; I was deeply depressed by the place in which I lived in. For their part my tutors told me to do more exercise and perhaps I should have cycled more. I didn't know how to cook; I told my girlfriend of the time that I wanted to make pasta but I was unsure how much water to put in. It was only later in Berlin that I learnt how to, toiling away for hours under the lamplight to get the burnt rice out of the pan. Back in Oxford I lived on sweets and stayed up every night.

'So on that day I was due to meet Woodford and Thwaite I just lay in bed reading. But that missed meeting took on a greater significance, or at least does considered now. It didn't seem so important at the time but my absence – I see them now, Woodford and Thwaite waiting for me outside the pub, looking at their watches, realizing the depressed man was not going to show; I wondered how long they waited – this hapless snub in the vicious playground of Oxford compelled them to form their own sketch group, *Not the Oxford Revue*. They presented a show at Oxford's second theatre, a massive, sell-out success, all of which didn't have a good effect on me.

'Each year, the Oxford Revue and the Footlights met up to do a joint show at the Oxford Playhouse. Now the Footlights had things like professional directors and ample rehearsal time and are basically much better comedians than Oxford. Oxford who would, at least in those days, turn up with their sketches on a piece of A4 paper and proceed to forget their joke. Cambridge, meanwhile, would come out for the second half, gambol around the stage being brilliant and send the Oxford public home asking why couldn't we have been more like them. It was a kind of ritualized home defeat.

'But by my time Oxford had been too bad for too long. The year before my arrival, a nadir had been reached with a Star Trek sketch at the Playhouse in which the participants, dressed in fake Starfleet uniforms with cardboard badges, had all simultaneously leant in one direction then the other in simulation of a shaky spaceship. 'Phasers on stun!' etc. So awful, so utterly, life-negatingly shit had they in fact been that upon assuming the Presidency I was summoned to a meeting with the artistic director of the Oxford Playhouse, Les Thorpe. Les was a short man in a polo neck with a receding hairline and a brown flannel jacket. He informed me that, due to years of falling quality, the annual Playhouse show for the Revue would have to be cancelled. Of course, said Les, looking at me behind thick pricey glasses, the decision would be subject to *constant* review.

'This was an early experience of a most British phenomenon, having to apply for your own job. Still I set about courting Les Thorpe assiduously. I wrote him applications, met him for tea and steered the contacts I had in his direction – I knew who I could get to drop a kind word. And in the end, in a brief email received that spring, he relented; there would be a Playhouse Revue show after all. Only it was now unfortunately too late to book the Cambridge Footlights, who were apparently shooting a documentary about themselves for Japanese television, and so the proposal was made to replace the Footlights with 'Not the Oxford Revue', and did I know their President, Arnold Thwaite? A charming man – you know, he could be the next Rowan Atkinson.

'The show was to be called 'Not the Oxford Revue vs. The Oxford Revue' – what a good idea that was. Take a group of over-competitive student comedians who'd slit each other's throats for a little sniff of success and encourage them to fight it out amongst themselves as to who was the funniest and, of course, invite an audience of their peers to judge who was the better too. A brilliant plan. I for my part, strung out, deep in my affairs, off booze but always stoned, threw myself into writing and rehearsing the Revue show. It would be a narrative show – again and again the Revue had been criticized for, unlike Cambridge, failing to provide a coherent narrative and I was determined to give them the sketch show equivalent of a thriller.

'Soon another controversy arrived. The atmosphere between the two sketch groups had been bitter from the start. The division of the show was fairly simple; some stand-up, the first half Not the Oxford Revue, the second half the Oxford Revue. But somewhere within pitching Thorpe his idea, Thwaite claimed, I'd agreed to include a sketch from Pippa Dryslade, about a rapping crocodile if I recall. Well, for obvious reasons, I wasn't about to let Not the Oxford Revue start the Oxford Revue show, any more than I expected to be able to start theirs. But Woodford and Pippa both insisted, again and again, that I'd agreed.

'Eventually it was called before the head of the Oxford University Drama society.

'I think,' said this later-to-become famous actor, looking at me, 'We're going to have to drop it. Mainly because I don't think *you* are going to compromise.'

'Anyway the upshot of all this was that by the time the show came round you had two casts entirely alienated from each other... And I was very sick. And not just depression; by the final week of rehearsals I had a heavy cold. Regardless the day of the show, long ringed on my calendar, arrived. May 21, 2003. Yes, I remember that day very well. Let's call it the day I got my comeuppance.'

V.

At Oxford, over the river, there is a long road which winds into Cowley, the multicultural sink estate where most of the students live out in their second year, very far from the play of dreaming spires and punting rich.

Stuart Holmes lived there for a time too in the early 2000s. He lived on a suburban street called Boulter Street, a shabby little tumble of houses, a haphazard cul-de-sac. One May morning he shut the 50th one of its doors and walked away from it, pulling up his jacket. It was very cold and bright. He passed a house in which a few days earlier a man had died, his face having been burnt beyond recognition by indoor fireworks. A journalist had come round to interview Stuart and asked him to confirm that was what had happened – 'if

86

you say it, I can write it' – but Stuart had somehow felt compelled to refuse doing that.

He walked along the street to where Boulter met St. Clements Street, the long thoroughfare which led on back to the centre of town, towards the Oxford of history, of virgins and bookshops. It was also the Oxford of extremely expensive sandwich shops and, if he ever had occasion to write a memoir of this time, it would surely have been called 'Baguettes.'

Walking along the road – for Stuart was a habitual walker in this town of bikes – came a figure he knew well, a rotund, bulge-eyed man dressed as ever in a waistcoat. 'Stuart!' called the man, lifting his arms exuberantly as he did and performing a mock-stunned stumble backwards, 'Stuart Holmes!'

'Peter.' Peter Lowel.

'Oh my God! I love you!' said Peter, moving round in a kind of weird dance, his eyes fixed on Stuart the whole time. 'I love him. I love Stuart,' Peter shouted to a passing cyclist.

'How are you Peter?' asked Stuart.

'Nomnomnomnom.' Then Peter flinched suddenly, and looked at him almost angrily. 'I hate you,' said Peter. The little dance resumed but now it had grown almost vengeful, animalistic. 'Hate you!'

Stuart was already walking on towards the town centre. 'See you later,' he called to Peter.

'I love you!' he could hear Peter calling back.

Stuart walked on. His mind was turning to the show tonight – of course it was. He had received a text from his producer, Julia, that a London West end promoter was due to come; they didn't know exactly where the promoter was from, or what they indeed looked like, but they were definitely going to come. It would be nice to be famous Stuart thought. He pictured it now; being able to peremptorily quit Oxford, a place he despised deeply, and move straight into a theatrical career; that, anyway, was his ambition. And he wasn't sure he was going to be staying here anyway. He had recently applied for a scholarship to study Old Finnish at the University of Helsinki. It had been that or Icelandic scalds in Reykjavík.

Though of course, there was always Nellie, his actress girlfriend, who loved Oxford.

And Oxford *was* beautiful, in its rococo arches, and cold medieval courts, and curved bridges under which the punters glided, and Stuart couldn't see it. Stuart could only see as far his own nose, which was today incidentally full of cold, streaming down onto him, onto his green corduroy shirt. He needed to get to the Playhouse, though first grab some lunch, so he stopped at a busy sandwich shop on Oxford's main shopping street.

Flo Doherty was there, sitting upstairs with a friend.

'It's Stuart!' he called as Stuart moved into the room and sat with his sandwich and caramel square. Stuart looked over, pale and sweaty.

'Hi Flo.'

'Excited for tonight?'

'I am.'

'Nervous?'

'I don't get nervous.'

Next to Flo was a British-Asian man with bloodshot eyes. 'What's tonight?' the man asked.

'Shaf, this is Stuart Holmes,' said Flo. 'Stuart's the President of the Oxford Revue. And it's the annual show tonight – this year it's the Oxford Revue vs. Not the Oxford Revue.'

'Where is it?'

'The Oxford Playhouse,' Flo smiled. 'Are there still tickets?'

'Yes, but they're selling fast.'

'It's going to be amazing,' Flo continued. 'The reviews were brilliant.'

'One of them was. The Oxford Student one was done by a German and he just said that we made too many jokes about paedophiles.'

'Yeah, but everyone knows the Germans have no sense of humour.'

Shaf said slowly, 'I was in Berlin recently. You can take a lot of drugs there.'

'Do you want some drugs?' asked Flo. 'We're going to have some coke later.'

Stuart didn't, and in fact his chicken and sweet mustard sandwich was just about done. 'Guys – much as I'd love to stay here chatting, my actors need me.'

'It's going to be a smash. Everyone's going to be there,' said Flo.

'I'm not,' said Shaf.

'Everyone's going to be there apart from Shaf,' said Flo.

Now Stuart was out of the cafe, walking along Magdalen Street, turning onto the main boulevard. It was tourist central here, the buses crowding along the road, the tourists hoping to catch a little of that Olde English charm behind the blackened facades. But Stuart still didn't see all this, felt only the dribble of his nose and the swirl of his dreams of glory. And he bent to check the screen of his ancient Nokia, which was telling him he had an unread message in its small black font. He unlocked the keypad; the message was from his production manager, Jonny.

I HAVE COMPLETED MY PROPS LIST

Stuart sighed. Jonny was a genuine, bona fide idiot, a man who a few days earlier had texted saying he couldn't find a button. Imagine a production manager who couldn't find a button, and who had also several months previously won student production manager of the year. Lost in mental criticism of others Stuart came now on his left-hand side to the Playhouse, where he had last performed a year previously in the Oxford Revue's show 'Gonads', in which he had portrayed a gonad. In the world of student comedy this counted as paying your dues. But tonight he would be judged, on his Revue, on his contribution to British comedy history, to his playing – him, the boldest and most radical student comic – the Andy Kaufman in a sea of Dudley Moores. First, though, he had to find the correct entrance.

He made his way round the back, which extended out

onto a concreted beer garden. There was a door slightly open out of which a man was heaving a keg.

'Excuse me,' said Stuart.

'Yes?' the man said.

'I, erm, have a show here tonight.'

'Oh, you're one of the artists. Let me show you to the dressing room.'

'It's OK,' said Stuart. 'Just through here, right?'

Stuart, who had never been called an artist before, entered the corridor. The man continued to walk behind him, while ahead of them Thwaite approached, the sound of flushing behind him. 'Sorry mate,' said Thwaite, 'wouldn't go in there. Major post-shit situation. Absolute stinkoid.'

'I'm actually just going through to the main stage.'

'Correct decision matey.' The flushing roar continued as Thorpe leant in, shouting 'Good luck for tonight.'

The hangar-like backstage gave way to the main auditorium and the beautiful sight of an empty heritage theatre with its hundreds of red-upholstered seats. Stuart paused a moment calming himself. There were actors on the stage talking, though not his actors. Several of those actors were there already though; Tubby Rikes, a magnetic young baldie who was his leading man, and Paul Talbot, a huge muscular Welshman who greeted him with a roar of 'Stuart!'

'Did they call you an artist too?' Stuart laughed.

'Come here,' said Talbot, taking him in his arms and walking him slightly to the side. 'Tonight is going to be so unbelievably brilliant.'

Stuart was smiling as he looked over he saw Nellie. His beloved Nellie. He looked over at her; her expression was stern.

'We can't rehearse,' she said.

'What?' said Stuart, moving swiftly out of Paul's hug. 'Why can't we?'

'Because 'Not the Oxford Revue' are in there.' She dropped her voice lower. 'They're blocking literally every cue. I don't know when we'll get on. If we can get on.'

More people were coming now; Cathy Lambert, Sophie Parkin, Jeffrey Dambo. All the main female and cameo roles. Stuart had for his part been seized by a horrible hacking cough, much to the perturbation of the assembled cast.

'Are you alright mate? Want a tissue?'

'No – I've got one...' Stuart straightened, his teeth gritting: the deal had expressly been that Revue would be allowed in at one pm. And his watch now showed five past one. He said 'I'll deal with this.'

Stuart marched through the auditorium, past the hundreds of seats which would soon be filled, seeing none of them – well, perhaps he took time for a cock of the head and a prideful inhalation. Then he bustled up the stairwell to the sound booth.

Rupert Ruffles was bent over the mixing desk with a technician, wearing a black polo neck. He was leaning over the techie giving detailed instructions in a perky whine. Stuart just stood at the entrance.

'Stuart,' Rupert said noticing him at last. 'OK, that's good Andy. Just a little more spot.' Rupert looked up. 'Sorry about this Stuart. We'll be done soon. Excited for tonight?'

'When are you going to be done?' said Stuart. He took a step towards Rupert, a much smaller man.

'We'll be finished, ah-ha,' said Rupert, giving a weaselly laugh, 'when we're finished.'

'Because we have curtain call at 17.30. And you've had all morning.'

'We've had since ten actually,' Rupert said.

'Three hours!'

'We had a lunch break.'

'So what do we do?' said Stuart.

'I don't know,' said Rupert. 'I'm not your director.' Rupert leant into the mic. 'OK guys. Run the whole thing again from the top.'

Stuart stared for a moment. 'Best of luck for tonight,' he said at last.

'You too,' said Rupert, and looked up with a big smile. 'Ursula – starting position.'

Stuart walked into the auditorium; Ursula was onstage, dressed as a plum. He crossed past her and backstage to where his actors were standing around.

'They're blocking their whole show,' Stuart said angrily upon entering.

'I booked us the Graves room,' Nellie carefully replied.

'Thanks,' he said, and leant in to give her a quick,

professional kiss.

And so the group of actors made the journey across Oxford from the Oxford Playhouse to St John's college, back along the main drag, so that they could use the Graves room, a small turquoise-walled chamber where they had been rehearsing for the last months, repeating until deep in the night at which point one of the grumpy porters would usually appear to toss them out. In a pack they strode: the American Gary Price, already bearing the long stage cloak he wore for the role of the villain Fumhat, was walking ahead of them with two of the actresses, Sophie and Cathy, both in green dresses, explaining to them as he did the intricacies and humiliations of archaeological digs in New York: 'And this guy comes up to me and says – you guys digging for gold?' Talbot was laughing with his actress girlfriend – but in a fine, safe way, he'd trust Talbot with his life – and Tubby was hauling, in its big worn case, his tuba, which was to be used just for a single joke. Stuart looked over to them proudly as he walked; he was very young and had a gang.

They came marching round into St. Johns, laughing and shouting, receiving baffled looks, and not just from tourists, as they moved down the corridor and to the little room, bounding through the door and then inside, taking up positions around the room, conversing, loosening, ready. 'Alright,' said Stuart with authority, 'Let's run the kazoos.'

Yet just a few minutes later all was chaos and rabble. Tubby was dozing besides his tuba, and Gary had gone to get coffee with the girls. His girlfriend was reading a magazine.

'What – is going on?' said Stuart.

'We've outgrown the Graves room, that's the problem,' Talbot rose to declare. It was true; they couldn't block their movements here, and this little carpeted square was very far from the vast stage they were soon to play.

'Did you see it,' Jeffrey was saying. 'It's big, isn't it? I mean, there's going to be an awful lot of people there. Like a large number.'

Nellie looked over to him. 'What?' she said to Stuart.

'I think we should go back to the theatre,' Stuart said. 'Where's Gary? Where's Marie?'

'They went to get coffee.'

'Well somebody go get them!'

Twenty minutes later Gary returned, sipping coffee and eating something out of a grease-stained bag.

'Sorry,' Gary said. 'Did you want coffee?'

'No,' said Stuart. He didn't drink it. 'Is everybody here?'

'We're missing Caps.'

Caps entered. 'Sorry. Was phoning my girlfriend. Things look bad.'

'Alright. Everybody here?'

'I think so.'

'Stuart!' It was Tubby.

'Yes?'

'I think I lost my kazoo.'

Stuart flashed a look to his girlfriend.

She looked over, coolly chewing nicotine gum. 'I told you. I'm not the production manager on this production. I'm purely an actress. Phone the production manager. It's his job.'

'Fine, I'll phone him,' said Stuart.

He did; the familiar nasal whine answering. 'Jonny's phone.'

'Hello Jonny.'

'Ah Stuart. I did send you a text earlier. I have now completed my props list.'

'Yes, Jonny, I got that, thank you so very much. But that's not the right issue now. It's that – could you get us another kazoo?'

'I have said props should be left at the theatre at all times.'

'Yes, Jonny, I totally agree – I think you're absolutely right about that – it's just, it's, the show tonight you see and we really need an extra kazoo.' He looked over at his girlfriend. 'And a sign, right?'

'Laura's making the sign.'

'Does she know that?'

'She said she was…'

'Somebody phone her!'

'There's no need to shout,' said Jonny.

'I'm not shouting!' Stuart shouted. 'Just get us a fucking

kazoo will you? Thank you.' He ended the call and launched into a hacking cough which ended with a yellowy burst of sputum into his handkerchief. 'Let's go to the Oxford Playhouse.'

When they arrived back at the Playhouse Rupert was *still* rehearsing.

'Nearly there,' Rupert said before Stuart had even got through the door.

'How long is nearly there?' said Stuart in the doorway. 'It's almost three-fucking-thirty.'

'Run that again from the top.' Rupert looked over but didn't stand up. 'Sorry Stuart, we're busy.'

Stuart went down and sat in the auditorium. Julia, his producer, came and quietly sat next to him.

'We've sold 400 tickets.'

'400?'

'We're going to get at least 450 in. BBC Oxford is coming. And that Oxford website.'

'That's good. You know, I'm just really proud of the show.'

'Excited?' asked Julia.

'Indeed. I've been working my whole life for this moment.'

'Well – it's an amazing show.' Julia hadn't actually seen it but, whatever, Stuart would take it.

'Thanks.'

'Finished!' called Rupert, bursting into the auditorium from the back. 'Right everyone,' he cried, 'Let's go to the pub.'

And Rupert and his little mob went off stage, laughing and joking and bounding out the door. Stuart stared at them with his sourest look and then sprung up.

'Nellie! Cathy! Sophie! Marie! Positions ! First scene!' Stuart spluttered and shouted. 'Come on, come on, we only have just over an hour!'

By the time this hour was up they had blocked exactly forty-five minutes of their two hour show and certain actors had never set foot on the stage at all. The result of all this was that the audience would in effect be watching their dress rehearsal.

About then Andrew the technician entered. 'You all have to get out right now,' he said.

'But we've only just started,' Stuart said.

'That's not my issue. Playhouse regs are quite clear; everybody has to be out of here by five thirty at the latest. It's five thirty.'

Stuart took a spaced-out pause. 'Alright everyone, clear the stage.' Tubby and Talbot, dressed as a bee and a priest respectively, shuffled offstage together, talking in low tones. Stuart for his part shuffled together his tawdry, coffee-stained script, saying despondently to Julia as he did, 'I can't believe this.'

Jonny was approaching.

'I have a kazoo,' Jonny said.

'Great Jonny.'

'It cost 65p.'

'Just sort it out with Nellie, will you?'

'I've told you, I'm not the production manager!' Nellie called back.

'I don't have any change,' Stuart said quietly. A new man was standing in front of him, with a huge shock of curly hair.

'Hey.'

'Hello.'

'Tig.'

'Hi Tig.'

'Cool. I'm a comedian. For tonight – you know, from the Cambridge Footlights. Well, alright, I'm not technically a Footlight but I'm representing the Footlights. I'm representing Cambridge. How long do I have?'

'Sorry but - who said you were on tonight?'

'You did. You're Stuart Holmes right?'

'Yes, I'm Stuart Holmes but…' Stuart thought back; he dimly remembered sending an email at 4am, some months ago, enquiring if the Footlights could send someone down. But he didn't remember receiving a reply any. 'Oh, *Tig*,' he said. 'Have you got five minutes?'

'I can do 15.'

'Five will be fine. I'll tell Rupert – or, if you find him, you can tell him. He's a small fat man in a polo neck. He talks a lot.'

Laura burst in, holding something large wrapped on a stick. 'I've got it!'

'What have you got?' said Stuart.

'The sign!'

'Right,' Stuart said.

'And about my cameo today – I practiced saying the line. Can I try it? "Hello sailor. Hellooooooo sailor." What do you think?'

'It's great Laura.'

'Or is it more – 'hell-o sailor'? And I thought I could wear this cap.' She popped a white woollen cap on her head.

'I already saw Rupert,' said Tig, standing to Stuart's left. 'He said I could do 15, at the start of the second half.'

Stuart sighed. 'Did Rupert invite you?' he said, standing up; some of the actors were calling him. 'Please do five. And keep it tight – we've got a very long show tonight.' Of which his part, the Oxford Revue, was to form the second half. Laura was standing in front of him.

'Lose the cap,' Stuart said.

With the auditorium being cleared and hoovered for the 7.30 start, and Not the Oxford Revue, plus Tig, safely ensconced in the only available dressing room, there was nothing for it, as Talbot suggested, but to go to the pub.

Stuart didn't drink. Indeed he disapproved of drinking, living for his part on a diet of marijuana and 50p mix. Gary sat opposite with a pint and a chaser, and Stuart didn't approve, it seeming to him a bad omen, imagining sloppy line deliveries to come. But nobody was getting paid, so how hard could he be on them?

They were sat in the yard behind the Oxford Playhouse, near the small Burton Taylor theatre, where Emperor Penguin had been staged. He remembered Nellie selling the tickets, newly together and so happy to give out the stubs. Kissing when the last one was sold. Now the sky above was very black, cracked almost, in a May as dark as winter.

'Come on everybody,' said his girlfriend.

'I'll see you at the start of the second half,' Stuart said.

Stuart moved to the theatre foyer, which was already filling.

His Mum was stood near the entrance with a concerned smile. 'Stuart – Pam's come down. Isn't that good of her?'

Pam was an old retired friend of his mother's who now spent her days photographing dogs.

'Thanks for coming, Pam,' Stuart said.

'I hope it's good,' said Pam with an unimpressed frown. 'The train ticket was expensive.'

'Thanks so much for coming, really,' said Stuart. 'This is a very big opportunity for me. This is probably the biggest venue in British student theatre,'

'You have done very well,' said his Mum.

'Stuart,' said his dad, approaching with a plastic pint cup.

Laura approached, dressed in her college scarf. 'Hello sailor!'

His dad said, smiling, 'Lively this one, isn't she?'

'Laura, these are my parents.' Stuart showed her his parents, together as so rarely. The two of them, little old people in Marks and Spencers wear, stood smiling back.

'You must be proud Mr. and Mrs. Holmes,' said Laura.

'Miss. Sachs,' said his mother.

'Stuart,' said Laura, standing a little too close to him, 'I made Italian fig cake for the after party.'

Stuart nodded. 'Thank you Laura. Now, if you excuse me, I have to go. We'll be starting in five minutes.'

'Good lad!' they all said, or words to that effect.

*

Stuart moved into the main auditorium. There were hundreds of people streaming in, coming into the stalls, friends, acquaintances. The strangers were often older and louder, and had a coarseness to their speech that the students, the reedy needy students, did not.

'Ready for a good laugh?'

'Am I fucking ever.'

'Hope it's not shite.'

'Students though innit. Wankers.'

Stuart took his seat towards the rear of the audience, directly before the main left entrance. Julia was already there, and excited.

'We had to open the dress circle,' she said. 'Biggest student show of the year.'

'People always want to see comedy,' Stuart replied.

'We're a hit!' said Julie.

In the pit to the right, Stuart could see his mother and father, and his girlfriend's family too. 'My mother likes you,' Nellie had said. 'I think she thinks you're the only genius she's ever met.' And his girlfriend's little sister, there in a tasselled cinnamon dress – smiling in anticipation of success. Now the lights were beginning to dim, and he noticed other familiar faces dotted around as the dark fell upon them.

'Good luck,' whispered Julia.

Arnold Thwaite came onto the stage first. He was wearing a black waistcoat and a silver bow tie, and said, raising his silver-topped cane – 'Welcome everyone to Not the Oxford Revue vs. The Oxford Revue.'

They went wild.

'We've got an amazing night of comedy for you tonight. But first, I want to talk to you. You know I read a headline recently that said 'Porn is being literally pumped into Britain's homes. And I thought,' Thwaite squealed, 'Really? Porn is really being pumped into Britain's homes? Like –' Thwaite, thin and red-haired, made a gross squelchy noise. 'Scwurppp.' Then came Stern Dad voice, Thwaite's specialty. 'Oh no dear. There's porn being pumped into the house again.' Generic Posh Woman: 'Oh no darling! Can you turn it off?'

The audience laughed for about five seconds straight, savouring this joke on the most radical of subjects, porn. It normally took the audience five minutes to warm up but with such excellent tech specs and at eight pounds a ticket, these people were like butter waiting to be spread.

Where had Tig come from? This detached Cambridge

Footlight, this man who seemed to end up on stage almost by accident, and was now there again, blethering bollocks about penguins and, once more, porn, and of course, that indispensable comic trump card, his possession penis. Tig seemed to go on for hours, shouting about doing 'a number three, a poo-wee', but there was a God, he was at his closer now. 'Can all the black people put their hands in the air?'

Nervous laughter into which Tig bellowed 'Come on!'

A few hands.

Tig said 'I still can't see you.' Then he said, 'Welcome to Oxford admissions.'

And with the ghost of satire securely slain, off went Tig.

Thwaite reappeared. 'Wasn't that incredible! Stealing my porn jokes, though. Ooo-er! Being pumped into our homes! Scwurppp! Now, are you ready for your first main act?'

What the hell was that, a first main act? You were either a main act or you weren't.

'I didn't hear you! Come on now!'

The audience roared louder.

'OK guys let's do this! Let's bring onto the stage – NOT – the Oxford – REVUEEEEEEEEEE!'

Stuart checked his watch; they had already been running for twenty-five minutes. He felt uneasy.

For now, a groovy little piece of pop funk began, and 'Not the Oxford Revue', these glorious specimens, these dancing clowns, these accessible fools, bounded onto the stage. Such enthusiasm! Here was Jerome Woodford, blonde and juggling, here was Ursula Blade, twirling and sashaying across the stage with her dress blown up by a fan. And here was Thwaite himself, who had expressly changed into jeans and a T-shirt to feature in the show he had himself warmed up for, and who was blowing bubbles.

It was a hell of a start and of course the audience loved it. They wanted to be entertained. The cast members twirled off, always in character, and the first sketch began, with Ursula emerging, dressed again as that gigantic plum. And now she began to pun, discharging a litany of fruit-based puns upon the audience in a way which left them rolling and gasping. Fruit puns! It would ever be thus; English audiences loved a juicy pun.

There followed funny videos of people dressed as cows, a song about soup, and not a single joke with bite or edge until, upon the finale – which featured all the cast dressed as rapping nuns, the laughter thinning now after over one hour in – 'Not the Oxford Revue' were dispatched to rapturous applause.

Stuart looked at his watch. Fuck. It was 9.15 with a twenty-minute interval still to come.

The Oxford Revue's turn; Stuart's turn. Triumph's turn? He walked out the foyer and round to the auditorium, to the apparent 'artist's entrance.' When he got backstage his whole cast was waiting for them, this numbering about twenty people.

Nellie was abuzz. 'Where's the oboe? The tuba? The

dart?' Various things were being found and tested, and some things couldn't be found at all. Jonny stood at the side of the prop's table with an air of inert pride.

'OK everyone gather in,' Stuart said. It was time for his motivational speech; the actors for their part moved into a huddle.

They all leant forward so their heads were at the same level looking over to him. But it suddenly occurred to him that he had prepared nothing, and he suddenly felt very sick, cold and frail. So all Stuart did was throw up his hands and say –

'It's there if you want it.'

And his arms fell back.

Then for a few minutes he strolled around, watching his actors, his heroes; Grimes was explaining medieval scholarship to Tubby, Paul was singing a rugby song; Jeffrey Dambo was practicing his line. Stuart suddenly felt greatly proud of them; perhaps they could pull it off after all. He kissed Nellie, he touched her hand, offered everyone a few last words of well-wishing, and walked back to the auditorium.

He passed his dad emerging from the toilet.

'Stewie, good luck,' said his dad.

'Thanks Dad.'

And Stuart's show began.

The plot of 'The Jokes Don't Work', written and directed by Stuart Holmes for 'The Oxford Revue' in 2003, is difficult to remember now, and those who were there do not remember it either clearly or with fondness. But for the sake of the record it was something as follows: Nelson Marvellous (Tubby Rickles), a teenage tearaway, is discovered to have an incredible gift for playing the oboe. Sponsored by his priest and music lover Father Toby (Paul Talbot) for entry to an elite oboe conservatorium, Nelson however refuses the patronage of eccentric but corrupt billionaire Artur Fumhat (Gary Price), inspiring as such the latter's wrath and seeing Fumhat resolve to kill the young man by hiding poison within his oboe. The whole narrative, which, when performed in full extends to nearly two hours, is interspersed with interludes such as the deadpan commentaries on the action of Gray and Carey, two middle-aged men, a recurring double act between the detectives Shaft (Jake Caps) and the Napoleonic TV soldier Sharpe (Cathy Lambert), and the energetic clowning of the one-lined jester Jeffrey Dambo (himself). All fairly conventional, then.

The opening scene depicts Nelson's theft of the oboe, which was until then being used by one Widow Downes (Nellie Cohen) to store the ashes of her dead husband. The tension of said scene is as to whether and when Nelson will in fact blow into said oboe, which he of course does, scattering the dead man's ashes all over the stage, this the scene's punch line. Before all that though the lights come up on four actresses seated on chairs, Stuart having thought it was a bold move to start this, his most high-profile show to date, with four funny girls.

From the very first line, however, the first and greatest problem of this to-date-only performance of 'The Jokes' was more than evident: namely, you couldn't hear what the actors were saying. Or you could but your ears had to work overtime to make them out. Still the first scene got some good laughs, particularly one exchange, played beautifully by his actress girlfriend, Nellie. Nelson's mother (Marie Smith): 'I must bid you good day.' Widow Downes' reply: 'Thank you.'

It felt good, that, hearing five hundred people laugh at once.

The next scene was intended to be a comic high point. The idea was that young Nelson, having kept the stolen instrument and practiced it incessantly, was being talked of as a musical prodigy. Father Toby, played by Paul, visited the house to verify the rumours and if so facilitate Nelson's access to an elite conservatoire. But the joke was that Nelson was in actual fact utter shite on the oboe, able only to play a dodgy version of 'Moonlight' from the musical Cats and 'The Saints Come Marching In', though his playing was still greeted with rapturous acclaim. 'Nelson!' Father Toby cried. 'That's just the kind of excellent music I've come to enjoy!'

During this audition scene each cast member – Nelson's mother, sisters, even the ghost of Widow Downes – were each to join in on a different instrument, from saxophone to miniature harp, building up a ridiculous sounding ensemble which ends with Father Toby whipping out a tuba and stomping around stage blasting it atonally.

But comedy, you see, was always in the small details. And the issue this night was that said tuba had already been positioned front stage left by an overeager stagehand, and was as such prominently on view throughout the scene. Meaning the topper on the joke, the sudden appearance of this huge instrument, was spoilt. Stuart sat there, increasingly agitated, thinking: If only he could run up there and remove it from the stage!

And these missed cues mounted. Lines flopped, or went unheard, props got lost, or extras moved to the wrong places. To mark the end of the first act, with the show approaching an hour now and the clock on 10.25, Jeffrey Dambo was to come onto the stage and sneeze, exaggeratedly, like, 'Atchoooo.' And then a sign would be raised: 'Act Two.' But when the sign was produced – and how had Stuart not seen this before? – it read 'Beginning of Act Two', and the already obscure joke, the acoustic similarity between 'Two' and 'choo', was rendered straight-up incomprehensible.

To start the 'second act', there having been no fresh interval, a parade of portraits took place at the villain Fumhat's house, drawing titters from parts of the crowd. But when you were painting entire portraits to get a giggle then there was a problem and by now the actors seemed very small and alone up there on the Playhouse stage. Whole passages were playing to silence, and the narrative was unclear, obscure, seeming like Stuart's giant avant-garde 'Fuck you' when in fact it was all simply unrehearsed. It was like university sketch comedy filtered through the medium of German symbolist drama.

By now people had begun to walk out. First a few, then more, tens, twenty, thirty at a time. The whole show was over two-and-a-half hours long now and some people went loudly jeering, some looking at watches and saying 'Last orders? Quick pint?' Amongst them, too, came Pippa Dryslade, Woodford and Thwaite, all just metres away from him and laughing and smiling in some kind of triumph. Stuart leant back in the darkness and felt very alone.

By the time Sharpe and Shaft came back for their reprise the mood had turned flat-out ugly. The air was tense while over the PA came his girlfriend's voice.

'Next week on the Oxford Revue. Is this the end for Sharpe and Shaft?'

And a male voice in the audience shouted back, 'Let's bloody well hope so!'

Applause and cheers broke out in the remaining crowd.

But that was actually the next joke! The lights came up and there were Sharpe and Shaft, dead.

'Yes,' said his girlfriend flatly over the PA.

'One step ahead of you mate, one step ahead,' shouted Stuart in the darkness towards the audience member.

And then a truly bizarre moment. His girlfriend spoke again; 'And there's some unbelievable news for Gray and Carey.'

Gray and Carey were seated onstage. Gray: 'Have you heard the news?'

Carey: 'I can't believe it.'

A huge laugh, and even some applause; it was like a bullied child doing a fart.

Now we are at the curtain call. Stuart is watching it all

as if from very far away. It was like, he thought later and before, and then, watching the mind of an ill person placed up there, a dishevelled, dismembered mind put on show for all to see. Like watching a sick man's mind.

Tubby is at the front of the stage, along with the rest of the cast, Paul, Nellie, Gary, Cathy, Sophie, Marie, Jeff, the extras, at least twenty of them there. The idea was that Nelson, his T-shirt still bloodstained from his death by oboe, was thanking everyone in the manner of the 'Wizard of Oz', saying that he'd had this amazing dream and, to the principals, 'you were there, and you were there – and, speaking to Fumhat friendlily 'and you' and then Gray and Carey, 'you were there and -'

'And you were all shite!' comes another male shout.

But this time there a different response from the crowd, a kind of gentle female exhalation, as if to say, that's enough now. Leave them alone now.

'Wuthering Heights' by Kate Bush was playing as the cast took their bows. Stuart stood, not looking over to his shocked producer; instead he walked straight up out the foyer of the theatre. He went quickly through into the cold night.

His plan – before he got the text messages and phone calls from his girlfriend, his parents, before he got just enough love – was to end his own life as quickly as possible. First though he had to get out of Oxford. As he headed to the bus stop he passed a figure.

Peter Lowell had just come out of the theatre. He looked over at Stuart intensely but said nothing now. He just raised his hands and gave Stuart a look – a look of a mixture of shame, revulsion and above all, sheer confusion, a look at Stuart which said – 'What *are* you?'

A lot of things were to happen after that. Stuart became a standing joke, derided in the student press, debunked, unwelcome now at the parties he had never wanted to attend anyway. Nellie would up and leave him, marry Flo and move to Indonesia. Later she would have two kids though not with him. Stuart would descend very deep and largely recover, but for now he sat in his girlfriend's room at St. John's college, reading a student creative writing magazine.

He was reading an article written by Laura, his former flatmate. The article was called 'When Comedy Goes Wrong' and was about how spectacularly the Oxford Revue had failed that spring. It decided, after various clichés of people 'leaving in droves' and audience jeers 'ringing in the actors' ears', that the cast and crew had been too concerned with making themselves laugh and not the audience, and as such cooked up an 'impenetrable turkey'.

And it was all Stuart's fault.

He sat, the pain screaming round in him once again. At which point his ancient Nokia began to shake. It was Thorpe, the Playhouse programming director. He answered.

'Hello Les,' he said. 'How are you?'

'Hi Stuart. Is this a good time?'

Stuart was sitting in his pants, covered in stale sweat. There were various unread books on the floor and he smelt of his own piss. 'Yeah, it's fine.'

'I wanted to phone you to talk about the show. We got your letter. Thanks for that.'

'Good.'

'How are you?'

'Obviously – I was – very disappointed.'

'Of course. It must have been a very wounding experience for you.'

'No one expected it to go like that.'

'No.'

'People who saw the show before said it was great.'

'Right.'

'And you know, I think, er, the professional standards we discussed beforehand were met. Because we rehearsed very hard, you see. Very hard. So if we're talking about professional standards, I think those were met.'

There was a pause. Thorpe made a little sucking sound then spoke.

'Funny you should say that Stuart. Because I've been listening to you for a while now, and do you know what I think?'

'Yes?'

'I think you sound earnest. Yes, earnest, Stuart, earnest. What you want doing comedy are words like wacky, zany, bonkers and fun. Not earnest. That's not a word you want. I saw your show; to be honest, I didn't laugh once.'

'Oh.'

'I mean, obviously, everyone at the Playhouse is very disappointed that the show went so terribly badly. But I think the problems were largely due to an unwillingness to listen on all sides.'

'Right.'

'Particularly yours.'

Stuart felt a lump in his throat. 'Well, thanks for your opinion, Les.'

'No problem. What are you up to this summer, anything nice?'

'I was thinking of visiting Germany.'

'Oh, you'll enjoy that, won't you. Did you ever think about going to France by the way? I think they'd quite like you there. They have more of an absurdist tradition.'

The conversation came to an end.

Stuart sat on the edge of the bed for a while, very quiet. He could hear footsteps and happy talk outside, people enjoying being at university. His girlfriend was at a Free Palestine meeting; he saw her lipstick on the side. Stuart rose over and picked it up.

Ten minutes later Nellie returned, carrying a tote bag of obscure-looking books – Nellie always did the reading. She put the bag down and turned; Stuart was sat upright in bed.

'Oh sugar what have you done?' she said.

On each of Stuart's arms he had written in lipstick in crude capitals 'FAILURE', and then underlined it with deep red strokes above his self-harm scars. She moved to him and took his arm.

'Come on,' she said, 'Let's wash this off.'

'It hurts so much,' he said.

'I know it does,' she said. 'It hurts me too.'

She ran the tap.

'Sorry,' he said as the water became clearer.

'I saw Thwaite,' she said. 'In the Eagle and Child.'

'What did he say?'

'He said, "Tell Stuart I'm sorry."'

'How nice of him.'

She handed him the towel and he dried the clean arm. 'Now the other one.' Cleaned, he sat down again. 'And I spoke to my sister. She's worried about you.'

'I think that we should do the show again,' Stuart said.

'Where?' she said. 'We've already lost Edinburgh.'

'I shouldn't have run off,' he said. 'Like a wounded animal.'

'But why does an animal run away, honey?'

He looked over at her. 'I don't know?'

He thought about it more.

She smiled at him.

'To survive?'

'Got it kiddo.'

There was a pause. 'Did you phone Darsh?'

'I did.'

'What did he say?'

'He said that if the Oxford Revue President leaves town after the Oxford Revue show, it's news.' She frowned. 'I told him that you were mentally ill, that they shouldn't be printing stuff like that about you.'

Stuart paused. 'They shouldn't be. Fuck!' He let out a howl but, just on the verge of being terrifying, turned it into funny, into a weird mad roaring noise.

He then said, 'Although I do kind of want them to.'

'Well, you can't have it both ways.'

'Mmm. What do you think of me?' he asked.

'What do I think of you?'

'Yes, what do you?'

'I think you're kindly and egotistical.'

'Anything else?'

'Just kindly and egotistical, all the way down.'

'I feel so bad,' he said.

'I know. I know sweetie. But let's be honest,' Nellie said, dipping into her bag to produce a carton of menthol cigarettes, 'It's not Palestine, is it? Here. We did a play. And we really loved it, and it went really badly. But we're still here. Nobody died.'

He looked at Nellie, his girlfriend, who smiled, her brown-stained upper tooth on show, a stain he loved.

'I'm sorry.' He bowed his head a little. Then 'Do you want tea?' he said.

'Yeah, wouldn't mind,' she said. 'I'll put it on.'

'No, it's fine.' Stuart paused before standing. He slipped on his trousers and went over to her little kettle. 'Put some music on,' he said.

'You confiscated it all,' she said.

'Only that one Travelling Wilburys CD,' he said. 'I'm not having you listen to that.'

'Bob Dylan alright?'

'Perfect.'

She pressed play, and a soft pedal steel shuffle began.

'OK?'

'I fucking love this song.' He was now at the teabag-stirring stage, really stirring and putting his soul into it. He wanted to make this cup of tea with real love. Next he added some milk from the fridge, drops spilling onto her floor.

'Sorry.' He wiped the drops with a towel, and finally handed her the tea, deep brown in her favourite stainless steel mug. 'It's a bit hot.'

Nellie took it, the hot base and cold handle, in her hands. 'Thanks, sweet,' she said.

'I don't deserve you,' he said. 'You're the best girl in the world.'

'Cheers.' Her grin was broad; her pale cheeks flushed a touch.

'Come on.' Stuart gestured; Nellie came to him. He hugged her and felt her lovely warm body in his arms and they began to dance. Stuart led, shakily, sweatily, but soon they began to speed up, making gentle little twirls across her student-halls floor, almost-waltzing in the quiet gloom, Stuart holding Nellie to his dirty body, their feet moving ever smoother and more perfectly together through the early summer night.

VI.

'So that's my story. Did you like it?'

'I liked some of it,' Claudia said.

It was late; they sat in his hotel room. She looked across the room at him from the chair beside the bed, a beer in her hand. 'And how do you feel about it now?'

'Oh you know,' he said dutifully, 'It made me a kinder person. But also a more conservative one. More timid, less original. It changed my relationship with my country forever.'

'Perhaps you only want to believe that,' she said. 'Because you can always go back.'

'Maybe. Nobody remembers it apart from me.'

'Exactly. You must have really learnt a lot from it.'

'Not really. I'm not actually sure you ever really learn anything from things. By the time you've learnt something you're already forgetting the things you learnt previously.' He shrugged, adding after a while, 'I'm aware of how ridiculous I was, by the way. How ridiculous I am.'

He listened to the hotel lamplight hum a moment and thought about his confession; he had done it once more, poured his heart out once again. He had it down pat now. It was amazing, for such a reserved man, how many times he had recounted the tale – whether pouring it out in bars in the Ruhrgebiet or Hanseatic hotels. He felt ashamed of himself.

Claudia spoke after a long silence. 'What happened next?'

'Mmm? I went to London after my exams. But there was nothing doing.'

'Nothing doing?'

'It didn't work. Then I visited a girl I knew in Berlin, and thank God I did. I don't know what I'd have done without Berlin.'

'And that's why you stay in Germany.'

'Yeah – I suppose. I'm successful here.'

'Really?'

'Yeah, I mean, I've been on TV –'

'Yes, you said, but I thought you wanted to be a writer. Is it really so successful to be doing something you don't want to?'

'I've found a niche...' he said. 'Listen, most people are happy to have success wherever they find it. What do *you* do, anyway?'

'Events management. That's why I'm here, remember.'

'Oh, of course.'

'I also sell gloves online.'

'Do you make them?'

'A friend of mine makes them – I do the sales. It's OK. Actually, do you still write?'

'I've tried a few things. But I sent them to a publisher in England and they told me they weren't of general interest.' His brow furrowed. 'Which meant: they were set in Germany. Namely the biggest country in Europe, the economic motor of the continent, its most spoken language... To have work disqualified just by dint of it being set in Germany – I mean!' He paused, hearing the anger in his voice. 'Maybe we shouldn't talk about this.'

'No, it's interesting. You hate England–'

'I don't hate England –'

'So you're proud to be English.'

'Are you proud to be German?'

Claudia smiled. 'It's just a coincidence. How can you be proud of a coincidence?'

'I don't know how you can. I suppose you're proud of parts of it, the parts you like. No one asks you to be proud of everything.'

'Well, I like Königsberger Klopse.' Meatballs in a white caper sauce; they weren't Stuart's idea of a good time. 'But there are things in German history – you know what they are. There are these things, and sometimes I wake up and lie there thinking about them, or I'm at a party and it's international and I say "I'm German", and it's a shame to say it, it's really a shame to speak the words out loud. And are you?'

'What?'

'Proud.'

'Yeah – I am... I love Shakespeare, and Kate Bush, and James Gillray – he was a cartoonist. I'm English. But when something like that happens to you at an early age you feel very – rejected.'

'But you feel accepted here in Germany.'

'Well –' he hesitated, although the answer had long been clear to him. 'I mean, what language are we speaking?'

'We can speak in German if you like.'

'No, it's alright. I'm much more charming in English.'

Yet he didn't feel he was being charming in any language; he felt he was whining.

'I think,' she said finally, 'that for we Germans it is very difficult to understand why a British person would choose Germany over England. But there are always more of you coming so – I don't know. Maybe Germany isn't so bad after all.'

'Germany's alright,' he said.

'You're happy here.'

Such big questions this night! She spoke to him as if she were interviewing him, but there was no position being contested, rather an objective assessment of the motivations of his soul was being conducted, her voice level, coming from one side, as if he were a job candidate for his own life. 'I don't know. When I'm back there I miss Germany; I miss the bike lanes and the bread. And the whole narrative of my adult life has been here.' He thought. 'I guess I'm looking for a reason to stay.'

He had meant it sexually, but that hadn't seemed to register with Claudia; German flirting was so subtle as to be missed by most microscopes. It seemed to normally consist normally of lengthy conversations about saving the world, or minute cultural differences, followed by the sudden onset of ferocious sex. But that didn't seem to be happening here; in fact at this moment, Claudia briskly stood and brushed down her trousers.

'So. I should go.'

He nodded. Seated in the hotel chair, beer flecks on his lips, 'Yeah,' he said. She craned her body to him a little.

'It was nice to meet you,' she said.

'You too.'

Was there something coming? She spoke. 'I think…'

'What?'

A pause. 'Oh, why not. Why the hell not.' She saw his eyes flicker – would she…? 'No, I don't want to have sex. Actually I want to show you something.'

'Yes?

'I want you to come with me.'

'What now?'

'No tomorrow, when you're not here. What time is your train?'

'It's at 08.06. It's two now so – in six hours.'

'Plenty of time. Come on – I'll get the car again.'

'Well, do I need anything?'

'Just bring your coat. It'll be cold there.'

'Where?'

'It's a surprise.' She had used the German word,

123

Überraschung, an overrushing, an ambush even, and it rang in the air. He looked over searching for clues in her face.

All she said was 'I'll meet you outside the hotel in twenty minutes' she said and left.

When Stuart arrived back in their shared room Dougie was already in bed though not sleeping. In fact the main light was on and Dougie was lying on top of the bed sheet eating croissants out of a plastic bag.

'So it's come to this, huh?' said Stuart.

Dougie looked up, and, chunks of breadstuff clearly visible in his maw, said 'These croissants are awful.'

'Serves you right for buying them.'

'Aye.' Dougie belched.

'How many people do you think were there tonight?' asked Stuart, moving to hang his suit jacket on a chair.

'Must have been twenty-five, easy.'

'I think it was more like twenty,' said Stuart.

'Still, hey, twenty people coming to watch English comedy in Kettwig on a Saturday night, it's not bad eh?'

'It's not bad,' said Stuart and farted. Dougie gave a little, hysterical, full-mouthed laugh and then ate more croissant.

'They loved you, man,' Stuart went on.

'Aye I did well.'

'Seriously – watching like you I thought, I'm going to

have to up my game tomorrow. You've got a lot better.'

The praise was begrudging but honest, as much challenge as compliment. Dougie's eyes were bright but he restricted himself to a reserved 'Thanks, man.'

'Yeah well. Enjoy your croissants while they last. I'm going to be funnier tomorrow.'

Dougie gave a big croissant-pulping laugh and then popped another one in his mouth. In the meantime Stuart was ready for bed in a T-Shirt and boxers. 'Are you going to sleep like that?' he asked.

'What? No, no, give me a minute.' Dougie reared up slightly and brushed the crumbs off his lap. 'Alright.'

Stuart said, 'Ready?'

'Pronto,' said Dougie.

Stuart slipped off the light and, slightly mirthful, lay in the dark on the bed. There was no sound in the room except for a quiet residual munching.

There was a pause and then Stuart began to laugh, a wheeze impossible to restrain.

'Wha'?' asked Dougie, grin audible in his voice.

'Nearly finished?'

'Mmm. Croissants.'

The dark had irresistibly increased the comic tension, and the pair of them began laughing now, Stuart struggling to enunciate even the simplest of phrases.

'What?' said Dougie, laughing.

'Nothing you twat.'

'Aye,' said Dougie and, after a moment, farted.

Both men were wracked in laughter now, wriggling almost uncontrollably across the bed, Stuart with his face hard against the pillow and feeling his whole body shake. It was as another wave of mirth rose again that a loud snuffling noise interrupted them from the back of the room.

'Jesus!' said Stuart bolting upright.

There was a further moan.

'Jesus!' Stuart snapped the light on.

Standing there, clad only in a small pair of briefs, was Malcolm, with a sober and mournful expression. As if drugged, 'Guys, I can't sleep,' he said.

'What?' Stuart pulled the bed quilt towards him.

'I can't sleep with all the laughter. Are you going to keep it down?'

'Sure, aye man,' said Dougie, bare-chested and upright in bed. 'Really sorry.'

'Yeah well. You should be Dougie McCallum. Why I've a mind to give you a good thrashing.'

'Go right ahead pal, I'm all ears.'

Stuart glared at Dougie, saying, 'It's alright Malcolm, we'll keep it down.'

'You better.' Malcolm stood, almost glowering, then broke to a smile at Dougie. 'You were so funny tonight.'

'Thanks man.'

Malcolm paused. 'Why, don't you look a picture.'

'Was there something else, Malcolm?' asked Stuart.

Malcolm blanked him. 'Night night Dougie.'

'Night mate.'

The big Canadian left the room; his steps echoed down the hall, and a door was shut.

'Jesus,' said Dougie, 'He's a big fella. I'm surprised he didn't crush you.'

'Yes, well. I'm turning the light out, alright?'

'Aye.'

Stuart turned it out. 'Shall we invite him back for a cuddle?'

'Only if you want to. He's not my type, unlike your good self. Anyway, what about Paulie?

'What about her? `

'She was all over you man.'

'No mate, she's not right for me.'

'What's wrong with Paulie?'

'Nothing's wrong with Paulie, just –'

'She's too old -'

'No she's not too old. I love older women. It's just – we've got girlfriends.'

'Aye man, we have. I for one got the best one in the world. Far too good for me; I'm like a fucking pig in a china shop.'

'A bull?'

'Bull, pig, whatever.'

Stuart laughed, but faster now; he was growing tired. 'Pig in a china shop. Pig in a... Good night Dougie - today was really fun.'

'Aye it was.'

There was a long pause, and the dark grew more serious now, more intent on taking them away. Somewhere within it, Dougie farted, and that was the day's last laughter before they slid into sleep.

VII.

They woke early, needing to take a bus in just a few hours from Essen *Hauptbahnhof* to Heidelberg. Outside the window the air was already clear to a wide distance; the cobblestone street was without occupant. Stuart packed up his things and, moving down the cramped stairs, paused; the door to the guest bedroom was empty.

Downstairs Pauline too was gone; recovering, no doubt, from that one cigarette too many. The bar was empty, tidy and smelt slightly of cleaning products. No doubt it too would soon close like a great many bars before it which had meant a great deal to a few people but not enough for it to pay its own bills. On the bar sill was a card marked 'Stuart.' Having already been paid, Stuart was confused; nonetheless, before Dougie noticed, he pocketed it.

His friend had sat at the bar. 'You ready aye?'

They had no keys, so needed to check they had everything before leaving.

'You got your phone charger?'

'Aye, it's in mae bag man.'

'And your phone?'

Dougie patted his jacket. 'Then let's go,' said Stuart.

'Wait – just let me do one last check.'

'Alright.'

Stuart ran up the stairs, and looked over the room where they had slept. The duvet had been made; there was nothing but the croissant bag wrapper on the floor.

He returned. 'Good to go.'

Dougie rose and they walked out to the street; the main door shut; they were outside again.

They walked down the little hill from the house; ahead, a dog yapped. It was Sunday morning and the small town was desperately quiet – and they had been likely its latest revellers the night before. In places such as Kettwig and those like it, history had yet to show up, and life proceeded oriented by a set of simple rhythms, of birth and work, love and death with no particular unnecessary complications in between. The welfare state took care of those.

'Nice place man. I've got to come back here with Anja. She would love it.'

'Sure.'

He thought about his phone, without a single message all night.

They had moved away from the main drag and were now into bland residential space, big chunky houses of some forty years standing. Stuart's heart dropped a little, as it always did when he was trying to get someone to criticize someone else. 'Weird that Malcolm just vanished like that,' he said.

'Yeah man, but he's an odd guy, right?'

'Yes – I think he came down just to show he wasn't speaking to me.'

'Ha! He's alright man. He'll soon forget it.'

'It's a good job that man wasn't born a king,' said Stuart. 'A lot of people would have been losing their heads.'

They walked on, and, as they approached the station, Dougie paused. 'Do you mind if I pop in here and get a cup of coffee?'

'Not at all.'

Stuart stood outside the bakery a moment; the roof was low – a sign of West Germany – and the interior dimly lit. The goods on offer were displayed in a large, fly-ridden cabinet, though not much was left; an *Apfelkranz* (a twist of sugary bread), the *Amerikaner* (the American, a cake of separated chocolate and icing coating, apparently intended to symbolize racial segregation in the States – only the Germans could come up with a pious cake) and a solitary, dry-looking donut. Not a single one of these cakes looked appetizing and as Stuart looked up at the large sign above bearing the legend *'Die bunte Bäckerei'*, he wondered if any nation presented itself less stylishly than Germany – seen here in its dry, cream-free cakes left over from yesterday and sold at full price.

Dougie emerged. 'Coffee machine was off.'

'Right. Couldn't they turn it on?'

'Not for foreigners.'

'Makes sense.' The two of them continued smiling up to the path to where, after a few minutes, they reached the small station. They had a wait of ten minutes, it being a Sunday morning; this time, they bought tickets.

When they reached the centre of Essen it was virtually deserted and they were just under an hour ahead of time. So they walked a while to find somewhere for a coffee, eventually finding a large café with chrome-coloured furniture. They took up two seats in the corner, the only people present.

'I think as you get older,' said Stuart after a while, 'the break-ups get easier and the hangovers get worse.'

'Aye man, you are looking a wee bit peaky there. Sort of like a fucked-up badger.'

'Thank you. I must say you're looking fairly flabby

yourself. A bit late-Elvis, you know, when he was dying on the toilet due to all his enormous drug problems.'

Dougie smiled, 'Thank you very much.'

The waitress brought them two coffees at which Dougie said *'Danke schön.'*

Stuart had taken off his glasses and was wiping them with a moist rag. 'Your German's not bad, is it?'

'Aye, it's not bad, it's alright... I never feel the Germans take me very seriously with it, you know.' Dougie sipped some water. 'I think they take you a bit more seriously.'

'Perhaps.'

'No, it's good man, your German's good. It's an achievement. Listen, man – have you ever seen a ghost?'

Stuart considered it.

'No, I haven't,' he said after a while. 'But my Mum claims to have.'

'Really?'

'When she was a kid. She claimed that one day she was walking through the woods – she grew up in the countryside you see, in Cornwall – and she came through into a clearing. And there was a crop of trees, dense foliage – and she waited a moment and, as she did, all the trees started shaking at once.'

'Whoa. Was it the wind?'

'That's the point. There was. No. Wind.'

'Christ. That's a little extreme.' Dougie thought about it all a little more. 'And was there, say, a sinister voice or apparition?'

'No, nothing like that. Just the foliage moving of its own accord.'

'Christ! So what does your Mum think?'

'Well, that's all she's ever said about it.'

'Really?' Doug nodded. 'You close with her?'

Stuart bent forward a little. 'We don't speak much. I think she misses me.'

'Aye? What's she think about you being out here then?'

'I mean, it's a bit lonely for her now, not having anyone. My dad and her are divorced - he used to love to come and visit; he used to come and drink in all the *Eckkneipen*.' The corner bars. Stuart had often had to fish his father out of these dives, a portly little Welshman swaying on strong salty beer. Nowadays the journey was a little bit too much for the old man and they spoke mainly on the phone. The most incredible things were happening in Stuart's life and they talked mainly about football. Sometimes Stuart would talk about his father in his sets, his obsessive punctuality, his weird military attitudes, his strange telephone manner – but never in those rare and precious occasions in which the old man had been in the audience.

'What about your folks?' Stuart asked.

'I don't see them so much, you know. You know my dad's dead, right?'

'I didn't. Was it recent?'

'Just a couple of years ago.'

'I'm sorry mate.'

'No, it's alright. We said goodbye.' There was a pause and Dougie cracked back into the story. 'I went to Glasgow for the funeral. And you know what right, they were burying the old man, and my Uncle Derek –'

'Is he the one whose insanely Scottish?'

'No, that's Uncle Archie, I'm talking about Uncle Derek, he hates the Nationalists. Anyway, they're lowering him in and my Uncle Derek is standing right next to the pallbearer. And my dad remarried, right, girl called Laura, lovely Scottish-Jamaican lass. And they're bending low over the grave to throw a wee bit of earth on the grave, Laura is too right, and I hear my Uncle Derek saying, quite low but very clear, "What a magnificent arse."'

'Really?' Stuart smiled, then shaking his head added, 'That's unbelievable.'

'It is. And that sir is the bunch of reprobates from which I hail. Me, who made most of his savings working as a barman in a brothel.'

Stuart had heard about this in stand-up, Dougie's brief but intense stint as a bartender in what the old Germans called a *house of joy*. Not that according to Dougie's accounts there had been anything particularly joyful about it.

'How was that, anyway?'

'Oh it was alright man. I mean – it was pretty sad actually. You'd get guys coming there with like 1000s of Euros, ordering champagne, big tips – all on company accounts. Sometimes I'd go into the rooms to collect the empties, right and I'd see them and I'd think – I'm not going to lie – "that looks fucking amazing." But other times I'd see the girls crying, doing their make-up, and I'd be like "This is really sad." Yeah, you're right, a lot of the girls have drug problems. Something has to have gone wrong for a girl to get into that kind of work.

'I was doing too many drugs meself. One time I was busted by the police at four in the morning for riding over a bike light. And I had about a gram of cocaine in my pocket. Bastard gave me a fine of 69 euros. I could have paid him out of my pocket but that'd have been a giveaway.'

'You make me feel square,' said Stuart after picturing the scene. 'My joke was always that I took cocaine at University but I didn't inhale.'

'You ain't missing much man. I don't think it's a coincidence that you and Ben Prank' - the most famous comedian on the Berlin English-speaking circuit, a nervy Jew from Florida with a handlebar moustache and lots of jokes about the fact that he looked Turkish – 'I don't think it's a coincidence that you and him perform sober. A lot of the guys'd kill to be as good as you two, you know.'

'I think that's true. I think they would literally kill.'

'Aye well they're just jealous right?'

Stuart thought about it; he lost himself in what he said. 'The audience knows the moment you walk up there. And you can't fake it. It's all decided in the moments you walk up to the stage, how you take the microphone, how you face the crowd. And then you make the realization, the realization that...'

'What?'

Stuart said, 'I forgot what I was going to say.'

Dougie gave a short laugh. 'We must be about right for the bus now, right?'

'Yeah, looks like it. I'll get these.'

Stuart was placing his money on the table, weighed out, with tip, in advance. He spoke again, 'Have you, though?'

'What?'

'Seen a ghost.'

Dougie thought about it and frowned.

'No man – but I think I'd like to. I think it might make a few things clearer for me.'

They moved back to the bus stop where they had dismounted the previous day. It was set next to a central road; after a few minutes, the bus itself could be seen approaching in the distance. Just minutes earlier Stuart had received a text message informing him that the bus for today's journey would be a 'non-standard bus', meaning, in effect, it was to be a different colour from the company's usual green. The Germans really did go in for attention to detail.

'This is us,' said Stuart as the bus approached. As it did, the passengers around moved to a closer circle of it, without automatically forming a queue. A couple of students dismounted, embracing their lovers by the bus stop.

Soon they were on the road again.

'How much did we make last night, anyway?'

'50 euros each.'

'That's not bad, is it?'

'Dwight and Malcolm got a 100 each.'

'Yeah but they had more people. I mean, we're already covered for the weekend. How much were these tickets? I mean, that's nothing, is it. Everything from here on in is pure profit. Pure gravy!'

'I hope so,' said Stuart.

'I'm telling you man, we're going to be up to our necks in birds and booze in Heidelberg. It's going to be carnage. The town will have to close.'

They had a shorter journey this afternoon, across the west German flatland, to where Germany began to burst into its southern beauty, the gorgeous depths beneath the country's beige midlands. Specifically they were travelling to Baden-Württemberg, an artificially-created, prosperous little bolting together of two former duchies: the Baden-land, of old school money, wealthy villages holding miniature wine festivals, and solar panels glinting on the roof of exquisite yet functional houses; and Wurttemberg, which was somewhere near it.

For now they were still driving Germany's beat-up industrial edge, and in fact the most densely populated part of Europe, the *Ruhrgebiet*, from the *Ruhr* valley and river, *Ruhr* also meaning, incidentally, dysentery in German. Twelve million people lived in this region, thronging its factory towns, supporting its football teams. Twelve million people – another London – crammed in these great cities across just two thousand miles, dreaming, hoping, talking, recovering – and who in England gave a shit about them? Who in England cared about Germany?

After about an hour of silence, Dougie suddenly cried out, 'Look at that man!'

Stuart did and saw out of the window a huge wind turbine banked in a lay-by, propped up on a huge long truck. It looked absurdly large and impractical, a great white needle of steel hallucinatory against the bland-hued motorway.

'So that's how they transport them,' Dougie said.

'*Windturbine*,' said Stuart. Tur-been-ah. 'Did you know that one day last year Germany got 50% of its energy from solar power alone?'

'I did not know that man. To be honest with you I don't know much about solar energy.'

Stuart indicated the carrier bag next to him - they sat now on seats one behind the other, exploiting the sparsely-populated bus. 'Do you want the rest of these croissants?'

'Nae man,' said Dougie, 'I think I'm all good with croissants. Actually I think I'm going to listen to some music for a bit.'

'Do it,' Stuart smiled. Dougie was already beginning to plug in his earphones.

In any journey there is a period of dead time, between

habituating to the journey and seeing it draw to an end, the only time in the journey where your cares are truly forgotten, where you are truly *away*. Somewhere amidst their getting comfy and sharing of residual snacks they had fallen into this period, looking out the window on the *rheinländische* countryside, both thinking about their gigs, talking almost automatically when they did talk, noticing their surroundings only as pure image; such absorption might be called the journey itself.

During this process the bus continued across the flat West German countryside, the day growing colder and greyer and the rain resuming. Dougie munched on croissants, and listened to music, while Stuart looked out of the window. There had still been no text message. Sheathing his phone, he watched drops slide on glass and recalled deep incidents from recent years, things people had said to him, things he should have said. 'Nothing interesting has ever happened to me in my life' – he would never be caught saying that.

Sometimes trigged by obscure connections he stumbled upon pockets of memory he thought forever lost. Sometimes he found memories he never knew he had, so utterly lost had they seemed to him, and remembering them was like having things happen to him to for the first time. And yet when he tried to remember his childhood again and again he felt like he faced an enormous blank, an absence. Where had all the time gone? He felt as if his life had only begun as an adult. The dull landscape beyond the glass had now brought to mind the landscape of Kent, and one summer day on a train where he had headed south to visit friends together with Pippa Dryslade.

'You're the first person I've met at university who's like me,' he remembered her saying.

Next to them on the train table they had a bottle of chilled vodka which Stuart had brought back from Russia. He remembered saying to her, maybe not directly after that, maybe another time, or maybe he never said it in fact, because he often continued conversations with people years after he had ceased to see them; 'I don't see why I have to choose between writing and comedy. I could imagine doing stand-up at the Booker prize ceremony.' And saying: 'The Booker prize should be open to comedians.'

'I do think you're a funny guy though,' said Pippa.

'He's a craftsman,' Mark Worship had said – yes, that Anglophile American been there too, sat next to them on the train in his cashmere scarf and sheepskin jacket.

'He's better than that,' Pippa had said.

'Tickets please,' said the conductor.

'Me, I'm just worried that people in the industry will still remember me after I'm finished with my studies,' Pippa had gone on. 'I mean – three years is a long time in the business.'

'Oh, I'm sure that people will be waiting,' Mark had said, helping himself to a little thimble of the vodka. 'I think people will always be talking about you. You fill an essential comic *need* for the British people – you could be the new Victoria Wood. And you Stuart well, you have the potential to be this generation's Stephen Fry. I say, this is an awfully good nip, isn't it.'

And then she not been able to find her ticket, he

remembered, and had needed to root around while the ticket inspector stood over them waiting. Pippa had hunted through her things, and, as men do when a woman's bag is widely exposed, he and Mark had looked away, in his case onto the view hurtling past of the window of the flatlands of Kent.

'You didn't do your Obama joke yesterday.'

'What?' It took him a moment to come back to the present.

'Yesterday. You forgot your Obama joke,' said Dougie.

'Yeah, and Cloud 9.'

In effect he had failed to tell his two best jokes, which probably hadn't helped matters. Yet Stuart was an experienced enough comedian to know what the solution was: another gig.

'Aye, man, they were loving it last night,' said Dougie, apparently feeling chattier now.

But Stuart was now falling into more precious memories. Finally, he was finding some from his schooldays; the time he had busted his head trying to catch a padlock, or when he had been a history prefect – perhaps he could find the blue badge when he went back to Nottingham, it would look good on stage – or the time he had scored a fantastic basket at school and had in his euphoria for some reason elected to celebrate with a fascist salute. The ball had arched beautifully from the very back of the court to drop through the hoop and as he recalled as had wheeled away in delight for some reason his left hand going above his lip and his right hand flipping into a little *Hitlergrüß*.

Even now Stuart had no idea why he had chosen that particular celebration and Mr. Hart had asked to see him afterwards.

'Take a shower first,' said Mr. Hart.

But there had been no abuse, just a kind, sympathetic man in a puffer jacket peering out from a tiny office crammed full of ping-pong bats and swim floats. Mr. Hart had rooted around for a mug to pour himself some tea.

'I don't know why you did the, what do you call it, *heil Hitler*,' said Mr. Hart, 'But I don't think you're a Nazi. Aren't you Jewish anyway? Right, on your mother's side. But that doesn't matter – that's not what I wanted to talk to you about. Because I've been seeing you mooching around recently and I must say you look very sad. I want to know what's wrong. Are there problems with the other boys?'

Stuart had nodded.

'Well, first of all I want you to know, it's going to get better. What you have to remember is that it's a difficult time for *everybody* at the moment. You know, you probably feel that things are terrible, life is meaningless, that you want to die, and I just want you to know, it's going to get better. You won't be at this school forever, and a lot of the things which you think are problems now – you know, being a bit *different* and that – are going to be a great asset for you in your future life. You will find people who are more like you, you know, artistic types. Have you thought at all about University? Oh you want to go to Oxford. Well I think that would be brilliant for you and for the school.

'Now some of the things you do aren't age-appropriate – Mr. Falkirk has told me about what you wrote in your English book and I have to say that's not on, to depict members of staff in those kinds of situations, even in the context of, you know, an adventure. But nonetheless we want you to know that we do want to encourage, I mean the school wants to encourage you, to be creative. We want to encourage that. In fact when I was your age I was in a rock band – called 'The Hemlock Stones' - and between you and me, I think we could have made it. I really do. But obviously I went down another route – you know, teaching. What I'm saying to you though, is, that you've got to take care of that. That little spark of creativity, what we could call your "humour", you have to look after that. Because once you've lost it – well, it doesn't come back. No it doesn't.

'Do you get what I mean? You do? Good. Then we don't need to talk about it anymore. Because what I actually wanted to talk to you about something else. I've talked about it with the other members of staff, and we really think you can do this. So what I want to know – and you can still turn me down if you want to – what I want to know is: How would you like to be the host for this year's Senior Citizens' Party?'

Stuart was disturbed by the music coming out of Dougie's headphones; it was tinny and electronic and he recognized it. 'Kraftwerk?'

'That's right man. The Model…'

They sung the chorus together.

'They're from Düsseldorf.'

'I know man I know.'

'It's also home to the biggest Japanese community in Europe. *Tokio-am-Rhein* they call it.'

'Is that right?' Dougie said. He thought a moment. 'I really like Japanese women.'

'Do you?' Stuart said, and then, 'I was just thinking about my first ever gig.' But Dougie had lost his gregarious spirit; he needed a restorative nap to be on full form for tonight. Still his friend was still conscious on some level for, when they reached the sign saying Düsseldorf an hour later, he murmured dozily, noting the character's beneath the city's name, 'Japanese. Like you were saying, man.' Then he slept again.

VIII.

Alone on his bus seat, a more recent memory came to Stuart. One day a few years earlier he had begun tweeting jokes and, to his surprise, saw them being retweeted beyond acquaintances, taking on interesting half-lives, being seen by luminary eyes. The jokes themselves weren't much, just stray thoughts on the cultural artefacts he consumed ('Writing a film about a fly which turns into Jeff Goldblum') or epitaphs upon relationships ('whenever a girl I don't like likes me I just give her my novel. Usually does the trick') but they came from somewhere between his comic and cultural personae and became read beyond circles. Such were the wonders of Twitter.

It was in these conditions that he received a message on twitter from @SteffenHerz ('London literary agent. Van Morrison fan. Mine's a double') stating that

> @BerlinComedian Been reading your tweets. Top drawer – and the girls in the office agree. In London any time soon?

In reply to which he lied that he would be there at the end of the month visiting in friends. Perhaps they could grab a coffee. In advance of which, if Steffen had a mail address, he would send over some of his stories.

So it was that he found himself back in his old home town on a cold March morning. Everyone was working, the hordes stampeding along High Holborn and the Kingsway. In the distance, great buildings rose, buildings barely built when he had last lived there. Berlin was for its sins only now reaching the heights London was currently surpassing, these gherkins, toasters and shards, giant 'fuck yous' of wealth, of frozen money. Meanwhile Berlin argued whether to build the new castle the same as the old castle. He clung to images of his new city as he walked around his old one, thinking that his adopted city was, compared to London but perhaps also inherently in itself, very small beer.

The office where Steffen worked – he had done some research about the agent, and it seemed he was pretty junior, his LinkedIn profile stating he had been in Hamburg studying 'Global Literatures' a few years previously – was wedged onto the fourth floor, reached either via the narrow stairwell or the cramped lift. He opted for the former, tapping up the stairs in his shiniest shoes. The average British office worker dressed as smartly as the most extravagant German comedian, so he had just worn one of his stage outfits, substituting only for his habitual bright floppy shirt a stiff white one. Anyway, it was publishing. Did they still take four hour lunches and dress in tweed? He doubted it.

The secretary took his name and he took up a seat on the couch. There were a pile of magazines on the table, each leaving him uniquely incurious: Golf Today, Men's Fitness, MoneyWeek and at least a Marie Claire which he raised to his nose to smell. Almost as soon as he did, though, a tall German man came out of a side office;

Steffen Herz. He had a few sheets of paper in his hand and he stopped to chat a little with the secretary.

'Really?' Steffen was saying. 'And Peregrine too?'

'All of them,' she replied. 'And then they started doing shots.'

'God – and I missed it.'

'It'll happen again.'

'I just couldn't, you know, because of the Benson book. Such a pain. Yeah, Artur Schopenhauer's Guide to Dating. Is it good? It's a fun idea. But too long. At the moment. Anyhow, we going for one after work tonight? The Perseverance!' Steffen turned, at last acknowledging his presence. 'Stuart! Now excuse me, *we* have a meeting.'

'Hi there.' He rose and took Steffen's hand, the smell of Marie Claire still in his nostrils.

'Thanks ever so much for coming. I know it's early, but I thought we could pop out for a coffee. There's a Café Nero around the corner. It's just a bit hard to hear in here over the noise of that bloody photocopier.' Steffen shot a humorous glance over to a large, droning hulk of a copying machine, from where an unglamorous man in a pale blue shirt shot back an arch smile.

They moved down the stairs in a London hurry, Steffen doing the talking. Stuart held back, but when he did speak he felt his desire to impress, subjugated in Germany to the need to communicate, flaring up again. A few times he volunteered a sentence in German a few times, for example stating his fluency in the language *in the language*, but Steffen, though replying with an enthusiastic 'Good for you', had clearly left all that behind. He was indeed, in his Burberry jacket, brown leather gloves and flopping brown quiff, more English than the Queen. This was never more evident than in his accent, a learned generic posh with occasional German interference, a slight mistuning of the vowels.

'Right!' They had seated inside the Nero and were unpacking their drinks from the tray. 'I love this place,' said Steffen.

'Really?'

'It's so convenient,' said Steffen, raising his buxom white Nero mug. 'Anyway you're living in Berlin right? How do you find it?'

'I like it very much. It's very convenient, to use your phrase.'

'A lot of people are moving to Berlin from London, actually. You know, artists.'

'Yeah. A lot of Israelis are coming actually.'

'How ironic.'

'A lot of Israeli DJs. It's a big discussion in Israeli society, going to Germany of all places.'

'Would you believe it?' Steffen gave a sharp laugh. 'And why did you move there?'

'I wanted to write,' he said. 'I have this joke: I've been living in Berlin for nearly ten years. I came to Berlin as the first stop on a world tour.'

'In German we say Berlin is always the city which is becoming and never the city which is.'

'*Berlin ist immer die Stadt die wird und nie die Stadt die ist.*'

'That's it. You know it.'

'I do but I don't know who said it. Where are you from in Germany anyway?'

'Berlin.'

'Oh, right. And how long have you lived in London?'

'Now I think it must be – five years. Do I like it here? Sure, I like it enough. I mean, there isn't anything particularly special about it. But sure, it's fine. Friends, parties, pubs; it's not half bad you know? Anyway, I read your stories.'

There was a pause. He stared at his interlocutor. 'And?'

'Well, tell me a little bit about them first. What do you want to do with them.'

There was another pause; Steffen was smiling.

'Well, I want to get them published, obviously,' he said. 'Or... um... do you mean artistically? I guess – well, I think I said in my email I'm aiming for a kind of contemporary "Goodbye to Berlin". Only I don't leave.' He grinned and went on. 'You know, tales of the decadent *bohème*. Not that my life's very bohemian but... Well, what I mean is I – I - think there's a real interest in Germany in England at the moment and...'

'A real interest in Germany, do you think?'

'Haven't you noticed?'

'Can't say I have. I try to avoid Germans. They're so *boring*. I mean, Berlin's a great city, but it's hardly London is it? All those people complaining about multiculturalism? Huh, I mean I'm sorry that's not multiculturalism, that's just Germans and a load of Turkish people.' Steffen dipped his biscotti. 'Anyway, your stories.'

'Yes.'

'I thought they were brilliantly written. Very stylish and actually, I know it's a big word, rather beautiful. I really liked the one at the end about the relationship which didn't work out – full of humour and sadness. I definitely think you're a promising writer,' Steffen said. 'But - there are problems. The first is nobody reads short stories anymore. And the second is yours are set in Germany.'

Stuart sat in silence.

'People don't know the references, you see. I mean I do but I'm German. And you have characters who say things in German without translation. Germans do that? It's possible. Maybe you and I might understand them but – the audience for these things is really extremely tiny. You need to stop writing bilingually. Really, mate, you do.' Steffen wiped his mouth with a serviette. 'I mean, obviously you should write about what you know, but what you know also has to be the right thing. What people want is stories, big stories, big books containing epic stories. To be honest, this kind of stuff – a young writer struggling for prestige, fame, break-ups, it is pretty unremarkable stuff. This is pretty standard experience.'

Stuart sat very quietly with a frozen smile. And suddenly realized he should have been speaking with Nellie, who had texted him – that all this talk was an avoidance of that. He should be in front of *her*, as he opened his awful cramped heart and apologized for everything he'd ever done to her, at the dreadful failure and rotten moods he'd inflicted upon her after the Oxford debacle, and that he was just so truly sorry.

Nellie looked at him now from across the table.

'You hit me you utter bastard. You don't get to behave like you do and come back and want your name to be anything utter than *mud*.'

'I was ill,' Stuart said.

'So was I,' Nellie said, 'And was I a despicable cunt?'

Stuart said nothing.

He just lowered his head.

'And was I?'

'I'm really am very sorry Nellie, with all my heart.'

'You can be as sorry as you like. You're an absolute fucking joke of a person.'

Meanwhile Steffen was still going on, voice completely unchanging.

'Anyway – I hope that doesn't seem too harsh? Does it seem too harsh? I did actually like them you know. And I loved your tweets. After that I followed the links to one of your stand-ups – mate, hilarious! Is it really true that the Germans have no sense of humour?' Steffen shook his head. 'You seem to have really found your niche over there. Good stuff! God, Germans need to laugh a bit more, that's for sure. I think we're done, right? Thanks so much for the coffee.'

They walked back together, Steffen talking volubly

about his adoption of cricket, his first attendance at the Proms, his continuing inability to fathom lamb with mint sauce. He estimated Steffen was about twenty-five. For his part, he would spend the day drifting around central London, failing to meet with friends, finding no one had a bed for him, checking into a hostel. At this point they reached the door to the office.

'So lovely to meet you,' said Steffen with a jolly smile. 'Do keep in touch – and keep writing!'

It was not the first of such escape attempts but it was perhaps the most urgent seeming. He had really wanted to get out of there. Nor was the rejection in itself unique; countless times he had received his work handed back to him with praise, begging the question that if he was indeed such a brilliant, incisive, original writer, why the fuck won't you publish it then? Money. Nor were a single one of Steffen's - Steffen this perfect simulation of the English social gatekeeper, who had learned so perfectly the language of cultural exclusion and clique, from the eternal 'promising' to the dreaded 'but' - nor were a single one of his points disputable. It was simply apparent at that moment and beyond, as he watched the young German disappear up the stairwell and the great crowds broke upon him once again, as the great world city, the hub upon which a great empire had collapsed, where the action was, which made Berlin look like a sleepy little provincial backwater, it was simply apparent just how much he wanted to come home.

He took the train up to Nottingham to see his father.

His mother was by then elsewhere and his father lived alone in a downsized house, fine for his needs. The old man met him at the ticket barriers, smiling beneath a green cap; it was, he could not fail to notice, the one he had gifted him for Christmas last year.

'Stewie!' said his dad and hugged him as he let go of his case. His dad took his other bag, the snacks one, with the customary refuse of banana peels and sandwich boxes he had generated on the journey, and for his part he wheeled the case to the car where it stood in the short-stay parking bay. A few years later the station was to be remodelled and improved but those were still the days of the scraggy station front and people dropping and dashing.

They were soon on the grey roads heading away from the station. It had been snowing in Nottingham recently and oddly enough the majority of that snow still remained. 'It snowed on Tuesday,' his dad was saying. 'I don't know what they're going on about with all this climate change. If anything it's getting colder. I reckon they're being paid off.'

'Who?'

'The weather people.'

'Meteorologists?'

'That's them.'

'Right. Because that's why people go into metrology, for the money. For the chance of glamour and fame.'

'Bloody wind farms,' said his dad. 'They might as well piss the money up the wall.'

He sighed and smiled in equal measure, asking 'How are

you Dad?'

'Never better. I feel right as rain. The doctor had me in the other day to give me my – what do they call them? – statins. They give them all to the old buggers these days. And I couldn't remember something so they did the tests if I'd had a stroke. Well, I don't think I've had a stroke, and I told them that, but they did all the tests anyway.'

'And?'

'I didn't hear back from them. But I certainly don't think I've had a stroke.'

'You do seem alright.'

'Exactly! I'm as lucid as I ever was. Nonetheless, at my age, you do start fearing the dread hand of the reaper. My mate Brian went last week; he had a fall at the pub and then he died at home later that afternoon. Poor old sod.'

They were next to the old Raleigh factory on the roundabout. Just past his window a cyclist was beating around, wrapped in fluorescence, bunched up in the English grit and dark. I don't think we're in Berlin anymore, he thought. Now they drove past the old chip shop, which had been the further perimeter of his nocturnal walks as a teenager. If he had reached here on an adolescent evening it was probably following one of his sporadic announcements that he was leaving home.

'How long you here for?' his father said.

He looked across at the old man. 'Oh I don't know – just the weekend,' he said.

'Well, it'll be lovely to have you,' his dad said.

In the neat small house his father set him up with a cup of tea. Gone were the days when he would lose his passport on the way home, or the key to his suitcase lock and his father and he would have to saw through the hoop of it together. He was becoming, if not exactly good at life, at least vaguely competent at it. He wheeled his suitcase upstairs and he had placed it in the small guest bedroom, a slight sweet lavender smell in the air, on the side some dried out potpourri. Mother.

'Thanks Dad.' Downstairs he drank the tea from a mug he recognized, a leaving present to his dad upon retirement. There was sugar in it.

'So was your meeting alright?'

'Oh you know, same old.' He sipped. 'To be honest they didn't really like it.'

'Why on earth not? They want bloody shooting!' his dad said, raising his glass of John Smiths righteously.

'It's just publishing these days. There's no money and everybody's living by grace and favour. It's like manoeuvring round a medieval French court. At least in stand-up you can turn up and do it. Here, it feels like they tell you you're promising forever and then you're dead.'

'At least you're still promising,' his dad said. 'Things are going well out there though?'

'They're just fine.'

'I bet they are. Getting your own place, I mean, that's a big step. Brilliant. You can have birds over. So do you feel, you know, Germany is completely your home now?'

'Sort of. I mean – it's been good to me.' He paused. 'Actually Dad that was sort of what I wanted to talk to you about. I was thinking about moving back.'

'That surprises me.'

'Really?'

'Well,' his dad said after a moment, 'The UK isn't a good scene to be honest. I can't stand the place these days. To me it's lost many of its advantages.'

'What were its advantages?'

'Oh, you know, it used to be a place where you could do things.'

'But you can still do things! All sorts of things!'

'Well, yes, but you know what I mean.'

'No I don't! I have absolutely no idea! Anyway,' he continued, 'I'm really ambitious. And I don't know if in the long term Berlin is going to satisfy that.'

'Mmm.' His dad sipped. 'It's your decision. All you need to know is that whatever you choose I will support you in it 100%. And I say this to all my kids – I don't care what you do, as long as you're happy.'

'Right.' He waited, cuing up a bit. 'So you're basically saying you don't care what I do, as long as you solve the central problem of philosophy? Don't care what I do, as long as I solve a question which has defeated Plato, Aristotle and the Rolling Stones? Couldn't you give me a more realistic target like – I don't care what you do, as you long as you always match your socks?'

'Ha!' his dad was laughing, his gnarled baggy hand shaking and a little John Smiths spilling onto his cords. He had always been able to make his dad laugh; after all, once upon a time and for a long time, his dad had been half the audience.

He woke the next morning in his small comfortable bed. Today would be idle; he had long ago abandoned the idea of getting any work done back home due to the amount of cultural artefacts he had left there. In his late teens he had bought a huge amount of global literature, Mann, Dostoevsky, Camus, in translations, read some of it and then, in his early days in Germany, resolved to read it all in original. The end of result of this was that he now had two unread copies of most of the foundational texts of European literature; two Plagues, two Crime and Punishments, and two Magic Mountains.

'Stew! Breakfast is in fifteen minutes.'

'Alright Dad,' Stuart called from the bed. It was ten o'clock.

He quickly showered, noting the weaker English water pressure, and came down into the small scruffy kitchen. His dad, a working class man from North Wales, was moving around the room in pyjama bottoms and a white vest. The radio was playing sport reports, interviewing managers about the upcoming games, upon which his father would pronounce one of his two habitual verdicts, that said interviewee had either spoken 'well' or 'very poorly.' There were no distinctions beyond this; simply poorly, or very well, had never to Stuart's knowledge been employed.

'Bacon sandwich,' said his dad. The kettle was boiling in the background loudly now. 'And tell me – do you take sugar in your tea?' asked the old man for the thousandth time.

'No Dad. And thanks; the bacon is just how I like it.'

'It's good, isn't it? Actually there's a new butcher just opened. And I do have to say, and everyone in the pub agrees, he really is first class. I've got into the habit of buying two lamb chops and having them every Sunday with Downton Abbey. Do you have a TV?'

'Never.' He nibbled his bacon. 'Have you heard from Mum?'

'Oh, what do I bloody know about it all,' his dad said. 'You know what she's like. Probably off in Nigeria or somewhere for all I know.'

He smiled, saying, 'It's Liverpool-Wolves today isn't it?'

'It is indeed. What time? It's at 12.45. It's at Molineux. I wondered if you wanted to go watch it.'

'Of course I do. I still watch every game. I always say you can change your job, your wife – well, I don't have a wife, but anyway – but you can't change your team. Where's your normal haunt these days?'

'At the moment I usually just go over the road to the club. The beer's quite cheap there – it's not too bad. The screen's a bit small but it's not too bad. You fancy it then?'

'Sure.' His tea was with him now, Yorkshire; served, amusingly enough, in the Jungle Book mug he had drank from every morning of his schooldays. Why had that ended up here? 'I was wondering if you wanted to

159

go for a walk beforehand.'

'Sounds good. You'll need some better shoes than those though.'

'What's wrong with –' he started, ready to become piqued, when he noticed his dad was pointing below the table to his fluffy blue moccasins, saying 'No – I mean those ones.'

'Ha,' he said, shifting in his seat, 'I suppose you're right.'

So it was that about an hour later the two men began walking along the small suburban street which led them across from the main entrance to Wollaton Park. Stuart had grown up a few streets from here, before his parents had downsized a few years previously, before the epic altercations of his entire family life had finally led to an ongoing separation. Now his father, retired and alone, spent his time watching sport, cooking fry ups, and drinking John Smith's bitter which he burnt off with occasional power walks around the park they now entered.

It being Saturday, and the suburbs ticking to an earlier rhythm than Berlin, there were plenty of people about; lone men and dogs, families hauling sledges and young couples revelling in their freedoms in that ecstatic time before the baby years. A large hill reared before them, atop which Wollaton Hall loomed, and below which the red and blue of darting sledges could be seen.

His dad set the pace as ever, the old man a surprisingly wiry figure, a kind of strutting tribesman in a cloth cap. He and Dad walked up the path on the right, looking up at the gothic mansion on its perch. 'As a kid they told me it was haunted,' he was saying. 'By the White Lady. But I never believed them. And there was another one, too, a man on stilts who used to walk round the hall. He was looking for his dead child. I remember scaring David Underwood when I told him about it. Admittedly, I embellished a few details. You know, I scared it up a bit. Have you ever seen a ghost?'

'I can't say I have,' his dad said. 'And if I did I didn't recognize them.'

'So in fact you could have done?'

'Well, they didn't tell me if they were. They would have been undercover.'

He was smiling.

Now they were moving through the court at the industrial museum, past the museum café, the gift shop were you could, at all times of the year and at generous opening hours, purchase a Robin Hood hat. For his own part he had always been rather on the side of the Sheriff of Nottingham, evidenced in a childhood photograph of himself dressed in a black and red cloak, raising his plastic broadsword at forty green-jerkined Hoods. The villain's role had always come naturally to him; perhaps that had explained his attraction to Germany, a country of which growing up the adults had only ever spoken ill.

'You don't want a coffee or anything?' he asked.

'You know I think I'm alright. How about you?' his dad asked. 'Let's just keep going, shall we.'

This took them back behind the hall, to the smaller rear slope, which went down to the cold silver lake. There was snow on the pathways again here and as they crunched along a figure hailed them ahead.

'Hello Sean!' the lady said in a broad Notts accent. 'And Stuart – my God you're tall. How are you?'

'Oh we're fine,' said his dad. 'Just taking the air.'

'And is this one back for good now?'

'Just the weekend,' his dad said.

'He's tall now, isn't he,' she went on.

'He is.'

She turned to address him directly now. 'I remember you when you were very little.' She was middle-aged, wearing a frilly woollen scarf, her hair lightly sprinkled with frost. 'I remember you singing "What Shall We Do with a Drunken Sailor." You loved that song.'

'Still do,' he said. 'I want them to play it at my funeral.'

'Oh, he's funny isn't he?'

'He's a comedian,' his dad said.

'Is that right? How lovely!'

'And are you alright?' his dad asked. 'I saw Matt in the Wheelhouse – well, it must have been about six months ago now.'

'Well he's doing very well. He's working in IT now, in Beeston, but he sometimes works out of the Chilwell office. And apart from that Sarah's married, you know. No kids yet. I think her and husband want to take a year out to travel the world.'

'It's a good thing to do,' he said.

'Isn't it?' she said. 'I wish I had done something like that.'

'Well, as long as they're all healthy that's the main thing,' his dad said. 'Listen, we have to go – we have a date with the football.'

'Oh who's playing?'

'Liverpool and Wolves,' he said.

'He's a big Liverpool fan you see.'

'Well you enjoy it,' she said smiled, before, about to turn, saying several times, 'Lovely to see you both!'

They walked on, the snow crunching beneath them. After a while he said 'I have absolutely no idea who that was'.

'That - is Shelia,' his dad said. 'She used to look after you at nursery. She always liked you, said you were funny. I never saw it, personally.'

He laughed and his dad smiled. By now they were nearing the lake; before it was a bridge over a small stream, which they crossed. Shallow water could be seen at its bottom.

'So you were talking yesterday about maybe moving back,' his dad said.

'I don't know,' he said. 'What do you think?'

They were walking on to the lake, along the muddy ground of its shore. His dad turned to one side as if addressing the question.

'Well, you're happy there aren't you? For most people it would be a dream – your own place, all your friends.'

'I just feel if I stay there nothing will ever change. And one day I'll be forty.'

They had stopped at the lake, just a little short of the water. His dad looked at him quizzically as he spoke on.

He said, 'You know in a way I feel I'm still running away from Oxford. I still feel very hurt about the way people treated me.'

His dad smiled and, raising up one brown leather glove, said with defiance, 'Well fuck 'em! All those people criticizing you at Oxford, where the bloody hell was their play? Look at your mate Harold Pinter – look at the shit that man took over the years. Those wankers at Oxford – and they were wankers, because I met some of them, and they were wankers – they didn't like you because you were the wrong kind of person to have

164

success there. That was the long and the short of it. And the fact is the things that you did there – those plays and shows – they were phenomenally successful. It's them that had the problem.'

There was a long pause. He blew his nose and said, 'Thanks Dad.'

'There's no downside to you as far as I'm concerned,' his dad said. 'And whatever you choose to do I will love you all the world.'

'I just want more, that's all,' he said.

'What do you want?'

'Just a generalized more,' he said, and then: 'I want to be famous.'

'Well, that's as maybe,' his dad said. 'If it's like that you just have to get on with it. You just have to be resilient and show 'em what you've got. Be so good they can't ignore you, that's right isn't it?'

'Thanks Dad,' he said once more. 'You've been a good Dad.'

'I'm freezing my bollocks off,' said his dad. 'Can we get out of here? It'll be kick off soon.'

They walked on through the final section of the park, the slushy fields where normally deer were to be seen. Today it was just long flats of ice, and a steady stream of people moving to the park exit. His dad spat occasionally with the cold.

'What do you think about Hodgson?' he said as they made the park gate.

'Well, he's a bloody idiot isn't he?' his dad said. 'The man was completely out of his depth.'

'I agree,' he laughed. 'He was always like – "well, I thought we played very well for the first five minutes..." Laughing they headed out the gates and over to the pub where they watched the game and he ate crisps and drank coke with lemon. On the Monday, his dad drove him to East Midlands airport, where he took the Ryanair flight to Berlin; they didn't speak about his coming back.

IX.

As Dougie and Stuart entered Düsseldorf's asphalt downtown a crackly announcement, made by someone with limited experience of both the English language and microphones, came over the bus's PA system.

'Ladies and gentleman we make a short stop now. One moment please.'

The comedians looked at each other; below them, the bus ignition was turned off.

They went outside to stretch their legs. On the pavement outside the bus, the driver - a tall German with a moustache, clad in a white shirt and green company tie – was frantically talking into a mobile phone. His conversation, which they followed, was betraying his anxiety as to the further course of the journey; it seemed they were to be held up. Finally with a curt harrumph of acknowledgement, the bus driver finished the conversation and hung up.

'Is there a problem man?' asked Dougie.

The bus driver looked over at them. 'You can say that. Sure there's a problem. We can't get to our pick-up point. It looks like we'll be held up here for – in the worst case – three hours!'

'Three hours?' said Stuart.

'Yes, and there's nothing we can do about it.'

His colleague, wearing a brown leather jacket over his white shirt, approached them now. 'It's the Düsseldorf Marathon,' he said, 'and there's no way through. We've already tried four different ways through.'

'It's not our fault!' said the bus driver.

'Not saying it is, man, just wondering if there's anything we can do.'

'We've phoned the company and are awaiting further instructions,' said the white-shirted man.

'Three hours,' said Stuart. 'That'll be tight with the gig,' he said to Dougie.

Dougie spoke to the drivers, 'Can the people not come here, you know?'

'Hah!' said the bus driver, even brusquer now. 'That's a great idea. Do you want to tell them where we are? Where is our address?'

'Well, I don't know,' said Dougie.

'Exactly! Look around you.' Behind them was a cluster of steely office blocks and a gigantic empty road; they were indeed at something of a blank spot. 'We are next to the buildings, on a road,' the driver said. 'Good luck explaining that!'

'We've done everything we can,' said the colleague. 'It's not our fault.'

'No, I'm not blaming you man.' Dougie looked to Stuart, saying in English, 'Do you fancy a pint?'

Stuart nodded. 'A coffee, certainly. How long will we

be stopping for?' he asked the jacketed man, who was emerging as the cooler interlocutor.

'We don't know. Maybe twenty minutes. Maybe four hours.'

'So we're just going for a wee drink, aye,' said Dougie.

'No,' said the white-shirted man, suddenly as ashen as his colleague. 'Please don't go away. We could leave at any time!'

Stuart nodded, paused, and said, 'Right you are then. Alright?'

The last word was addressed to Dougie, who said, 'Alright.'

The two of them stepped back and out of the conversation, moving away from the bus. As they did, the bus driver was on his phone again and the colleague looked over a final time. 'It's the Düsseldorf marathon,' he said. 'Nobody told us about it.'

So they walked along the kerbside, round a bend, and suddenly, surprising above all in its volume, found themselves in front of a restaurant. With the weather quite warm, the place was full, and they stood a moment before the families and the chatting tables.

'D'you fancy a pint?'

'I'll have a water.'

They went inside; the restaurant was cool and dark. In the middle of the room was a huge green birdcage, itself next to a green vase with water trickling down it, set on a brown mahogany stand. Waiters in gold aprons crossed through the huge space, past a melange of old furniture, mirrors and tables shoved against the emerald-streaked walls. The two travellers surveyed the space; almost every table was full.

'I'm just going to take a leak,' said Dougie.

Stuart nodded. 'Shall I get you a drink?'

'I'm alright man. I've some water in my bag.'

'Alright then. I'll meet you outside.'

Stuart vanished in the direction of the bar; Dougie waited a moment and, as a waiter moved by, asked him where the toilets were. The waiter said nothing and just pointed authoritatively up the stairs. Dougie looked back to Stuart and the two of them parted with brief mutual smiles.

Dougie moved up the stairs, the boards creaking beneath each step, his hands in his pockets. He was tired. There were books piled up at the top of the stairs and, at one point, what looked like a pornographic magazine, a woman's head turned to the side on the cover, wearing her blond halo. He bent down and flicked through, but it was erotic sketches, nothing really of interest to a man with a porn-choked iPhone. Further up the stairs was a large briefcase, its buckles undone; inside were other, smaller briefcases.

The gents was at the top of the stairs, behind a crème door marked with *Herren*. Dougie hated that, the presumption of German knowledge complicating something as basic as a piss. All toilet signs should be in English out of consideration for the drunk. One night he had been steaming in bar and got stuck in front of the lavatory doors, trying to work out whether he was an X or an XY. Luckily a woman had emerged to resolve the question.

As Dougie approached the door handle, he became aware of a slight noise emanating from the green door down the corridor on the left. It was a strange noise, a kind of dull throbbing breath, reminiscent, at the moment he had first intercepted it, of a female orgasmic moan. His subsequent consideration made this seem less likely, and then there it was again, a little pant, that little gasp of a woman being penetrated.

Dougie zipped his fly – he usually unzipped before entering the bathroom, a sign of his habitual confidence, confidence genuine though, deep within him, concealing an anxiety, a fearfulness formed when he stood as a beautiful, wide-eyed child at the table in parents' bedroom watching them scream across the room, the bright light on those angry faces, suffering – and moved to the door where the sounds were emanating from. He stood for a moment listening but it left him none the wiser. There was a keyhole beneath the door handle, this gold-leafed, and very slowly he bent forward to look. His eye touched the keyhole and there he stood, squinting. He could just about make out two shapes; arching his back up, he saw legs, standing in front of what seemed to be a selection of furniture, moved slightly to the room's centre and draped in a long black cloth.

Suddenly he felt a hand on his shoulder; he turned back, already apologizing. He had witnessed something he should not have; he had transgressed. He would never find out what he had glimpsed behind that door, although on the sadder erotic evenings of later years, alone in his trailer, a bottle of whiskey before him, his mind would sometimes turn to speculation upon it. Stood in front of him was a waiter, himself clad in the white shirt and black aprons of those below. The waiter made no sound but simply placed his hand upon Dougie, taking his wrist and placing his other arm behind the upper part of his back, to literally push him, wordlessly and without regard, to the toilet and indeed, with a helpful push on the toilet door itself, steer him into the place he should be.

The waiter's steps echoed down the stairs. 'Fucking hell,' said Dougie, listening to his own breathing in the silence for a moment. He took out his iPhone and said, 'That was weird.'

Stuart sat in the garden, bathed in beautiful sunlight, when he remembered Malcolm's letter. He reached inside the pocket of his jacket and extracted the envelope, this a little crumpled now. He started at the orange envelope with its central blue squiggle of 'Stuart' and then read.

Dear Stuart,

People in Berlin have told me that you've been complaining about the way I treated you. Clearly, you have a very high opinion of yourself, as you showed once again last night. Sorry, but I just don't have time to deal with your behaviour as I have twenty dates in the next two weeks. I'm busy, and you're making a much bigger deal of this than you need to, treating me like I'm some kind of Aids terrorist. I will not be reading your emails, texts or Facebook messages in future.

I sincerely hope you become a better person.

Malcolm

There was also another blue streak of pen next to the final name, as if the author had begun a kiss but then decided the recipient did not merit one. Stuart stared at the paper a while, trying to work out what he felt, apart from the dull ringing blow of abuse.

'Love letter, is it?'

The man spoke in English; a clear, stagey English which sounded like it was always lilting towards an anecdote. Stuart looked round to where a large, bald-headed man sat. He had a savagely angular face, like some woodcut medieval peasant.

'Actually the opposite – it's a letter of bitter recrimination.'

'Oh, you're British,' said the man, piqued. 'From London?'

'Nottingham.'

'Goodness – then what are you doing here?'

'I'm waiting for a friend. We're comedians; we're on tour.'

'Really?' said the man. 'How interesting!' He turned over from where he was sitting. 'And you're performing in Düsseldorf?'

'No – in Heidelberg. We're just waiting for a bus.'

'Gosh; that must be exciting, mustn't it?'

'Waiting for a bus?'

'No, I mean really. You must be having a brilliant time. I can't imagine how much fun you must be having.'

Stuart paused. 'I guess we are. We did a gig in Essen yesterday.'

'Wow!' The man paused, then played his trump card, apropos nothing, except that he had clearly done it many times. 'I used to be on television myself. On WDR, you know, *Westdeutscher Rundfunk* – and my show was called Johnny Ausländer.' Literally, Johnny Foreigner. 'It ran for fifteen years.'

'Is that right?'

'Oh yes, we were the biggest variety show on a Saturday night for nearly all that time. In the last seasons we dropped off a bit – MTV, you know, we couldn't see that coming. That it would be so popular. Honest to God, if I told you some of the fan mail I used to get...'

'I bet.'

'Oh yes,' said the man, presumably the Johnny of the show title, leaning over, his big broad face alight, 'the girls used to *insist* on anal sex.'

At this point Dougie entered with paleness spreading across his face. 'Making friends?' he said to Stuart with an attempted bravado which revealed a quaky voice.

'This is –'

'Carl,' said the man formerly known as Johnny Ausländer.

'Pleased to meet you man,' said Dougie.

'Carl here's a television personality,' said Stuart.

'Was, darling, was. I don't have it any more – in fact, I couldn't get arrested these days. They don't want to know, you know? These days it's all up on bloody BoobTube.'

'He had the biggest show in Düsseldorf for nearly fifteen years.'

'Aye man, really? What was it called?'

'It was called *Dem Vaterland mit Johnny Ausländer*,' said Carl. 'And I could tell you stories about that time, I can tell you. We used to get fan mail from girls who - '

'I bet you did, man.'

'We had all the stars; Roger Whitaker, Howard Carpendale – even Jethro Tull. I actually have one of Ian Anderson's flute cases, which he left in my recording studio.' Carl lowered his chin. 'Say – do you boys fancy a drink?'

Stuart attempted to communicate his disapproval to Dougie who completely misread his expression. 'Well, I don't see why not.'

'The bus, remember!' said Stuart. 'It could leave at any minute.'

Dougie said, 'Oh, right, yeah. You see the thing is, we have to take a bus. It could leave at any minute.'

Carl nodded like a man schooled in dealing with disappointment. He raised a hand; 'Ah of course. You must go. My partner and I Otto Kaltes – do you know him? *Badezeit mit Papa*? – used to go down and do road shows in Heidelberg every summer. Amazing times! The girls down there, now I'm telling you – they used to...'

'That's our bus,' said Stuart. The two young men were rising up, brushing themselves down.

'Have fun in Heidelberg! Give my love to the Neckar!'

'Thanks man!' said Dougie, and then quietly to Stuart, 'Is that the river?'

'Where are you boys playing?'

'O'Reilly's Irish pub,' Dougie called back as they rounded the corner.

'Never heard of it!' Carl called back as his voice gradually became too distant to hear.

The two men walked briskly towards the road.

'Jesus man, the weirdest thing just happened to me...'

'Weirder than Carl?'

'Aye. Carl's alright man, you're too hard on him.'

'You didn't hear what he told me. Anyway – what happened?'

'I think I got caught spying on two people fucking. By one of the waiters.'

'Think? How can you *think* you got caught?'

'I didnae get a very good view, like, but it looked like a woman was giving a man head in this weird white room full of covered furniture. Like they'd been decorating and she'd started sucking him off like.'

Stuart laughed. 'Sex seems to follow you around, Dougie. I wish it did me.'

Dougie considered. 'No man, it was weird. It wasn't right.' He didn't elaborate as to why not, which had to do with the sudden, embarrassing way the waiter had laid his hands upon him, a true invasion of his personal space, and the shame he had felt in being caught peeping. Dougie felt dirty. 'Let's get back on the bus, if it hasn't fucked off already.'

But it hadn't and, after they seated themselves again it was another fifteen minutes before it, without warning, clicked into its massive life. Within minutes they were on the motorway and neither the marathon nor the restaurant scenes were ever mentioned by either of them again.

X.

One hour later the bus stopped at a motorway station for a fifteen-minute break Dougie and Stuart got out to stretch his legs. The bus driver and his friend – for some reason bus drivers, like chatty teenage girls, always felt the need to travel with a companion, even just to sit in silence with – were drinking coffee and smoking outside. '*Aber jetzt ist alles OK,*' the driver was saying to his friend, now everything is OK.

Dougie stood in the queue at the McDonalds, wondering what to buy. He was still a little dry-mouthed from the night before, to be honest, so a quarter pounder'd suffice; just a quarter pounder, aye. Or fries? The queue was moving up. He still, he recalled, had a chocolate bar in his pocket from the night before. Burger then chocolate – or should he save the latter for later?

He took the purchased burger out to the seating area, where he sat on the bench and watched the cars pulse by. What'd really make this nice now he thought would be a beer – maybe one of those Becks Lime concoctions. Jesus he thought drinking beer on your own by the motorway. He might as well go home now. Where was Stuart anyway? Still, it was good to take a break from him the wee cunt. Don't get me wrong he liked Stuart but everyone's company got tedious after a while.

Interesting to speculate on the difference between

McDonalds in various cultures. Like – there was dampness to the bread here in Germany. And in China there had been a – Dougie had been to China once, to his brother who'd been working there, and had lost his virginity to a prostitute on his brother's dime, if you were interested, a lovely smiling girl – sweetness. A weird, sort of fatty sweetness. It was the same shite everywhere to be honest with you.

Hard to overstate how much they had all hung out in McDonalds as kids. There had been something powerful about it, honest to God, gesturing with the chips, ordering a further round of burgers. No discount coupon had gone unused. Sometimes four – alright, not four, but two, two-and-a-half easy – hours in there at a time. Bank Holidays, school inspection afternoons, they'd always head into town and order two Big Macs each.

Later there were pubs. They blended in over time, like, first came the initial carefully prepared excursion to purchase alcohol. You'd be thinking for days in advance about whether they were going to serve you. Taking a bath beforehand, doing your hair with shampoo and conditioner. Trying on a black T-shirt, your older brother's jacket. The fuss in the house if people found out where you were going. And then the drink – cider and black. He'd be spoiling for some chips after a few of those for sure. They'd all go down to Magical Kebab and it'd be bedlam, the sporty kids lining up next to the indie boys, he being the latter; he wondered if that indeed magical establishment was still there.

But quite soon it was becoming just the pub. Like the summer where he had just messed up his mock exams and he was in the Brunswick Cellar with Olly and Darren Fitzpatrick. His friends were playing pool and drinking lager while he tried to read Kafka's 'The Trial.' It was a slow process. Probably it would have been 'The White Stripes' on the pub jukebox, they were obsessed with them then. But they liked older stuff too, The Cure, The Band, Morrissey.

'You want to play Doug?'

'Ah I'm alright. Trying to read.'

'Are you really? You haven't turned a page yet.'

'Ah leave him alone,' said Olly. 'What's it about?'

'It's about a man who gets banged up for no good reason.'

'Sort of like Callum, aye.'

'Callum stole a lawnmower.'

'Yeah I know but it was a joke, he was going to give it back.' Olly smiled. 'Put something else on will you?'

Dougie looked up from his book, the corner already folded. 'Aye I will man.' He got up and went to the jukebox, found the song 'Sparky's Dream' by Teenage Fanclub, and slotted in 20p. The big chords clanged into life and the pool-playing boys sang along.

Dougie was moving back to his seat when a voice cut through him.

'Like this song, do you pal?'

It was a harsher Glasgow voice, a rough voice, a voice with experience and suffering and cigarettes behind it. A man sat in the snug in a black and white check shirt.

'Aye, it's not bad. It's one of our anthems you know, we love to sing along with it.'

At this Olly struck a pool ball and raising it, chorused in sync with Darren 'I took a wrong direction!' while the ball trundled into the hole.

'It's good to have songs. The music's much better now – in my day it was a load of shite. Well, it wasnae shite, but most of it was. Fuckin' Tears fae Fears. Everybody wants to rule the world, except me, I just want you to shut the fuck up.' The man smiled; his glass was empty. 'You boys have a good time, yeah? You get up to much?'

'We certainly have a laugh.'

'What do you do?'

'Ah - we taxed a Wall's Ice Cream sign recently. You know as swag. But then somebody stole it off of us.'

'Ah it happens man. We used to steal fuck loads when I was a kid. We stole a car once, and we got caught. How old are youse anyways? 17. Enjoy it pal. Those are the best days of your life.'

'Are they?'

'Oh absolutely. When you get to my age – everyone wants something aff ye. It's true. Everyone wants a piece you know, all these fucking chisellers. At your age you have no responsibilities.'

Dougie was thinking about his brother, his father, his home. But he said nothing. Instead he smiled and said, 'Alright', moving back to pick up the library Kafka.

'Is it good then?' the man said, his gaze undiverted.

'It's alright.' Dougie lowered the book again, looking at

the blocky 70s cover. 'To be honest I haven't really read much of it. Seems very – I don't know. I like something with a bit more action, you know?' Dougie considered; no, that wasn't quite it. 'It is pretty cool that you don't know what he's done though. I think that's like we all feel. In life.'

'Ah I wish I'd read more son. I left school at 16. Keep going young feller – you don't want to end up like me. Drinking pints in the afternoon at the Brunswick Cellar.'

'Well, I am too. And my life's great, remember?' Dougie smiled.

'Aye but for you it's different. Schools out; you've got the whole summer. It's a beautiful feeling – a sensation of almost endless freedom. Freedom.'

'Aye,' said Dougie, marvelling at the almost infinite six weeks ahead. They were planning to go to festivals.

'Say what's your name?'

'Dougie.'

'Dougie, I'm Mark. Would you care to join me for a drink?' The man smiled. 'What's the matter? Your friends seem pretty occupied.'

In fact, Ollie had gone outside to smoke a joint, and Darren was on the phone to Lisa.

'Come on. You've just finished your exams, right?'

Dougie stood up, and, as many a young man feeling nervous, tried to appear enthusiastic. 'Alright Mark. That's very kind of you. I'll have a Jack Daniels and Coke.'

'JD and Coke. Coming up. Just take a seat.'

Dougie was closer to Mark now, catching him at close quarters as he headed to the bar. His hair was closely cropped, and he was thin, body and face exuding a kind of rangy addictiveness. A tattoo poked from beneath his second-top button.

'Did I introduce myself? I'm Mark,' said Mark, returning with the drinks and a packet of crisps.

'Aye you did, aye. Dougie,' Dougie repeated. The crisps hit the table. 'Thanks very much mate.'

'Go steady though hey? You've got all summer to enjoy these.'

Dougie tasted the black salt and sweetness. 'So what did you do, aye, when you were my age?'

'All sorts of shite to be honest. Stealing traffic cones, graffiti, selling drugs. The whole kit and kaboodle. Or I was just sitting at home watching TV. And I had this hamster right, called Pig. And sometimes Pig would go into what can only be described as a coma. But we'd find that we could always wake him up. Like, we'd splash some water on him, or on another occasion – right, I know this sounds really cruel and you're already looking at me like I'm a sick fuck – but on one occasion we stood him on the grill and in a few minutes he was right as rain. It is cruel if you think about it now. Well, it was at the time too actually.' Mark drank. 'But effective. Got a job?'

'Actually I'm looking for work in a bar. But I'm only 17.'

'Hah, you look older.'

'Exactly. It's fucking shite.' Dougie sipped a bit more. 'I'm telling you man, I was made to do bar work. Made to. I'd be a really good barman, because I'm charming.' Dougie paused, almost embarrassed. 'What do you do?'

'Jack of all trades. Been like that since I left school. I wasnae like you – wasnae bright. When I was 15 they asked me what I wanted to be and I said "unemployed." At least that didnae happen.' Mark grimaced a little; it was hard to tell when he was joking; sometimes he seemed to fence with the words. But this was before a time in Dougie's life where he was able to gauge ages, or be aware of what people were supposed to be doing with their lives time at a given age. Here all Dougie was thinking is 'this is an older man.' There was even a sense of honour in being talked to by him.

'So you are looking? 'Cos I need someone.'

'Me?'

'Yes you pal. Not your funny friends. No offence mate, but I wouldn't quite trust them with this. I need someone to help me with a job.'

'When?'

'Tonight.'

'Right.'

'What, you busy?'

'No, I mean – what's the job?'

'I need someone to help me pick up and transport some roofing. Just get it to the van, like. 50 quid cash in hand.'

'Roofing?'

'Well, things which are on roofs at least. We'll need to clean it afterwards as well. But I'll show you how it's done, it's really no bother.'

Dougie thought of his home, of his absent desire to return early today, his father, the latest from the divorce, the booze. A vortex of shite was waiting on him back there. And Mark – well, he needed help with some roofing. 'I think I can manage that,' Dougie confidently said.

'Great. I'll pay you tonight, don't worry about that. Give you a bit of money to take a lady out on the town. You got a woman? Can't imagine you have many problems, dashing young feller like you. Don't blush pal! He's blushing!' Mark called to the returning, baffled Ollie. 'Me, I'm single. Better that way. Better to be on your own.'

Dougie said, 'It's nice to have someone though aye. I think it's the best thing, a woman with you like. The way she smells, the way she looks. Aye, I think that's the best thing.'

Mark said, 'What a fucking poet. Now let's get a few pints down us and then we'll drive off over to the site.'

Dougie looked over cautiously to where Ollie and Darren stood chatting, their cues lowered. Mark cast a crooked eye over them.

'I don't think your friends are going anywhere,' Mark finally said.

They drove across the city, the suburban roads, the small fast-food shops. It was a damp summer day. They passed the swimming pool, and Dougie saw the mums lining up outside, the young children with them, plastic bags in their arms. They carried on along the Clyde, through the South Side, heading on to the Gorbals.

'You got your license yet?' said Mark after a while.

'Nah. But I can drive though.'

'That's such a Scottish answer!' Mark laughed. '"Nah but I can drive." I love it.'

Mark continued driving and after a while, and all of a sudden, slotted a cassette into the tape deck. Fast dance music started mid-track.

'I used to go out listening to this shite every weekend,' Mark said. He turned to Dougie, manically beating the air with his fist and, when Dougie laughed, laughed himself. Then he snapped the tape off. 'Load of shite.'

The drove in, the city getting thinner now. 'What's your ambition then?' Mark was saying.

'I don't know man. I think I'd like to get out Glasgow you know. Mebbe live in London for a while.'

'London's shite man. Don't bother. My dad's from down there – it's shite. Too expensive, people are cunts. At least you know what you're getting with Glasgow.'

'Aye, misery and smack.'

'Fuck off, Glasgow's a great city.'

'Aye I know son I'm only kidding on. I really appreciate it here man, don't get me wrong, it's world-class. I have this joke that if you cut me I'd have Glasgow written through my entrails like a stock of punk rock.' Mark did not react. 'But don't you ever get the urge to you know, see the world a bit?'

'I lived in Inverness for two years.'

'How was that?'

'Alright. But I missed Glasgow.'

Dougie leant back; as the car accelerated he felt an excitement rising inside him. Just seeing a road sign to Edinburgh gave him a tingling in the groin. It was all so infinite, so exciting; America! Scotland! Europe! The adventure of the world.

The car was now crossing a large industrial park and now came to a sudden halt. They were a speck on a field of unpopulated concrete. Mark raised his head; 'Here we are.'

'Where are we?'

'We're east. How are you feeling? Do you want a Red Bull before we get started?'

'I'm fine.' Dougie suddenly felt clumsy, scrutinized, middle class. It had suddenly become very hot in the car.

Mark meanwhile stepped outside the van leaving Dougie alone. He waited him; behind him he heard a scraping of metal. Dougie turned; the older man was holding a toolkit and a Red Bull. 'Sure?'

'Aye, go on then,' said Dougie, taking the can and stepping out.

The Red Bull tasted like blood as they walked across the park. A few hundred metres, approached from a slow distance, a large fence rose. A whole had been cut, or worn, into it, and Mark stepped confidently through. There was no sign in him of anxiety or trespass. Dougie shook the last droplets from the can and, gently, almost like an offering, laid it down at the fence entrance before slipping through the hole.

They were now in an area of office space dominated by large, low-roofed sheds. The distant sound of traffic could be heard, like the sounds of the beach far away. They walked along below a low wall and, as if from memory, Mark suddenly sprung up onto it, and soon the two men were walking the wall, finally reaching a little ladder up onto a small rectangular roof. On the centre of the roof lay a pile of blue solar panels, unfixed.

'Here we are.' Mark moved over to the panels. Now wearing black gloves, he leant down over the panel and fiddled with the back of it, apparently loosening a screw. 'Got it. Give me a hand, would ya?'

Dougie stepped over. He was surprised at how calm he felt – no, not calm, out of his fucking skull. He felt like he'd taken a load of glue and dope and been drinking black coffee at bedtime. He walked over and took the opposite end to Mark.

'Right, we'll just lift and then tilt, right? Then all the way to the van. Be careful – it's no good broken.'

'Like this?'

'Aye but walk a bit slower.'

'Aye. Like that?'

'Good, good – now tilt. Tilt!'

'I'm tilting!'

'Alright – just one step and - that's it, that's good.'

The two men were down on the wall now and

Dougie found himself almost ready to fall, just crash on the concrete below, but he didn't, instead hopping assertively back and overseeing the sliding of the panel down. There was something about the panel, the preciousness of this weave of glass, aluminium and glue, which seemed worth protecting. More than if they'd been stealing – because this was what they were doing, wasn't it? – say a car or tyres. Some of the other lads did that; Dougie couldn't imagine it having this sacred air. This was a quasi-religious experience.

Mark closed the car door. 'Alright. Let's get the next one. We could try lifting too but I don't know, they're heavy.'

'They're heavy.'

They walked back to the roof in silence.

As they lifted the second panel, Dougie spoke. 'Mark – I feel bad man.'

Mark said, 'You want your fifty do you pal?' Then he laughed, his same friendly laugh but sounding now, in this different context, blunt.

'Look mate, these panels have been forgotten. It's council overspend. You know what they're like. They buy them up and they don't even know how to fit them. But I do; I fix them up and....'

'Sell them.'

'Aye, and fit them too. Now you gonna lift?'

Dougie was acutely conscious of the space behind his head; the Red Bull blood taste, the swimming pool sounds of the road, and the cool summer light splitting his hair. 'Aye,' he said and lifted.

They walked back to the car and slotted the panel in. Mark strode on ahead. But Dougie paused just a moment, trying to sort out his trembling emotions. He stood a moment to listen the distant traffic, he heard voices coming from behind the fence.

'Naw man, I'm just looking –'

'Shut up and put your hands up.'

And then sounds of a scuffle. Punches, kicks, shouts. Dougie had paused at the fence and his body seemed locked. He felt fear, paralysis, older, his throat swollen with extra saliva sometime. Now he pushed himself to look across at the car, stuck in the middle of the concrete like a toy, and at last from nowhere he burst into a run. Past the car, past his can, and out of the complex, as fast as he could to the main road and beyond.

Dougie arrived back home late that night, creeping down the driveway, slipping his key into the lock. Its dark frame made it seem like an obelisk in the night. Inside the hall there was silence, the house's hum, the fluffed-up coats. Unsorted, just summer coat over winter coat and his own red jacket, which he hung up now.

He stood a moment in the hallway. Between the fear of arriving and the residual fear of his flight in his stomach, he waited. Then he went to the kitchen to get a glass of milk. All the little actions became sensitized at this time of night; the hums of the kitchen, the scrape of the drawer opening. Living in someone else's house, you know. Then he moved to the living room to watch TV.

'Y'alright.' His dad was sitting in the living room, a glass next to him, in utter darkness.

'Y'alright Da,' Dougie said. 'You sitting here watching TV all on your lonesome aye?'

'Aye I was watching TV but there's fuck all on. Then I was just sitting here thinking.'

'Pretty depressing Tuesday night isn't it? Sitting on your arse in the dark watching the TV. I mean literally watching the TV – it's not even on.' Only the red standby dot was visible.

'In an hour they're going to be showing Angel.'

'And you're staying up for that one are you?'

'Would you like to watch it with me? It's not bad. It's the feller from Buffy the Vampire Slayer.'

'I know who it is man. He's always up on a rooftop being emotional. Always with the big soft rock on the soundtrack too.'

Dougie caught sight of another glass on the drawing sill.

'Your Uncle Billie was round.'

'Really? How was he?'

'Oh you know how he is.'

Dougie sat down on the sofa next to his dad, picking up the remote.

'What channel's Angel?'

'It's on Four but it's not on yet. There's still some shite documentary about, I don't know, ladyboys or something. The way they live their lives - it's quite interesting actually. Aye, you know how Billie is. He's a man a few words and most of those are 'Nae bother."

'He is very keen on that phrase.'

'Nae bother. Nae bother. All fucking night. So I do a massive fart next to him and what does he say?'

'Nae bother.'

'Nae bother, right.'

Dougie was looking over at his dad, or at what he could see of him, the worn little face in the dark, the puckered nose, the little crop of tufty hair and the freckles in the dark.

'Where's Sharon?' he asked.

'She's out tonight with her bowling club, hopefully that'll do her some good.'

'So she's not back yet?'

'Oh you know she sometimes like to hang out with them afterwards. You know they like to smoke dope.'

Dougie smiled in the darkness. 'How're you two getting on?'

'Not so good, son, I've got to be honest with you son. We've not been getting on for a while, you know. We just can't seem to – get on. Put it all aside. Let it all flow under the bridge. It's like things keep boiling over; I don't want to argue, but it's all just seething under the surface. You know, not just now, but everything that's ever happened, that's ever gone wrong.

'When we met it all seemed so good. After your mother died I was feeling pretty pissed off for a long time. I was so angry with God, you know. And then I met her and she was the most beautiful thing I'd seen in so many years. And so friendly you know? Ten minutes after you'd met her it was like she was your best friend. In that way women have you know. They make you feel at home.'

'Aye, I know.' Dougie grinned; he longed to tell his dad his recent escapades with Sarah, before he realized he already had done so, last Friday night, on the same sofa.

'Anyway life took an upturn; you liked her, and we married. And I realized yes, there is a God. He can just be a right numpty sometimes.'

Dougie laughed; he liked his dad's jokes, especially the darker, late-night brew, which he suspected only he and his dad's mind got to hear. Certainly not with Sharon with whom his dad was always a little gentler, a little more polite. Sitting there he felt freer than usual in the little room, where so many of his nights ended, where only the most memorable didn't.

'I tell you son,' his dad was saying, 'if you can find a way to live without women you should do, because they raise a lot of problems, problems you wouldnae have if you were just yersel'.'

'You know Woody Allen says that marriage is an attempt to solve problems you wouldn't have had if you were on your own.'

'Aye, Woody knows what's going on, even if he is a paedo.' His dad shifted, the sofa giving a leathery groan. He was leaning forward. 'Oh Dougie I tell you – another divorce is going to be hard tae take.'

Dougie looked over. His eyes were growing used to the dark now and he saw his Dad bending forward, his empty glass.

'You want a drink?' he said at last.

His dad turned. 'You getting one?'

'I'm going to have a milk, so, if you want something.'

'Well, a wee whiskey would be nice.'

Dougie thought a moment. 'No, I've got an idea. I want to make you one of my specials.'

There was a pause. 'Alright,' his dad said.

Dougie walked to the kitchen. It was still quiet in there, the hum, the little windows; he made himself a milk and quickly knocked it back. Then he began to work; taking down the glass, the liquors, the ice, and going to the cupboard were he kept, behind a scales and baking books, the thermos flask top which served as his secret shaker. He poured the whiskey. Minutes later, after measuring and cracking and stirring, he stood back to survey his work; it was good. It was all you needed really, a good drink, maybe a lovely lady, a nice meal too.

He brought the glass back into the room. Entering, the sofa was clearly empty, evoking a sense of disappointment. But, in fact, his dad was over by the TV, popping a DVD back into the box.

'I brought you a drink,' he said.

'What kind of drink?'

'It's a cocktail.'

'What kind of cocktail?'

'It's a Manhattan.'

'What's in it?'

'Whiskey, vermouth. You're supposed to use bitters but I just used a bit of orange peel. Thought you could use some, you know, vitamin C. Help you see in the dark.'

'And you made this yourself?'

'No, I bought it from the bar in the kitchen –' Dougie stopped himself. 'It's a piece of piss making them, aye. I think I'm really good at it. I like doing it. It's a passion of mine. I mean, I can't yet but I honestly reckon I'd make a really really good barman. I don't want to work in Budgens Dad. I want to be a barman and make really good cocktails.'

His dad said nothing, but Dougie could now quite clearly see him in the dark, all 5'8 inches of him, standing head cocked and, reaching out a hand to take the drink.

'And this is your speciality is it?'

'It's one of the first ones I learnt to make. But I also do fantastic Bloody Marys.'

'Well I'll be. You're like a regular Glasgow Tom Cruise. The Tom Cruise of Pollokshields. I'll expect you want me to try it now?'

'If you want. You don't have to – I mean, it's strong.'

'Cheers.' The glass glinted; Dougie listened to his dad make little sipping and slurping sounds in the dark.

'And?'

There was a further pause.

'Dougie,' said his dad, 'that is a truly delicious drink.'

Dougie couldn't help but grin a little.

'Really? 'Cos you can tell me if it's not.'

'Honest to God, it's delicious. Make one of those for a girl and she will fuck you like a stoat.'

Dougie laughed. 'Sit down man, it's time for Angel.'

'Ha,' his dad laughed back. 'But I think you'll have to watch it for me tonight. I've got to be up for work at six.'

'Oh alright.'

'But thanks so much for the drink.' In the darkness, his father touched his elbow. 'You'll have to give me the recipe.'

'No I bloody won't!'

His dad laid the cocktail down on the sill. 'Put that away for me would you? And goodnight Dougie.'

'Night Dad.'

'It's not every day that you're sent to bed with a Manhattan. I'm not totally square you know, we were drinking these in the 70s. Takes me back. I had big sideburns then, just like you. I was just like you. Just think of my poor wee heed in the morning. Goodnight son!'

His dad left the room and Dougie sat down. He pressed standby on the remote; the TV flickered into life. He brought up Angel; it was early, he hadn't missed much, credits still scrolling under the early scenes. As the plot thickened and Angel stood on the rooftop he finished his milk, placing the glass next to his dad's glass, and he couldn't resist, seeing it, dipping his finger to the bottom, finding, to his pleasure, nothing left in there but a residual orange slice.

XI.

Ten years later, after the many and varied adventures that had led him to Germany, involving love requited and unrequited, a brief cocaine addiction and a frankly outrageous interlude in Dakar, Dougie greeted Stuart at a service station urinal. But Stuart didn't want to talk to his friend now. Instead he moved out of the garage across the kerb, looking across the low level car park, a space between spaces, an uncelebrated corner of the world, towards a large evergreen hedge behind which he couldn't see. The rain was coming down quite heavily now. He turned back, looking across to the *Autobahn* where the cars roared past, relentless cars unrestricted by speed limits. The ground was incessantly flat and he hadn't seen a beautiful thing all day. This was Germany, the utopia of the functional, and perhaps it was precisely this monotone aspect, this nondescription, which appealed to him as a subject for his life and comedy.

He had lived amongst the Germans for many years and they would not let him in. Hence the comedy. But what did *in* mean here? Perhaps they did let him in but once they did there was no conviviality, no welcome, just distanced talk about prejudices and facts, variegated judgements passed on foreigners dependent on their land of origin, and always the sense that his hosts were more excited by the idea of the foreigner in their country than the reality of their presence. Sometimes, he felt that his German friends, such as they were, would return home from their stilted, awkward conversations, ones always tensed by the threat of a sudden and unnecessary switch to American English on their part, and present to their families excited descriptions of their new British friend and the new, open face of their country. That it all came out behind closed doors. Perhaps so much of the alienation and isolation he felt here were just the Germans being well, German.

Dougie was standing across from him and had purchased a hamburger, which he held in his hand. 'Y'alright man?' Its wrapper was shaking in the wind.

'I'm fine. Just thinking.'

Dougie nodded. 'I was just thinking too man.'

'Yes?'

'I was thinking we should get back on the bus.'

Stuart nodded and walked back with Dougie to go on to Heidelberg.

They continued on past the cities of Germany's Western edge and its post-war heyday, on by countless flat fields, cutting south now along the concrete-lined motorway. They were becoming late and Stuart glanced at his watch occasionally.

'Where are we staying tonight man?'

'I don't know. Dwight said they'd stayed with Luigi.'

'Can we stay with Luigi?'

'I don't know. His number's here.' Stuart indicated the printed-out email which contained the itinerary Dwight had composed for them, and a number written on top in black pen. 'I'll send him a text.'

As Stuart did so, 'Aye, well we don't want to end up in a hostel, do we? That's all our profit gone,' said Dougie. Strange as it seemed, the hundred Euros they might earn each for the weekend would keep them going for a couple of weeks in Berlin, the Eldorado of broke people.

'No we don't. What'll we do if we can't stay with him?'

'Aw, something'll work out.' Dougie paused and thought a moment. 'Tell you what – we'll ask after the show if anyone wants to put us up.'

Stuart smiled instantly. 'Honestly?'

'Aye, aye, they'll love it man. Two dashing young neds like us, what's not to like?'

'What's a ned?'

'A ned is a person.'

'Right.' Stuart lowered his head. 'We can ask if we kill it. I'm not asking the audience if we have a bad gig. Then it becomes like – pity these poor clowns. They're not funny *and* they've got nowhere to stay.'

Rain continued to fall gently as they came into Mannheim, a city famous for its chessboard layout, although one Stuart only learnt about later, reading about the places they'd been to following their trip, although nothing of what he had seen would have suggested order to him. The bus crawled round the main station and moved into an industrial parking lot.

Dougie looked out the window, deep in thought. Eventually he spoke; 'Jesus – what a shithole.'

Yet people's lives were going on here. For some people, Mannheim was all they knew. Stuart was sure there were famous people born in Mannheim, though that would have to be your connection to Mannheim, being born there. You might say the same about Nottingham.

It was a quick drive from there down the motorway to their destination. Half an hour later, on a Sunday afternoon at five o'clock, they arrived in Heidelberg.

'When I mentioned this place to my dad, he started singing.'

'Aye?'

'When it's summertime in Heidelberg...' It was a line from a 1950s musical, the Student Prince; Stuart continued to sing.

'*When the Frauleins wear*

Flowers in their hair...'

'Right – just wait a minute will you man, I'm going to buy a pie.'

Stuart nodded and, with Dougie disappeared into the main concourse, watched the train station before him. It was the usual shabby mix of crammed bakeries and tourist shops with stuffed towers of overpriced postcards. Pedestrian traffic was considerable and taxis were crammed along its circular parking bay; others cars sought a drop-off point. Mark Twain had called Heidelberg the last refuge of the beautiful, having presumably never been there on a grey afternoon in early April.

'They didnae have any I like,' said Dougie once back with more disgust in his voice than Stuart had ever heard before. 'I like the *Apfelpflunder*, you know, and they only had the *Apfelkrapfen*.'

'You're an *Apfelkrapfen*,' said Stuart.

'What?' said Dougie.

'Nothing.' Stuart had already been staring at the map, largely incomprehensible, which had been mounted on the bollard ahead. He pointed straight across from the station. 'I think that's the river. We have to cross there.'

'Let's get going then.'

They began walking directly on from the train station. Stuart had been to Heidelberg before, but just for a day. He had been crammed into a tiny car with a German girl, Maria Spatz, visiting her friends across multiple German cities while she returned a book here, visited a relative here, one of those long passionate days of involuntary chastity which had characterized his early years in Germany.

After about ten minutes walking they had arrived at a slightly raised road bridge, a large American-looking structure of apparently brand-new concrete. There were no cars about. 'I don't think this is right,' said Stuart. 'I think we're going away from the city.'

So they walked away from the motorway and over a smaller bridge, where a woman was coming towards them.

'Excuse me, we're looking for the *Altstadt*,' the old town,

Stuart asked.

The woman looked over. '*Altstadt*?' she asked, thinking apparently deeply.

'I think it's over this way,' said Stuart.

'Yes, I think you're right,' she said.

'So over the bridge and keep going?' Stuart asked.

'Yes, that'd be it,' said the woman. 'That sounds right.' And then she said, with exceptional friendliness in her Badeian accent, 'Have a nice day!'

'So. Straight on this way.'

'She said keep going, aye?'

'She did indeed.' They started walking forward. 'I like her accent; I had a girlfriend with that accent.'

'Aye? You never told me about that, man.'

'A gentleman never tells,' said Stuart. 'She was my longest ever German girlfriend. One month. Her name was Elvan.'

'Typical German name.'

'Her Dad was Turkish but her mother came from Karlsruhe. I think having sex with her was the only time I ever felt integrated.'

They had now moved away from the roadway and were in kempt residential streets lined with exceptionally elegant homes. Certainly, the houses were old, but more in a wealthy stockbroker way than being of historical providence: was this really the *Altstadt*? Was it really *alt* enough? Stuart suspected not as beside him Dougie went on talking.

'The one thing someone told me about Heidelberg is that there's an emergency contraceptive service. Like, if you've got a lassie home, right, and you realize you haven't got a condom, then you can phone them up and they'll bring you one. You know, like how some cities do an after-hours booze delivery.'

'You think they'd be part of the same service,' said Stuart. 'I think we're lost.'

At this point a man walking a dog was passing them, a tall man in a black hat and green raincoat. Stuart addressed him formally. 'Excuse me,' he began, 'We're looking how to get to the *Altstadt*.'

The man took an almighty suck of breath in. '*Ich denke, ich denke*,' he said, 'I think, I think – the Altstadt, there's lots of ways you can do it. How far are you prepared to walk is the question? Because there is also a bus. And there's also the question of *where* in the Altstadt you want to go. And obviously, how long you've got to actually get there. You just came from the train station, you say? I'm trying to think. It's not easy for you to do it from here; I'd say it's a long way. Yes, it is very far.'

The man looked over them smiling. His little pea-headed dog had also paused, its head seemingly cocked as if also waiting for their response.

'Well...,' said Stuart. 'I'm sure we'll work it out.'

'Really?' said the man. 'I have a map. I can go home and get it.'

'No, that's fine, really. Thank you. Many thanks.'

'OK – have a wonderful day. *Ciao!*'

The man, after first politely then with a yank of

his chain notifying the dog that they were to be moving again, pattered off round the corner. As he turned out of view, Dougie and Stuart's laughter began, great wheezing laughter at their incompetence and the uselessness of their received advice.

'Let's walk back to the station,' said Stuart.

Back there, Stuart looked at the useless map bollard again and, as he did, Dougie, stood behind, suddenly and forcibly suggested a left turn.

'Are you sure?'

'Aye man.'

'How do you know?'

'It's this way.'

It wasn't. Within a few minutes they were stood next to a hard shoulder even more exposed than before, with the odd Sunday driver roaring past. Strange this, how quickly the cities gave way to roadways, like when you walked round the façade of a theme park funhouse to find only staves and wiring behind. The illusions of society never went deep – not in a country like Germany, which had been built up again from ashes based on drawings of its old self; from this perspective, Germany had become a theme park of itself.

Stuart repeated the phrase he had been saying with variations for the previous five minutes, only this time as a genuine bookend to a sentence. 'This isn't right.'

Slowly Dougie said, 'No. No man, you're right.'

When they got back to the strain station there was only one remaining direction they had not yet gone in, veering immediately left upon exiting the station and, sure enough, after a few minutes down that path, they found themselves walking a magnificent tree-lined avenue. Tall poplars broke the sky; the air was cold and slightly damp. They approached a large bridge, with wide swathes of concrete for the cars bordering roomy bike and pedestrian lines, and there, to their right, was the city of Heidelberg, spindly, brown-hued and, golden lamps lining its water-bound rim, remarkably intact.

'It's pretty man, it's pretty.'

'Yes,' said Stuart. 'It's the last refuge of the beautiful.'

They descended to walk along the river, past little allotments and through small tunnels. 'Did you text Dwight?'

'Not yet. But I've got the address.'

'And they said it was good yeah?'

'They said it was amazing.'

'How many did they have?'

'About fifty. Mostly English speakers apparently.' Stuart contextualized, 'It must be all those American bases. Heidelberg still has a large troop presence, I believe.'

'Aye, I heard that. Hopefully we can get a few of that crowd in, like.'

'I can imagine them, the soldiers, watching Dwight and Malcolm' Stuart went on. He began to imitate a Southern drawl, one of the comic voices which lived within him, 'Saying "We didn't care much for fat boy and his Jewish friend. No, no, we didn't like them boys much."'

'Ha!' said Dougie, then adding to the riff, stomping his feet, called '"We made fat boy dance."

'Dance, fat boy, dance!'

'Squeal fat boy! Squeal!'

'Squeee!' Stuart laughed. He mimed the bartender lowering his rifle and looking into the distance. 'Yeah, them boys won't be coming back in a hurry.'

They passed a botanical garden, beautiful in the moist twilight. Someone had taken such pains over this little rectangle of dirt, sowing it with flowers or perhaps cucumbers which they presented to friends at organic dinner parties, asking them if they could taste the difference which you could. The Germans had returned from their romantic dream of domination through violence to cultivate their own garden, like a nation of Diocletians, the Roman *Kaiser* who gave up his empire to grow cabbage.

'It is time to ascend,' said Stuart, and they walked up a set of stone stairs. According to the address written on a piece of paper, the venue was located right next to the river, but they couldn't instantly find it, and Dougie's smart phone had no signal.

'O'Reilly's Irish bar, right?' said Dougie.

'Pub,' said Stuart.

'I'm having a Guinness tonight,' said Dougie.

They had already walked along the busy commercial street without finding the venue. Now they stood on the corner looking back over a bridge.

'Shall we ask somebody?' said Dougie.

Stuart paused. 'Wait a minute,' he said diffidently, then moved them on back to the riverside, peering down at several empty-looking riverside office blocks. Then he moved back to the side street behind them. 'I think it's here,' he said, matching the street name to his instructions. They walked on down the road, doubt growing a little as they went further and further before there, on the corner, next to a moist expanse of grass, down by the riverside in the falling twilight, was O'Reilly's Irish Pub.

'You fucking beauty!'

They had made it to their final destination as the clock struck seven and with the show at eight.

In the bar they asked the attractive barmaid where they could find Luigi and Luigi emerged.

'Guys! You - are really – fucking late!' Luigi was anxious, short and bearded, but smiling. He was also wearing a large comedy Guinness hat, which for some reason did not detract from his evident distress, making him only seem more desperately and legitimately confused.

'Nice hat,' said Dougie.

'Oh yeah,' said Luigi. 'From St. Paddie's day last year. It was fucking *wild.* I'm telling you it all got very messy – very messy - I'm talking tequila shots at 4 AM. Oh my God I was fuckin' steaming. Anyway, can I get you guys a drink?'

'Mine's a Guinness, man,' said Dougie.

'No problem. You're Dougie right? And Stuart,' said

Luigi, who had immediately relaxed. What was in it for him to remain annoyed? He had his comedians now, who brought no great technical demands, aside from amplification, and all he had to do now was lubricate the audience and take as much of their money as he could.

Meanwhile, Stuart ordered a mineral water and sipped at the top of it. He still pretended it was Scotch. Luigi handed the finished Guinness to Dougie – like a true adoptee of Irish culture, he had taken his time pouring it, pushing back the pump to give it its nitrogen head.

'You guys have a good journey down? I'm glad. We're happy to have you here. And tell the girls if you want anything to eat, right – there are menus in the bar and we've got a good cook, Jean-Marc. He's French so he must be a good cook. How are your friends? Dwight and Malcolm, right? Those guys were great. Particularly the big feller. Come on, let's go see the room.'

He took them to the large back room; a broad, almost cavernous space, focused on a large elevated stage, overhung by a large banner saying 'Comedy in Heidelberg' and, to the side of it 'Live Six Nations Rugby.' The whole place smelt of beer. Stuart moved to the back to look at that stage, which Dougie was already standing on.

'Yeah, so this is the room. What do you think?'

'Very nice.'

'It really is.'

'We have everything here; music, sports, you name it. Comedy,' Luigi continued, and then, 'I don't know why

I'm still wearing this.' He took off his hat. 'Nice though isn't it?'

'Fantastic.'

'Wunderbar.'

'Wunderbar, right.' Luigi indicated a tall bald man in the corner. 'That's Terry, he's the technician.'

'Alright Terry.'

'Alright guys,' said Terry.

'Alright,' said Stuart.

'How many d'you think we'll have tonight?' asked Dougie.

'Don't know mate to be honest,' said Luigi. 'Last time we must have had a hundred. Last time was brilliant. Made so much money at the bar. Oh - do you want to test the microphone?' he asked.

'Aye, I will man,' said Dougie, beginning to talk into the mike, which switched on as he did. Mike testing was, for what it's worth, always excruciatingly embarrassing; doing a joke would never get a laugh – there were usually just a few people listening anyway, and those cleaners or technicians unsure whether to laugh even if the joke was funny – but it was somehow impossible to play it completely straight. Dougie for his part elected to sing the intro to 'Maggie May'.

It was already clear, as Stuart looked at him, just how famous Dougie would become. He would be on chat-shows, television programmes, at film premieres, and when the pretty young reporter asked him a question he would always know instinctively and exactly where to pitch his answers between bemusement and charm; the simultaneous 'What am I doing here?' and 'Who else could be?' of the famous working-class man. It was all there, the work, the little Glasgow fighter who had pulled himself up by his being funny to a life of wealth and fame; the girls, the drugs, the love.

Dougie had finished singing and walked down off the stage. 'What's it sound like?'

'It sounds great,' Stuart replied. 'The whole set-up is perfect.'

'What about an introduction?' said Terry, briefly exiting his little booth. Luigi was rooting around behind him.

'What?' asked Dougie, snapping along the space front stage. He was prowling, getting into his groove.

'You can announce us if you like,' said Stuart, also feeling it.

'Can I?' said Terry, close to them now, bald, lonely, looking in the mood for a longer conversation, but absolutely without the resources to make it happen. ''Cos last time they didn't want us to – you know, the skinny guy and the fat lad, what's his name, William – Malcolm, right, that's it – last time they didn't want an introduction. And I thought that was really weird, you know; they just like, got up on stage and started.'

'Aye man, you're very welcome to introduce us,' said Dougie.

'I think it's better.'

'No man, you go right ahead.'

''Cos it's more of a show, you know?'

'I think we're done, right?' Stuart said.

Luigi had finished rooting around although still, for some reason, wore the hat. 'I think so. Is there anything more I can do for you? Want another?' he asked Dougie.

'Is there somewhere to change?' asked Stuart.

'I show you,' said Luigi. Coming out, the door had already been set up, a table bearing a money box and simple piece of card saying 'English Comedy 5 €.' They would not be retiring on their earnings just yet.

They moved into the kitchen, passing Sandra as they went. Luigi stopped, smiling 'Hey Sandra.'

'Hey Luigi.'

Luigi looked back to the comedians who were reading the menus. 'What do you guys want to eat?'

'Can you get me the Irish Stew please Sandra, and another Guinness?' Dougie smiled.

'Shepherd's Pie,' said Stuart.

'Sure that's no problem fellers,' said Sandra, in a West German accent which had been weirdly spliced with an Irish one, the words starting metronomically than veering up into a lilt. 'The Shepherd's pie is fuckin' beautiful.'

'Come on.' Luigi took them downstairs, further and further down the heavy stone steps. They moved past a fridge where cheap meat loitered before being cooked above. There was a loud electric hum. Then further down, down another level filled with carpets and crates before reaching the bottom, a tiny corner with toilets, a spare room and a large silver-lidded oil drum.

'You can change down here, alright?'

'Sure,' said Stuart. 'Thanks Luigi.'

'And just ask if you need anything, right?'

'Thanks Luigi.'

'Aye thanks man.'

'I'm looking forward to the show,' said Luigi, and disappeared up the stairs, his steps rapid, a young man busy in his job.

'You gonna change, right?'

'Of course I am,' said Stuart who had in fact already begun unbuttoning his shirt.

'I'll see you up there then. I'm going to go through my notes,' said Dougie. He vanished up the stairs.

Stuart moved into the cubicle, already slipping off his trousers, walls banging his elbows as he struggled to undress. But he was to look good tonight, black shoes, clean socks, suit top and tie, and would not get annoyed when the trousers got mixed in with the socks or he could not find where he had put the shoe covers. He had played in worse places; he would play shittier gigs. Punch by punch you became a stronger comedian and besides, in all his time in England, no one had ever offered him a Shepherd's Pie.

XII.

As luck would have it, years later Stuart would become a very well-known comedian and years later you could even say a star one, with his German developing to the point where he could host his own Saturday night *Talkshow*, *'Die Big Show mit Stuart Holmes.'* He would meet the painfully limited pool, endlessly repeating, of German celebrities, interviewing book critics and preachers who would never have got such a look-in in the UK, displaced there by visiting Hollywood stars of the kind Dougie would bed but not keep, and finally have enough money after taxes to afford the drugs he had so little interest in now. One time he would even interview Dougie as a guest, primetime, and the two of them would just sit there a moment at the beginning of the interview, laughing endlessly inside at the bizarreness of it all, at the sheer distance they had travelled, and some of it together.

So Dougie McCallum, how are you?

I'm very well how are you yourself Stuart Holmes?

I should just explain for the benefit of the studio audience – *switching back to German here* – that Dougie and I are old friends.

Yeah, we used to be lovers.

Laughter from the audience.

But it ended very badly.

There were tears! You left me –

Aye I did.

For the Queen. How is she?

She's deid.

Anyway, I'm glad you're so successful now that you can come back to honour us with your presence- Tell us about *Mr. Schottisch III: Schottendicht!*

To be honest I haven't actually watched it yet. But I imagine it's very very similar to the other *Mr. Schottish* movies – which by the way, have a combined total of 5.7 million unique cinema visits in Germany alone – *applause from the audience, though not whoops, the Germans being not as automatically deferent to financial success as other nations* – But in this one I play Doogie, yeah, I know, a real stretch. I run a heritage printing shop in Glasgow. But we actually shot this one on the Friesian islands, near Holland, just to give it extra resonance for all our German fans.

So in a way Germany just keeps dragging you back.

You could put it like that. But Germany's great man, it's nae bother.

We're glad to have you; we only have three celebrities over here; Boris Becker, Heidi Klum, and the other one. Now let's watch a clip from the movie.

A clip was played. Dougie, or rather his character, Doogie Macanchees, was stood in a print shop, wearing a kilt, when he, shutting the press, managing to accidentally trap his kilt in its spokes. He was struggling to free himself, electric parps and drumbeats sounding, when a beautiful tall dark German entered saying, 'Entschuldigung,' excuse me, 'I want to print these flyers.' Dougie turned to her and the kilt tore, at which point he scampered to cover himself, but stumbled, accidentally falling into a huge stack of paper, where he lay prone, his pale white arse exposed to the camera, finally saying: 'What size do you want them doing?'

The audience laughter was jolly and polite.

That's comedy. And that's Silke Engel in the clip with you right?

Right.

And how was it working with her?

It was fantastic, she's very professional.

Because we heard a little rumour...

Dougie's grin was still as toothy and effective as ever.

Aye?

He's not changed a bit ladies and gentlemen – Dougie McCallum! We'll be back after the break.

Well.

You alright man?

I'm great.

That went well. Oh, we're back already.

After the break they were to be joined by Germany's horseshoe tossing champion, who demonstrated his craft to electrified German ballads and jaunty audience clapping. For some reason Dougie was presented with some bagpipes and had to try and blow into them which, to massive audience hilarity, produced only a tiny farting sound. But in a moment the show was over and Dougie and Stuart were standing alone in the huge emptied auditorium together.

It's good to see you again, Dougie.

Aye man, it is something of a pleasure. How longs it been?

Years. Five years? At that party in London right. God, that was awful – that hostess was so *eindringlich*, you know? I can't even remember what *eindringlich* is in English. Are things alright with you?

Aye not bad you know. Just finished an Australian tour – it was a bit mad. Lots of drugs, to be honest.

But you're well.

I'm well.

How's England?

I'm always on the road to be honest with you. But man – this show's amazing. You've done well for yourself. This is a big deal!

Yeah, I suppose it is. We've been doing it three years now.

Three years! And all in German. Respect.

Yeah well, I made my bed. We're trying to do a modern take on the traditional German Saturday-night revue format. We're aiming to target both a young urban and more rural demographic, trying to have a social cohesion element too. Jesus, will you listen to me.

So you think it was the right choice then, stopping here.

Well… But it seems it was definitely the right choice for

you to go.

I guess. I mean, the UK though man – I mean, with Scotland being separate now they're really making it suffer and London, it's like a Victorian theme park. I just keep thinking – what I mean is – I've made it, right, that's good, but somewhere so nasty, you know? So what does it mean that I've succeeded in a society which is cruel. Does that mean I'm a wee cunt, right, because lots of other wee cunts think I'm the shit?

I think, *said Stuart after a moment,* that's what's we know as a luxury problem. Now look what I've got for us. *He indicated the table where two glasses and a champagne bottle stood.* Let's have a drink. What shall we drink to?

Dougie thought about it.

To Germany. For all it has given us.

Yes, to Germany. For all it has given us.

The two men drank.

Or, Stuart imagined, something like that. Right now though, at this exact moment, he was stuck in a basement in Heidelberg, next to an oil drum, barelegged and forcing his trousers into a tote bag.

He looked at himself in the cubicle mirror; floppy collar, black jacket, dandruff-spotted shoulders. He looked like a comedian, or at least a man who could do a passable impersonation of one. Looking in the mirror he found himself humming, mugging, sounding little vocal loops and practicing the comedy voices he would be doing in the set tonight. 'That'll do pig,' he said to himself.

Coming back into the bar Stuart found Dougie sitting

there, faced by a large steaming bowl of Irish stew and a pint of Guinness down to the last third.

'Few people coming in already.'

'Yeah?'

'Yeah.' Dougie sipped and said, a broad grin on his face, 'I think tonight's gonna be amazing.'

'I hope so. How's your Irish stew?'

'It's delicious man. Mmmm. Did you get yours?'

Sandra looked over from the bar. 'I'm so sorry there friend – we're out of the Shepherd's Pie.'

'No problem.'

'Can I get you anything else?'

'A portion of the Irish stew,' said Stuart.

'You won't regret it,' said Dougie. 'Mmm yumm yumm yumm yumm.'

Stuart paced back to Dougie, standing over him. 'I'll go second tonight, right?'

'Aye mate, no problem at all.'

Half an hour before the show and both men became consumed by their rituals. For Dougie, that meant solitary communion with a pint, for Stuart an antsy stroll around the venue. It was like he had to swing his body into some kind of comic groove, warm up like an athlete but because he was a comedian the warm-up had to be funny too, daft little squats and arse shakes. Tonight Stuart's prowl took him outside the pub; it was another rule with him that he always had to sample fresh air for a while before a show although, unlike in

Berlin, the pub itself was smoke free.

He found the exit quite near to the river and in fact walked down to the bank side. Night had fallen, and across the water the lights of the other bank could be seen. The river lay between them rippling and black; there was a gentle sound of lapping and rustling in the air. He took a moment looking over the lights of the newer town and imagining the philosopher's way, a famous walking route, above.

He remembered Twain's words on Heidelberg again; 'the last possibility of the beautiful.' And how amazing it was to be here in a Europe at peace, with an apartment in Berlin and fifteen good jokes. Amazing that fifteen good jokes could feed you. Thinking of this, of the struggles behind and ahead, he realized that these would likely be the best days of his life. The thought filled him with sadness. Perhaps, his mind went on, that was why so many people avoiding being happy – in fear that, having found happiness, they would lose it, like a football team coming so close to the title but watching it slip away. Better for some to be solidly mid-table amongst the contented underachievers. But not for him – for him, it was top of the league or nothing! He felt the jokes move within him, descending like weights in water, breathed in the deep peace.

Back inside Dougie was leaning against the pub's snugs with a slightly worsened air. 'It's filling up in there man.'

'Excuse me,' said a man next to them, black and sitting next to a blonde woman, 'What is happening in there tonight?' He spoke English with a strong German accent.

'It's a comedy show, man.'

'And is it funny?'

'That's the general idea,' Stuart responded.

Dougie spoke, enthused. 'It's brilliant man, brilliant. We come from Berlin, right, and there's a great English comedy scene there. This guy's great,' he said, with a slant of his head towards Stuart.

'And you are making jokes about the Germans?'

'Yeah,' said Stuart, although by now Dougie had established himself as the man's chief interlocutor.

'And what do you say about them?'

'That you're very – competent,' said Stuart.

'What does competent mean?'

'*Kompetent*,' said Stuart.

'And how much does it cost?'

'Five euros,' said Dougie.

'Bwaah!' The man turned back to the silent blonde next to him with a sceptical air. 'I mean, if it had been four euros, I can imagine it – but five euros for just people talking? Bwoah.'

'Shall we go in?' Stuart interjected.

'Aye,' said Dougie, and rose. As he did though he checked, turning to stay to the man, 'Listen pal I've got a comp ticket if you want it.'

The man looked up. 'Thank you.' And that was his entire refusal.

Dougie, opening a hand, said, 'Suit yourself. Come on, friend, let's go in.'

They did, passing Terry, who had now set up at the entrance – at this level of the circuit technicians were doormen and doormen technicians – and was stamping people as they entered, himself now wearing the large Guinness hat. 'Like the hat?' said Terry. 'You've got a few in there now.'

And when they entered it was true; there really was a substantial crowd gathered, huddled around tables, eating and drinking, loudly chattering and clearly ready to be entertained. They had come to be made to laugh! And at some point in a comedian's career you realized that they actually *wanted* to. A comedian's own obsessive rehearsals and OCD rituals were a long way from their minds; they wanted the people they saw to be funny, or at least so outrageously bad that watching them was an event.

That was the same in Heidelberg as anywhere else on the comic map. At moments like this Stuart felt vindicated in the obscure path he had followed; no one else would be having these experiences, in these places. One day he would have to write them down.

Stuart set up the camera behind a table with an older couple from Chicago, wearing baseball caps and, for the man, a Blackhawks jersey. 'This won't disturb you, will it?' he asked.

'Not at all,' said the man. 'You one of da comedians?'

'I am.'

'Oh sure,' said the man. 'You sorta look like a funny guy.'

Dougie wandered back to where Stuart was setting the camera. 'I tell you man, tonight's going to be brilliant. I can just feel it.'

'I hope so,' he replied. Dougie would go first; Stuart wanted, intensely, to be better than him.

XIII.

Hamburg. Dougie was gone; Stuart was still in Germany. And Claudia was behind the wheel as they traversed the night-time city. The North German city had a reputation for a wild nightlife but, as in most countries north of the Rhine, it was presumably all happening indoors. Around them were large, almost American-wide highways under a streetlight glow less intense than in England. Occasionally a middle-aged cyclist whirred along the bike paths or a few cold revellers crowded around a late-opening kiosk; otherwise the streets were depopulated.

'Quiet,' said Stuart.

'Not where we are going,' said Claudia. 'Actually it will be.'

Soon they pulled up outside a glass cubicle at the entrance to the car park. Claudia said 'Wait' and exited; upon her knock the door to the office opened and a man appeared. The man wore a long black jumper and greeted Claudia with evident pleasure, before returning to the office; after a moment he returned with an envelope which he handed to her with a smile.

She closed the car door behind her, clicking on her seatbelt. 'OK.'

'Who was that?'

'Alex.'

'What did he give you?'

'The keys.'

'Keys to what?'

'Where we are going.' She started the car again. 'It's about ten minutes drive.'

Stuart looked at out the window again as they sped along in the direction of the docks. 'So, d'you live in the city?'

'Yes, not far.' Claudia spoke, 'So you don't write anymore, huh?'

'There's no money on it. Comedy pays. Tonight I got 600€ plus all my costs for fifteen minutes. Sure, I did twenty but – You can earn good money doing comedy.'

'And that's it – only the money?'

'I still write,' he said. 'Sometimes. I put it away in a drawer and I don't bother anyone with it. Thing is, I realized a few years ago, I'm a foreigner, and foreigners are intrinsically funny. It's a way of making them harmless, to laugh at them, their accent. Your living circumstances dictate the form you choose. And mine are funny.'

'Mmm.' Claudia had the air of someone used to dealing with artists as logistical problems. 'I think it's a shame. I think it's better to be a writer. Comedy is always the same thing, you know; you say something and then the people laugh.'

He couldn't argue with her definition. Contemplating her words a memory dislodged within him, of back at

University when Nellie had painted him a picture of their lives together.

'I'll be out working, you'll be at home writing. And every day I'll come home and you'll read me what you've written. You'll write the most beautiful things, plays, poems, stories, novels. And I'll earn the money for us both. Later, we'll have children – you're going to be a wonderful Daddy – and you'll read them your stories. And in the summer we'll drive round Europe in an old camper van.'

Back in the car he went for it. He reached to touch Claudia's leg.

Her response was clear. 'No – I don't want that.'

He removed his hand. 'I'm very sorry.'

Claudia smiled. 'It's alright. I have a boyfriend. You met him tonight – Udo.'

'Udo?' he said. 'You're with Udo?'

'Yes, him. We've been together four years. But anyway it's not that – I don't find you attractive.' He nodded understandingly; in fairness, he had heard it before. 'But listen, forget about all that.' She turned to him. 'I want to do something for you much better than that. We're here.'

They had arrived at their destination, pulling into an empty industrial car park in what seemed to be dockland. There was a large rusty, almost hangar-like, structure ahead, with a small black door set onto its black side. Claudia brought the car to a stop and sat looking at the structure for a moment with an almost paternal air. He was still brooding as she spoke. 'Come on. Let me show you inside.'

In Heidelberg, Dougie had started. Stuart sat at the back of the room, monitoring the image through the small portable camera he bought with him to all his gigs. It was often a Sisyphean task, as the only gigs worth watching afterwards were the good ones, which you enjoyed but could never exactly repeat. Bad ones were for their part swiftly deleted.

But this was a good one. Dougie was being funny, slipping in and out of jokes and, for the first five minutes, doing very little but banter the crowd into a frenzy. 'Is it true right,' he said, his beer in his hand, another contrast to Stuart who performed as soberly as a Victorian judge, 'that you guys have a late-night delivery service just for condoms?' There was complete silence from the audience, which response they then themselves laughed at. 'I'm talking to you pal.' The tanned German, a little man in a red and black jumper with a huge chin – Germans always seemed about to burst out of smart clothing, looking like horses in suits - said, 'What? You mean me?' 'Nae, the invisible feller just next to you. Of course you. Anyway,' Dougie said after a tiny pause and to big laughter, 'I don't think you'd know much about the emergency condom service anyway.'

Dougie was doing it. He was talking to some French girls, asking 'Where you lassies from, eh?'

The girls tried to speak and ended up just giggling, at which the audience again laughed.

Dougie paused, 'Right. You're not exactly a tough crowd, aye,' he said. 'If you think your own names are so funny wait till you hear some of mae jokes.' The girls were still laughing volubly; Dougie looked back up to the rest of the audience. 'Reckon I'll be needing that condom service myself,' he said.

From here Dougie strode into his material, doing the set he had performed in Kettwig only still sharper, still better, strengthened by the further confidence last night had imbued. 'How do you say that in French?', he'd ask the girls from time to time, or switch back to gain the man's assent, whose reluctance to respond only made it funnier. 'Have you ever seen a Scottish person get drunk?' On this he became a whirl of straggly hair as he paced the stage, squeezing every comic drop out of the air and audience.

Stuart found himself thinking about Fraser, a former friend who he had known back in London, in that little burn-out interval between abandoning England and embracing Germany. He had seen Fraser performing comedy one night and held it as one of the great performances he had been able to witness in any medium; a shock-haired, mutating crow who regaled the audience with bizarre, melancholic aphorisms and impersonations of fictional Ugandan hip-hop artists.

One of his best bits involved asking the audience if they liked James Brown, to which a few of the cool kids would usually respond in the affirmative.

'You see my theory about James Brown,' Fraser would say, centre stage, 'is that he's an engineer. He's always shouting out things you only say on a construction site like 'Work it!' and 'Hot dam!'" Fraser snapped into the persona of a fatigued construction worker. 'What shall I do with this pivot, James?' 'Take it to the bridge!'

Then Fraser would give a wild scream as if the Godfather of Soul were taking him over, upon which a fabulous whirl of strings would come crackling over the venue's PA – this was in the time before smart phones – and Fraser would begin to sing.

'This is a man's world

This is a man's world

Man made the tampax

To absorb the menstrual flow

Man made the Gender Studies institute

To discuss patriarchy

Man made the forceps

To pluck the emerging babe

Man made my little pony

To amuse the older child

This is a man's world

But it wouldn't be nothing, nothing, nothing

Without a woman or a girl

Man made a brightly-designed pinny...'

And so on, and so on, across a raft of such masculine inventions as lipstick, rom-coms, dark chocolate and 'a selection of herbal teas.' The impression was reliably dead on, the yelps hilarious, the performance deadpan, and it usually finished to bemused applause. Many of them presumably didn't know who James Brown was.

Perhaps you had to be there, and even Fraser himself wasn't there that long. He had revealed one night after a gig over a drink – Fraser being one of the few comedians who treated Stuart civilly in his recovering, failure-stained state – that he was doing a law-conversion course and planned to take the bar the next year.

'And what about the comedy?'

'It's just a hobby.'

'But you're so good!'

'Thanks,' said Fraser with a smile. 'But other people will do it even if I don't. Oh look – is that Frank Sanazi? I love that guy!'

He had never heard of Fraser again. And perhaps the lesson here was that the funniest people weren't always those who carried on. Those who did were the ones who could take it; take the grotty, itinerant life of dive bars and endless travel and having your mind on pause all afternoon to prepare a twenty-minute working day. Of gigs in tiny backrooms before audiences entirely composed of comedians. Of producers who, if you didn't want to play to empty venues, locked you up backstage until you agreed. No wonder smart people like Fraser went away from it. Why struggle on when even the greatest reward possible was to be a paid clown? For all he knew Fraser was a top lawyer by now, in a jumper at home with a child bringing him drawings from school, placing down his gleaming smart phone to look down at his offspring's work. But perhaps Fraser also lived with a sense that he was neglecting the truest part of himself.

Dougie had now arrived at one of his longest and most showstopping routines, a frantic parody of supermarket cashiers and their inability to deal with individual items of fruit.

'Have you ever seen someone look at you with such disdain? when you hand them an apple? And they're like –' a quintessentially annoyed face – 'And, 'Tomatoes. Right. I'll just have to look in my weird little book. You know the weird little book, with all picture of vegetables and codes.' Dougie mimed through the cashier flipping through their weird little book, growing increasingly infuriated. 'Well I'm in the supermarket the other day and I'm standing at the checkout. And I'm a single guy who lives alone, right, so I've got like five tins of *Eintopf* chilli con carne.' Producing a cute little chilli tin. 'And the woman on the checkout is German, right, and I'm not kidding – she looks at me with mae five *Eintopf* chilli con carne and she says I'm not kidding, the most German thing I have ever heard. "Why didn't you just buy one big tin?"' Now riding the laughter onto the closer.

'Alright guys, I just want to say, I've loved talking to you today, you've been amazing. Just want to share something with you before you leave. It's a bit embarrassing actually, but have you, like ever had your girlfriend put your finger up your bum? I'm talking you're shagging and she just slips it up there. Ooh I say. Well my lassie did it to me right and then she's pulls her finger out and she's what's she like – Eeew! And I'm like, what are you expecting man, that it comes out with sweeties and chocolate sprinkles on it? Aye. And what do expect man, I had to eat five tins of chilli con carne!'

The call back, then rolls of laughter, which Dougie held. 'Thank you very much. We'll have a wee break and then you'll be back with your headline act, Stuart Holmes.'

A nice touch there, the word headline. Beneath his cursing, his ribaldry and his excess, Dougie was an old-fashioned gent.

Dougie came off the stage grinning; he would be high without drugs for hours. 'Man, they're fantastic. You're going to have so much fun up there.'

'I hope I am.' Stuart nodded. He had no excuses; it was a good crowd. He turned off the small camera in front of him and began to slide his mind into gear.

Years later, Stuart stood inside a derelict building with Claudia, barely able to see in the general dark. She was rummaging around behind him, going to find a power switch or a flashlight or a power switch. 'Just wait,' she had said, multiple times. Just wait.

'I'm waiting.'

'Good.'

He did, trying to see what he could. After a while his eyes began to acclimatize to the large, rectangular room, the floor empty as far as he could see, though they were dim shapes stacked against the wall. Old pianos? Broken baskets? Or mannequins which came, at this time of night, to life? He looked at his one source of light, his smart phone; it was 3:15 AM.

'Are you ready?'

'I'm ready.'

There was a clunk; a big satisfying sound of a generator whining and levelling into life. When the lights came it revealed a theatre; a small dilapidated theatre, with only a few broken seats and only a small, tattered stage – but a theatre nonetheless. There was a high bar sill beside him, and more and more junk the longer he looked – an unplugged lamp, a pile of clothing – but still.

'What a beautiful place,' he said.

'Yes, exactly.' Claudia spoke German now. 'I had to throw away some of the chairs but still, those which are here are original. They're still good chairs, I think.'

'What was this place?'

'It was a strip club and peep show. I think they had live sex shows on the stage. It was very popular in the 70s.'

'The 70s?'

'Yes, and then the 80s. But then with the rise of the Internet it closed. People watch more pornography online these days.'

'I did hear that. And what's your connection to it?'

Claudia laughed. 'It belongs to me.'

'Really?'

'My father was good friends with an industrial speculant who he bought it from at an extremely reduced rate. He planned to develop it into a showroom for SUVs, which were quite popular here in the 90s. Now not so much. But my father died last year and it was left to me. He always trusted me the most in the family; he thought I had the business head.'

'Wow.' He had found himself a seat and sat there savouring the audience's view. 'I love how intimate it is; these kinds of spaces are always the best.'

'You like it?'

'Sure.' He looked again. 'Actually I love it.'

'So. It's yours.'

'What?'

Claudia stood watching his reaction. 'It's yours.'

'Excuse me?'

'I'm giving it you.'

He paused. 'Look, I really don't need this. I know I'm a comedian but... I really don't get this.'

'It's yours.'

'For how much?'

'Nothing. It's a gift.'

'Come on. This place is worth money.'

'I have money.'

'Well.'

He wanted to speak but she was silent in a way that suggested, as far she was concerned, everything was accounted for. 'Well. Well.' He couldn't believe it; not any part of it, and would not for a long time. But perhaps questioning would help.

'So what do I do with it then?'

'What do you want to do?'

'Ah. Well, I could do a thousand things with it. It'd be amazing! It's always been my dream to own a theatre. To have my own company of actors and write plays for them. To write.'

'Well, do that then. Do what you want.' She smiled. 'I thought you might open an English-comedy club.'

'I could do that. I could do anything.' He spoke again; 'Listen – are you serious about it not costing any money?'

She looked over the space herself. 'You'll have to find out a way to pay the heating costs. And clearly there's renovation to be done. But perhaps you could apply for grants. You could even make it a community project.'

'Why don't you want it?'

'Me? It's not really my thing - I'm more into events management. I might borrow it off you for an odd evening here and there. So, you accept?'

'You're really being serious.'

'Why wouldn't I be?'

'Then of course I accept!'

'Next we'll draw up a contract. To give it to you as an unconditional gift.' *Ein bedingungsloses Geschenk.* 'Yes,' she went on, 'Otto understands these things; he'll go through the legal technicalities and then I'll send you an agreement for it in the post.'

He paused, knowing the feebleness of his next question. 'Does this mean I have to move to Hamburg?'

'If you want. It might be a good idea. Or you could come down a few nights a week. But I keep telling you – it's your choice. Consider it a gift from Germany.'

'A gift from Germany?' He looked over the tattered seats, the stray lamps, the shoe-worn stage. 'It's beautiful.'

In habitually useful fashion she had found a broom and was sweeping a few shards of broken glass into a corner. He stepped towards her. 'Claudia; this isn't a joke, is it?'

'You said we Germans had no sense of humour.' She smiled, continuing, 'Listen, it's no use to me. Have fun with it; you look like you need it. The whole time I've been looking at you I've been thinking, that man needs a new project. He needs to find his enthusiasm again. Now however,' she said, propping up the broom, 'We should go. I have another event in the morning.'

'Of course.' He stood, happy, marvelling.

'Take one last look at your theatre.' She opened the door to the night, on the little outside light visible.

He did, stood for a moment just looking at his imminent realm.

It was enough, it really was. He walked over to her; as he neared the exit, she threw down the light switch with a solid clunk.

They walked back across the car park he would come to know so well. There was just the cold night, still intensely dark, the sound of their steps and the hum of the odd streetlight. He looked over at the silent, skinny German, and found himself giddily thinking: a bit of sex would really make this an evening now. But, he laughed at himself, even without it was all too wonderful; there was no part of him unelated.

'Claudia.'

She looked over, key in the car lock. 'Yes?'

'*Danke unglaublich sehr.*'

'You're welcome,' she smiled back.

XIV.

'Don't you sometimes get the feeling,' said Stuart, years before on the stage in Heidelberg, 'that if Barack Obama had been German it wouldn't have been "Yes We Can" but "*Nein das geht nicht*"? No you can't. 'Everyone would have been chanting it – No you can't! No you can't! Of course in this version Obama would not have been black.'

Stuart was closing in on the kill.

'And this very lack of optimism,' he said, treading across the stage, limbering, into the really good stuff now, 'is actually built into the German language itself. Like for example, when you're really happy in English, you say "I'm on Cloud Nine." But in German you say, "I'm on Cloud Seven." Does this mean that even in their happiest moments the Germans are two clouds less happy than English-speaking people?'

And after developing that bit, which meant moving into a depiction of an exemplary German, Hannes, in his German heaven, with an allotment, board games, juice and an *Autobahn* heading directly to Mallorca, he noting, somewhat wistfully, the celebratory Anglophones on Cloud Nine who were dancing to 'Video Killed the Radio Star', which was an excuse to sing it, following which they – the Anglophones – called down to Cloud Eight "Hey Hannes man! Come and join us here on Cloud Nine" and Hannes replying "No thank you. Everything on Cloud Seven is perfectly satisfactory" then moving on to speculation as to the occupants of the other clouds, the French on Cloud Eight living it up, their motor scooters floating off the cloud and down to Cloud Zero where the Greeks were and below them the Cypriots who'd had to sell the cloud, and were just falling – after all these and other jokes, Stuart had them where he wanted them.

'Isn't it funny that, since the Second World War, the Germans have been like', change voice, German accent, '"We Germans. We have done so many things wrong and there is no way we can ever put them right." And now Greece is like,' pause, turn of the head, "Well, *actually*..."'

They laughed, and laughed, and laughed.

They got it.

And after the joke about Germans inventing steel, and German bread being the best, and the obdurate refusal of Germans to speak German with foreigners, leading to absurd and often protracted linguistic battles known as 'German Offs', where the hapless foreigner tried to overwhelm their Germanophone interlocutors with increasingly baroque learned sentences *auf Deutsch*, only to be congratulated in ever more banal Americanisms, and after the banter with the Canadians and the Americans and the Germans and the one Greek there, it soon became time to close. Just as that night much later in Hamburg he had finished again with the story of the policeman, only this earlier time competition-crazed he did it better, his voice crisper and fresher, and his moments more stoutly baffled as he imitated the pussycat cop: 'Why? We're all really nice!'

The joke landed well and he left to huge applause. He walked off the stage in a way calculated to be normal but in fact concealing great delight. Grittily, with faked elan and internally reasserted will, he had fought Dougie to a draw, Dougie, the future comic megastar. It had taken his best jokes in his best order but that night there had been nothing to choose between them. Stuart didn't begrudge Dougie an iota of his inevitable success; he wished him every woman and line of coke and massive appearance fee in the world but he would not, just would not, be worse than him – and most of all not in Germany, his home turf.

'Man!' Dougie bounced towards him with a massive grin on his face. 'Don't forget to ask about the accommodation!'

'Accommodation?' said Stuart. 'Jesus you're right! I completely forgot. Do you want to do it?'

'Let's do it together,' Dougie said.

'Sounds good.' They ambled back onto stage, Stuart saying, 'You do the talking, alright?'

So Dougie moved and took up the microphone again. 'Alright ladies, and gentlemen,' – they laughed, that was all it took by now – 'I hope you enjoyed the show tonight. Did ye?' They gave an unruly but affirmative bellow, some of them already buttoning up their coats. 'Thing is, right, we're actually looking for somewhere to sleep tonight so if anyone has anywhere to offer us, please let us know. We're both really, really nice.'

Callback! As Dougie relayed this message, perfectly

charmingly, every phrase moist in his Glaswegian knicker-dropping brogue, Stuart clowned around in the background, making little weird stumbling movements and gurning. It took all sorts.

'Alright, that really is it now.' Message done, they walked from the stage to a final spasm of applause, the audience's thoughts now squarely on drinking and getting home. Monday now loomed. They headed to the bar; Dougie got himself another Guinness and Stuart ordered a large Pils. Raising their glasses, the two friends looked to each other.

'Cheers.'

'Cheers.'

They looked into each other's eyes; their drinks clinked; it was the German way.

'Man, that was fantastic. They loved it man, they really loved it. Ayayaya!'

'Both of you were great,' said Luigi behind them. 'I'm sure next time we'll have even more people. But I think they liked it a lot. Really like your jokes man,' he said to Dougie.

'Aw, thanks man. Really – thanks so much for having us.'

'It's no problem.' Luigi had finished setting a tray of drinks for one of the tables, which he now went to take over. 'Just give me a minute to sort out this out, then I'll be back to you with the money.'

'Really man, nae bother, we're in no rush.' Luigi disappeared into the other room with Terry who as he exited flashed them both two thumbs up, leading the two comedians to briefly smile at each other.

'Hi.' A woman approached – Stuart had joked with her during the set, when she had told him she was from Canada. 'Great work guys.'

'Thanks,' said Stuart. Dougie smiled; and then both smiled in anticipation at the beautiful girl before them.

'I'm the girl you picked on in the first half. Remember?'

'Of course I remember.' He was trying to slide into his game, always easier after a gig.

'Sharon,' she said. 'So you've had luck with Canadians then?'

'The odd success. Do you live in Heidelberg?'

'I do. Actually I play the cello in the orchestra here.'

'That's amazing! ... Do you enjoy it?'

'Yeah, I guess do.'

'You sound unsure.'

'To be honest, Heidelberg's a bit of a drag.'

'It's pretty though, aye?'

'It sure is that.' She kept looking at Stuart. Her eyes were intense and dark. 'Listen – I'd love to invite you guys over to my apartment but I'm afraid it's just too small. But I wish you luck, honestly, in finding somewhere to stay.'

'Oh that's most kind. And thank you for coming.'

'No – it was my pleasure. I really laughed. I actually had a really shitty day with German bureaucracy, so I'm actually really glad I came.'

'Thanks.'

'No, thanks to you. Good luck. You're funny.'

Sharon left; the men stood very quietly again. 'What a beautiful woman,' said Stuart after a while.

'Aye, and right into you man.'

'You reckon?' Stuart smiled.

'Oh aye. All day long.'

Stuart smirked. 'Maybe. Who knows?'

At this point, another girl crossed the room towards them. She had also been in the audience tonight and in fact Stuart had spotted her, sitting in the audience with a poker face which belied not a mere lack of amusement but actual incomprehension, and, discovering she was Slovenian, singled her out. 'Is that how they flirt in Slovenia? Sit there in silence all evening then come up to someone and strike them? You! Me! Threesome!' It was crude and he would never have said it away from the stage but it was effective in getting the audience onside; for her part the girl, Lenora, seemed to have made a complete recovery.

She moved to them head slightly lowered. 'You guys were saying you needed somewhere to stay right? Well here's my address. You have to – to ah – to take a tram. To very end of line. I have written it down.' She had; the script was minute, the route described via arrows, numbers and extensive illustration. It would take forty-five minutes. 'I will go home now, but you are welcome to come by tonight.'

'It's Lenora, right?' said Stuart.

'Lenora, yes.' She smiled, showing a brace on her upper teeth.

'Lenora, this is really most kind. Dougie and I are having a drink now. But do you mind if we come later?'

'No, my number is there – just give me a call.'

'Really, we can't thank you enough.'

'Ay Lorena, it's really good of you.'

Lenora gave a shy smile, a slight spasm seeming to move through her thin frame. She grinned, mouth slightly open, 'You're welcome.' And then, as if having sought and failed to find an exit line, she just walked off smiling.

'Looks like we've got ourselves somewhere to stay, buddy!'

'Sure,' said Dougie quietly.

At that point Luigi returned from the background beaming a wide, somewhat ecstatic grin on his face. 'Hey, fellers! One of you want to come with me?'

Dougie and Stuart looked at each other, but Dougie volunteered. 'I'll do it; just a sec.' He took a gulp from his drink and set down the glass. Then he disappeared along with Luigi.

Stuart looked around. Most of the audience had gone. Ahead of him a group of younger people had remained, playing pool and drinking. In a corner Terry was setting up his DJ booth for the few other people; this was the peril of the Sunday night DJ set, with people returning tomorrow to jobs and classes to a country that had it together squarely enough that even a few hours comedy seemed an exotic treat.

Stuart was stirred by an approaching figure; now

sporting a white woollen hat and a red and brown scarf, it was Sharon. 'Listen,' she said, 'I've been thinking. I feel bad – you guys are actually welcome to come and stay at mine.'

'Really?'

'Honestly - it's alright. I live right next to the station, so it's convenient for you guys tomorrow. Do you have a pen?'

'I do.' Stuart always had a pen on him and handed it to her; she wrote down her number in his notebook, tore it out and handed it to him.

'There – that's my number. Give me a ring later.'

'Sure. I think we're going to have a drink first. You know, we've got to celebrate. We spend a lot of time on buses.'

'Oh, do take your time,' said Sharon and then smiled. 'I'll stay up for you.'

Stuart gave a little expectant laugh. 'Ha!'

'Then - *bis bald*,' said Sharon, German for 'until soon.'

'Bis bald,' said Stuart. And then: 'And Sharon.'

'Yes?' she paused.

'Thank you.'

'Oh, it's no problem,' she said and smiled.

Dougie came back with a preternatural grin and an envelope. 'Here's your dough brother.'

'We do alright?'

'Very nicely bro. Very nicely indeed.'

Stuart peeked into the envelope, and then snapped a look back to his perky friend. 'Not bad. We're in profit for the weekend. Fuck, by quite a lot, actually.'

'And,' said Dougie, 'it's been a lot of fun.'

'It has. It has been an epic amount of fun. And – look what I have.' Stuart raised the piece of paper Sharon had torn.

'What's that?'

'Sharon's number.'

'No way man!'

'Yes. And also we're invited to stay with her. She says just to send a text when we're coming down.'

'Alright man,' Dougie laughed and gave a primal shudder. 'Al-fucking-right!'

Stuart hesitated. 'What do we do about Lenora?'

'Who's Lenora?'

'The other girl.'

'Ah right, of course.' Dougie gave the matter some thought and proposed his strategy. 'This is what we do brother. You listen to me. You send Lorena a nice wee text saying thank you so much for the offer but we've found another option. And then cool as you like you write to Carmen – Sharon, right -- and accept, but you keep her waiting a little while I play a game of pool with these nice people. Hello nice people!' He said, indicating the table of young Germans ahead; who were potting and chatting in low tones. A girl moved amongst them, sliding and stroking the cue with the greatest of ease. 'And when that's done we rock on over there cool as you like and enjoy the delightful company of a lovely young lassie.'

'A lovely young lassie,' repeated Stuart. 'She said she lived about fifteen minutes away.'

'Ay but we'll take a taxi right? We've got the money remember.'

'Okay, okay,' said Stuart. 'Just let me get my stuff, alright?'

'Take your time brother. We are in no rush whatsoever. We are the kings of this town.'

Stuart descended the steps to the basement once again, now though filled with the warm pulse of a decent gig. In the old days it had been a giddy vertiginous high which had seen him floated up to the ceiling for days, but in these days it was more a mellow glow, the temporary satisfaction of a job done gone, coupled with the knowledge that another performance, and by necessity a good one, had to follow the next night or the one after. In other words his addiction had gone deeper. The addiction to the jokes and the motorways and the friendships – it was a job, a way of living, an idea of freedom.

In the toilet or changing room Stuart took out his phone; seeing that the handset, cheap and tatty just as he liked it, had received a new text.

'Glad gigs going well!!! I'm fine! Xxx!'

He breathed in; Dougie, his counsellor, had been right; her silence had likely indicated nothing more than a busy weekend. He breathed further, deeply, like an astronaut finally returning to an airlock, the helmet loosening on his spacesuit, the relief of another evaded death. He stood without trousers in the grotty changing room free to once again imagine the possibility of a successful love.

XV.

Much later Claudia drove him back to the hotel. They didn't talk much, conversation impeded by occurrences, and eventually she flicked on the radio. The music was a scratchy little ambient doodle, occasionally threatening an ambling techno accelerando, and then fading to an out-of-tune sitar loop; the rasping announcer came on afterwards, sounding like they were broadcasting from some distant boat, to give the name of the track as 'Ted' by Clark in the Bibio remix.

Music was the pulse of life. And comedy was the pulse of life too. The moment you sung a song, told a joke, wrote a book, you committed to life. True depression was silence, he thought; a comic who was still performing was never really despondent.

'I have to get up really early tomorrow,' Claudia was saying. 'And do you know what the worst thing is? My coffee machine is broke.'

'Hashtag first world problems,' he said reclining. 'Do you live alone?'

'No, in a WG.' She used the German word *Wohngemeinschaft*, a living community, a flatshare. Germans, even if they had the means to live otherwise, often shared flats and kept to cleaning rotas, budgets, house meetings, building up little empires in their clean and spacious apartments. 'It's nice - we're always cooking and holding parties.' This was very German, an attempt to create a functional Utopia in the absence of a need to do it; to improve the world for its own sake. Often said attempted utopias unravelled into arguments about cleaning rotas and the ethics of purchasing a dishwasher but as so often with Germany it was the thought that counted. Meanwhile, he lived alone. That was what he worked for, wasn't it?

'I live on my own. I need somewhere to rehearse for my gigs.'

Her leg was still just close enough for him to touch and perhaps she would reward his persistence. Yet, delicious as that leg looked, he wouldn't try to touch her. He wanted to do nothing that would undermine the unfathomable gift she had given him; in other words, he was happy to style her refusal of sexual favours to him into his noble sacrifice of them. Besides, he was sobering up.

The car pulled outside the hotel. 'Look – I want to thank you. How can I thank you?'

'It's really alright. I quite enjoyed your comedy. Take it as thanks.'

'So.' He looked over to her. 'So you'll be in touch?'

'Yes. I'll be down in Berlin in a few weeks and we'll sort out the formalities. I'll be less busy then. Maybe we can go get a beer.'

'I'd like that,' he said. At least in Germany whatever happened the beer would be good. He leant in and kissed her cheek then turned back to where he, unused to the mechanism, fumblingly opened the door. 'Sorry.'

'Thanks!' Now he stood on the street.

She looked up and smiled coolly. 'Bye bye!' she said and drove off.

Entering the lobby, he further considered the possibility that the whole thing was an elaborate joke and that he would never see Claudia again. As he entered the bronze-lined lift a man in a sailor's cap entered behind them and stood next to him in utter silence with his lip quivering. For a moment it seemed that all Hamburg was in on the gag.

'Night shift,' said the man.

'Yeah?'

'Tomorrow I'm going to Delmenhorst,' the man went on.

But after that the man had no follow-up and just stood there intensely until his floor dinged where, with a conclusive nod, he exited.

When he arrived into bed it was approaching 4:30 AM. He sat on the edge of the bed shirtless breathing deeply. Something important had occurred and nothing had changed; it was too soon for the ramifications to be truly felt. As he lay down he thought for the first time of the gig tomorrow, a performance at the launch of a new e-books company, corporate, English and comfortably paid. There would be no need to rehearse – he would do the same jokes again.

The two comedians did indeed take a taxi over to Sharon's, after she had confirmed on the phone in a short and upbeat conversation, she laughing at him not saying particularly much, just that, and what an old chestnut this was, she liked the way he said her name, even though actually, he couldn't remember it at first, and him laughing, then inside taxi moving onto the lamp-lit streets in an initial prideful silence. Dougie had immediately engaged the cab driver in conversation, telling him that they were comedians and had performed the show, which led somehow – things had got a little boozier now – to the cab driver telling them that he had purchased a new coffee machine, and Dougie saying that he had worked with coffee machines all his life, that coffee machines were his passion, his *raison d'être*, his *Leidenschaft*, and the cab driver suddenly launching into a Karlsruhe FC song. Stuart for his part leant back in the cab and watched the lights of the city on the tall solid houses; it was so pretty, the world.

They paid the cab and got out alongside a small lane lined with plain concrete benches.

'She said down a lane, away from the main road.'

'Did she?'

They walked on a bit, went too far, and had to walk back to where a grey block of flats stood. It was built in that supremely functional West German style; smaller, uglier and more human in scale than the gigantic, rotten houses he had found so lovely out East.

'This must be it.' Dougie followed him down to the second door – 'She said second door' – and, with the light of Dougie's smart phone, found the surname; 'King', Stuart said, 'she said King.' He buzzed.

Her voice came out almost immediately, plainer and huskier than the tone she had sounded on the phone. 'Hey!'

'Hi, it's us,' said Stuart.

'Come on up.'

Dougie grinned over at him; he was bending his neck forward, hunching himself up in some kind of weird anticipatory strut. 'Open sesame!' he said. The door opened and Stuart himself went into some kind of weird little leprechaun dance.

Dougie's face clouded. 'Steady on man.'

'Sure. Sorry. I'm still buzzing.'

'Aye me too.'

'You know I got her name wrong on the phone?' They were walking up the stairs. 'Yeah – I called her Carmen.'

'No way. What did she say?'

'She was really nice about it. Seems like a nice girl.'

'Very nice indeed.'

They were at her door. It was pale white, metallic and shut. Stuart nodded and Dougie stepped forward with his fist bunched; as he did, the door opened.

'Hey.'

She had changed, was wearing a thin black nightdress, legs bare, and her folds of black hair were falling over her shoulders. She was very beautiful. Seeing her like that Stuart was seized by that deep desire which is one of the most profound emotions a human being can feel. 'Sharon,' he said.

'Come on in, guys.'

XVI.

They entered the apartment, seeing the whole thing from the doorway. It was indeed small but also, despite her protestations – 'if you'll forgive the mess' – utterly orderly and clean. The back half of the room was cut off by a large screen which could be drawn back to form the bedroom, where a small balcony looked out on the dark night. The furniture was well chosen and perfectly spaced, forming an expert little stage set for the party; three chairs had been set. On the table next to the chairs stood a bottle of wine and three glasses. Next to these was perched a laptop and speakers through which graceful, classical music was playing and three candles lit. It was all ready, all prepared – although just one of the candles was lit.

'This is so nice, Sharon. This is really lovely,' said Dougie.

'Where's your cello?' said Stuart.

'In the bedroom,' said Sharon with a smile. 'Now come, sit.'

They moved to take their seats; she stood in the centre of the room, barefoot. Stuart stared into neutral space.

'This place is lovely Sharon,' said Dougie as she poured him a glass of wine. 'Is it a student flat?'

'It is – but I'm good at making the best of small spaces. I

used to live in Manhattan. Try that.'

Dougie sipped. 'It's very nice. Very refreshing.'

Stuart asked, 'Manhattan?'

'Yup, that's where I studied. At the Juilliard. I had what was probably the teeniest tiniest little loft apartment in Manhattan, but I loved it so much. It was on the fourteenth floor. What do you think of the wine?' she asked him.

'It's good,' Stuart said.

She smiled. 'I'm glad. I've been saving it. Actually I have a photo here.' She walked over to the sofa, stepping briefly up to be able to reach a shelf where several frames were perched. She stood with her bare heels showing behind them, if you looked over that is, which Stuart did; sat in the chair with his glass of wine, Dougie raised his eyebrows smiling.

'Well, it's there somewhere,' she said, coming back down to them. 'It was the cutest little place.'

'This wine really is lovely, Sharon,' said Dougie.

'You should listen to him,' Stuart said. 'He works in a bar; he knows a lot about alcohol.'

'We sell a lot of French wine,' said Dougie. 'In fact we have over a hundred bottles.'

'And they trust you with that? – Being Scottish?'

'Aye, that's right. It was two hundred at Christmas.'

'Well there you go. Now tell me,' said Sharon, 'About yourselves. You don't do this full time?'

'We can't live from it, no,' said Dougie.

'Give us a few years,' said Stuart.

'Well I think both of you could. I like both of you! I should sit down,' she said and did.

Now they formed a small curve in the candlelight, each taking their position, the Scottish dandy, the beautiful cellist and Stuart, the anxious wit. Stuart looked at Dougie and listened to him talk – 'I know a lot about alcohol man. In fact that's mae plan. I'm going to make some money – say 20,000 pounds. Write a stand-up comedy show, practice it for weeks and then make 20,000 pounds with it. I'm going to talk about my mother, Glasgow, women, all the stuff that's really under my skin. All the stuff you never get finished with. And then when I've done that I'll have some money and I'm going to buy a vineyard in Portugal, and I'm going to set up my wee chair, and I'm going to sit there with a glass of wine and just think about it all', feeling as he did an enormous surge of love for his fellow man, or at least this particular one.

Stuart spoke, slowly. 'I love this music.'

'Do you?' Sharon asked.

'Oh yeah. I'm a baroque nut.'

'I also love baroque,' she said, pronouncing it the North American way, barrock. 'It's such fun to play.'

'The people who say it's cold don't know what it's talking about.'

'No, they don't. Do people really say that it's cold?'

'My mother does.'

'Your mother lives in Nottingham.'

'No, she lives in Brighton now.'

'Oh, I know Brighton! That's a coastal town, right? And Nottingham, I haven't been to Nottingham yet.'

'It's the most beautiful city in the world. Hands down. Once you've seen Nottingham, that's it. It's over. Why the cello then?'

'Oh, I just loved them from when I was little, from the first time I saw one. I used to borrow the school one. So when I was eight my parents told me if I studied hard for my math exam I could have my own, and I studied so hard they gave in. I think they were getting worried about me. I was staying up a lot.'

'That's adorable.'

'It's not that adorable – it was mainly down to Adderall. I mean most everybody at music school is on that stuff. Or anti-depressants. I mean it's not like rock music, you know, where if you fuck it up it's part of the charm. If you fuck it up your career is down the tubes. A lot of people can't take it. A friend of mine cut his wrists open in a recital. That kind of thing.'

'Sounds like Glasgow,' said Dougie.

'Does it?' Sharon said. 'What about you, do you play any instruments?'

'I play the ukulele.'

'Wow! That's amazing.'

'Yeah, well,' Stuart said, 'it's partly practical. My hands were too small for guitar. Dougie, do you play anything?'

'Drums.'

Stuart went on. 'I'm very passionate about music. I couldn't live without it, actually; it's essential for me. It's the life force you know.'

'Yes, it's the same. I couldn't live without music. Well, of course I couldn't – I've devoted my life to it.'

'One time in London I was on the bus to work and I realized I'd forgotten my iPod. So I went back home to get it.'

'Really?'

'An hour on the bus without music? Forget it.'

Sharon shook her head. 'What were you doing?'

'Then? Oh, writing advertising copy. Before I moved to Germany.' Stuart tilted his head. 'How did you end up in Heidelberg, then?'

'Actually I've been in Germany for three years. I was in Cottbus before.'

'*Cottbus*?' A small, ugly, reconstructed town in Brandenburg, about an hour east on the train from Berlin; a border town. To imagine this woman, Stuart thought, in Cottbus...

'Yeah I know. Looking back it's pretty weird that I ever lived there. I was playing first cello in the ensemble; it was a one-year contract. It wasn't the happiest time of my life to be honest, and the weather was awful. Fifty shades of grey – haha!'

'I did a gig there once,' said Stuart.

'In Cottbus?'

'Yes. Half the audience were East German; the other,

Chinese. Nobody spoke English.'

'Sounds about right,' Sharon laughed. 'All the international students, right. Oh god – all I can remember about the place is the *Metzger*.' The butcher. 'My flat was above one and they used to leave sausages outside my apartment door. They were trying to integrate me I think. They really hadn't heard of vegetarians. A friend of mine visited who was vegan and they kept giving her just lettuce. When were you there?'

'Two years ago.'

'We were there at the same time, then,' said Sharon. 'I mean back then. Before that I was in Manhattan, and originally I'm from a suburb of Toronto.'

'I've never been to Toronto. Is it nice?'

'It is very nice. That's exactly what it is. You know we say our hockey team sucks and our Mayor smokes crack.'

'Is that what you say?'

'It is what we say.'

Stuart nodded. 'How are you finding Heidelberg?'

'It's alright. Well actually it's kind of small.'

'Pretty though, aye.'

'It is pretty. When I was cycling along to the show today actually I was thinking wow – this is really pretty. Really cute. That's what I pay my money for.'

'It's expensive here?'

'Oh it's ridiculous. And the taxes!' She raised her glass,

legs now folded neatly over each over and nails, Stuart could see, painted black. 'I mean, look at the size of this place. For what I'm paying it's ridiculous. It's like New York only everybody's white. And racist. I can say that right? I mean, I'm brown enough right? Even though I'm actually really white – my mother says I'm a coconut, you know, white on the inside. Isn't that awful? Now you both think I'm a bad person, I'm sure. You don't? That's good. I'm actually really glad I met you guys.'

'Likewise,' said Dougie.

'The show was really funny,' she said.

'Stuart was saying after the show,' said Dougie, leaning forward from his leather chair, 'that we both got the audience laughing today in very different ways.'

'Yes, that's right I think. You're very different.'

'Aye – so how are we different exactly?'

'Well.' She gave a little laugh and thought about it a while. After a long time she spoke, looking over to Dougie first. 'I think you're very much the best friend.'

Dougie smiled, 'Aye?'

'Yes. Very charming. Very funny, but like – well, the best friend.'

Dougie grinned as he usually did when he could detect himself being undermined.

And now for Stuart. Their eyes turned to him, he smiled, and a moment later they all laughed.

Sharon said, 'And you, my friend, are dry as a bone.'

'But you're very welcoming on stage,' said Dougie.

'Sometimes I feel I dare them to laugh,' said Stuart.

'You could say that,' Sharon said.

'Best friend, aye?' said Dougie after a pause.

'So what's the plan for you two,' said Sharon, business-like. 'You can't possibly be wanting to stay in Germany performing in English for the rest of your lives.'

'Well, they only discovered comedy here recently,' said Stuart. 'You know – like oil in the 1930s. I was actually in Germany when the first joke here was ever told, in 2008.'

'Yeah you did that joke tonight.'

'Did I?'

'A friend of mine calls German comedy Guantánamo,' said Dougie. 'Anyway you're right. I'm going back to the UK one day, aye. Germany's all about learning my trade, you know. I mean – if I was in London, even Glasgow, I'd have to work all the time you know. And I don't know if I'm prepared to do that.'

There was another pause while Stuart considered. 'My set only really works in Germany. It's kind of an existential joke, and also my life.'

'Sharon darling – where's your bathroom?' Dougie had stood and Sharon pointed to the door at the entrance, warning him that the flush was a little resistant. 'It's been like that since I got here.' She laughed nervously, and as she did the baroque music, which sounded like thinking in notes, resolved its final knot of suspensions to roll to an end. 'OK – music requests guys.'

Stuart thought, what can impress this woman, but it was Dougie, swiftly returning, who spoke. 'John Maus, Hey Moon.'

'Hey Mood?'

'Moon. "Hey Moon." It's from the album "We Must Become the Pitiless Censors of Ourselves."'

'Great title.' Sharon fumbled around for a moment and then a beautiful minor key piano sequence ambled into their ears; suddenly the room was gripped by music.

'That's it,' said Dougie, 'Aye.'

Around now the vocal began, a deep, distorted male voice.

They listened to the song, a beautiful electronic lullaby to the moon, for all of the five minutes of grace it afforded them, their minds in reveries. Then it finished.

'Yes!' said Sharon.

'That's beautiful, man,' said Stuart.

'Aye,' said Dougie. 'I play it when I want to throw people out the bar. Go home you bastards! Get the fuck out!'

After they finished laughing – they were getting along famously - Sharon looked at Stuart. 'So – your choice, Mr.'

'How about 'Hey Moon' again?'

Dougie and Sharon gave a little cheer. Sharon pressed play again and it was the same magic slightly drunker. During it, Stuart had time to make his next selection, and as soon as the song had finished he cued a piece by Couperin, 'Les Barricades Mystérieuses.' Stuart had played it to his actress girlfriend on their first date; they had sat in his student bedroom listening to it, the door open on the freezing winter night.

'I like this piece so much,' he had said.

She had said, 'Tell me why you do.'

'Oh this is nice,' said Sharon, having listened to it for about ten seconds. 'What is it?'

'It's Couperin.'

'Couperin. Yes, it's very pretty. I keep meaning to get into this period.'

'I love it,' Stuart said. 'It's just a very profound experience of time.'

'Ever the poet,' said Sharon.

From the chair, Dougie flashed him a cheeky, drowsy grin, slipping into real inebriation now. The music, this piece shorter, finished. Stuart loved this music.

'What next?' Sharon asked again, apparently ceding control of the playlist to Stuart. This was an honour and a challenge. He cued up a track.

'Oh, I know this,' Sharon said, mildly enthused. 'Into your minimalism, are you.'

'Yeah, I like it. I really like John Adams too. Do you like him?'

'Do I!? John Adams man! John fucking Adams! I played in a production of his in Stuttgart.'

'Which one?'

'Nixon in China.'

In the background, a piece from Glass' opera 'Einstein on the Beach' had started, namely 'Knee Play 5', a song built around rhythmic counting, electronic drones and, later, a violin. Following the beautiful violin solo came the impassioned recital of a poem, playing tribute to love, that force which it has been said moves the stars.

When the poem overlaid the solo Sharon said, 'Don't you kind of wish he'd shut up?'

'It is beautiful though, what he's saying,' said Stuart.

'Sure.' For Sharon the music was enough. 'You boys look like you could use another drink.'

The poem stopped and the music did so too, instantly in fact; Sharon having gone to the kitchen, the boys were left sitting in the room. They looked to each other rapidly and, with agitation, Stuart stood and swept towards Dougie.

'Jesus Christ!' he said.

'I know...'

'Candles and...'

'Wine. Good wine. This stuff's not cheap, I'm telling you.'

'Is she trying...?'

'She's trying to seduce us.'

'But me or you? Or both of us?'

'I don't know,' said Dougie. 'But I reckon she's more into you.'

'No man – I think she's thinking more ambitiously than that.'

'You mean?'

'Yes. I mean... that's the logic here.'

'So, should we?' There was no sound from the kitchen.

'I don't know man.'

'I've got a girlfriend,' said Stuart.

'Aye, me too. She's really into us though.'

'So what do we do?'

Stuart was conscious of the slightly Laurel and Hardy quality to their dialogue.

Meanwhile, Dougie was by now practically shaking. 'I dunno man – I just dunno!'

Sharon came back in, hair tossed back, catching Stuart slightly crouched and rising as she did. 'Do either of you like Spanish wine?'

'I adore Spanish wine. Gives me terrible hangovers though. Earthenware hangovers I call them. Doesn't the city look pretty,' said Stuart, wafting his hand towards it.

'Doesn't it?' They had moved to the window, looking out to the balcony. 'Want to go out?'

'Sure. Dougie?'

Dougie had sunk further into the chair and looked increasingly and conveniently sleepy. You go on ahead, his eyes said, or at least the cat-like slivers which could still be seen. Still, 'Fill up my glass,' he said.

They went out onto the balcony. Before they did so, Stuart selected John Maus, 'Hey Moon' once more. He clicked and there it came, that blessed song, trotting itself into life once again. The song always did the same thing but it also always grabbed the human heart, particularly the drunk one.

The small balcony affected a still better view of the lights and towers of Heidelberg. Sharon leant to one side; she had put on a shawl. 'The train station is just round there. You can see it, right? Just there.'

'Right.' There was a pause.

'I enjoyed your show.'

'Thank you. Listen, it was really nice of you to put us up.'

'It's no problem.'

'Too nice, really. I mean, we could have been rapists.'

'Are you?'

'No.'

'You don't look like rapists.'

'What do rapists look like?' Stuart asked.

'Not like you. You look – well, British.'

'I am British. This wine is great by the way.'

'Right? So you guys are doing like, a mini-tour.'

'Yeah – we were playing Kettwig last night.'

'Kettwig?'

'In Essen.'

'Oh, Essen. *Eat*.'

'I call those the verb towns – Essen, Gießen, Siegen...'

'... Baden Baden...'

'So good they named it twice. Did I do that joke as well?'

'No it's not that.'

'What?'

'It sounds really dumb to say it.'

'What?'

'No...'

'Tell me.'

'I really like your accent.'

The wine and music echoed in his mind...

'Thank you. I have the same one in German. It doesn't work so well there. I imagine you have less of one, given your musical ear. Actually, I think there's a lot of similarities between music and comedy.'

'There are.'

'Right – it's about hitting the beats, getting into the right rhythm. When you're right the audience laughs without processing. Or it's also like playing cricket. Do you have cricket in Canada?'

'I don't believe we do. Hockey's the big thing. Is this what you really want to do then – comedy?'

'I am doing it.'

'But you know.'

'What? They need to laugh here as much as anywhere else. Perhaps more so.'

'You're funny.'

'I love making people laugh. That's the big thing you

realize – it's about them. All those people, come to have a good time. And when you get them – it feels so good. It's like taking, what's that drug you like, Adderall, right? Intense focus. What about you?' He tried to pull back from his blurry self-involvement. 'What about you – do you like playing professionally?'

'Yes but – it's a very hard life. But I do, I really do love it. I'm incredibly lucky to be in Germany. I'm genuinely blessed. The support for the arts here is really amazing. It's just –'

'Just what?'

'Well,' said Sharon, with a deeply conflicted air, 'well, if you must know, it's the people. They can be a little –'

'Touchy?' he said.

'Yeah, touchy, that's one way of putting it. To be perfectly honest I think they're bunch of assholes. It's like today, before I came over to the show, I had to pick up a form. So that I could be here for another season. And I appreciate that it means going into the theatre on a Sunday – but the woman was just so rude to me. She was just so rude to me, as if she was doing me a favour finding the stupid form, even though it's probably the only thing she had to do all day, you know?'

'I do. I know exactly what you mean. It's like they smell out an opportunity to make your life difficult.'

'Totally. And this kind of thing just keeps happening to me. I mean, I don't want to sound ungrateful; it's totally amazing that I get the chance to live here, to play and get paid. Most of my friends in New York can't even make rent. But I just sometimes wonder if they'd have told me back at music school just how hard this was going to be, just how much I would have to sacrifice... And then I realized that they did tell me. They told me repeatedly, and I just told them to go to hell, I will do whatever I want to do, and if you tell me I can't do it, I will just redouble my efforts to do so. And that's been the same all my life. Do you get that? I guess you do, right? I was terribly ambitious... You know I wanted to be the best cello player in North America, you know. And I am definitely working towards that. Anyway, that's how you end up here, I guess – I mean – on one side I have everything I've been working towards, on the other... I'm sort of stuck.'

She continued talking but Stuart couldn't really focus anymore. Other people's ambitions were boring. Or rather something was welling inside him, beyond wine, something perhaps we only feel when in the presence of someone we desire immeasurably, a sense of the wondrousness of it all. How wondrous to be here, on this planet, on this stage, looking up at the sky, full of this euphoric wine and so close to a beautiful woman he could even reach out and touch her. And wondrous too that we weren't allowed to say it, were only allowed to let out this tiny squeal of our joy when drunk, or at our children's parties, when really, if we considered the possibilities, we should be reeling round the whole time shouting 'I'm alive!' and 'You are too!'

The other thing he felt was a sudden and urgent desire to be sick. There it was, the familiar lip-smacking saltiness and excess saliva which signified that his diet for the day, in all its variety, had not sat well. Sharon was for some reason saying the words 'YoYo Ma,' which seemed to describe precisely what he needed to do and, nodding politely, Stuart said, amiably but somewhat too loudly, 'Excuse me, I have to go the bathroom.' He then turned and walked to the bathroom where, with a brief, neat falling to his knees, like a soldier who had just taken a bullet, he leant over and evacuated the contents of his stomach into the toilet bowl.

He then flushed the faulty toilet several times until the puke sank and stood to wash his mouth in the basin. The water felt very cold and he paused to look at himself. Apart from an encroaching paleness, he did not, he believed, look like someone who had just been sick. That was the hope anyway. In the background, as he wet his hair now, the music turned back to the Cello Suites. What an evening.

Stuart fetched himself a glass of water from the kitchen and turned back into the living room where, on the chair ahead, Dougie had fallen asleep. It was a most sensible response. You were as Chris Rock suggested only as faithful as your options and Dougie had simply extricated himself from said options by seeking refuge on the Isle of Nod. Asleep, his colleague looked peaceful, well-fed, well-loved, a man who would never be short of friends. He did though look a little cold, and Stuart lifted a rug off the sofa-bed to drape it over Dougie's shoulder. The sleeping man strained a little at that, and, wriggling a touch, muttered a single but clearly audible word, 'Puffins.'

Stuart walked back into the bedroom where Sharon was waiting. She turned to him and said, 'OK?'

'The Cello Suites.'

'No 4. My favourite.'

'Mine too.'

'Really?'

'Yes, really. Dougie's asleep by the way.'

'Is he?'

'Like a baby. Listen...' Stuart began.

'Yes?'

Sharon looked at him and Stuart realized that he had arrived, without having made one, at the point of decision.

Turning to later again.

Much later, after his comedy career had begun to blossom, after his father had got sick, after he had long since separated from Deborah, and many others after her, after Heidelberg, London, Oxford, Nottingham, he woke in a hotel room in Hamburg after little sleep. He saw that his iPhone was shaking not due to his alarm but due to Tina, his girlfriend, phoning.

'Hey,' he said, not yet awake.

'How are you baby?'

'I'm asleep,' he said.

'You didn't call me last night. How was the show?'

'It was really good. Actually it was kind of a crazy evening.'

'Yeah? Why?'

'I – I'll tell you when I get back to Berlin.'

'What time are you back?'

'I should be at Hauptbahnof at midday. Shall I come back to yours?'

'You can do. What time?'

'Later. I need to take a nap. I've got a gig too; it's on a boat on the Spree.'

'Yeah, I remember.'

'But I'm sure I can bike it. I won't be drinking.'

'Sure honey.' Tina always said honey in English, like an American. 'I'm looking forward to seeing you.'

'You too darling. I've got to get ready now; my train is in –' he checked his watch – 'forty minutes.'

'Forty minutes!? Forty minutes?!'

'It's OK – I'm right next to the station.'

'Well. Is there anything special you want for dinner?'

'Make that thing with cabbages and nuts, the one you made last time.'

'Fine. I'll make you some fig cake too.'

'You don't have to do that.'

'OK, I won't.'

'I do like fig cake,' he said.

She laughed. 'Alright, I'm going.'

'You're sweet,' he said and hung up.

He then moved to pack his things together, hungover and sore-faced and vacillating between absorption in this task and occasionally remembering, for the first time after he had cleaned his teeth, the second after he had checked himself in the mirror, and last and more deeply as he exited the hotel, that he had apparently been given a theatre.

Years earlier Stuart awoke in a small apartment in Heidelberg. Sunlight was falling through the windows and there was a strange, sweet smell in the air, either pot-pourri or unknown flowers. Outside the window the quiet sounds of a German Monday, quite early, could be heard, gliding cyclists and light rail systems delivering polite commuters who sat in thoughtful silence and still read print.

He lay looking across the empty bed and its tangle of sheets. Now sounds could be heard from the kitchen, the tiny roar of a kettle, the clump of cups being set. Stuart pulled himself across the bed, his feet dangling over, and sat there for a moment feeling punch-drunk though not hungover. Wine was always better in that regard. Finally, eyes blurry, he rose, slipped himself into his dirty clothes, and stepped into the main room.

'Hi.' Sharon turned from the stove. 'I'm making some porridge. Would you like some?'

'That's very kind,' said Stuart. His spectacles had been, he now saw, left on the living room table, from which the wine glasses had been cleared.

'What time is you guys' train?'

'About half an hour,' he said. 'But it's not a train – we're getting a lift.'

'*Mitfahrgelegenheit*?' Germany's car-sharing network. 'I've been meaning to try that for a while, but I've not been sure about it, you know, as a woman travelling alone.'

'Oh it's quite safe. They vet the people in advance. Can I give you a hand?'

'No, it's fine.' Sharon had her back to the stove and as she cooked Stuart found himself staring at her ankles. She had really lovely ankles, he thought, and then how much he liked the word ankles, and then he thought nothing.

At this point Dougie stirred on the couch.

'Aw Jesus what time is it?'

'It's 07.45.'

'It's time I got up, right.'

'I think so.'

'Aw man it's a shame. I was dreaming I had been made King of this small African Kingdom, right, and I had the most amazing harem. There must have been 1000 lassies in there, easy. Morning Sharon.'

'Good morning Dougie. Would you care for some porridge?'

'Aw no thanks Sharon, but thanks very much.' Dougie had sat upwards now, his brown locks falling over his face like twisted string.

'Where was your kingdom?' asked Stuart.

'Me? Oh I don't know – in mae bumhole for all I care.'

The boys were still sniggering as their porridge was served, Sharon handed it over and then waved something silver, saying, 'Spoon.'

She sat next to him and they tucked into their porridge, Stuart also being presented with a cup of green tea. Dougie was looking at him almost forlornly.

'What – you want some now?'

'Yes,' said Dougie.

Stuart nodded. 'First the croissants then this. Here.' He pushed the bowl towards Dougie, who had taken another spoon.

Sharon blew onto her spoon. 'Be careful; it's hot.' She popped the spoon in her mouth and withdrew it cleaner. 'I was meaning to ask you Dougie. What do you think of Scottish independence?'

Dougie paused. 'I dunno Sharon. I can't vote in it you see, I'm in Berlin.'

'But how would you?'

'If I could? I honestly don't know. I think what it is, right, is someone's just looked at the maths and thought, aye, we make this much from tourism every year, we make four billion from whisky, we have so much oil – we could survive on our own.'

'As long as people keep boozing and wanting to look at castles,' said Stuart.

'Aye – and that seems a relatively constant demand.' Dougie laughed, but gave off the sense that he didn't find this the funniest of topics. 'Why do you ask?'

'Just interested. I like Scotland.'

'You've been?'

'I've been to St. Andrews. My boyfriend's Scottish.'

The scraping of a spoon on the bowl bottom.

'Oh right, is he?' said Dougie.

'Yep. He's living in London at the moment.'

Stuart rose from the table and over to the kitchen sink, reaching to turn on the tap. Sharon spoke suddenly and almost irritably; 'No Stuart, please leave it. I don't want that.'

'It's done now,' said Stuart, lifting the still-flecked bowl onto the drying rack. He paused for a moment facing the kitchen wall. 'I think we best be going, Dougie,' Stuart said.

It was indeed time. Dougie rummaged himself straight, pulled on his trousers in the same swaggering fashion he had moved across the stage, and laced up his shoes. Stuart, by now dressed and ready, slipped into his old coat.

'Well, thanks so much for having us,' Stuart said.

'Oh – no problem. It was actually quite fun.'

'Let us know if you're ever in Berlin.'

'Aye, let us know if you're ever in Berlin,' said Dougie, putting his dirty T-shirt into his bag.

'I will do. You guys know how to get to the station, right?'

'We'll be alright I think.' Dougie stepped over to her and gave her a kiss on the cheek. 'Sharon.'

'Dougie. A pleasure.' She reached over and hugged him, a wide smile spreading across Dougie's face. Stuart was next, saying 'thanks for the wine' and leaning over to hug her for a long, warm instant.

'Are you guys sure you don't want to shower?' Sharon said.

'We'll be alright, aye,' said Dougie. 'See you later.'

Outside the door Stuart turned back, seeing her standing in the door frame ready to close it. There was a last moment of contact between them before '*Tschüß!*', cheerio, she said. 'Good luck in your comedy careers!'

The door closed.

The two men turned to each other and then began to silently descend the stairwell. They walked onto the road and began the brief crossing over to the train station, the fibreglass carbuncle ahead to the left.

It was only after a minute's walking that one of them spoke. 'What a beautiful woman,' Dougie said.

Stuart just nodded.

They stood in front of the Heidelberg railway station waiting for their lift to Berlin.

Stuart looked over the busy station parking. 'You were talking in your sleep last night.'

'I was talking in my sleep?'

'Yes you were.'

'What did I say?'

'Just the word "puffins."'

'Puffins?'

'Yeah. Any idea why?'

'I don't know man, I don't know,' Dougie said. 'Listen – I'm going to go and get myself a pie.'

'A pie? But you just had half my bloody porridge.'

'Aye, and I fancy a wee beer to be honest but I'm not making a big deal of it.'

'Alright get on with it then,' said Stuart, and Dougie moved off with a little maniacal laugh.

Stuart stood there; a man in a cagoule passed by, looking like a possible driver; Stuart approached him, asking, *'Fahren Sie nach Berlin?'* and the man said, with a big beaming smile, *'Nein.'*

Stuart walked back to their starting point, trying to find the calm to depart this small town. Now out of the corner of his eyes he could see a car where a young man in a black T-shirt was helping a young woman place her suitcase in the back of a tiny car. Stuart walked over to them.

'Excuse me,' he said – 'Are you?'

'Berlin, right?' said the man.

'Yeah, that's it.'

'Great. Johannes.' They shook hands.

'Lotte,' said the girl, who was tall and handsome.

'Stuart.' They shook hands. Then he raised his bag towards Johannes. 'Got room for that?'

'Yeah – but you've got one more person, right?'

'Yes, he's just getting a pie.'

'No problem. We're not in a great rush.'

'That's good. And you got the money?'

'Yes, thank you.'

'Because it should have been transferred in advance.'

'It arrived, thank you. And you also know we're going to make a little stop in Frankfurt on the way.'

'Yes, you did say. That's fine.'

There was a pause then. The German language had, with its habitual precision and disinclination to equivocate, executed all the practicalities in no time. There was genuinely nothing left to confirm. All that remained was either strained small talk or long silence for the ride north. It was a good time, then, for Dougie to emerge, walking briskly with his head bent over a pie.

'Hello there,' said Dougie, flakes dropping from his chin.

'Johannes,' said Johannes.

'Lotte,' said Lotte.

'Dougie, pleased to meet you.' He transferred the pie to another hand to bite into, raising a hand but not shaking theirs.

'Did Stuart tell you about Frankfurt and making a stop there?'

'Aye he did, thanks.' Dougie continued to eat.

'It shouldn't take long. That your case?' Johannes swooped it up from where Dougie had placed it on the floor, and busied himself a second arranging the cases for maximum space.

Then there was nothing more for it; it was time to go. They opened the car doors, Johannes and Lotte taking the front and the two comedians squeezing into the back. The car was truly tiny, a little marvel of steel engineering heft, and both men were truly cramped in the back with their knees pushed high up and the Germans close enough to touch. It felt like the car was a tiny space pod which would be shot straight to Berlin, perhaps through a continuous underground tunnel, propelling them into the heart of their home neighbourhoods.

'OK,' said Johannes. 'Berlin.' He started the car and they drove out the car park.

Stuart looked over to Lotte. 'Why are you going to Berlin then?' he asked.

'Oh you know – see some friends, have some fun. Just chill, really,' she said.

'And you live in Heidelberg?'

'I'm studying nursing here.'

'What are you studying?'

'Nursing.'

'Oh right, nursing.' Stuart shifted his head a little. 'What about you Johannes?'

'Yes, I live here. I teach photography.'

Dougie was less accomplished in German than Stuart,

but by no means silent, chipping in with 'At the University?'

'Yes – I'm a teaching assistant. That's why I'm going to Frankfurt actually, to pick up some pictures. And what about you guys?'

'We're comedians,' said Dougie.

'Really?'

'We did a show last night in Heidelberg; that's why we're here.'

'Ah I see. And where was the show?'

'O'Reilly's Irish pub.'

'Ah yes, I know where it is. Have you been there?' Johannes asked Lotte.

'Yeah – it's where all the expats hang out, isn't it?'

'That's right. All the *Amis.*' Johannes addressed them again. 'Were there many people there?'

'Must have been about fifty.'

'That's pretty good. Did they laugh?'

'They did,' said Stuart.

'And the show,' said Lotte, not turning back, 'was it in German or English?'

'In English,' said Stuart. 'Most of our shows are in English – there's a really good English-comedy scene in Berlin. You can perform virtually every night of the week in English there. I'm much funnier in English,' he said.

'I think it's normal, no?' said Johannes. 'I mean – telling

jokes in a foreign language. I think that would be very difficult. Right?' he said to Lotte.

'When I went to Chile I found it was the hardest thing, understanding the humour,' said Lotte.

'Really?' Johannes drove on a moment. 'You were in Chilé?'

'For one year, yes.'

Johannes continued to nod, then spoke to Dougie and Stuart again. 'And is it true that Germans have no sense of humour?'

'Oh, I think everybody has a sense of humour,' said Stuart. He spoke with conviction, although perhaps not sufficient conviction for a man devoting his life to the question.

They drove on, and gradually the conversations separated itself into a German section at the front and an English one at the rear.

Dougie spoke, tired but still full of ebullience. 'Did you make it with that girl after I fell asleep, then?'

Stuart gave a light smile, 'No.'

'Really? I think she was into you.'

'I think she was into you.'

'Or maybe both of us?'

'Maybe.'

'Aw man – I'm sure if we'd have asked she'd have been up for it.'

'Well, now we'll never know.'

'No, we won't.' Dougie thought a moment. 'Unless you send her a text asking her.'

'What?'

'Yeah, go on, send her a cheeky wee text.'

'Saying what exactly?'

'You know, if you'd have been interested in us sexually, how exactly would that have worked?' Dougie grinned. 'Na man, I think she was definitely more into you.'

'I think she was more into me,' Stuart said.

'Aye? And what's going to happen to me? Sit there in the dark watching your bonny little arse bobbing up and down listening to 'Hey Moon'?'

Stuart was laughing. 'I can just imagine walking out from the bedroom and you're sitting there on your chair in the dark.'

'And I'm like, "Shitter's broke."'

'Ha! Just on your own in the dark – "shitter's broke."'

By now the two men were sniggering so loudly that the Germans turned to look at them. 'Everything OK?' Johannes asked.

'It's all fine man, it's fine,' said Dougie.

'And what about her boyfriend!' Stuart went on. 'He was conveniently forgotten alright. That was one hell of a boyfriend bomb. I can understand it from her perspective, though. I mean, two guys rock up from out of town – they're really funny –'

'Aye, we were really funny last night. You were great,

man.'

'Only because you had them absolutely cooking for me first.'

'Thanks. I was good, wasn't I?'

'You were great. Anyway, imagine,' Stuart continued, 'two guys, good-looking young guys, show up from out of town, they're funny, and she'll never see us again.'

'Right man. It's the perfect crime. I mean, it's actually kind of sad in a way; a beautiful girl like that being all on her own. Lonely, you know. She needed a good pumping,' Dougie concluded.

'Well, we do have girlfriends,' Stuart said.

'Aye – I've got the best one in the world - but I just want to find out, you know? Whether she wanted one of us or both of us or neither. Send her a text will you, go on. Send her a text and ask her exactly what she was imagining.'

'I can't send her a text mate,' Stuart laughed, 'What am I going to say? "Excuse me Sharon I was just wondering..."'

'Your comedy gets you girls, man,' said Dougie. 'It was the same in Hannover with that girl – what did she say – "can I take him home with me?"'

'Firstly she was about 15. And in fact, I only get girls when I'm with you. It's because I look like the intelligent one, which is very compelling for some people. I think it's kind of like a Pinky and the Brain dynamic. And you're Pinky.'

'Pinky's up to his knees in pussy man. That's how he

gets his name.'

By now they were having to calm themselves as their mirth became almost painful; wheezily, they slowed the conversation down and then to a halt completely. To calm himself, Stuart looked out at the motorway, a narrow clean strip with barely a vehicle around.

'What a beautiful woman though,' said Dougie after a while.

'Oh yes. It was her hair, wasn't it?'

'Aye.' Dougie sighed. 'And now we'll never know.'

Sharon would for her part even on that day barely think of them, as she sat on the tram in Heidelberg, looking out the window, absent-mindedly rummaging for her ticket as the inspector came down the carriage, or later that year when she decided to return to the United States, and struggled to get a place in an ensemble and taught, and then one day at the encouragement of a friend entered an 'America's Got Talent' style show but for classical music, and won, and became famous, and released an album which won a Grammy, a copy of which eventually found its way via a friend into Dougie's hands, who then sat years later at the North Sea listening to it remembering that distant night. But she *would* think of them later that day when she returned to her apartment and saw three glasses, already sparklingly clean, and feel a wave of loneliness overwhelm her.

They watched the road speeding by; Johannes drove the tiny car remarkably fast. There were no speed limits on the autobahn, only the ones the cars themselves set, and it just felt so good to be in a car again after the long cheap bus rides. During the journey, he found himself drifting into repeated thoughts of Sharon, who he would never see again, feeling certain she would be an important figure in the rest of his life.

They stopped in Frankfurt; Johannes picked up his photographs, official in a fine brown envelope, and they sped back up the motorway north.

Dougie looked half-asleep and Stuart said to him, not even sure the other man could hear him beneath his earphones, 'There will come a time when we look back at these times and think of how free we were, how lucky we were to be so free.'

Dougie, although clearly sleeping, seemed to register, and stirred against the car door.

And so the little car sped on to Berlin. Johannes cranked some Rolling Stones up on the radio, *da-da, na na na*, and within what seemed like moments they were already reaching the flatlands, the swathes of dark, black plain, which marked the entrance to the federal state of Brandenburg, and within it, Berlin. Pretty soon not only the landscape but the road signs were familiar, that you could drive on north to Hamburg, east to Poland or make the turn in to West Berlin Charlottenburg, which they duly did. Lotte was being dropped off in Moabit, an unfashionable district to the northwest of the city, and Johannes asked them if it was alright to let them out there, to which both men agreed.

So it was that they stepped out of the little vehicle beneath the rundown tower blocks of a part of their city only ever rumoured to be becoming gentrified. The scene outside was high rise, corner parks and luminescent kebab shops. They got out the car, said goodbye to Lotte, who Johannes had assiduously chatted up throughout the journey, and Johannes himself who, in the last contact they would ever have with him, gave them a handshake entirely out-of-keeping with the level of interest and warmth he had shown to them during the journey before.

'Have fun guys!'

And Johannes went back to his car to drive Lotte to her door.

They stood in the rain in Moabit.

'Should be an U-Bahn station quite near,' said Stuart.

They walked on. It was starting to rain and they passed bright, somehow essentially *west* Berlin shops, these squat dark premises with their brown plastic chairs and elderly Turkish men smoking within them. Dougie made little snotting sounds.

'You getting a cold?'

'Mebbe.' Easy to, in this weather. As their conversations thinned, Stuart began to feel the final shift in their intimacy of the last days, from a developed camaraderie to the resumption of their separate lives. Now they would once again get to do all the things they had been looking forward to and had only a few hours before begun to wish they could postpone a little longer.

Dougie spoke as he walked. 'Aw man – I remembered what it was about the puffins. You know, what I was talking about in the night. The puffins. I'd been meaning to talk to you about it the whole time anyway. It was when I went up to Shetland, you know. In my dark times.

'It was after I was up on Unst, aye, just after I'd been chasing the cash machine – you remember. And Unst is the most northerly part of the United Kingdom, it's the inspiration for Treasure Island, this weird little rock, I told you right. Closer to Iceland than to Manchester. And at its tip right was a nature reserve, and that was the northernmost point of the United Kingdom – I mean, you couldn't get more North than that. And for some reason I had to see it.

'So I hitched up to the top of the islands, and if I remember correctly I got a lift off the park ranger. And he was living up there because he said he liked the freedom, that there weren't a lot of rules up there. And he drops me off at the entrance to the reserve.

So it's that way, I say, aye?, looking out the van on this windswept plain.

And he says, aye, you just need to go on up that way. There are puffins there, he adds.

Really, puffins aye. And I haven't ever seen a puffin but I'm thinking at that moment that's what I want to see more than anything in the whole fucking world.

'So I start hiking across to the top of the island, right, and I'm crossing this plain. And it's raining on me just like now and suddenly there's this big fucking bird swooping down on me, this huge bastard of a bird, they call them bonxies right, they're like angry flying testicles, and they're making this cawing sound, *skua*, *skua*, and coming down on me – because they're very protective of their young right, and they thinking that I'm interfering. Even though I'm not, I'm just trying to get to the North.

'And I go on right and I'm just about past the bonxies and I get to the cliffs and then this really thick mist comes down on me, swirling down me, and you can see where the water might be but you cannot see it very well. Basically I could fall in at any time. But I keep going on because I'm determined to see a puffin.

'Then after a while I can only see a little further than my own nose; I'm literally crawling on my arms and legs and it's so misty I actually nearly topple down an incline. And I realize that I'm going to have to go back; I've come all this way, I'm literally metres away from the most northerly point of Scotland – and I'm going to have to go back. I don't want to go back, but I do.

'Now as I'm walking back the same way, away from the sea, I see a couple walking together, this older man and a woman in a green cagoule, a very attractive blonde girl. And I say to her, "Listen, you're going to have to turn back, it's too misty to keep walking up there, you will die."

'At which there's a pause and the woman looks at me and says, in a strong French accent, "But is there puffins?"'

They walked on for a while before Stuart spoke. 'So you spend your free time walking around bleak depressing landscapes in the rain. A lot's changed, hasn't it?'

Dougie laughed.

'I was thinking man,' said Dougie. 'What you said. Maybe things won't always be this good but – you know – maybe they will be. I mean, the rest of life, it might be good, it might be shit, right, but you've got to give it a go, surely. No sense in giving up now.'

They had reached the U-Bahn station Leopoldplatz and descended the steps to the functional underground. On the wide platform Dougie moved to the ticket machines.

'You can have my spare,' said Stuart.

'It's OK man – I need to buy myself a *Vier-Fahrten-Karte*,' a pack of four tickets. 'I'm not taking my chances in Berlin. I got busted at four o'clock in the morning once.'

'Three fines and you get a criminal record,' said Stuart.

'Is that right? I just pretend I don't understand. It usually works.'

Their train, a squat yellow snake, arrived, and they boarded leisurely, taking up a seat opposite to each other. Next to Dougie sat a young woman in a headscarf with her child.

'You're doing Mumbles' show on Thursday, right?'

'That's right – I've got 20.'

'New stuff?'

'A best of. You remember in Hannover when –'

At this point Dougie's phone went off and he answered it briskly, giving a slight smile to Stuart to indicate the conversation would soon continue. *'Hallo Schatz,'* darling, Dougie said.

He proceeded to have a conversation with Anja appearing to vary not only between German and English but gentle lovingness and low-level, breezily delivered insults, such as, as Stuart couldn't help but overhear, *du bist eine kleine Fötze*, you're a little cunt. Somehow the way the Scotsman employed the phrase appeared to convey genuine affection; Dougie, his immediate plans now clear, ended the call.

'Sorry man – my lady. I'm going round to hers now. She's going to make me some noodles. Pasta, I mean. I'm telling you man – this girl, she's the best I've ever had. I don't know what I'd do if we broke up.' Dougie shook his head. 'What about you; are you going to see your sweet lady soon?'

'Oh, I'll see her.' Then: 'I don't know.'

'But you like her, huh?'

'What's not to like?' said Stuart.

'Listen, did I ever tell you about the time I lost a grand? I didn't? Oh, it's a good story.' But they had come to Dougie's stop. 'Well I'll tell you next time man - I'm changing here.'

'Sure.'

Now the two men faced each other; there didn't seem enough room to hug, particularly under the watchful eyes of a small Turkish child.

'See you Thursday.'

'Yeah mate. Come home safely, huh?'

'You too.'

The train stopped; the doors opened. 'See you Thursday,' said Stuart, watching his friend Dougie waiting at the doors, looking tired, weekend-heavy, but still full of great life force.

'*Tschüß*,' Dougie said, '*bis Donnerstag.*'

'See you Thursday mate.'

And then he stepped out, Stuart watching him for just a second walking the platform before the train rolled into the blackness again.

XVII.

Later once more, several years later in fact, before Stuart would become owner and impresario of Germany's first dedicated English-language comedy club, and offer a home, a lodestar to those Dwights, Malcolms and Mumbleses, this new breed of international comedian who toured lands non-indigenous to stand-up, making jokes principally about their own unlikely presence in them, and before he made the decision to stay in Germany for good, his birth island and its slights seemingly floating away from him forever, before marriage, before children, before love, if it ever came, before various incidents and accidents which make an ordinary human life, in this case Stuart's life, but possibly any life, sumptuous and elegant, and which made Stuart feel that even the most typical human existence if there were indeed such a thing would be worthy of countless plays, poems and novels, that a day where he just say went to the shops and then drank a cup of coffee with his friends, his friends, his beloved friends, could inspire a year's worth of material, at least; years later, then, Stuart exited the same train, getting off at the *Platz der Lüftbrucke* stop, the site of the Berlin airlift and the station closest to his flat.

He moved down the hill towards his beloved *Chamissoplatz*, along *Fidcinistraße* and then taking a left down *Koptischstraße*, and onto *Willibald-Alexis Straße* itself, the street where he lived, to the small apartment where he had already lived for several years with its pale pink facade and red window frames.

He had been away only a night, but already there had been Monday post: bank statements, Amnesty International newsletters, not to mention all the emails slumbering online. After nearly ten years in Germany, and despite the country's rent control laws which protected him in its social democratic embrace he still feared coming home to an eviction notice. It was the constant low-level anxiety of being a foreigner. He unlocked the door to his ground floor apartment – it was good, for a comedian, to live on the ground floor, because it allowed you to hear random snippets of other people's conversation, like the women disciplining their boyfriends or the kids announcing their plans to behave abominably – and walked into the tiny kitchenette. He hadn't had time to clear up his pre-departure breakfast and facing him was a banana peel and cold cup of tea. He stepped through the lounge over various things into the main room, and then just sat down there on the edge of the bed for a minute in the silence.

A song was still echoing around his head, one by The Cure, a song he had recently heard leaving a café, striking him so powerfully he had stood to hear it all, and written the words down to later Google search the title: 'Pictures of You.' It began with a tremendous, rhythmic bassline, which he retraced in his head now, and his memory reconstructed it to fluency he found himself first leaning back, and then gradually lying on the bed, his legs bucked up, like some kind of stunned and gigantic bug.

He could already imagine what he was going to do with the theatre. He could already picture the opening night in his mind. A room filled with all the reprobates and geniuses he had seen slogging their guts out across Europe; German media there, maybe getting Dougie over from England, resplendent in a tux, his grin. He imagined low-lit tables and Katrina attending, and good money, and being interviewed about it in German afterwards saying something like, '*Also, wir können nur versprechen, ihr werdet* very amused *sein*', 'we promise you, you will be very amused,' selecting the relevant German cliché, because that was how German discourse worked, at least for him, the foreigner: he simply had to select the correct cliché and repeat it to the citizens of his adopted home who would then applaud its reproduction. He saw all this and more. But what he still couldn't quite work out was why Claudia had given him the theatre in the first place. Why? Why had she? He pondered it as the song coursed through his head again, wondering what she had seen as he crouched before her in the hotel room so very tired – broken, even.

It was only later, too much later in fact, that he realized that Claudia, seeing the trajectory of his life more clearly than he, its liver, ever could, had given him the theatre as a joke; and it was these cosmic jokes, jokes for their own sake, which the Germans did so well and which were perhaps the funniest of them all.

And there came that incredible intro once again. It really was tremendously exciting how the bassline came in, and the singer sang.

He listened.

And there was Stuart listening to the music inside, on his back on his bed, in raptures, ready to catch his lucky break.

INTERVAL

You could see the bar all the way up the street, its lit front, its plastic furniture. There was even a bench still outside though more forgotten than placed, this being the deepest part of winter. This was the time when you entered bars from the cold and suddenly found large rooms of people talking, as if mutually waiting the winter out together. This was the time when spring felt furthest away.

On the stage Dwight was talking. He was bearded tonight, his facial hair a fair barometer of his recurrent attempts to reform himself; often he would appear at the nights he hosted – and there were many – clean-shaven, fresh-shirted, to announce that he had either quit drinking or was moving back to New York or both.

But even if he had tried he couldn't leave; he belonged here, in this netherworld, in the comic potentate he had created and now himself administered. In Berlin he could be free. And though he had work the next day, designing avatars for relentlessly violent online games, he would almost certainly be at Poe's Bar for another five hours yet, standing on the plastic furniture, coordinating the vodka shots and generally presiding over the customary later Bacchanalian turn of this evening, the Tuesday-night Open Mic. Of which Dwight was singing the theme tune now.

It's the Poe's Bar

Open mic

Get on the stage

Do what you like

Colin sat murmuring along, one of the quietest voices, but definitely one which knew the words. There were about ten people in the room, slumped around on the orange chairs, indolent, along with the newcomer at the bar. A young man, he wore a black suit and held a long drink in a whiskey glass at the top of which an olive sat. Poe, the bartender, would have delighted in laying that olive; he for his part stood a little back, in black trousers and white shirt, a cloth hung over his shoulder as he watched and laughed at Dwight's excessive sallies.

'Herpes!' Dwight was saying. 'Her pees! They call it that because it hurts her pees. My God that was awful, somebody kill me. Oh my God this is going wrong.

What do I care, there's like ten people here. What do you think random German guy? What's your name? Torsten, OK Torsten, I cannot pronounce your German name so I'm going to call you Bob. Is that OK? Good Bob. I think we are going to be very nice friends. OK – listen up everybody 'cos I have an actual joke now. I want to start a German dishwasher firm called *Ich liebe dishes*. You know when I first came to Germany I was actually dating this German girl called Agathe – and Agathe was blonde and beautiful and we had period sex, I don't know what that is in German, *Blutzeitficken* or whatever, and, she used to say, *you know Dwight, you are a very nice guy and ich liebe dich*. And I'd be like: Who's Dick? I mean, do you love him more than me?

'It's good that you're laughing. That makes this all so much easier. Are you guys ready for your next act? He's a very good friend of mine.'

The next act was Stuart Holmes, a glum-looking Englishman who had a bit of a reputation around these parts and was apparently permanently on the verge of leaving town; he was also notable for being just about the only man in Berlin who wore a collar shirt. Tonight he was working on material about toothbrushes, and their incorporation into relationships; it was funny enough, but Colin was more just enjoying being stoned, the marijuana sitting either on top or below of the alcohol, depending on how you thought of things. Colin was also thinking vaguely about his music career, though he didn't like to call it that; he had been gigging all autumn and was starting to learn this season's recurring characters; the tattooed girl who kept returning to Canada and returning back, the long-term

British Berliners who wore black T-Shirts and insisted they were integrated even when sitting in expat bars, and the enormous blonde Germans who hung out with the English speakers and laughed at all the right moments a second too late.

Colin noticed too how much he had been drinking. Drinking in the week, entering nightly vortexes of alcohol which robbed him of whole weekdays, repeatedly, drinking at the weekends which saw him making his way to his shared flat as dawn cracked over Prenzlauer Berg. He was 33, which would have been problematic elsewhere, not that he was telling anyone here, certainly not the impregnable chain-smoking barmaid who sat impassive behind the counter and with whom he had slept twice, each of them a mistake. It was bohemia, lost time, or found time you could say, as when he had an early flight back to England and instead of going to bed, spent the whole night through at the club Berghain. Why not get what you could out of life? Why not live in Berlin?

'OK,' Dwight was saying. 'OK Big German guy. Okay random Italian students. Are you guys ready for your next musical act? Yeah? This guy's a favourite here at Poe's bar. So I want you to give him a really warm Poe's Bar welcome – starting at the back – and going to the front - for Colin Heinrich Wilson!'

Colin was already making his way to the stage. Dwight was still up there smiling, the beer-stained American leaning down to briefly loudly whisper, 'Attaboy!' You could smell the beer on his beard. Colin's guitar was propped up at the side of the stage, and as he leant down to retrieve it he smiled, there being no need for an amp in this tiny room.

'Everyone alright?' said Colin. 'Good. I'm having a bit of a crazy week – it's Tuesday and I've been out three times already. Not sure how that happened. Anyway, this is a song by a German guy called Joachim Witt with new words.'

He began to strum, his hands moving through the few simple chords with ease, minor G, B flat major, F, repeat. Then he began to sing.

'On the outskirts
Before the start of the town
There's a plastic-surgery clinic
You'll not find the like around

The town's tourist centres
It can easily outclass
And if your nerves are faulty
They'll make you a new man'

A firm stroke and onto the chorus.

'Hey hey hey I was the middle-aged singer
Hey hey hey I'm a child of this town
Hey hey hey I was so far up the river

But then I came down

Then I came down'

Back to the verse.

'On my way to the clinic

I saw the lights shining all around

They burned like coals in my eyes

I felt so lonely - I felt a clown

Hey hey hey...'

By the time he had sung the chorus through again some of the audience was clapping; some of the Germans were smiling, but they didn't join in. It was enough for them to be registered as present.

Colin finished, to a smattering of polite applause. 'C'mon, it was better than that' he said. The audience returned a laugh and a question.

'What's that? Yeah, I actually translated it myself.'

There was a whoop from the audience. Peter, the rotund rugger-bugger Englishman who usually made an appearance around now, had indeed surfaced and was saying loudly to his thin neighbour, 'He's amazing, right? Isn't he amazing?'

'It's no big deal,' Colin said, and then to Dwight, 'Two

songs right? Right. I don't know why I asked that, I'm here every week. I think if Lou fucking Reed showed up here he'd get two songs. Anyway, this is another German song by a guy called Herman Brood – he was Dutch actually, he lived in Berlin for a long time. He was actually a heroin addict and then a few years ago he threw himself off the roof off the Amsterdam Hilton. Yeah, heavy. Anyway the song's called *'Berlin Schmerzt'* in German but this is my own version.'

Colin paused. "Berlin Wounds."

'I still have a suitcase in Berlin

That's why I'll keep going

I'm homesick for Mehringdamm

Berliner Tempo, music and drag

Kreuzberg waiting at Mustafa's Kebab

Neue Welle washed up long ago

Come little man why you looking at me

The world's spinning outside

Just like back home in E17

Why are you weeping new Berliner

Tonight we're going again

Fresh faces and dark history in Friedrichshain

Everything'll be dandy, just not

Just not for our dreams

Your 20s go so quickly

Like the streams in Tarkovsky films

The chorus.

Berlin wounds

Berlin wounds

Berlin wounds

Berlin wounds'

He played the outro and, with a palm, stilled the echo of the final chords. There was a deep silence in the room before the applause began.

'Thanks guys,' Colin said. 'I've got some CDs at the bar, if I remembered to bring them. Have a good rest of the week.' He was interrupted. 'How much? Three euros I think. But make me an offer.' Then he made his way from the stage, smirking.

The applause continued as he did so, and he bowed his head a little, noting the diminutive blonde at the table who didn't smile at him in a way which somehow conveyed her attraction. Or was Colin imagining things? What he wasn't imagining was Peter who, as he passed, put one enormous hand around Colin's head and pushed it towards his ribcage, saying in a quite but most intent voice, 'You hurt me. You hurt me.'

'Who likes anal sex?' Dwight was back. Peter released his headlock and made a loud moaning noise. 'I know you do Planetoid. You *are* anal sex.' The insult made no real sense but something about its timing provoked the biggest laugh of the night so far. In response Peter emitted his catchphrase donkey moan, followed by a cricketing bellow of 'You sir!'

'OK quit laughing assholes. You guys ready for your next act?' A small roar. 'You are *clearly* ready for your next act! Well that next act is all the way from London. Let it never be said that we are not international at Poe's Bar. So ladies and gentleman, give a big central Berlin welcome to – Mr. Teddy. Fist!'

The tall stranger from the bar milled through the crowd to the stage. There were a few more people now. You could see his full elegance now; the black suit trousers, suit jacket over the white T-shirt, and the hair. Also his youth; his skin was smooth as gel. He took with him onto the stage a small case which he laid down next to the stool and, bending down, took from it a tiny instrument. Colin's eyes narrowed as he did and as Teddy turned back to the audience the thought swam up in him, 'Not another fucking ukulele.' For they were everywhere in the early 2010s, ukuleles; at weddings, on adverts, at every open-mike, soundtracking the age with their perky toy-like strum. Once, long ago, they had been cool.

Teddy spoke. 'I'm actually German,' he said in a clear, and clearly feigned, East London accent, at which everyone laughed. 'I'm not really,' Teddy said and, after more laughter, took an iPhone from his pocket and laid it on the stool. Teddy scrolled around at it for a minute, broad face above the slim device. 'I always fuck this up,' he said and then laughed nervously himself, before at last 'Got it' he said.

He was rehearsed, was Teddy, every ramble calculated, every vagueness tested. You couldn't pinpoint exactly what he was trying to be, just that he was exactly it, and had decided young. 'OK – I'm going to play my songs together,' he said, and then 'Hope this works.' He hit the screen of his iPhone from which the techno-infused peal of a mariachi band arose, followed by a snatched, shouted 'Ja!' as Teddy began to strike familiar chords on his ukulele.

The smartphone was emitting an electric *boomchika* beat, a powerful one occasionally collapsing into little shards of percussion, while Teddy sang of that sweet taste of love. His voice was dark, fruity, rich, like an unexpectedly mannered bouncer at a London pub. And as Teddy sang Colin thought on England, its dense rows of homes, its stout, private gardens. He saw the sun beating on the window of the central office where he had worked there, before he had come to Berlin, before... On Teddy sang.

The beat was segueing now, transforming itself, and suddenly it stuttered into a series of notes; *dum dum dum de de dum dum, dum dum dum de de dum dum...*

There was a wild scream from the audience; it was Peter, who was now yelling, 'Holy shit!' Teddy was focused; people were into it. The first girls got up to dance.

Suddenly the beat burst into a little crystal shower of smaller beats, like a party popper exploding, and Teddy shouted a cappella

'Altogether!' he shouted.

And they sang the chorus back: It was 'Just Can't Get Enough' by Depeche Mode.

All around the people were dancing now, and Teddy too, throwing and twisting moves on the stage, the beat trundling into life again. All eyes focused on him, Teddy bounded from the stage, into the crowd, wiggling at a small Italian girl, bouncing arses with the lanky German. 'Yeah!' shouted Peter. Teddy made his way through the room, the beat continuing on stage, now towards the bar, a small line of dancing people following him as he moved out, still singing loudly as he made his groovy way out onto the cold street.

Poe was laughing, preparing a drink for Teddy's return. Peter was just standing there braying into the air, 'My God! My God! Jesus!'. Dwight had already regained the stage and the microphone, saying to those left, 'Wow! Pretty amazing huh? Give it up for Teddy Fist.' Who you could still see through the window, talking to the gathered crowd outside, playing another song on the ukulele, jiving in the freezing night.

At the end of each Poe's Bar Open Mic one of the performers won a bottle of the bars own brew 'Chafe' vodka, a truly noxious concoction of chillies and pure alcohol. Tonight there was no real question as to its recipient. 'Ladies and gentlemen – Teddy Fist!' Teddy took the bottle and the applause again and, as he and Dwight left together the latter said to him in a low voice 'You share it with everyone, that's how it works.'

Colin sat at the bar as Teddy poured out the liquid into about twenty plastic shots, laughing as the audience members came to help themselves. Free alcohol. After the last was gone, Teddy sat back at the bar himself, taking the shot and, with a look to Dwight, Peter and Colin around him, downed it. 'God – that's disgusting,' Teddy said.

'Yeah, it's a speciality,' said Colin.

'I need a poo,' said Peter, and kept standing there.

'Great,' said Teddy. He put the shot down and offered Colin his large hand. 'Really enjoyed your stuff, mate.'

'Thanks, you too,' said Colin.

'So you live here?'

'Yeah.'

'It's great here isn't it? I mean it really is.'

'I like it.'

'I mean, I've only been here a few days but it seems like such a fun town. You just feel so free here. Like I could, I don't know, take a shit on the street or something and no one would care. Ha! I'm playing a few shows, right, I've got one on Sunday at – is it Dub Club? Bud Club, right. Yeah, I've been having a great trip.'

'So do you do music full time?'

'Trying to mate, trying to. I mean I've signed a record deal and I've got a manager and everything – but London's tough, you know? You're from there, right. It's a slog mate. I mean, just that I was given that free vodka then, you know? That would never have happened in London. Never in a million years.'

As Teddy spoke Colin realized he was younger than he

had thought, just in his early twenties. He suddenly seemed like some suit-wearing extra in a production of Bugsy Malone. Colin smirked at the thought; at the bar, Maurice and Peter were engaged in some form of hug.

'So do you find it easy to get opportunities here?' Teddy was saying.

'It's OK. Well – it's a bit of a Catch 22 really. You know, it's really easy to get attention, but it doesn't go anywhere. It's sort of like working in a small Royal Court. One of the 18th-century Grand Duchies, you know? I keep thinking about going back to London actually.'

'I wouldn't do that,' said Teddy quite seriously. 'No – I definitely would not do that. London's really hard. Everyone's really depressed; there's a recession on. Do you do music full time?'

'I teach English. That's what most people do here. They teach English, or they translate, or both.'

'Oh that's good. I'm crap at languages,' said Teddy.

'But everyone in England says they're crap at languages. Surely we can't all be?'

A girl had approached them at the bar. She had a nose and tongue piercing and a German accent. 'I was wondering – do you have a CD?' she said to Teddy.

'Yeah I do,' Teddy said. He reached next to him on the bar.

'How much is it?'

'Nah it's alright,' Teddy said. 'That's for you.'

She laughed. 'Thanks.'

Colin caught a glimpse of the CD; it was Teddy with his ukulele on an arena stage.

'I was on the X-Factor,' Teddy said. 'I got to the semi-finals. I did the same thing you saw tonight. Just like ironic cover versions. God, I can't believe I just said that. But yeah, I did play to an audience of 20,000 people. It's actually really easy, because if a small part of the audience likes you, that's still a huge crowd.'

'But you didn't get through.'

'There were these teenage girls dancing,' said Teddy. 'They were like elastic the way they moved. Moving round in a little synchronized herd. Like aliens.'

At this point, Peter had begun to move a few steps away from them, moving to the music coming over the bar's speakers.

'Hey,' said Teddy, looking at Peter.

Peter looked at him. His head tilted forward. 'You hurt us,' he said.

Teddy looked at Colin. 'Is that good?' he asked.

Colin nodded. 'It's his compliment.'

Peter looked over at him, and said again, 'This guy. This guy hurt us.'

'He did,' Colin replied. Next to him Teddy was laughing hysterically; the girl moved away.

Peter spoke to Colin now. 'You hurt us too. You hurt us! But he, he *really* hurt us.' And then he moved to take the two men into his enormous beer-scented embrace, pushing the two musicians together in a little bundle of straggly hair, Teddy laughing louder and louder as the armpits closed in.

Another night at Poe's began to wear on. The conscientious attendees left, the hardcore established itself and stayed. And as ever a few waverers were sucked into the murk, avowing their midnight beer would be their last before being sighted again an hour later doing shots with people who had only recently been strangers to each other. Velasquez showed up, a thin-faced Venezuelan who lived just round the corner and changed into rockabilly clothes after work. He entered the bar with a calculated Fonzy 'Hey guys', but was soon arguing with Poe about some recent slight. Stuart was last seen drinking his one too many with Dwight saying to him, 'I can't get my cat joke to work,' before eventually and smilingly parting by giving Dwight a fierce bear hug. After which Dwight for his strolled around the bar like a satyr encouraging various girls to sleep with him and somehow remembered the line he was spinning with each, like some industrious hairy sex spider.

Colin was down in the toilets, toilets which were genuinely sordid, two tiny little cubicles next to a pitch-black, unused dancefloor. There was a strong odour of faeces. Colin had his nose under the cold tap and as he raised his face it was hard not to look in the mirror. There was no doubt, he thought, looking at his cheek veins, his sunk sockets, the aftershocks of a recent shave, that he was aging. He was not handsome anymore but somehow felt only he had noticed yet. Somewhere this winter he had become stuck in a Dantean loop, getting up each night to play gigs whose modest proceeds he reinvested in alcohol the same evening. Occasionally he would meet hale-faced Germans in boardrooms and attempt to insinuate a respectability to the rest of his life. 'You're a musician?' he heard Herr Bielmann saying now and could he live from it? No, but he could live *for* it.

Teddy had appeared behind him. 'Man, it really stinks of shit down here.'

Colin turned.

'I look like a vampire,' Colin said.

'Are you?' Teddy said.

'No, I'm just in my 30s,' Colin replied.

Teddy gave a little uneasy laugh. 'In London everyone'd be home by now. I can't believe this place. Fucking wild. Really man, again, honestly, really enjoyed your songs.'

'I'm glad.'

'You should be playing bigger rooms than this, you know.'

'I would like to.' Colin stood up. 'But you know.'

'What?'

'You know.'

'The second song – what was that called?'

'Berlin Wounds. I mean, *Berlin Schmerzt* is the German.'

'What's the German?'

Colin repeated the words.

'*Berlin smertz*. Sounds so cool. I'd like to do a cover of it.

'You would.'

'Yeah, I actually really liked it. I mean, when you were playing I thought, someone should cover some German songs and do them in English, that'd be amazing.'

Colin said, 'Yeah, that's an idea.'

Teddy nodded. 'Say – how about we meet up tomorrow? You can bring the lyrics to the songs and we can record them.'

Colin smiled.

'Come on man. I can take them back to the record company, and we can get them released. Do an album like – Teddy Fist Sings Berlin. What do you think?'

Colin paused. Finally, 'I'm teaching tomorrow,' he said.

'No problem, I'm here till Friday.' Teddy looked around. 'Go for this whole you know Weimar Cabaret vibe. "Live in Poe's Bar". Well, maybe not that but I mean, this place is amazing. It actually has red curtains! Where has red curtains these days?'

'Funeral parlours,' said Colin. 'Please.'

Colin stepped out to the dancefloor and Teddy took his place in the bog. As Colin stepped away Teddy turned back to catch him. 'Well – take my card anyway,' he said.

Teddy reached his card towards Colin, who stood smiling, not taking the proffered square.

'What?' said Teddy.

Colin nodded.

'You're not going to take it?'

Colin said nothing.

'Why are you being like this?'

There was a pause.

'Don't you want to collaborate?'

'I don't want to collaborate.'

'Is this about money? I'll give you a credit, of course I will.'

'It's not about money.'

'This will open a lot of doors for you. I know people in London mate. I know the President of EMI.'

'Fantastic,' said Colin. 'It's got to be nice for you to have those kinds of contacts. I'm sure you'll do very well. You're really talented. But this - is *Berlin*. Alright? Now come on; let's go and join the party.'

Teddy stared at him for a moment, the frowning young face younger and more anxious than ever. He looked about fourteen. 'I don't get it,' he finally said. 'Why don't you want to hang out?'

The two men emerged into the front of the bar which was almost empty now. Moritz had poured himself a red wine. On the stage, an informal show had developed. Velasquez was playing fluent flamenco guitar and singing while behind him Peter was dancing with the lanky German, both of them now shirtless. For some reason every few bars the men were shouting 'Like a pony!' Teddy crossed over to the front of the stage and took up his drink, defeated. Dwight, near the centre of the room, looked over to the silent Colin.

'Hey Col, we're doing an aftershow! You want to do a couple more songs? Sure you do! Attaboy!'

Colin looked over to the audience, which now consisted of three Italian exchange students and a single man sleeping. 'Sure,' he said. He walked over to the stage to retrieve his guitar from against the wall, and when he turned back, tuning, he saw Teddy was already leaving, walking out into the cold alone, at which sight Colin himself turned back to play to his friends, to plunge once more into Berlin's world-class nightlife.

PART TWO

I. THE BERLIN EQUATION

The world is a most unsentimental place. It is intensely unavailable for comment, with a tendency to continue come what may. So it is with the end of love, even of great love. How interesting it is to live in a time where the inseparable has become separated, where two lovers who wanted to spend forever together have failed after a mere few years, where people who really should have had beautiful children together have had none and instead embarked on separate lives, invisible to each other and, at least for his part, unsure as to the extent to which their lost partner even still imagined them.

As such, and to turn to a specific case, it was with great surprise that Dave received Anna's mail informing him she would be in Luxembourg at the end of February and asking him if he would like to meet. He would, but didn't know if he should, so deferred on replying. In the year since their break up the wounds had healed about as well they might be expected to – enough, anyway, to weather the news of her impending marriage and, he presumed, her subsequent pregnancy. All summer the thought of her conceiving had been like a gun held to his head. It was nauseating waiting for someone to procreate, especially as, as he sat there in his jogging bottoms holding a teacup, there seemed to be no evidence of imminent reproduction round his parts.

He wished he had the ability to incorporate time travel into his relationships. When she turned to him, in front of a sunset, and cooed, 'I will love you forever' – which meant she would love this moment forever – there would be a puff of smoke up ahead. His future self would emerge and say, head very still, 'You'll break up in seven months.'

'Who is this?' she'd ask.

'I don't know,' he'd say. 'It looks like me with greyer hair.'

'I'm your future self,' the older man would say, 'and I'm here to save you a lot of bother. You're going to break up down the line and it's going to hurt; break up now, at this perfect moment, and spare yourselves a lot of grief.'

After a pause he'd reply, 'But future me, breaking up now is a logical impossibility. If we'd have broken up now you wouldn't have had to have come from the future and as such we couldn't be having this conversation.'

Another pause. His future self shook his head, observing: 'I finally understand what Facebook means by "It's complicated".'

Despite the email it seemed best not to reply, to appear overeager, and besides he had rehearsal today. At the moment he was taking on the role of Jake in a film adaption at the city's one English language theatre. Said theatre was within walking distance of his house but somehow this proximity only facilitated his greater lateness.

Berlin had been his city and occupation for his adult life. He knew these streets so well and indeed, after initial dreams of Berlin as point of disembarkation for a world tour, his life had contracted to what he now knew as the Golden Square. This meant *Bergmannstraße* at the top, *Gneisenaustraße* at the bottom and *Zossenerstraße* and *Mehringdamm* forming the bookends. In this square could be found all that he needed in life; supermarkets, a cinema, delis and a swingers club which he had never visited. The English theatre was to the geographical south of said square and as such non-essential. You could live many years without English theatre.

He was passing his local bar, *Kollo*, the red sign bright against the rapidly-darkening sky. As his life continued, as relationships ended, as he aged a little, he surprised himself with his capacity to drink at the same places, to simply brush down his lap and start again. Two summers ago, he had sat there with Anna and good red wine and toasted their future plans together. Yet just months later he was there once again there with friends and surprised himself at the joy he had felt just to return, drinking on the candlelit tables in the early-autumn chill. Maybe good bars were harder to find than good love affairs.

He had arrived in Berlin for some obscure reason, some attraction to the idea of the city, and was continually resolving to leave it. But celebrity had found him: local, unobtrusive celebrity, that of say somebody who ran a shop with guide-book featured coffee, but celebrity nonetheless. About two years ago he had begun a daily newsletter to his friends, headed at that time simply 'Bad News,' with a quote from Camus on the letterhead;

'The principle question of philosophy is whether to commit suicide.' In the letter he had compiled evidence of the suffering and pain of the world: dog savagings, women found rotted in London flats, viral strains mutating to antibiotic resistance. Of course, most media news was already bad, but he really furrowed, went to the lengths of obscurity – searching YouTube to find images of people bitten by spiders, reading the obituaries of the most obscure provincial newspapers to learn of the premature deaths of local youths. And after all this, his friends told him, his newsletter had a cathartic effect, expressed some longing in them for despondency merited and rare, and they forwarded it.

Soon the newsletter was going small-scale viral and he began to amass a gigantic mailing list. He consulted his friends as to whether they would like to see a daily version and, receiving an equivocal yes, contacted a graphic designer to create a cool beige interface. Within this form the worst could be exhibited. Add some limited advertising revenue, mainly at first from heavy metal nightclubs and tattoo parlours and, one year ago, the newly christened 'Misanthrope's Digest' was born.

It now boasted 50,000 subscribers worldwide. People from all over the world ordered and forwarded his email compendium of the worst the world had to offer; accordingly, advertising revenues, as well as the workload, increased. It had quite the cachet for a band or book to be given a mention on the Digest and, now more than ever, he received enquires to use his list in exchange for useful sums, which he inevitably accepted.

Of course, it was difficult for him to do the research.

He was tested as he waded through reports of prison rape, dictatorial cruelty and the inability of turtles to lay their eggs in sand overheated by climate change. But he was the man to do it, especially with his current deadness; only he could traverse the Internet with such glassy remove. As for the rest of his money, with a little acting – he had trained as an actor for a term before arriving in Berlin – copy-editing and teaching the odd German 'Imaginative Skills', he could live comfortably as a Berlin 'artist:' A mildly dissatisfied, undertaxed young creative in the city of Berlin.

He was ascending the hill to *Fidicinstraße* where the English theatre stood. Anna had not liked the Digest, even as acquaintances flocked around them to heat their hands on the tiny sliver of his fame, a sliver which shone amongst Berlin's swamp of obscurity. She couldn't understand why he would want to devote so much time to the misery of the world. He didn't tell her about the times he had received mails from people saying the Digest had helped them through their own sadness, disillusionment, sense of redundancy. 'A large percentage of my readers are in the United States,' he said. 'I'm admitting the sadness their culture won't.'

'There's plenty of sadness in the U.S.!'

'Yes, but it gets lost in all the 'rugged optimists' bullshit. It's much more acceptable to be sad here, to think life is intrinsically sad.'

'And that's why you want to stay in Europe? For the sadness?'

'I do think the sadness is better in Europe, yes,' he said.

'But why would you want to be sad?'

'I don't. I'm quite happy. I just don't think it's a problem if I am, that's all. When my mother died I didn't need pills, or a doctor. I just needed to be sad.'

'I know that. You let time do its work.'

'Right. You respect your wounds.'

They had this conversation at the window of his small apartment, looking over the courtyard in a dull grey afternoon. It was February and neither of them had to work.

'Did you listen to my songs?' she said, raising her coffee cup.

'Yes, I did,' he said.

'And?'

'I think they're sad. You had your heart broken?'

'Sure,' she said. 'You heard them!'

'And didn't you sort of enjoy it?'

She gave a very dry smile, taking a step closer. 'Do you want to go for a walk?'

'I would, but I have to do my Digest…'

'Oh, because they're so waiting for it.'

'You'd be surprised. Monday morning is one of our most popular days.'

By then the Digest already had 3,000 subscribers and he despaired of it. Warhol had been right that in the future, everyone would be famous for fifteen minutes, failing to add only that nobody would get paid for it.

'I don't know, *gloomy Gus*. I think you might just be

bored.'

'You think?'

'Yeah, I think you're bored of Berlin.' She went on, 'I think you're too good for Berlin, too.'

'Maybe. But I'm not unhappy. And that's because of you. I mean it – you really cheer me up.'

She smiled. 'That's adorable,' she said, and gave him one of her trademark kisses, small, clean and precise.

He could still feel the ghost of it now as he walked into the theatre. 'I think you'd like it in the States,' he could hear her going on.

'And if I don't?'

'We'll work it out – we'll find somewhere. I'm sure there's a place for us two in this world.'

'But where?'

In the rehearsal room Jakob Denisovic sat alone, forlornly eating a sandwich amongst the empty seats; he came and sat a few rows lower down from his director.

'Privjet, Dave,' said Jakob.

'Privjet, Jakob,' he replied. Jakob had taught him some Russian phrases.

'So where is everybody?' he asked.

'This scene just you and Laura. Laura is not here and you are –' Denisovic looked at his cheap phone – 'fifteen minutes late. We cannot act without you both. Do you want sandwich?'

'No, I'm alright thanks. *Ee ty – kak dela*?'

'*Normalna. No, znayesh, sevodnya chut-chut gruzni.* Homesick.'

'Really – despite everything?'

'Because everything!' Jakob went on. 'I think it would be good if Putin died. If I were in Russia, I could kill him. But not here.'

'No, here the opportunities are limited.'

'I wonder how I kill fucker Putin! Perhaps with firm blow to testicles. Mister President! Then he will cry like wounded child.'

He was laughing at good, outrageous Jakob.

'Tell you what. Why don't we cancel rehearsal today and go kill Putin?'

At the moment Laura entered, flustered-looking and apparently at war with her bag.

'Sorry, sorry,' she said.

'No rehearsal today,' said Jakob.

'What? But –'

'We're going to go kill Putin,' he said.

'Oh, right,' she said, moving to sit at the table set up on the stage. 'Listen, I learnt the scene in advance...'

'OK, OK,' said Jakob. 'Let us start. Putin lives another day, I guess. Dave – ready?'

He went down to the stage and prepared for his entry line. Laura took up position at the bar.

He entered; Laura, cast as Sam, asked him what he wanted to drink. He looked around the imaginary bar.

'Scotch,' he said.

'Not bad,' said Jakob. 'But less – Billy Big Bollocks, yes? More like the man with no balls.'

He paused. 'You mean… weaker?

'Yes, yes! More weary, more life-castrated. You know what I mean. This is life, Dave!'

Laura looked at him. 'What it'll be Jake?'

She poured him another shot of water and he moved to the table, looking up at her to give her the next line. 'Of all the bars in all the world…'

'Fine!' Jakob stood up noisily. 'Take break! Five minutes we run whole scene.'

He moved over to Laura, attractive in a Joy Division T-Shirt.

'How are you?'

'Oh, I'm alright,' she said. 'Having a bit of a time of it actually. Finding it a bit difficult to get out of bed in the morning you know, not having any reason to do so and what have you. Weren't you supposed to be leaving?'

'Yes,' he smiled.

'Oh right – I thought you…'

'I was gone for a few weeks. But I missed the Berlin lifestyle.'

'Yes, I can see why it might be appealing…' She looked around. 'I'm thinking of going home.'

'For good?'

'Just for a few weeks, see what happens you know.'

'Sooner or later everyone leaves,' he said. 'Do you know what the Germans say? *Wer nicht weiß, was er will, geht nach Berlin.*'

'What does that mean?'

'People who don't know what they want go to Berlin.'

'Oh.' She seemed taken aback by it. 'Do they say that?'

Jakob entered and clapped his hands. '*Horosho*! We ready to run shitty play again.'

'We sure are!' he said, rising to his feet. Before him he saw Laura, having a moment of young female confusion, the Berlin lostness, the expat malady.

In the mid-2000s, people from all over Europe, primarily young, flooded to Berlin to make albums, write novels, concentrate on their creativity. They came to Berlin because the rents were cheap. But here the paradoxes began: the city had no money for art and certainly not in languages other than German, while only a minority of said expats took the trouble to learn said tongue, balking at a language with sixteen different ways of saying 'the.' After a few years most of them returned to their home countries, discouraged, or stayed too long, plunging themselves into an underworld of drugs and sex clubs. Those integrating, for their part, disappeared into regular, uninspiring jobs, which, by the way, they were very grateful to have. He had friends as proud to be secretaries in Berlin as they would to be lawyers back home.

But he – where was he in this equation? He had done his years of drinking, made a moderate success – and was still here.

In Berlin there was room to experiment. Unimaginable room; great parts of the city still stood empty. London had put a premium on space, and in New York the occupation of a private park had presented an act of cultural radicalism. One evening recently Jakob was telling them of his plans to deliberately direct a show badly. 'I will! I do everything against my instincts, misdirect, make all stupid! Fuck success! Because who knows, maybe I am frequently wrong. Maybe this way I will stumble upon inadvertent genius. Maybe I am bad director and will become, by doing this, good.'

Thing was, in Berlin Jakob could actually try this and whatever the outcome continue working. And a very serious young man from a Berlin newspaper – even newspapers had some dwindling afterlife here – would come interview him about his *Konzept* – in which interview Jakob, being Russian, would be expected to speak German, unlike the Anglophones who got a free pass – and print it up without a red cent changing hands. One hundred people, mostly friends, would turn up to the opening, after which Jakob would declare great plans for tours and revivals while earning his beer money for the week. That was the Berlin bargain: you could get them done, your wildest dreams, albeit on the cheap – but you would never earn a living doing it.

Tolstoy, a believer that all art should remain amateur, would have approved. But despite the success of the Digest, Dave was getting tired of the bargain – and also of saying goodbye to a thousand Lauras, getting tired of men like Jakob whose talent was impossible to prove in the vacuum of creative infrastructure in which they lived and worked.

So when Anna asked him if he wanted to live in the U.S. he said yes. He felt ready for a change, and he loved his American girlfriend, with her goofy Midwestern mannerisms and deep random melancholy and thought that, if it produced such people, the U.S. couldn't be half bad. Of course, the choice of location, Austin, Texas, wouldn't necessarily have been his first but he had heard great things about the place and, in an encouraging sign, a translator friend of his had moved there after her years in Berlin.

Later, as he walked over the longest road he had ever seen on one of the smallest pavements, and realized people did not walk in this country, to the extent that walking had become a political action, fired on by countless activists who had blogs called things like 'Walk Austin' and fought furiously for their right to totter along in a straight line, where groups of armoured cyclists filmed themselves on high-quality digital mini-cameras as they inaugurated additional strips of pavement or when he, standing in a Wholefoods store, flashed back to images of Albert Speer's plans for Germania, did he realize that the city of Austin, and by extension the state of Texas itself, was likely for him a personal hell.

They had gone there in May and the heat was sweltering. Even if there had been walking infrastructure you wouldn't have been able to. On the way there had been some residual romanticism to the trip, recalling those American girls with whom he flirted at parties who, when they spoke, evoked stretches of unimaginable vastness, denoted by tribal names evocative to him in their unfamiliarity: Wisconsin, Illinois, Ohio. And Texas – even Texas, a place without boundaries, Lone Star shining, and Austin the little liberal island within it. Only it didn't look like that in reality. It looked like a post-industrial nightmare, a sea of concrete, sun-burnt gas stations where pop tarts were vended and air conditioning blasted your skull.

Certainly you could join the SUVs and pick-ups and follow the freeway out into nature. But it was scorched nature, burnt nature, tarantula down your trousers nature. It was a confidence trick based on ventilation to live here at all and those who did, including Anna's family, seemed both alien and exuberant. How amusing it must have been to them to watch him struggle. He could see the slightly baffled violence in Uncle Jack's eyes, the visible intake of breath when Anna's Dad got his confession that he didn't have a driving license. Oh, he did his best, but he felt small and shrivelled in the States and it was strange to watch Anna, always somewhat cowed in Germany, become limber and assertive in her homeland. It was in the way she talked to waitresses, made use of special offers, or explained to sales clerks the meanings of their own German surnames. Her time abroad had distinguished her from the average American.

Meanwhile he fled from the sales clerks and forlornly counted Smart Cars. There was one a day at best. And they were still cars; it was unfathomable to him, a society based on the automobile, a society where the simple pleasures of walking and congregating outside had been denied to the populace by the way things had been built, this environment where you spent your time either at home, work or driving in between. And yet he liked Americans! He liked them! He didn't understand why their country – or at least this part of their country – had this effect on him.

He was lying in bed, leafing through a Spanish dictionary, as she entered.

'Listen,' he said quietly. 'I don't think I'm going to be able to do this.'

'I figured,' she said.

'I'm really sorry.'

'No. Thing is – I don't really like it here either.'

'Really?'

'I like it more than you, and I can drive, but it feels kind of small. Obviously it's nice to be near my family.'

He found it odd to see this person, so clear in memory from those February talks in Berlin, in such a strange and unknown place. It was strange, this, how relationships could be wonderful right up until the moment you discussed the big problem, like when you remember bad news when drunk.

'We could divide our time,' she said. 'Live in Berlin in the summer and...'

'I have no interest in living here,' he said.

'Right.' She nodded. 'Then we have to find somewhere else.'

To their credit they tried. They loved each other, they really did, and saw futures together, little mental oases amidst their many struggles. He for his part plunged into research, and she remarked that more and more items on the Digest, itself growing in popularity in her country, related to the United States. He now realized that from that night in Austin as they had lain in the heat listening to the exhausting suburban freeway they were still together but had begun letting go of each other, a funeral procession to the moment when they finally parted, albeit one done in the brightest of liveries.

Next Chicago in early June. She had just returned from a run and was adjusting her bicycle against the wall when he spoke. It was their second attempt to live together in the United States.

'I don't think it works for me here, Anna.'

He had been there almost four weeks, ostensibly looking for a job – although with customary U.S. friendliness you were warned entering the country you were not allowed to – but in reality working through her extensive library and watching football online. Everything important to him, everything he valued - languages, cycling, socialism, the treatment of sadness not as a disease but part of human life - felt worthless here, and he himself trapped, a little husk of Europe accidentally forgotten and brought home at the bottom of a moving box. Without gaining much sense of them he walked the Chicago streets, beneath the rusted underpasses, past the sprinklered lawns. People greeted him. What was he interested in? Renewable energy and world politics. Did he know the Mayor has solar panels on his roof? Meanwhile, the summer wore on; he wrote, read, and day by day worked up to uttering the rejection he had just pronounced.

Hearing it, she broke off from leaning the bike; her face, still sweaty from her run, blanched a little. Then she crinkled her nose and walked through to her bedroom. In a moment he heard the notes of the keyboard sounding, and he rose, standing a moment before going through.

She was seated at the table spreading her hands very softly on the keys. He paused at the entrance and leant back against the wall, looking at her where she sat. The first time he had seen her she had been onstage, singing in a bar owned by a friend of hers, face soft beneath the bright lamps. That night she had told him of her plans to leave and they had made jokes and later, sang together. Then they had begun a love based on a deep love of the same things and a hatred of certain others.

Anna would sing to him often and once ended a conversation with a perfectly trilled 'I love you' down the phone. Now she was playing 'Hey Love,' one of his favourite of her songs, singing;

'Hey love, what you doing round the house?

Were you out playing catch with your friends again?

Hey love, so good to see you

Didn't know you'd be dropping by today.

Hey love – why you looking so sad?

Is it because you know what lovers think when they say?

Don't be sad love, we know what we're doing
Everyone down here knows they're playing a game.

Hey love, sit down beside me
Let me sing you the truth in a song my friend
There's no use weeping, I knew she was leaving
I guess you think you let me down again.'

He nodded, moved, as the notes stilled. 'I'm really sorry,' he said.

And how he was. Is it really necessary to tell of how they parted? How she threw her hands to him, how they kissed at the airport after their final abortive mission, to make the Midwest work, had come to naught? And here was the deal breaker: if he did not like Chicago, the centre of so much good about the United States – its wisecracking populace, store-front theatres and fair public transportation – if he wouldn't have been content to write the Digest here, stroll around the Downtown and bicycle over to Pilsen – then it was beginning to look like, at a basic level, he didn't much like the United States.

That was it; that was the root of it. He just didn't want to live in the United States.

How to explain then that he still dreamt of it? Still told friends he'd live there one day? Still intimately followed its forthcoming election? To hate something was to grant it a power over you, after all, and he could never claim to have been neutral to the United States. In fact, he willed it on; he delighted in its stylish President's re-election – the thought of the election of his opponent had been a major contributing factor to his rejection of the place – going as far as to title the edition for November 11th 2012 the 'Optimist's Digest.' This month he watched the inauguration speeches with a tear in his eye, ear grown expert in that patriotic jive.

In some way he felt that he had insulted the U.S. He had the distinct feeling that the country was annoyed with him, was lying with its belly curled round sulking and refusing to talk while he fluffed up its pillows saying 'Fine! Have it your way!' He had rejected a country not a girl – Anna remained dear to him until the final moment they had kissed at the airport, the tears rolling down her face, his face – and indeed the most powerful country in the world. That had consequences. He was a marked man. The U.S. would have its revenge.

There were reasons to go to Luxembourg, then, to see Anna, to see her engagement ring, to accept the deepest of deep griefs, 'the yardstick by which all other pain was measured,' to quote Alex James on his own separation. But not least of the reasons to go was to show her why he had stayed in Europe. All year he had been contemplating a decision he had made, weighing it and analysing it as time went on. Now in his flat in Berlin in winter he clicked send on an accepting email. It was only after he did so that he realized had never been to Luxembourg.

II. A TALE OF SECOND CITY

The Chicago sky was of a peculiar grey, something like a sky which had been washed through and then hung wet over the buildings, dripping down over the lake. A bird wheeled through it ahead, wings superimposed onto smoke issuing from the rooftops on the city's denser north side. Small deckchairs could be seen on a roof ahead, a little island of comfort in this most unrelenting of cityscapes.

She moved to the kitchen table, holding the coffee cup at its base and looking out to the chrome peaks of downtown. It was 9.15 and autumn in Chicago. She had a rare extra hour before work today, before a slow commute on the clanking train, as there was a general meeting and – as her deodorized boss had told her in the corridor – it wasn't imperative for the newer staff to come in. She had been working there for four months since her return at the start of the year.

She left the coffee cup and moved back to the bedroom. The sheet was still slightly crumpled; Steve had left about an hour before and his warmth could still be felt. Steve had to go fix people's computers but she would see him at the show tonight. She was his + 1.

It had been a few days since she last wrote to Dave and

she had heard nothing from him, though honestly she did not care too much. It was all part of her calculated meanness to him. Of course she knew he had not *exactly* done anything to earn it, but also that this was the only way things could be. She had waited for him to come, after all. She had given him a chance.

Steve was a tall, blonde Midwesterner with an enthusiastic way of speaking and broad hands. She had met him at a reading, and it was soon clear that he was his own man, fixing computers by night and pursuing a career as a stand-up at night. Chicago was good for that. She didn't care too much for comedy, capital C comedy anyway, and couldn't say that she would have voluntarily spent her evenings at comedy clubs. They were all a little soulless, with their two drink minimums and industrial-cleaned carpets. But it was fun to be dating one of the acts – and good, too, that he was good. Steve delivered wry monologues about customer service, night farts, relationship difficulties and driving in a bemused Wisconsin whine. Just occasionally he made political references. It was strange, she remarked, that so much of the country's political reality was accounted for by comedy. You could make a joke about how awful things were then move on.

Steve had gone to school in Madison, and they had driven up there a few months ago, along I-39. He had shown her some of his old haunts and they had met some of his pre-college friends. They all seemed quite tight still. Apparently they had made some kind of pact to stay in touch throughout life, and she definitely picked up a mild bros before hoes vibe, like when Steve knelt down to play Streetfighter with his old friend

Andy. But that was okay too. He still looked up every time she came into the room.

It had been one of those typical American weekends where you drive between enjoyments. Since her return, she had made an effort to keep up European walking levels, but was still worried about getting a little fat. Dave had hated the cars. She remembered once he had, staring out the window at the sea of traffic, seen a smart car. He had turned to her elated. 'Look how happy you are,' she had said.

It had been clear to her from the moment she had met him at O'Hare that he would be unlikely to move to the U.S with her. The Austin debacle had been bad enough, and though Chicago suited him more, she had seen him struggle to connect to her home. It was also clear to her that she would stay. She was back now, nearer her family, Uncle Tony in his Evanston house, her dear friend Laurel with her parks project on the South Side. Chicago was a nice city and she liked it. Dave flailed here, couldn't breathe as he put it, suffered; but that was not her business. She couldn't afford to be sentimental about this: She had things she wanted. And he would be, she knew it, fine, would thrive back in Europe. After all he'd have Europe.

For Anna Europe frequently seemed like a dream. She had lived there for four years happily, learning some German and French. But now she was back, and involved in things, the whole story seemed like it had been a delaying tactic. Dave once told her the Russians believed you could only be fully yourself in your own country. She agreed with that now. Living abroad was vanity. It reduced your place of abode to just another consumerist preference; removed that sense of having loyalty to a place come what may. The U.S. was her home and where the action was, even if that action was very fucked up indeed.

At work they often called her German girl.

'Hey German girl!' called Stuart.

'Hello Stuart.'

'Do you want to grab a beer?'

'I'm working.'

'Later. In the Loop.'

'Do you have ID?'

'C'mon. Quit being such a hardass.'

'We can discuss this another time.'

'Picky type, huh?'

'I have a boyfriend.'

'Bet he's not as fun as me.'

'No. I like him for his intense moral seriousness.'

'You're weird. The Germans made you weird.'

'I was already weird before I went there.'

This was true; she had been a strange high school child, fond of taking in frogs and birds and obsessed with hiding in obscure parts of the house. Her mother would frequently find her in cupboards or in the laundry bin.

'Anna, what are you doing?' She looked back, she liked to think, cutely from beneath a pile of dirty clothes.

One of her great passions at school had been jogging. She had been a quiet, head-down runner, ploughing on for mile after mile to commendable finishes in school runs. At interstate level she placed squarely in the middle, but the crucial moment came in a state race when, as anticipated but still inconveniently, she had found herself some way short of her usual powers. And somewhere in running that race, in that slight but evident deceleration, she had found herself asking herself a most un-American question: why did she want to win so bad anyway? For herself? For her parents? For her school? No answer had presented itself and she had placed eighth and soon after ceased to run.

Everyone in her family was a little off, a little odd. She thought frequently that many of the things that made her a weird American suited her for Europe. But she had not wanted to stay there. She had missed home. Home, she dreamed of a house – maybe not in the suburbs, maybe in the satellites of Chicago – with a train connection to the city and a back yard. Steve wanted kids. That was a good sign, especially after Dave had been so riddled and confused about it all. He always had to make things difficult for himself.

Dave, and Berlin, and European life. It all seemed very far away, so complete had her re-absorption into America been. Indeed it was strange to think of going back there again. She wondered how she would feel when she did.

Her Chicago neighborhood was beautiful, and walkable. She passed a series of large grand houses, neatly manicured lawns and polished expensive cars. She was the only person out walking.

Here was something she had to grant Dave. The adjective 'walkability' was a superfluous one. Making as basic a human activity as walking into some kind of statement – 'I walk, people!', proclaimed the pedestrian as activist – was pathological. You should just walk. But in lots of places in the U.S. you couldn't; there were no sidewalks, or what you could walk was bisected by endless freeways constantly furrowed by cars. Somewhere along the line Americans had got out the habit of walking.

It was cool on the L platform. The Chicago heat had been a trial, but a colder spell had arrived in the last few days. Here came the steel trains, carriages bearing the little U.S. flag, and the crowds of late morning commuters, mostly young people with jobs downtown. The old drove. She felt that Chicago was fighting itself, that the boomer polluters who had ruined America and created its endless wash of sprawl were in competition with the young who wanted dense, walkable neighborhoods. That word again.

Opposite her on the train was an elderly African-American, dapper in brown tweed and a felt hat. For a while, he sat smiling and then leaned forward in a way which made her instinctively drop her head.

'May I just say,' he said, 'you wear those pants really well.'

She smiled genuinely, but didn't, or couldn't, say anything in response. He got out several stops later and she went back to looking out the window, dreaming away.

At her office screen, instead of working, she read the Digest.

OCTOBER 2 2012

Ferry disaster off Lamma Island, Hong Kong: 39 dead, over 100 injured

Prophetic Anxiety: Children reporting psychiatric disorders due to climate change

From the Annals of Human Misery: On this day in 1812, the Battle of Rancagua (in Chilé: Desastre de Rancagua)

Thoughts on the death of Historian Eric Hobsbawm

(click)

So the twentieth century continues. Eric Hobsbawm, the Marxist historian and chronicler of the bloodiest century on human record, has left us, and the commentariat left and right are rushing to shower him with digs and plaudits, and excavate old and unsettled debates. The following exchange, from a 1994 interview with the historian and later calamitously unsuccessful Canadian Liberal Party leader Michael Ignatieff, has been repeatedly quoted in coverage of Hobsbawm's death:

Ignatieff: In any case [in 1934 - MD] millions of people are dying in the Soviet experiment. If you had known that, would it have made a difference to you at that time? To your commitment to being a Communist?

Hobsbawm: This is sort of an academic question to which an answer is simply not possible (...) I would have said probably not.

Ignatieff: Why?

Hobsbawm: Because in a period in which, as you might say, mass murder and mass suffering are absolutely universal, the chance of a new world being born in great suffering would still have been worth backing... Now the point is, looking back as a historian... I would say... probably not. The sacrifices were enormous; they were excessive by almost any standard and unnecessarily great. But I'm looking back at it now and (s)aying that because it turns out that the Soviet Union was not the beginning of the world revolution. Had it been...I'm not sure. After all, do people now say, "We shouldn't have had World War II because more people died in World War II than died in Stalin's Terror?"

Ignatieff: So what that comes down to is saying that had the radiant tomorrow actually been created, the loss of fifteen, twenty million people might have been justified?

Hobsbawm: Yes.

Hobsbawm has been criticized for the implications of what he is saying. But surely the more significant aspect of said implications is not that twenty million people dying would have been worth it in face of a good outcome - after all this is, as Hobsbawm states, exactly the justification that people use in talking

about World War II, namely that the ends justified the means, and in that case they surely did – but that twenty million people did in the end lay down their lives for an ideology, Communism, and a state, the Soviet Union, which proved to be not only no 'rainbow utopia' but in fact actively detrimental to the cause of human well being. The sacrifice which defined their lives was worse than being worthless: it was actually actively malign. Still at least a communist can argue their ideas sounded nice. There are even more dead in history who have given up their lives for ideas which were *prime facie* bad, those who sacrificed all *in the name of* tyranny and injustice, fought for racism or privilege and became part of the endless stream of villainous cannon fodder which history sends us and who we -

'Anna bear.' She looked up; Stuart was standing there again.

'Don't call me that.' She clicked.

'There's going to be a meet-up in half an hour. It looks bad.'

'What kind of bad?'

'Lay-offs bad.'

She hated her job, sure. But the fact of her hatred made no difference to her living in world capitalism. She took a sip of coffee and tried to relax. Having this job was one of her few meager signs of success in Chicago.

They were called to attention in the large company lobby. Peter Stanhope spoke with Suzy Lineham, the company CEO, standing next to him.

'Hello everybody! Hello!'

She got the urge to shout hello back, or call out requests, but it seemed it wasn't that kind of show.

'Thanks for being here everybody. I'm sure you're all a little concerned. And we at the company want us to know we share that concern.

Tech start-ups are fluid beings. I have a background in experimental theater and let me tell you, working for a tech start-up is not so much different. You try a lot of things. Some work, some don't. It's like if you throw some pasta at the wall, it sticks. Or it doesn't.

Suzi and I have been talking and we feel it's time to make some of the changes we've been talking about. Which is why we are going to have to – and believe me, this hurts us as much as you – let some of you go. This afternoon, we'll call each of you into the office and tell you if we're going to keep you or not. Those of you who aren't staying will finish out at the end of the week. And those of you who are staying, which is about a third of you, well, we go on together. Suzi – do you have anything to add?'

Suzi Lineham looked up. 'Obviously I won't get a chance to thank each one of you personally. But rest assured, we wish all of you the best in your future careers.'

On the train back she was thinking about having children, how it might not be easier just to get pregnant, and if one of her problems might be that she was not, not really, not in heart, a career woman. She felt the pressure to be career-oriented in the way others felt pressurized to settle down. At least Steve wanted children, which was, it occurred to her again, an upgrade on Dave, although in many other ways Steve was not an upgrade, and she missed him, especially on days like today when life bruised her.

The doorman at the comedy club was a statuesque black man with horsey teeth and an earring.

'Why hello,' he said as she moved to the front. 'You are looking sublime.'

'Thank you,' she said. 'My name's Anna Berry – I should be on the guest list.'

'Indeed you are. Indeed you are. You're Steve's girl, right?'

'Yes.'

'Well, that man is clearly charmed by you, I can tell you. He says you are *relentless*.'

'I guess. Just now though I need to pee really badly.'

'Don't let me stop you, lady,' said the doorman, and went back to displaying his upbeat charms to the other patrons.

The comedy club was lurid and glossy and had that slight septic quality to it as if there was nowhere in it where you could really relax, a room which screamed upscale amusement. She moved to the front and sat alone.

'Are you Anna?' A woman had approached.

'Hi – you must be Lindsey.' Steve's work colleague.

'Yes. Steve's told me so much about you.'

'That's nice. He's told me so much about you too.'

'Oh yeah, we have a great time together, ordering spare parts.'

'Have you seen his act before?'

'Only on YouTube. He's good, right?'

'I think so.'

'I mean, I don't understand all the references. I'm sure that makes a lot of difference.'

'I don't think it makes that much difference.'

'Well, maybe not then,' said Lindsey. 'Have you been here before?'

'No.'

'Oh I have. I saw Chris D'Elia here. He's such a badass. What are you drinking?'

'Just a beer.'

'I'm drinking a mojito! It's really good. The mojitos here are to die for – when I saw Chris D'Elia, I drank three of them, and then I laughed my ass off. What kind of comedy do you like?'

The truth was that she didn't like comedy much; she could appreciate a good comic craftsman, certainly – and it was men, she didn't hold much for the women in the profession, though that was not their fault but rather that of how they were presented and presented themselves, as if obligated to be representative of some kind of femininity whereas the guys could just tell jokes – but she felt other forms, like novels and songs, were richer than this one of people become joke machines –

though she said none of that.

'I like Eddie Izzard,' she said.

'Eddie who?'

'He's a very surreal English guy,' she said. 'You can check him out on YouTube.'

'Oh – I don't really like English comedy. I mean, I've seen some of Monty Python, but some of it I just really don't get.'

'I think Izzard's good,' she said.

There was a pause. Lindsey looked around as if for someone to flirt with.

'I got fired today,' she said quietly.

'What?' Lindsey turned and smiled.

'Today – I was laid off from my job.'

'Oh!' Lindsey blinked. 'I'm really – sorry...'

'No, it's fine. I hated the job. But even if you hate a job it's not nice to be fired – I mean I hate my job and I was bored with it but apparently I was bad at it too.'

'What are you going to do?' said Lindsey, focused now.

There was a pause. 'I'll talk to Steve,' she said.

'He's at work,' Lindsey said. They both smiled and, almost exactly on that, the lights began to dim and the host took the stage.

Host Eddie Burnside was a middle-aged man with frizzy hair in a dark T-shirt reading 'Vader was Framed.' He had a thin beard and for some reason snapped at the air with his left hand while holding the mike in his right.

'People of Earth... Welcome. How'd you all get here tonight? What about you sir, camel? Fucking Arab.' The audience laughed. 'It's alright, I'm a little retarded... You know, what they say, behind every great man is a woman telling him he's autistic.'

He rambled on for a while before running out of either momentum or material; judging by the response, though, the audience had definitely come to laugh, in that 'This has to be great' American way. 'You guys ready for your first act? Or as I like to call him your opening headliner?'

The audience fairly bellowed. 'Alright: Ladies and gentleman, all the way from Madison Wisconsin, Mr... Steve... Lloyd!'

Steve came onto the stage then, relaxed and casual in a plaid suit and neat – ironed? – blue jeans. They were so crucial, these moments of approach; how a comedian came to the microphone said so much about how their set would go – an abashed fumble was never a good sign whereas someone who, not to put too fine a point on it, grabbed it like a dick they wanted to suck was normally in for a good set.

'Hey ladies – where my ladies at?' asked Steve. Shrill cries came back. 'Oh good! Pleased you're here. Never seen so many women before. We don't really have them in Wisconsin.

'You know, I've got to be honest with you. I'm a pretty interesting guy. I juggle, fix bikes, and I read literature in French and understand everything except for the words.' A laugh. 'Yet none of these things have ever interested a girl more than the fact that I happen not to like tomatoes. What?' I hear you ladies call. That's right. I don't like tomatoes. I think they suck. But say that to a girlfriend and she's like What? HOW CAN YOU NOT LIKE TOMATOES? And I'm like, I don't dig them baby, that's all. They're not my kind of vegetable. And she's like: They're not even a vegetable. They're a fruit! There you are, all hating on them and you don't even know what food group they belong to.'

What was getting the laughs here was his voice and face. Steve was a good mimic, and here his voice was pitching up effortlessly, but not hysterically, to imitate the piqued girlfriend. There were comedians like this whose performance and presence sold weaker or odder material. Were they the best comedians?

Now he was changing his tune. 'At least if I was a girl I could call a girl and go – Hey Steve, you want to come over for some down time?', and it would work. It's like kinetic energy.' Laughter from the science geeks. 'Imagine if I tried that. Just ringing up a girl and saying 'Hey baby, want to get down? Oh, it's her voicemail.' In stride, he dropped his head to a spectator in the front row. 'Question to you lady. How many of the guys who want to sleep with you do you think you sleep with? Yeah. You know what that figure is with me? 100%. I have accepted 100% of offers of girls who wanted to sleep with me. I'm attracted to 100% of women who find me attractive. Guy relationship math is pretty simple.'

He was doing well and beside her Lindsey gave energetic, pre-sexual coos, apparently the kind of woman who found it flattering when a guy deigned to talk about her gender at all, even if in such mildly sexist tones.

Then a cheaper shot, the kind of thing he would eliminate from his act when more secure. 'You know guys have a reputation that we like to fuck and run. That's not true. I'll always drive you home. And you know, we get hurt too.' Ahh! 'Guys, you ever been with someone and they give you the old brain wipe? Yeah, that's pretty scary. You break and you can go round to see them all puffy-faced and they're like 'Who are you?'

'You're like, 'Uh, we dated for two years remember?'

They're like, 'I've never seen you before in my life.'

You're like, 'Oh – I just came for my duvet.'

And they're like, '*Your* duvet? Get your hands off *my* duvet!'

'It's like that bit in the X-Files where Mulder sees a UFO in a field and comes back the next day with a police officer and it's just a field. The UFO's like the relationship.' Clever idea; they just about got it, but he had to do a big shift into a well-rehearsed Fox Mulder impersonation to win them. 'Mulder's like, "There was a relationship here!" And the woman's standing in the field next to the police officer saying, "I've never seen this man before in my life." The policeman's like, "Is he bothering you, Ma'am?" He mimed a handcuffed Mulder being dragged away. "I saw it! With my own eyes! There was a relationship! Everybody was *involved*."

At the final pull of the arrested Mulder's body towards the imaginary waiting police truck a smattering, gathering to a general, round of applause began. Steve paused at the front of the stage. 'Anyway my girlfriend's here today so I don't think she's going to wipe me. Actually I don't think she's installed me yet.' It was funny how the tensions became jokes.

They drove back in Steve's blue Prius.

'You did so well.'

'It was OK,' said Steve, looking straight ahead.

'No – you did so well. They loved you.'

'Yeah well, you know how it is. What you're expecting to work never quite does. There were a few things I didn't expect to be funny. That joke about foreign policy for example. I meant that just to be true.'

'Yeah – that's why people laughed.'

'Can I ask you a question?'

'Of course. You can ask me anything.'

Steve drove for a moment. 'Do you think my material is challenging enough?'

'What do you mean, honey?'

'I mean, you're a real smart girl. Sometimes I'm up there and I think, God, Anna must hate this!'

'I don't.'

'It must seem so dumb to you, you know?'

'But people like it.'

'Well, people love Cheez Whiz. People love microwave macaronis. I just feel kind of a sell-out, you know, and you're so well-read and stuff...'

'I'm delighted to go out with you. You killed it tonight. You must have been one of the funniest acts.'

'Sure, that's why they put me on first,' Steve said and turned with a brief smile. 'I just sometimes feel like such a hick with you, that's all. I mean I'm just a boy from small-town Wisconsin. We don't have fancy things in Albert Wisconsin like public transportation and juice. It's a soda and cars kind of place.'

'Do you think I'd rather be going out with some kind of radical? Honey, I came home. I missed America. I chose this.'

'I guess,' he said. 'It just worries me that's all – there aren't many girls like you about.'

Back at his place he fetched himself a beer while she flicked on the TV. At Steve's place she allowed herself all the things that her own place, equipped with only a laptop and a bicycle, did not possess.

'You want to watch a movie?' said Steve.

'Maybe. Come and sit here.'

He sat next to her on the sofa and she gave him two small kisses on the face. She enjoyed the warmth of his body and his abundant brown beard, enjoyed the range of muscles on his chest, like a sculpted flowerbed. After a while though the foreplay reached a plateau of sorts. Steve was leaning forward on the coach, his eyes bulging peculiarly. He was waiting to say something.

'Steve?'

'Mmm.' Still waiting. At last: 'You're a swell girl, Anna.'

'I'm glad. You're a swell guy.'

'I'd like to make this real serious, you know.'

'Well, that's very sweet Steve.'

'No – I mean – I was wondering. Do you feel the same?'

She smiled. 'Steve.'

'I mean, I want to have kids with you.'

'How many?' she smiled.

'At least two.' He turned, going for it now. 'Jesus, I want that even more than I want to be rich and famous!'

He was shaking, blanched and adrenalin-crazed. But he was sincere. He was trying to be honest. She had felt this declaration – an explanation of love, the Germans said, explaining love just like you explained your taxes – brewing inside him for a while now, in the slightly excessive pauses following his jokes and his smiles. Sometimes she would find him standing furrowing in the kitchen as if thinking through complex mathematical sums.

'Oh honey, that's very sweet.'

She pushed into him a little. His hand went to her leg, and pulled at her thin, black stocking, pulling at the fabric right at the thigh. She helped him roll down the fabric.

Later, they lay in bed together, his broad contented face next to her with the look of a huge child.

'Goodnight honey,' he said, sleepy-voiced. 'Tonight was really nice.'

'I think so too.'

'I'm really sleepy now. And I'm really happy about the

gig.'

'You did really well,' she said. She kissed him goodnight. For a long while she lay in the dark thinking about what she would say to him tomorrow

III. THE LUXEMBOURG COMPROMISE

It wasn't much, but it was the only compromise he could think of, the only one that might work. He didn't know what he himself thought of it – only that on paper it had a satisfactory balance to it, like a settlement where all participants received an equal share. An equal share of the loss, you might say.

It had been cold on the train platform that morning. Hauptbahnhof, Berlin's central train station, afforded a backdrop on the industrial city in the deep winter dark. But it was an ugly building, a fibreglass cube with an arch banged on top, a wad of nondescript tunnels and overpriced shops. All in all a suitable entrance to what remained a pretty ugly city.

It was not yet light on the train platform, and the commuter trains were already sliding in and out, from the city, to the city. In previous years, when he had been interested in Berlin and not just the details of his own life there, he had loved to travel, often illegally, on the *Stadtbahn*, around the city's vital orbital ring over the grey-brown Spree and past the Pergamon museum. Now the tourist hordes had arrived and Berlin had become, to him at least, more international and less inspiring. In 2005 there had been still some defiant exhilaration in the air.

But there were still great love stories beginning, still people cycling the cold streets to work, still intensely moustached handymen boarding the trains from the Eastern suburbs to the city centre and still, waiting around him, international businessmen holding money newspapers and coffee-cups. On the info boards was a chart – he had worked this out only after several years in Germany – where you could align yourself on the platform to precisely where your seat's carriage would arrive. He did this and still had minutes to spare. It was a Friday in February at 06.49 as he boarded the train to Cologne changing for Luxembourg.

He had never been of course. A cousin had once told him it was like a place stuck in the 1950s; a friend that it was a hive of white-collar criminality. Apparently their friend, wanting to open a bank account in Luxembourg, had been taken into a back room with the shutters pulled down and asked what could be done for them. An acquaintance had visited and afterwards posted up on Facebook images of forts. He imagined plazas, girls in long dresses, sandstone banks. But again, destination had become incidental. He thought only of Anna and seeing her for the first time in a year and a half since they had parted at O'Hare with a confusing final kiss. At that time the door had been left open, but he had said that he might never see her again and had, until now, been right.

He had brought with him a small carry-on which he put in the rack above. He had packed very light, his only concession to his residual sweetness for her being to pack her a slab of her favourite chocolate. In him remained an urge to daughter Anna, his junior by a year. But in her emails she sounded hard and mature.

There was an older woman across the aisle, leafing through the *Bahnmobil* in-train magazine. Untypically for a German – respectful, private people – she pronounced a quiet 'Hallo' into the carriage calm.

'Hallo,' he responded, trying to combine the maximum of friendliness and distance into this short greeting and ensure no conversation developed. He had much to think about.

The Digest knew of his absence, with a message left on site saying he was away for three days. Traffic continued to grow and ironically, mainstream advertisers were increasingly in contact. It was often cited to him as an example of German wit that the country possessed a brand of toilet paper known as 'Happy End', and it was surely a confirmation of said wit that they had contacted him asking about advertising space on his website.

He was slightly haunted by his gentle success, by the sense of the time it drew away from the ambitions he had possessed arriving in Berlin to make art. Funny how the world wanted this specific thing from him, a misery blog, and seemed to anger if he made the slightest deviation from it. A while ago he had posted a small good news item on the blog, about a child rescuing its parents from a fire, and seen a furious, transatlantic reaction ('Where's the downside here? Stick to what you know, dude.' 'This is NOT what I come to your blog for.') And it was so difficult to relinquish standing in Berlin, a city where even the most moderate success marked you out as distinguished.

He thought it strange though that society took people of talent and used them principally as copy editors, English teachers and librarians. That society could understand them best on those terms. He could imagine Shakespeare flirting with some pox'd lovely at the bar, saying: 'Will Shakespeare. I'm the company manager, though I do occasionally dabble in plays. Most of my income comes from straw.'

The train had been travelling for about an hour across the monotone North German plain. The air was cold and misty, the ground frosty and cracked. The earth was going through it again. He had made this trip before, but never had the winter seemed so long, the spring so far away.

The ticket controller made their way round for a second time. He gave him a you-checked-me nod. After so many years abroad he was getting quite expert in non-verbal communication. The woman sitting opposite spoke, '*Alles schon in Ordnung!*' Everything in order. The controller went on.

He smiled.

'You travelling far?'

'*Nicht so weit,*' he said. Not so far.

'Oh, you speak German,' she said, switching to that

language. 'I'm going to Frankfurt. My son just got a job there. I think he's got a girlfriend too. First job and first girlfriend. What about you?'

'I'm meeting my last girlfriend. I last saw her a year and a half ago –' *einandhalb,* that was right, in German, wasn't it – 'this is the first time I'm seeing her since then.'

'But that is very difficult for you! Are you alright?'

'I was engaged to her actually. But yes, I'm alright. I think she's moved on, and I'm pretty sure she's engaged to her new boyfriend.'

'Oh, but I think you are better than him.'

'That's really very nice of you but…'

'No, really. I don't think he is very good at all.'

'Well, that's really kind of you.'

'Where are you from?' she said, hearing his accent.

'London – but I live in Berlin.'

'Berlin, hey. Why did you move to Berlin?'

'I guess I just really liked it. Is that an answer?'

She paused. 'I suppose so. It's a little bit strange, that's all.'

He smiled. 'My name's Dave by the way.'

'Anna,' she said, and returned to her magazine.

The journey took eight and a half hours and a few other, shorter conversations, plus his usual fascinated perusal of diagrams of the European rail network, his dreaming up of future expeditions, saw him through to his arrival at Luxembourg's *Gare Lëtzebuerg*. In addition to the local Luxembourgish, there were signs in the French, German and English he spoke, and he was able to easily negotiate to the exits where he began the walk to the central hotel he, and later they, were booked into.

It was a little warmer here, but the sky was still grey and nondescript; the buildings were handsome and spindly, with fine details on the window ledges. He walked past small, well-heeled shops, Cartier watches under small intricate lights. The streets were spotless, safe and narrow. One man stood, impeccably suited, staring into the window of a jewellers, apparently coveting a particular ring.

Somewhere in the distance he heard an accordion sounding; the city was gently bustling still. Later he would go out and drink a beer or two, sample the pleasures of Friday-night Luxembourg. Perhaps he would embark on a decadent erotic adventure and still be in time to meet the woman he loved.

The Hotel Business was located on one of the main pedestrian drags. He rung himself in and then hauled the little carry-on up the thin stairs. Inside the walls were yellow, run down not so much in spirit of desperation but in that no one particularly cared about this part of the world. The lobby was quiet with one aged businessman watching television and a young, heavily made-up woman sat at reception.

'*Bonsoir*,' said the woman, extremely tidy in a black blouse and white shirt.

'*Bonsoir*,' he said. 'Deutsch – Français – English?'

'*Comme vous voulez,*' she said.

He went on in German. Speaking it fluently, he was always keen to expand the range of its usefulness, an attitude to the language itself very unrepresentative of the modern German tourist. '*Ja,* I have a reservation. It's a double room. I should also have a reservation for someone else coming tonight.'

'Die Frau Perry?'

'The Frau Perry, yes.'

'Very good. Breakfast commences at 07.00. Here are a selection of leaflets. The room is 4B, up the stairs on the left. Questions?'

'Well – what do you do in Luxembourg on a Friday night?'

She paused. 'Many people,' she said, 'are tired on Fridays.'

He spread out a few items on the bed, periodicals, his jumper, his charger, and a certain sequence of thoughts came up in him once again. He looked over the quiet dignified street and gave himself to them.

The deal was simple; she would come back to Europe and they would have a child. It was the only deal where they both lost equally. He didn't particularly want to have a child and she didn't, he presumed on the basis of her curt emails, particularly want to return to Europe. Other than that the proposal made sense.

She suspected that in some way she still loved him but was not allowing herself to. They had shared so much together. Where had all that gone? Was it simply waste, a tiny historical blip? But that was how it was with young women, he thought, and perhaps that was the source of the wound that had conditioned the Digest: they simply couldn't afford, no matter how much things hurt, to hang around too long. Here he was, British, European, male, free to think about the futility and misery of life for years before eventually, in some wild naked moment, procreating and going soft at the resultant life. She in the meantime was on a tight schedule and needed to get back to the U.S. to breed.

But could she breed in Europe? They had spoken of it often.

'I want healthcare for my babies,' she said.

'We have that,' he answered.

'I'm sure,' she said as they sat naked together, 'You'll make a good and loving father.'

'Do you think so?'

'Oh, absolutely. You'll be a big hit at children's parties. Kids love gloomy men.'

To become a father, perhaps in Berlin, perhaps here – It had not been the life he had envisaged. But it would be with her. He would get Europe and she a baby; it was the only deal he could think of and was still unsure if he would offer it at all.

The receptionist had crossed on his map locations of several good drinking establishments, unsmiling as she did so, supplying only the most cursory of comments.

He began the walk along the darkening streets. He could already see Luxembourg was small, and this the whole country.

He came to a pedestrian crossing with a small café. From odd utterances, he gathered the group sitting at the table ahead beneath the heaters were American tourists. They had ordered the best beers, situated themselves on the prettiest square, arrived at a suitable time and were despite all this surprised to find the conversation did not flow of and for itself. Their whole lives were likely marathons of business which left them inadequately prepared for this, a moment of free time sat beside heaters outside in Europe. 'You mean we just sit here and talk?' One of them adjusted the rug on his lap. There were no intervals in American life.

Soon he arrived at the bar in question, *L'Alliance*. Outside was a hubbub of young people, well-dressed petite girls and broad-shouldered men plying them with cigarettes. Behind it was a sports bar devoid of people, just a few middle-aged men drinking blonde beers and smoking to themselves. Inside monitors were showing images from the Turkish league, the pick of the Friday football. He wasn't sure if Luxembourg had its own league, or where Luxembourgian teams played if it didn't. He walked over to the empty bar.

Inside, the owner, an olive-skinned man in a blue apron, was watching the monitor. The man turned to him. '*Abend.*'

One of the screens was showing activity; somewhere in Europe, a goal had occurred. Beer half poured, '*Was für ein Tor!*,' what a goal, exclaimed the bartender looking up.

'Ja – the Turkish league?'

'The Turkish league, right.'

'Are you Turkish?'

He had got into the unpleasant German habit of asking people where they were from.

'Nee! I'm from Portugal.' The bartender sat the beer on the counter. 'You like football?'

'I do.'

'You want some of these?' The bartender, eyes on the monitor, indicated a small bowl of olives.

'Please.'

'I'll get you some.'

He sat himself down. The bartender laid the olives at his table. 'Where you from?'

'I'm British, but I live in Berlin.'

'Mmm. Berlin. I've got a cousin in Berlin. Paolo. He keeps asking me to come visit him. Actually I owe him some money.'

'Berlin's a great city.'

'Say – if I gave you some money, could you give it to Paolo?'

'I guess – couldn't you just transfer it, though?'

'No, it's got to go via cash. Just a thought. Berlin's good?'

'I like it.'

'There's not so much going on here,' the bartender said. 'Business is really bad. Especially at weekends when everyone leaves.'

'It's pretty though.'

'Oh sure, it's pretty. Really pretty. You a journalist?'

'A blogger.'

'What's that?'

'I write for the Internet.'

'About football?' The bartender smiled down. 'You should write about the Portuguese league. Porto –' He pronounced the last o as a u – 'they're the best.'

A name occurred to him. 'Mario Jardel?'

'Great player!'

A woman entered; she was blonde and heavily made up, mature looking, in long black tights. 'Clara!' said the bartender. She come over the bar and leant slightly over to kiss him. Then she stepped back to him to ask for a beer in deep, Nicoesque German. German was a deeply sexy language to him; it sounded like a good girl asking if she could do something very bad.

She turned to him, saying in English. 'Hello.'

'Hallo,' he replied.

'Who are you?' she said.

'My name's Dave,' he said.

'American?'

'British.'

'But you speak German,' she said. Then she turned back to the bartender who had her beer already poured.

Even in those brief moments he had imagined an encounter with her, imagined the whole thing, following her home. She knew the city well and led him through her alleyways to her house, the family house, on the outskirts of the inner city. She probably lived with her ageing father, he pictured, and imagined her unlocking the door and then turning to indicate him he should be quiet. There would be no warmth or prelude of imminent sex in those moments. They would ascend the narrow staircase, passing her father asleep on the sofa as they did so, the television flickering in the dark. Upstairs in the clean bedroom they would make love and he would fall asleep next to her. As soon as the act would finish the pain would come back. But he would also be distracted by new senses and intimations of the city. At the dawn his hand would find its way around her flesh, touch her privately once again, but she would be busy and impatient to get him out. Perhaps he would get a coffee, which he rarely drank anyway, and with a quick final kiss – if even that – he would find himself back out on the streets in the gathering dawn. Upbeat but unchanged, he would walk over to a bus stop to arrive back at the hotel in time for Anna's eleven o'clock arrival at the hotel.

But she had turned back to the bartender and was kissing him. There was no one else in the bar; he drank the rest of the beer and, popping two euros fifty on top of the printed receipt, left unnoticed.

She was travelling to Brussels for a conference and would combine it with a meeting with her former partner at Luxembourg, a place they had both often spoken of, this orderly little duchy between France and Germany, one of those hundreds of places which were simply content to be European, to work from the default premises of liberal democracy, old buildings, multilingualism and good food. It had always been a joke between them that they would meet again in Luxembourg. She would see him and they would spend time together, and she knew it would be fine, that everything was as it should be, that she had been right to go, and that there had been no other way.

She did not know whether she still loved him or not – she had not thought about it in those terms – though she suspected she did not. She did not check that place within herself and besides, it would all be made clear spending time with him. She tried to imagine what Luxembourg was like; what their old joke, made after lovemaking, looked like in reality. She saw tree-lined avenues and rose gardens, black-suited gendarmes signalling people to wait at lights and gigantic, decadent cakes. Jokes always became reality in the end.

Waking early he took a picture of the street with his phone and uploaded it to his blog via Instagram. Rue des États Unis, Luxembourg; he captioned it 'No misanthropy here.'

As it was several hours before she was to arrive he went down to the breakfast room, sitting at the bay windows and staring out into the street. For his entire adult life he, a Briton, had lived and breathed Europe, and he found it deeply sad to come from a country so near to the continent yet content to talk such complete crap about it, an endless fuzzy calumny of half-truths and ignorance. And bad decisions were always made on the basis of ignorance. It wasn't as if the information wasn't out there; even a cursory glance at European history saw Britain perpetually engaged in this endless game of footsy with the continent, shooting admiring glances across the Atlantic; meanwhile time and again, in the midst of this arrogant display, events on the continent sucked the self-absorbed islanders back into them. How much better it would be to proactively embrace this state of affairs; how much better this would be than now, with Britain's contribution to Europe being to, like some weird secluded neighbour emerging from their basement flat, to occasionally embark on jingoistic, fantastical rants.

And now there would be a referendum on whether to leave 'Europe.' It was so pointless, like holding a referendum on whether someone was your brother or not. Whatever the vote the facts would not change. Your brother would still be there; and Europe would still be there too; Britain could never shrug it off. Why should it? Was there any part of the world richer? So rich in great cities? So rich in concentrated history, not all of it sad? Truly this was a great European breakfast; old people, great buildings and good coffee.

His thoughts returned to the meeting. Sometimes in the morning now he would wake and simply not be able to believe he was no longer with Anna, the feeling of something being out of joint pressing down on him. He ran through the various entry lines he had thought to offer her; a cool 'Hey,' 'It's good to see you,' exclaiming 'Anna' or, closer to the spirit of their earlier adventures a gentle 'Hey kid.' But by the end she had no longer wanted to be called that.

He wondered what she would look like, if she still had the same haircut, the same skin tone, if he'd recognize the clothes she wore – although this latter he doubted, guessing that her Berlin indie wardrobe would be exchanged for the uniform of gainful employment, just as her mannerisms had begun to shift in their post-break up Skype conversations, her accent growing more Illinoisan again, gestures more extravagant, more U.S. slang – 'Love. It.', with big, audible full stops, she would say – peppering her conversation. Any traces of the London accent she had begun to pick up from him were long since gone. He wondered if they would have sex, if the same Anglo-American spark which had seen them enthusiastically screw in Berlin would return as she grew more European and America intrigued him once again. Who knew? It was so difficult with real loves, because you loved them.

She had arrived when he came down from his shower and was standing at the reception speaking French. He came towards her, waving as he did so; while she did not break the conversation, she acknowledged him with a genuflection. Then she turned.

'Dave.'

'Anna.'

A pause. They embraced.

'Well.'

'Well!'

'What room are you? I'm room 18.'

'That's right near me!'

'Come, let's take my stuff up.'

'Have you had breakfast?'

'I had a coffee and some energy biscuits. Have you tried them? They're really useful. You eat these biscuits and they keep you going the whole day.'

'Sounds like astronaut food.'

'Astronette, in my case. Come, let's take my stuff up.'

They went in the lift, slightly disoriented. A person looking at them from the outside would think they had taken drugs.

'How was Brussels?'

'Great. I blagged it really. I'm far too junior to be here. But the company is looking for investments from the European Union.'

'What's the company?'

'ChicaGo. We're looking to encourage private-public investments in Chicago infrastructure.'

'You get EU money?'

'Crazy, right? But under EU law, Europeans investing public money in U.S. private projects beneficial to the environment contributes towards preventing climate change.'

'And your role?'

'I tell them why it's a good idea. Chicago's a bit like Europe after all - just less racist.'

Ding. The doors clunked open; they exited and went to her room. She opened the door and moved in while he hovered outside.

'What a great view! Hell, come in, don't be shy.'

He tentatively stepped into the room. There was a large view and the window caught the same view of the overcast Saturday street.

'Pretty, huh? I had a bit of a look about last night.'

'And?'

'It's pretty. It's Europe.'

'Ah, you've always been a sucker for that.' Her chin dropped a touch. 'I do miss it though.'

'Are you doing alright?' he asked.

'Yes. Very busy – American life, you know. I miss my Berlin existence.'

'Of course. Berlin's very addictive.'

'You still hooked? But tell me later. There's a lot to talk about.'

'So much.'

'Where do you start?' But she didn't want to yet. 'How about you freshen up and we'll walk into town together.'

'Sounds like a plan,' he said and, smiling, bowed out. Their eyes caught and just as he left, he noticed a slight tint of coppery red dyed into her hair; the morning light caught it as she ducked a touch and, with a small laugh, smiled.

His heart was racing as he retreated to his room. He stood very quietly in front of the mess he creased for a moment while he internally regained and regrouped, listening to his breathing for a while. It would be alright, he assured himself, his heart shuddering within. She was not wearing an engagement ring.

He was already seated in the lobby as she entered, reading the Spiegel off his smart phone. 'So!' she said. He scrambled backward, pocketing the phone to look at her. She had changed her scarf and was now also wearing a light blue blouse and crimson lipstick. 'So!' she said and then, gesturing to the receptionist, '*Au revoir, Monsieur.*' But it was a new man and her friendliness just confused him.

They strolled down into the street, he slightly checking his step to do up his coat. The street was starting to busy and there were small stalls set up by stout Germanic artisans trying to look French; brown crates of cheeses and fresh transported salad. The sound of an accordion drifted through the air. Walking, their bodies remained respectfully distant from each other but, if it was possible for elbows and eyelashes to flirt, they did.

They soon reached one of the main squares and the imposing national bank. 'It's so pretty here! Can you take a photo of me?' Anna asked straight away.

'Sure,' he said, and she assumed position. It was so quick; her body snapped into an open, confident pose, a smile broke her face and he photographed her before the clean baroque façade and surrounding market stalls.

'Thanks. Crazy how this place is a country,' she said.

'I'm sure it's mainly for tax purposes. These little places like Andorra and Lichtenstein – that's normally the reason.'

'I remember you saying. Didn't you go to Lichtenstein a few years back?'

'I've been to Lichtenstein twice,' he said. 'How many other people do you know who can say that?'

'I don't know anyone else who's even been there *once*.'

He smiled; her energy was having its usual enlivening effect on him. They had already decided they wanted to sit down and eat lunch – strange, these echoes of coupledom – and soon enough, on a street next to the square, they reached the brasserie where yesterday he'd seen the Americans. 'This place looks nice,' she said, and they checked the prices.

They sat inside next to the window looking out at the square in the grey and the cold.

The waiter came. 'Messieurs-dames…'

'Bonjour!' she trilled.

'Guten Tag,' he said with lumpy determination.

The waiter began in English, 'So, we have a –'

'No,' he said. 'You can speak German. Or French.'

'Which would you prefer, Madame?' said the waiter.

'Oh, I don't really mind,' she said. 'It's really this guy's thing.'

'*Bon. On parle français,*' the waiter said and raised his notebook.

'I take language seriously, that's all,' said Dave, handing back his menu. 'A green tea, please.'

'A hot chocolate for me.' She grinned at him as the waiter disappeared. 'Linguistic activist Dave Benthorpe.'

'Yeah well, someone's got to do it.'

'Crossing the continent – a one man Anglophone mission against Anglicisms!'

'At least *I* could hack more than one tongue,' he smiled.

'Touché.'

Both smiling now, they looked out at the square together. There were streamers and the Luxembourg flag, sporting its lion, hanging from the building ahead, as well as the EU standard. 'It's nice here,' she said. 'So – how've you been?'

He paused. There was a removed expression on his face; each statement came weighted with associations. And yet it was easy to talk. 'I'm well,' he said. 'Still in Berlin. Pretty sure I'll be moving on soon, though.'

'Still London?'

'Or Paris, yes. Actually I thought about Kazakhstan.'

'What would you do there?'

'First of all I'd learn Kazakh.'

'Is that what they speak there?'

'And Russian, yes. Very interesting culture.' His tea had arrived. 'How've *you* been?'

'Well, I'm engaged,' she said.

'Yes – of course. To – Steve?'

'That's right.'

'What's he do?'

'He's a comedian.' She sipped her hot chocolate, 'But to pay the bills he does IT work. I think he'll make it in comedy though, he's quite slick.'

'Sounds good.'

'Yes. Mmm, that's good,' She sipped. 'Berlin seems a long way away.'

'It is. 5,000 miles. But I'm curious - are you nervous?'

'What about?'

'Getting married.'

'No. Of course not. I've wanted to for years.'

'I do remember you saying.'

'Anyway – Steve's a nice person.'

'Yeah? What's his comedy like?'

'Observational. He notices things.'

'Tell me one of his jokes.'

'I can't, really. They're more like bits.'

'Do a bit then.' He smiled concertedly. 'Come on, come on, I won't get jealous.'

'Well,' she said, thinking, 'he has a good bit where he says have you noticed, if you pour chips in a bowl, it's impossible not to eat one straight away? Like just one.'

There was a pause. 'Yes, he's right,' he said, with little

amusement.

'Anyway – Steve's not here to do his bit. So it's not fair to talk about it.' She frowned at him.

'Alright, alright. What about yourself – are you working on anything?'

'Actually I wrote a new book of poems… But I've been so busy. I work full time, you know. I only write when I'm waiting for the laundry.'

'But it's good that things are working out.'

'Yes,' she said. 'They are. Do you ever miss Chicago?'

'I dream about it sometimes,' he said. 'It made a big impression. I quite liked it, actually.'

'But you don't regret your decision?'

There was a long pause. Very quietly, he said, 'No, I think that was the right decision to make.'

But now their food arrived; a bowl of onion soup and gnarled bread for him and for her a saucy beefsteak. Two small glasses of mineral water were also deposited by them. He looked over the spread and, to his own surprise, emitted a little gasp of pleasure. 'Guten Appetit,' she said and they ate.

They finished their meal and walked together through the streets of the city state, sometimes speaking a little German, sometimes a little French, but always speaking to each other. The old attraction, the old bond; it was still there, but overlaid with something else – the brevity of the present. She would go tonight, go and eat with him again and, he dreamily presumed, from her interactions with his arm, her laughing at his jokes and most of all her inimitable bluntness, spend with the night with him a final time before she departed in the morning to the airport. The U.S. was far away and they would continue their lives unseen by each other.

They came to a remarkable fountain full of coins and surrounded by tourists, the base adorned by mosaics of guilds. The tiny tiles were often quite worn and faded. 'Want to make a wish?' he asked her. They approached the fountain and their bodies grew quiet together; she took and tossed a coin.

'What was it?' he said.

'You'll never know.'

The afternoon had gone even greyer. A child was standing next to them and naming things in German.

'Süß,' she said - sweet.

'It's very presumptuous of children to speak such a complicated language,' he said.

She laughed a lot although he had made the joke to her before. Had she forgotten it? He asked, 'So you're really happy then – with Steve?'

'Of course,' she said. 'He's a lovely guy, and my parents will love him.'

'They haven't met him?'

'They'll meet him next month. We're going to take the train down.'

'How romantic.'

'Yeah, and get this – it costs 80 dollars!'

'*I* met your parents,' he said.

'You did. They liked you.'

'Yeah, it was weird… You know, you can tell me if you're not happy.'

'I am happy!' She said sharply. 'Well, what about you? What are you doing?'

'Women?'

'Or boys, if that's your thing now.'

He nodded, acknowledging the dig. 'Not as of yet. Anyway – in answer to your question – there's no one in my life at the moment. I'm happy with that.'

She looked at him.

'Really. I need a break from all you women. I'm concentrating on my blog.'

'The Digest?'

'Of course the Digest - plus I've been writing journalism. Political journalism, opinion pieces, that kind of thing. I wrote a comparative piece about articles on Obama in 'The New Yorker' and Spiegel. You remember that Spiegel article on Obama just before he was re-elected – with that picture of him and just the word *Schade*? I wanted to write about how Europeans love to read about how fucked-up the U.S. is.'

'It's not that fucked up is it, really.'

He said nothing. 'That's what I want to do, anyway.'

'Write?'

'Political journalism. It's not that much of a change from the Digest, anyway. But I want to expand the blog into the realm of politics. Build up a team of writers, that kind of thing.' He improvised, 'Interested?'

'Oh no. I can't deal with politics at all. It's much too exhausting.'

He paused. 'How do you feel about it?'

'What?'

'The politics – in the U.S..'

'I think,' she said, 'It's colossally fucked up.'

He nodded, and then asked: 'Yeah?'

'It's more fucked up than I would ever imagined it'd be. People have their big cars and their big TVs and they don't give a shit. They're stuck in some kind of primitive ideology, all based on internal coercion, all these individuals arriving separately at the same decision and priding themselves on their freedom in having done it. Real freedom, well, that's something different to me. So in short – I can't blame you for bailing.'

'But I did bail, didn't I,' he said.

'Sure, you bailed. I was angry at you for a long time.'

'Not anymore?'

'Less. I've moved on,' she said. 'Now come on – let's get ice cream. How often do we see each other?'

'I don't want to get an ice cream,' he said. 'I want to keep talking about this.'

'How fucked up the States are? You've already won, Dave. It's a catastrophe. We agree.'

'Then why live there?'

'Because it's my home.'

'And that will never change.'

'I don't think so. But I really don't want to talk about it.'

He stepped away and looked at the fountain, the coin lying there still. Pedestrian traffic had briefly thinned. 'I think politics is important,' he said. 'It was a matter of conscience. How can I live there by choice? How can anyone choose to take that on?'

He looked back at her – her reaction was minimal and difficult to determine but perhaps there were hints of tears. 'Of course,' she said. 'But it's my country.'

There was a long pause. 'You're right. Let's go get ice cream.'

They walked on from the fountain, both quiet together, and past a selection of attractive shops which they had passed earlier. There was a men's clothing with a collection of ties in the window.

'Nice,' he said, looking at the fine ties.

'I'd like to buy you something,' she said. 'I mean – I never had so much money.'

'Really?' he said.

'Yeah, a tie, a shirt, a bag. Just something for you to, you know, remember me by.'

He paused, went as if to walk then stepped back slightly. 'Would that make you happy?'

'Yes, it would.'

'Well then, be my guest.'

She took him by the arm and led him into the store.

Inside the cubicle, his trousers off, he contemplated his reflection. He noticed his eyelashes grown spidery and the sleeplessness in his face.

She had brought him a tie, a purple and red one, handing it over the top of the cubicle. This place was conventional enough to have a door; often in Berlin you changed behind a drape, or there was no division between the cubicle and store at all. He also inspected a new pair of socks.

She could see his bare legs in socks beneath the door. He had always been blithely unhip, she thought, and it seemed that the last year of bachelorhood had made little difference, though she was surprised how clean and resolute he looked meeting her in the hotel this morning. It occurred to her that he was a good man: this had become somewhere forgotten over the hundreds of miles and days of separation. But he was also strangely passive, trapped in his misanthropy, committed to a Europe he had voluntarily adopted and a city of idlers which he affected to float above. A cough came from the cubicle.

'What do you think?' he said.

He was wearing the tie, his black shirt, and no pants. A bold move.

'Try the socks,' she laughed.

Back in the cubicle he wondered about his decision to do the tie joke. Still, it had appeared to be received well; it was all in his embracing of it, the conviction of his delivery, and the oversized knot. She had laughed and how good it was to play the clown again. It was just so nice to be with a woman, a young woman, with her high voice and fine hair, in their old double-act, and goof about for a moment. Since they had split he had become, he saw more clearly than ever, detached from his life: Think of the excitement a trip to this Duchy would have awakened in him earlier, whereas in his current state he had sleepwalked here, remained interior even as he stared out the window the whole train ride down. She had changed deeply of course, had changed and become more like herself. Which raised the question of whether their love had been part of her problem, had been keeping her back, keeping her from her developing. He wondered whether to kiss her; he felt certain that, if he reached out, pushing the cubicle door wildly open, he could kiss her and push her against the changing area wall, could kiss her all the way down her neck.

But he didn't. He emerged, brushing down the shirt he had been wearing before. 'You can buy me the tie,' he said.

All over Europe couples were going out, meeting, eating ice cream, sitting in cafés and regarding famous sights. Shutters clicked on monuments, and in a Berlin rehearsal room, Jakob waved a pen. Beneath the Eiffel tower the tourists moved in hordes. An American high school student stared at a Czech window that had been the sight of a medieval controversy. Barges sailed across the Danube and, in London, a conservative businessman read a newspaper in French.

For their part, they were in Luxembourg. He was waiting for her to get her coat outside the art museum. The afternoon had brightened a little and he watched a steady stream of people cross the courtyard. Perched on the side of the fountain was an old man holding his gloves in his hands. He ventured some small talk, mainly to impress her if she re-emerged: '*Tolles Wetter, geh?*' Nice weather right?

The old man, dressed in a black felt hat, nodded. 'It's normally better than this.'

His accent was English behind the German; he recognized this. He asked, 'Are you British?'.

'English, yes!' the man brightened immeasurably. 'From Kent! Pleased to meet you.'

'Dave,' he said.

'Mr. Johnnie Walker,' the man said in a laughing voice. 'You've been to the museum.'

'Yes,' he said. 'I loved it – I love fin-de-siècle art.'

'Do you? It's a very good collection. Now, myself, Velasquez is my man. I love his dark palette, you see.'

'You live in Luxembourg?'

'Me? Oh yes, I've been here forty years.'

'You must have seen a lot of changes.'

The man laughed. 'Do you know what, I haven't. Constancy, that's sort of the principle of Luxembourg. *Dauer im Wandel.*'

Constancy in change: a Goethe quote. 'It's certainly very pretty,' he said.

'Pretty? Sure, it certainly is that. Perfect for the weekend. Where are you from, may I ask?'

'London.'

'Now I do like London. It's just not that good for cycling. I like riding my bike, you see.'

'What brought you to Luxembourg?'

'Love, dear boy, love! I fell in love with a Luxembourgian. You know what they say – *cherchez la femme.*'

'Right.' And then: 'I'm waiting for a girl too.'

'Oh are you. And is she also Luxembourgian?'

'No, she's from the U.S.'

'The U.S.! I was in Atlanta, Georgia for six months before I came here. Long time ago. Bloody loved it. Cheap petrol in those days. Where's your girlfriend from?'

'Well, she's not –' He paused. 'The suburbs of Chicago.'

'Chicago! Gangster town.'

'And your wife?' he asked. 'Oh right, Luxembourg.'

'Yes. And we're still together. Been forty-one years now. I always say marriage is for life – no chance of parole!'

Anna had emerged and was crossing the courtyard now. 'This must be her,' said the older man. 'Very pretty indeed.'

'Hi!' said Anna, with a broad smile.

'And do you still like her?' he pressed.

The old man cocked his ear. 'Who? My wife? No, no. Love, not like. If I didn't love her she'd have been dead years ago.'

'What are you talking about?' asked Anna.

'Mr. Johnnie Walker here,' he said, 'Is telling me the secrets of a long and successful marriage. You'll need to know that too.'

'You're marrying?' said the old man.

Anna nodded. 'I am, yes.'

'Now listen here,' the old man said, and drew them closer with a drop of his voice. 'I'm an old man and I've been married a very long time. My wife and I – I think you could say something of a symbiosis has taken place. I've had to – we've both had to – give up a lot for each other. But I've never regretted it for a moment. And when I look at you too, setting out on that journey –' and here there was a little tremble in his voice – 'I wish both of you the very, very best. There's nothing better in life than a marriage, not children, not family, not friends.'

There was a pause. 'That's so beautiful,' Anna said.

The old man stood there, impassive. He asked, 'Would you like to come for a drink with us?'

'No, no,' the man replied. 'I have to go and meet the Missus. How long will you be in Luxembourg?'

'Until tomorrow.'

'What you must do is go and eat at *Oporto*. Luxembourg has a huge Portuguese community and for that reason some very good Portuguese restaurants. Do you know where the train station is? It's right near there.'

'*Oporto*, right,' he said, taking a note of the name in his notebook. 'Near the station, right?'

'Thank you so much!' Anna said.

Mr. Johnnie Walker bowed slightly, before, in the act of stepping away, pausing to give him a leathery wink. 'Hang on to her,' he said, and ambled off.

'Well, that was weird,' he said.

'Oh – wasn't he so sweet?'

'He thought we were a couple.'

'Well – we were.'

'Were,' he said. 'It's over.'

She paused; there was a little sunlight hitting her nose. 'What if we were a couple?'

'What?'

'I mean – when we're in Luxembourg.'

He paused. 'Do you come here so often?' But then he spoke seriously: 'Anna, I can't deal with this.'

'Just for one last day. We could say a proper goodbye to each other.'

'Anna, I can't…'

'I think we could do it.'

'I don't understand this, Anna.'

'It was just an idea.'

'Well,' he said trying to draw himself up to full height again, 'We are already doing all the things couples do anyway.'

'I know. And isn't it so nice?'

He nodded. 'You – have a boyfriend.'

'Well, I'm sure he fucks some of his comedy girls anyway. I'm pretty sure a girl called Lindsey gave him a blow job.'

'Girls called Lindsey often do.'

But the joke made things awkward, or perhaps they had already been so. The pause became a silence, the clock slanted before four.

'I thought you were angry with me,' he said.

'I was – for a long time. You let me down.'

'I let you -?'

'I felt like you let me down! But I don't feel that looking at you now.'

'What do you feel?'

She bobbed her head, 'Fonder than I thought I would.'

He sighed. 'Why did you have to come back, Anna? I've been doing fine. The Digest has been going great. We have at least 50,000 subscribers now. There's money coming in. You're stirring things up.'

'I wanted to see you.'

'Why?'

'I just did.'

'Did you really have a conference in Brussels, or was that just an excuse?'

'Of course!' Her voice raised: 'How could you even suggest that!?'

'Well, I checked the train table and I didn't see how you could have made it to the hotel for 11.00.'

'I came,' she said, voice hard and sharp, 'on the 7.42 train from Brussels North.'

He thought it over. 'Well – then I'm wrong.' She stepped away. 'I'm sorry.'

'Yeah well, you should be,' she said.

'I'm really sorry –'

'Do you think I'm desperate enough to invent a story just to see you? Indirectness has never been one of my problems.'

'No,' he said. 'That's true. I'm really sorry and take back what I said.'

'Fine. Whatever.' Her whole body language had changed, her back straightened and eyes avoiding his. 'Let's go back to the hotel.'

They had never been a couple who argued frequently – his own troubled upbringing had deprived him of any desire for that, and she had clearly been well brought up, or at least knew that fighting got you little of what you wanted – so it was strange to find themselves at contretemps during their final time together. They walked through the streets in the late afternoon, her lips pursed and head down, he quiet but occasionally coming up with novel conversational entrées such as 'Did you see Django?', 'My dad was excited I was seeing you' and 'That's High Baroque architecture.'

'I like Baroque,' he went on. But there was nothing to be done, at least now; the rage had to be waited out. He had to be punished.

Now the thought that they were no longer together became a comfort and a sort of strength. One of the good things about being in a relationship was the sense that there was always another day; that all quarrels would be resolved, that the relationship sailed through great oceans of time. Sometimes it would feel just like that, like oceans; he would lie on his back next to her in the late afternoon – they often scheduled late afternoon cuddle sessions, before one of them had to go meet friends or work – and feel like a turtle crossing the sea, some instance of nature moving over the vast blue drink.

But now there was no time. She would leave, he saw with a glance of his watch, in about fourteen hours, and he did not believe he would see her again. Therefore this argument needed to be resolved now. But how? He grasped to old tactics, stopping her on the street with a tap of an elbow.

'What?' she said.

'I'm really sorry,' he said.

'Whatever.' Then: 'I just can't believe you'd think that.'

'Do you accept my apology? It's just – We don't have much time. This is probably the last time we'll see each other.'

She was impassive. 'I accept it,' she said.

They went on walking for a long time. A homeless man was standing at the street corner, pulling the strings on an old ukulele.

'There should be a *Ukuleleverbot*,' he joked, a ban on ukuleles. 'Particularly from open mic nights.'

She was talking, head down. 'I was angry with you for a long time. I can't blame you for bailing, but I was still mad at you.'

He said nothing. They had arrived back at the hotel.

'So that's why I didn't write to you. I felt like you'd abandoned me. And – I was determined that you'd have no power over me.'

'I don't.'

'Exactly. I was determined to make my life a success.'

'Sounds like you're doing alright.'

'Yes, I am.' She looked over. 'I can't believe that you think I'd make up a story just to see you. Do you really think you're worth it?'

He smiled. 'No. God forbid that.'

'I'm sorry. That was harsh. You're right; there's no sense being angry.' She smiled. 'Come here.'

They embraced in formal fashion. She was thinner then he remembered; her physique had grown leaner and been worked upon in some scramble for employable fitness. From behind them came the sound of an accordion.

'I'm going to go and freshen up,' she said, 'and then we'll go out.'

'We could watch a movie or something,' he said. 'I'd check the listings.'

'Let's think about it. I'll come round to your room in about an hour. No 21, right?

'That's it.'

'OK. You're still a jerk.'

He laughed, 'Yes. Speaking of which, I recently had some jerk pork in London ' which he told her about as they ascended the stairs.

In his room, he checked his emails on a miniature laptop.

She for her part ran a brush through her head, television running behind.

He read an email from Jakob, full of complaints and lambasting the play's progress.

She checked her emails for news of note, receiving one full of love and cuteness from her partner.

He idly played with his genitals, flicking his hand against his foreskin, staring at his hand.

She showered and stroked gel suds over her skin.

He stopped short of ejaculating and rose to put the kettle on.

She dried her hair and smiled at friends' photos.

He sat and sipped black milkless tea, thinking about the evening's potential course.

She looked at her body in the mirror and sat on the edge of the bed.

He caught himself in the mirror and decided it was time to shave.

She applied eyeliner, powder and tights.

He hacked at tufts of peppery hair and scissored at his beard.

She sang the bit she could remember of a song she recently wrote.

He swore he heard her voice singing softly once again.

She was dressed and ready to go out.

He had shaving foam everywhere.

She looked at the cover of the book she was reading, translated from German.

Bleeding slightly, he pulled a T-shirt over his head.

She gathered her things together and made for the exit.

He was not yet ready as her knock came at the door.

'I'm almost ready,' he said, opening up.

She nodded, smiling. 'Hey.'

'Can I have a look at your room?'

'Of course.'

She hopped in like a bird along a branch, holding a magazine. He stood to the side, buttoning his shirt, pretending to look in the mirror.

'Yeah, mine's a bit bigger,' she said, looking out the window. 'You've got a nice view, though.'

Similar to yours?' he asked turning to her.

'Oh identical. I miss the way Europe looks.'

'You're looking at it now.'

'I mean when I'm home.' She flapped the magazine. 'So I took a look at the listings, and I couldn't really find anything. There's a few movies that look really sad and Asterix.'

'Not a huge Asterix fan I'm afraid.' He was slipping a tie on at the mirror.

'You're wearing a tie?'

'Yeah, is that a problem?''

'No, I think it's cool.'

'It's the one you bought me.'

He had been nervous enough to almost avoid looking at her, but now viewed her from across the room, thin, clean and fibrous in a long black dress.

'You look beautiful,' he said.

'Thanks,' she smiled. She seated herself on the bedside chair and indicated a book. 'What are you reading?'

'Thomas Bernhard.'

'Good? Looks gloomy.'

'It's very good, yes.'

'Did you ever sort out that –' she said, perching on the chair, 'that guy you had a problem with?'

'Schopenhauer?' he asked.

'Yeah, that's it.'

He was popping on cufflinks. 'It's an ongoing process. I don't think about his ideas so much – I've got the Digest.'

'You're quite successful.'

'I wouldn't say that.'

'No, you are. For Berlin you're practically a rock star.'

He couldn't keep his eyes on the mirror. 'I'm not sure Schopenhauer's as important as I thought. I see him as very German; the bloke at the side of the swimming pool telling everybody they're going to drown because he can't swim.'

There was a pause. 'What did he write?'

'*Die Welt als Wille und Vorstellung*. The World as Will and Idea.'

'Should I read it?'

'I don't know, I've never tried,' he said. 'Listen, I don't need to go to the movies. I'm happy just to go out and eat with you.'

'Sure? Not even Asterix?'

'Not tonight.'

'What about that restaurant that old dude recommended – *Oporto*?'

'It's not too far from here.'

'Then that's just great then isn't it. Should we phone and reserve?'

'I'm sure we'll be alright.' This was Berlin thinking.

'Just let me comb my hair,' he said. She raised an eyebrow. 'Okay, okay,' he said, moving to take his coat instead. He hung a moment. 'It's really nice to see you.'

'Isn't it?' she said. 'In a weird way.'

'It was always going to be weird,' he replied.

Later, he would frequently remember their walk to the restaurant as an island of happiness amidst his passage of strife, in the new challenges he would embrace and the old ones he left behind in Berlin. They walked through the Saturday streets, the pavements lamp lit, a harpist playing near a fountain. (Only here could someone busk on a harp). There were revellers and street performers, stout banks and queues at cash dispensers and embracing middle-aged couples. Occasionally there were moments to pause and take it all in: they stopped for a moment on the bridge to look back over the darkened city, its clustered train tracks and surrounding roads.

'It's pretty huh – I like it,' she said.

'Is it how you thought it'd be?' he said.

'Better.'

They crossed a further street broken up by road works; here the houses looked a little shabbier, posters for violent films visible through windows on the street. He checked their location again on the smart phone; it seemed they had to turn right. But when they turned right the location remained unclear – 'It should be here,' he said.

'The restaurant? Yes, I thought….'

'Here it is; *Oporto.*' There was a sign in the window, *Geschloßen wegen Krankheit.* Closed due to illness.

'Alrighty – *sieht nicht gut aus*,' she said.

'Yes,' he said. 'Typical German restaurant – may as well put up a sign saying '*Immer geschloßen wegen der Schwere des Lebens.*' Always closed because life's difficult.'

'Yeah – closed because of the intrinsic sadness of human life. Ha!' She asked, 'So what's the plan?'

'I did read about a few places…'

'I'm hungry,' she said.

'Shall we try walking this way?'

'Fine. Let's go.'

They walked further along the street but continued to find nothing.

'Doesn't look like there's anything here.'

'My feet hurt,' she said.

They began walking backwards the way they came.

'Shame it's closed. It's supposed to be good.'

She said nothing and just kept walking, head down.

'I'd be happy with anything to be honest,' he said.

'What about here?'

He peered in at the prices; it was an Indian restaurant. 'I'm not really big into Indian food..'

She said, with weak emphasis, 'I just need to sit down...'

'Let's go that way. I saw some places up that way.'

Ten minutes of milling about later, they returned to the Indian restaurant.

'Are you sure about this?' he said.

'It's fine. Let's just eat,' she said.

They entered and the waiter approached them eagerly, towel in hands. '*Bonsoir, monsieur-dame...*'

The room was cavernous and full of drapes. Countless tables bore orange candles and cheap paintings of deities were on the walls. Waiters moved around the couples interspersed at tables, serving gregariously, chatter in the air though the place was far from full. Of all the Indian restaurants in all the towns in all of Europe, they had to end up in this one, and this for their last meal.

'What do you think of this place then?'

'It's - interesting.'

He laughed. 'Yeah – not sure about the décor.' There was now a glass of wine at her elbow. 'How's your wine?' he asked.

'Very sweet.'

'Still. Keeps their carpets clean I suppose.'

'Strange place this. Not sure that swastika is ready to be appreciated in context. Actually, did you ever notice that when Germans tan they look like Indians?'

'That's true! Kind of weird though.'

He grinned. He was doing well. 'So did you have a good day?'

'Yes – it's been good to see you.'

'Sorry about the argument.'

'It's alright. Did you enjoy it too?'

'Yeah - it was an *Auszeit...*'

'What's that mean?'

'A break. Sort of a time out of time.'

'Are you sad?'

'That we broke up? Sometimes.' He seemed almost confused by the question. 'Why did we break up, anyway?'

'Didn't we talk about this already?"

He paused, sipping his drink. 'When else are we going to talk about it?'

'I guess you're right. Well - I've thought about it a lot,' she said. 'I'm glad we went out. And –'

'Me too,' he replied. 'And?'

'I think,' she said, very carefully, 'The reasons were pretty much those we talked about at the time. The U.S.

was too much for you.'

'It freaked me out, yes,' he said.

'Poor thing. It doesn't help that you don't drive.'

'It's not that I don't want to – Have you bought a car, by the way?'

'I don't need one. Steve drives.'

He nodded. 'I always thought that was when I could finally give you up, when you bought a car.'

'Glad I'm holding up. But you can give me up already.'

'I did.'

'Good.'

He paused one more time. 'But you haven't thought anything new, then?'

'It's more that it feels different. Some feelings stay, other ones become more distant. What do you want me to say?'

'Do you miss me?'

'Of course. And you me?'

He laughed, 'You know I do. It's funny – you know I was unsure about having a baby, but when I think about you having another man's child, I get so jealous...'

'Well, you had your chance.'

'It's not like I said no, in fairness. I thought I made my position clear.'

'You were clear. I respect that. But I'm still not convinced you really wanted them.'

'Certainly not in the U.S.' He raised a hand slightly. 'But...'

Here was the moment, then, when he had to go all in, offer his grand bargain and declare his hand. The pitch was to be made, a revision suggested, the dull certainties of successful Steve circumvented. But he looked at her and he loved her; he realized that the U.S. was her home and, if she loved to walk the streets and squares of Europe, if she was a sophisticated American who would always be at home in the world – she loved them as places to visit and not, as for him, as home.

'But?'

He inhaled. 'It's very difficult. I mean, I write the 'Misanthrope's Digest', for God's sake.'

'You don't have to. You could write the 'Optimist's Courier' or the 'Positive Gazette,'' she said.

'That sounds like a HIV newsletter,' he said sarcastically, before continuing 'Sorry, cheap joke. Listen - it's just difficult if your body doesn't have any clear feeling about it. I've not got a womb. I remember, many years ago, I was on the U-Bahn in Berlin, and I looked across at a woman and I suddenly had this forceful, pressing pain in my stomach. It was the pain of feeling that I would *never* conceive. I think many men have that pain.'

Her mouth was already open to speak. 'Not many would admit to it, though. But isn't what you're talking about exactly the opposite – Your body was giving you a message to have children?'

'It's not like that,' he said. 'The world is not a kind place – and I think it's easier to recognize that without kids. That's what Schopenhauer argued – romantic love is a delusion designed to get you to procreate.'

'I think it's more complicated than that. Anyway, did Schopenhauer have a wife?'

He shook his head. 'He was rejected.'

'Then he's hardly an expert is he?'

'I think that he saw things clearly. But also that seeing things clearly doesn't mean you're not subject to them. I don't think seeing things clearly makes much difference to them in the end. It only means you can describe what's happening to you in a more accurate style.'

'Well, for me it's already clear.'

'I'm sure it is. I'm glad it is.'

'Maybe you should just go with the flow,' she said.

'What does that mean?'

'Just have a kid.'

'Just have a kid? Just like, go for it?'

'Yeah.' She shrugged. 'Why not? It just doesn't seem like that big a deal to me.'

'Mmm!' he said, and then, angered, 'Seems like a very big decision to make for somebody else, that's all.'

She thought, as he spoke, taking such pains to be equitable, to not insult all those who bred, as she had when they were together, that he would make a good father. She saw him blessed with a little dancing singing boy and that, for all his strategizing, fatherhood would be a part of his life.

'Anyway –' she said. 'It's not really relevant now, is it? We'll just have to agree to disagree.'

'Perpetually,' he said.

They looked over the plates, where just the occasional scrap of salad or naan could be seen. They savoured the residual flavours and spices as music drifted out across the restaurant; it was Phil Collins, 'Another Day in Paradise.'

'Not half bad, was it?'

'It was awesome!' she said.

'Do you want dessert?'

'Maybe some ice cream. I don't know – do you?'

'If you're having it.'

She paused. 'No, I think not.'

'Then we'll get the bill. *L'addition, s'il vous plâit.*'

She was smiling in front of him. 'What?'

'I'm just remembering that email you wrote...'

'Which one?'

'... you called it 'Chubbo got fired." She laughed.

'Oh right - when you lost your job. Thought you'd like that. I always liked that you didn't mind me calling you such names.'

'Not 'spudface,' though. I never did get used to that.'

' Still - it's worked out well for you though, hasn't it?'

'I got my new job straight after. Second application I sent.'

'What about writing?' he asked.

'I told you already - I don't have much time at the moment. But I'm always working on new things.'

'Will you send me some of them?'

'Well,' she smiled, 'You don't quite have the access privileges you used to.'

'True. I was practically president of your fan club for a while,' he said. 'A good president, if I may say so.'

'You were a good president.'

'I was your biggest fan. Still am, in some ways.' He smiled. 'It didn't hurt that you were so damn beautiful.'

'Mmm.' Their eyes met, and what passed between them, a mixture of lust, confusion, memories and resolution, was difficult to describe.

The bill had arrived. 'Shall we pay?'

'Dutch?'

He paused and then said, 'Sure. 50-50. A straight split.'

They walked back to the hotel together. They had touched each other just once all day and now, just before leaving, as he had insisted on supplying the tip, she had placed her hand, just for a second, on his shoulder near the collar bone. So now they walked close together and his hand made little forays towards her, never quite touching her flesh. Between them was the question, a pregnant, breathy one, of what would happen next.

At the entrance to the hotel they were approached by a tramp. *'Hunn Dir kleng*?' 'do you have money?' he asked, revealing his eyes bloodshot, arms scabby and veins bulging at the neck. She hesitated but he cut through with a firm 'Sorry, no' and, with a slight push on her lacy back, pushed her up into the hotel's front door.

'Poor man,' she said.

'Very poor,' he said. 'But I never give them money.'

She looked sad as she spoke. 'It's just so sad. I see it all the time in Chicago. I mean, I'm no socialist but I just think – we have the capacity to make sure these things never happen. Can't we do something to look after these people? There is no need for that man to be out on the street. Did you see his teeth? I mean Jesus!'

He stood there respectfully frowning. She came to a halt with a cry. 'Aargh! Let's just go upstairs,' she said, waving her hands at it all. They greeted the receptionist, the same man as the morning, who nodded sternly at them.

They stood in the elevator, in silence once again. Soon the doors opened at they exited at his room.

He opened his door. He turned to her; she leant forward, they kissed.

He withdrew, heart fast in his chest.

'Wait for me,' she said.

He went into his room alone.

It was midnight; the accordions had all gone still; the street window showed only lamps and drunks. He waited for her, seated in the plastic hotel issued chair, leafing through a magazine guide to Luxembourg which would no doubt soon be only available as an app. For some reason he found himself thinking about his father.

His father was old now, and older each time they saw each other, growing more shrivelled and shinier as each year passed. Dad and he would go out drinking, talking women, growing close. Their relationship had mellowed; there was little point in being unkind. All of this was a gift, but it was a gift with an expiration date, and quite soon his father would die.

It was the imminence, the expectation, which did for you; the feeling that the phone call would come from Carol. Carol was a slightly dotty woman nearing 60 who looked after his father during the week – and would be saying that Dad had, as anticipated, died. Somehow his life was being dominated by this waiting, this anticipation of the moment where he would once again witness the rougher aspects of life – where his pessimism would be confirmed. And then he would have no parents left, no unconditional love showering him in this world.

She had kept him waiting for half an hour; he was sobering up. Steve, who he had never seen, having hidden her on Facebook, flashed into his mind. The clock ticks elongated. Would she come? He realized, sitting there, that he had since their separation learnt something.

By the time there was a knock at the door about forty minutes later, and she stepped into his room in a thin black dress and shawl, her slender legs and bare feet touching the carpet, it had become quite clear to him what he needed to do.

'Take a seat,' he said. 'I want to talk to you.'

First she wanted to make out, and they did for a little while, half-heartedly, mouths soft. But they soon noticed something was wrong. 'What?' she gasped, making little fish gulps.

'I want to talk first,' he said.

'But – we're here.' They kissed a little more, heads still knowing which way to bend.

'We need to talk.'

'Do you not want to have sex?'

'Is that really a good idea?'

'I don't mind…' She kissed more.

'Really?'

There was a pause, during which feelings floated up. 'I'm not sure,' she said.

'What about Steve?'

'Yes, Steve,' she replied. Now she was still.

'Come on. Sit on the edge of the bed.' He patted her stocking thigh, holding his fingers a second too long.

She propped herself on the bed at the wall and raised up her knees up to her chin. 'I'm ready,' she said.

'Do you remember Arnold from Berlin?'

'Yes, I do.' Pause. 'The dude with the massive beard?'

'Yes, that dude. The musician.'

'I remember him. He was with Claudia.'

'Claudia *die Schöne*.' Claudia the beautiful.

'Whatever.'

'It was you who used to call her that.'

'Did I? I don't remember.'

'Well, Claudia loved Arno and, in particular, Arno loved Claudia, and the two of them lived a fine life in Berlin. She regularly attended his shows, playing the supportive girlfriend on the front row, black-clad and beautiful and encouraging him with minimal gestures. And when he gave up music for journalism she supported that too.'

'Oh yeah, I remember! Didn't you have a crush on her?'

'We'll come to that later.

'You see, Arno was caught up in the dream, the Berlin dream, the artistic dream, and felt he and Claudia were getting too close. She'd cook him minestrone soup, and give him great blow jobs, and when she spoke of children – which would clearly be a leg brace around any aspiring expatriate musician with no money and a newfound abundance of sexual opportunities – it didn't inspire him with the terror it should.'

'I remember. Those guys were really into each other.'

'Yes. It was love. They were the kind of couple it gladdened your heart to see. Babies – you know that's always been difficult for me. But I've also always relished other people's romantic success – I really enjoy watching other people kiss.'

'You're a lover of love.'

'Right! Of love without reason. Of love beyond the sexual or societal need. Of love for its own sake. You won't believe it, but that's one of the reasons I do the Digest – it's kind of an accounting of things.'

'I can see that,' she said. 'Just about, anyway.'

'Like Arno and Claudia. Two beautiful people, that strapping Iowan singer and his Silesian bride, together and happy in beautiful Berlin.

'But trouble soon reared its lovely head. Arno, like many small-town boys who come to the big city, couldn't keep his eyes off the delights of womankind, the thousand cherries he could pick. He suddenly had groupies. Plus the intensity of his feelings terrified him and, for a man who'd moved to Berlin with only two sexual partners to his name, that led to only one response.'

'He dumped her,' she said.

'At Barcomi's café. He told me he didn't even know he was going to do it before he went in there but there was a baby crying in the next room and he was struck by a vision of hell, which quite spoilt his latté. Meanwhile, Claudia moved into a small flat in Friedrichshain and started writing a novel called '*Mundtot.*'

'Mouth dead. Nice.'

'It means silenced, more or less. Back to Arno. He now plunged himself into the sexual carnival of Berlin nightlife. He slept with people in nightclubs, took moderate amounts of cocaine – I've never been able to take people taking cocaine in Berlin seriously, cocaine being a drug associated with success – and even contracted his first STD.'

'STD? Oh, STI, right.' She went on: 'Plus I remember something: Claudia dyed her hair blond.'

'She did. She fucked around too, but it was all a bit desultory. She didn't have the constitution for decadence. Or maybe she was one of those people who, surrounded by decadence, turn square.'

'Like you?'

'I've had my day.'

'Me too. I'm turning into a little old lady.'

'Chicago drinking not suiting you?'

'Back to your story.'

He resumed. 'Thing is, after about a year, and after having treated his dripping plumbing, Arno started to regret things a little – started to think he maybe hadn't made the smartest of decisions regarding Claudia after all. She hovered before his eyes, and he found himself mooning through Facebook, noting her beauty and how lovingly she'd looked at him in the few photos they'd had together. There was one image in particular, of him lifting a comedy foam hand with his other arm wrapped around her that frequently brought Arno to tears. Claudia had her problems, as you know, but she'd seemed to find her best form with him about – and

410

support his journalistic ambitions, even the time he failed to show for a date and called her to apologize from Iran.'

'He wanted someone who'd let him do such things,' she said.

'That's right – who found them exciting. One night – one morning – in *Bohngeld*, - a place you once described to me as "always a mistake", he confessed to me his undying love for her and swore me never to touch her.'

'Did you like her?' she asked.

He paused. 'I did. I met her at the same time as you, and always felt I'd be happy with one of you.'

'I always thought so,' she said. 'Maybe you picked the wrong one.'

'Yeah, well,' he said. 'Around this time, unknown to Arnold, I had begun spending some time with Claudia. Last Christmas I didn't go home – I mentioned it to you in an email – my father was drinking a lot, and I couldn't face Aunt Pam's remarks this year. So I found myself celebrating Christmas in a smoky Neukölln bar with Claudia and Carlo.'

'Carlo the religious shoemaker?'

'The very one – Godly Shoes, blue with a lot of sole. I have a pair, actually, but sadly the stitching's coming apart. Anyway, Claudia was resplendent as ever – she's a beautiful woman as you know – and I began to work on her. Not so much, you know, because my heart was still full of yourself, but we have to give men some credit here: In the area of flirting we can multitask indeed.'

She gave a thin smile. He responded embarrassedly and

resumed, 'Claudia liked my entreaties. We went to a sex club and she messaged me that I was hot. I watched her kiss a gigantic Aryan man and pissed off the bar staff by asking them for tap water.'

'Only you,' she said, 'could order tap water at a sex club.'

'From a man dressed as a gimp.'

'Did you like it there?'

'I eventually came to the conclusion it wasn't the best place to bring a girl on a date. Anyway – Claudia's signals were one minute flirtatious, the next confused.'

'And Arno?'

'He played no role in my thinking at this time.'

'You wanted to fuck her?'

'I wanted,' he said quietly, 'to get her into bed.'

'Say fuck. Don't be so British.'

'No.'

'Fuck. Fuck.'

He looked up coolly. 'It soon came to a moment where I had to stick or twist. But I was thinking of all the relationships I'd had which hadn't worked out – my last two relationships, you know, ended at airports. I asked myself: is there any reason why this relationship will be different? I didn't see it. So I wrote her a letter about love. Not a love letter. A letter *about* love.'

'What did it say?'

He took up the letter, still positioned on the table, and

began to read.

Dear Claudia,

I have never seen the point of unrequited love. Years
of passion for some unattainable person, years wasted
while a hundred other beautiful people, a hundred
other potential lives probably all equally as good as the
one denied to you go by – what a waste, like those
high school kids who eat only McDonalds while on a
trip abroad. Romantic fantasy is perhaps best left to
art, where, free from practical concerns and questions
of sustainability it can flourish beyond all measure and
generate the most unexpected consequences. Of course
giving a person up to the muse like this is also giving
up of the delusion of ever getting them back or indeed
having them in the first place. The moment you decide
to create work about someone life sells out to art, and
art usually pays it back in book sales, posthumous fame
or third party admirers far removed from the initial
state of affairs.

At the same time, you see the irony: to write or
create really convincingly about a romantic passion
almost inevitably means that said passion is dead or
at least unrealistic, or you would not have sold it to
art in the first place. If you really are realistically in
love with someone, you're probably not writing them
poems; instead, they are sitting in your kitchen, and
are probably planning what colour you're going to paint
your first child's bedroom. (Black I jokingly suggest.)

Still, I do wonder if art has ever made anybody change their mind about someone else. If, when what an ex-friend of mine memorably called 'the old humans' received letters from their suitors, say a poem or a novel dedicated to them – or for a scientist perhaps a particularly beautiful mathematical equation – I wonder if they ever changed their minds. To repeat the question: Do you think a poem has ever convinced one human being to love another?

The trouble is that a poem is nothing like its author; falling in love with someone on the basis of a poem is a poor indicator for loving the person themselves. Given this, perhaps the relationships that work are the ones we need to write about the least, the ones which just keep ticking over; as Chris Rock says, only bad relationships are interesting, given that 'You never know what's going to happen tomorrow in a bad relationship.' For my part, I see the state of contentment a good relationship brings as an artistic challenge; to write well of happiness, to depict the predictable progression of well-matched love, requires more skill than describing doomed passion, where everyone cries in the end.

You are looking, you tell me, for love. My question to you is: Are you prepared to be boring? That is how marriage vows should read, I suggest: 'Do you consent to be boring with me until one of us dies first?' 'Forever?' 'Forty years if we're lucky.' For real love is reliable; it may stink and it may moan but it will be there at the hospital, the nursery and the deathbed. It will be there at about the time expected behaving approximately as you expected it would and its consistency is its charm.

The idea of 'looking for love' is fundamentally strange to me. This is because, to elaborate upon my personification above, love just turns up. It moves into your house one day and sits there on your sofa smoking its filthy roll-ups which you implore love to quit. Love's head will be forever in front of the TV screen and it always has vague plans, meaning with love around you can barely watch a programme or even go out to see your friends without it getting all upset. Some things you can only do *without* love in your life. So why covet something, romantic love, which will make other things, and other wonderful things, impossible? Things like learning languages, travelling and having a small amount of money of your own. (Love is a terrible spendthrift). You could be working very hard at something and really starting to make progress when love turns up and spoils your concentration. So you throw your pen at love and shout: 'Love, now I'm in love with you and you've fucked everything up!' Your future mutated, your concentration shot, at this stage you may even begin to resent love.

It would surely be better to say: I am looking forward to the experience of love. Me too, and being in love is very nice. I am looking forward to a time when the forest of trees in my heart has been replanted, where the ashen foliage there is springing into verdant life again, when my heart's carburettor has been refitted and is chugging along like a freshly refurbished Volvo. I am looking forward to buying cakes for someone and cycling home to them. I am looking forward to the touch in the morning and the warm waking at night. I am looking forward to that time, but now is *not* that time, and it is easier for me to imagine that time now than it will be for me to remember this time then. Put plainly: It is quite possible to imagine being in love while single but almost impossible to imagine being single while in love. That's one reason it hurts so much when a relationship comes to an end and you have to get off the ride: You simply haven't been thinking of it coming to an end, absorbed in it as you were.

Romantic love, then, is sadly not enough. What does that make romantic love? It makes it *some* of enough. At the same time, it seems clear that the meaning of life is to love; to love, but not to be *in* love. I feel love frequently and often; I have been overwhelmed by love for supermarket cashiers. It is highly unlikely that I was ever in love with them particularly as none of them seemed especially memorable and the only affection they expressed for me was in giving me plastic bags. What I mean by this is that you need to find a love for, and in despite of all the deprivations we still insist on putting each other through, your fellow humans. To insist on one person as more important than everyone else is back to the child who only eats one food, or here perhaps the man who only listens to one album, believing as he does that Lana Del Rey will marry him despite the nice girl next door who actually wants do so.

Speaking of attractiveness, if you are very beautiful – which I am not - it likely makes it more common that people love you without really knowing you, that they feel the general joy I am advocating just at your very existence. I think we are too quick to disapprove of this kind of erotic love. To love people for their beauty is to at least love them for something. It is as not as if people stay beautiful forever, either. When are you going to tell people that they are beautiful? – When they are old and ruined and need to hear it because it is no longer true? I advocate instead the praise of beauty where we find it, without needing to damn the ugly with over-honesty; let us praise the beautiful and say nothing to the hideous. Though following my logic here, the ugly would know they were ugly because they would not be praised. And they would ask to be so. The ugly are insecure.

But I digress. I wish of course that you do find love. I wish everyone finds this. But I also view it, as a statement, as equivalent to 'I hope my birthday will be on day x this year' or 'This apple better taste of apple.' Why wish for something which will inevitably be the case? And why wish so hard for something which is, as an experience, equivalent to going mildly insane? It is exciting to be on a storm at sea but after a few years it might get a little distressing and plus you can't get any work done. Or, worse, you can, and you get used to the storminess, just lie there yawning as the waves crash around in all their wild beauty.

What I wish you is a love that can last and suspect as I age that the hardiest love is that which, rather than being invited, creeps up on you by surprise. Maybe looking for love is the least likely way of finding it. Why don't you look for something else, like a hairpin or a Harry Truman for President pin? Seen like this, finding love is often the accidental by-product of a search for something else entirely. Set out on a journey and love will be a character you meet along the way, and they will hopefully tag along, become involved in your story.

An ex-girlfriend of mine said something which stays

with me: 'The two lovers are not looking at each other but at the world.' More than romantic love, I wish you a love of the world, of its great cities, old trade routes and modern flight paths. I wish you to get in tune with the universe or at least learn to hum along with it. You appear to already love life – believing in love at all is a good indication of this – so love it more.

Strange that even in the smallest of flirtations there is an element of futurity meaning that, even when only talking drunkenly to a stranger in a bar, you subconsciously imagine marrying and having children with them: you see them stood at the altar approaching or arguing with you over moving boxes. Then they reveal they have a partner and your heart gives a little sigh. (I believe this is colloquially called 'the boyfriend bomb.' I once saw a girl drop it so thoroughly it destroyed a small German town.)

But now in these moments of emergent truth another part of me watches from a distance and feels as much joy at another prospective sale to art as if the love were to really be requited. I wonder if by now I have gotten too eager to do business, if I feel I know love too well, like a golfer who has forgotten the beauty of the links. As such I will close this letter in happy anticipation of one of my favourite loves, that of all which I do not yet know or will never know in the many years I intend to live yet.

Yours as ever,

Dave

After a while she spoke. 'I like it. Different from how you

normally write.'

He nodded. 'You think? It came from the heart.'

'And what about her?' she said. 'Did she write back?'

'Yes she did. I have it with me here.' He produced the letter, its handwriting visible, but then made a dismissive gesture waving it in the air. 'I'm not sure she'd want me to read it you that's all.'

'Oh go on! Who am I going to tell?'

He pursed his lips. 'Well – I suppose. I can't imagine she'd mind...' He looked down the page: 'Ah yes... Love...... She's written little headings in the margins, can you see? And drawn pictures. This one's called 'Ego & Eros.'

He read an extract, saying, 'Picture her saying this,' Claudia at her desk, looking out the window on grey East Berlin, writing,

'Dave,

Ranting about love is one of my dearest hobbies. Though, for me, debating love takes less the form of an essay and more of long contradictory phrases, disrupted sentences and perplexed interjections.

Not that I'm too cynical to feel it. On the contrary, I feel it much too often, but it's not meaningful... I fall in love (just as you do) every single day with at least five men, random people I see on the train to work or queuing for soya lattes in the morning or simply not giving a damn in some bar. And the best thing about it is that it rarely develops beyond a few fugitive looks - otherwise where will we end up. This inability to choose one over all others that appear just as beautiful and interesting and smart and driven and and and - well, it's unsettling. That is why I prefer to imagine their stories than to get to know them and thereby retrieve them to banality. The same applies for revealing my own un-specialness, as I too am not spared by the mundane. I do laundry, I have bad hair days, I talk about the weather, I waste time on Facebook etc...

For me, if love doesn't feel like a blindfolded *montagnes rousses* ride, suffocated with deliciously disgusting cigarette smoke, then it's not love. It can't be love, unless it takes you through both heaven and hell. Without stop. Exhausting love. Destructive love. But damn, it's all worth it. As love makes me ME, it awakes the ambitious me, the hungrier me, the creative me, the healthier and more active and attractive me, the better me. Which makes love also egoistic. But that is ok.'

'You get the idea,' Dave said.

'I like it,' she said. 'She's very cool; I remember her now.'

'Indeed,' he replied. 'Her English is good too.'

He resumed. 'So we had this exchange. And, as is the way of these things, it had at least in part the opposite results as intended; her interest was piqued. She thought it was cool – that there was a lot of truth in what I wrote – and I felt that if I kept my head clear now I could win her. You know, sometimes winning someone's heart becomes a task. Like with you.'

She was impassive.

'Around this time Arno and I met a few times and we were at the Indian Embassy one day for the launching of a new range of Indian spices – the milder spices given a higher heat level for plain German tastes – that he resumed his confession in full. He wasn't in a mess, was suited and clean-shaven, which made what he said convincing: he had seen Claudia for lunch recently and was certain, he said, that he had passed up on the love of his life.

Suddenly it became clear to me what had to be done. By a mixture of happenstance and calculation – in other words by living – the path suddenly became clear. Normally my advice to Arno's confession would have been dismissive; forget about her, move on, there are plenty more fish in the sea. But I saw that, however tiny, there was now an opportunity for him. He just had to go, as you used to say, balls out.

I told him to confess to her. She was single. He'd need to talk marriage and babies and property. A ring would need to be supplied ASAP. He'd need to self-immolate in her presence and beg her to put him out. He'd need to sacrifice a lot; forget journalistic assignments to the North Pole, forget freedom – for now anyway – and pack up the guitar for good. Forget fucking around.'

'What did he say?'

'He just kept nodding and saying, "I hear you bro, I hear you."'

'And?' she said. 'What happened next?'

And so he produced his third and final exhibit, a small piece of card displaying the following information.

YOU ARE INVITED TO / DU WIRST EINGELADEN AUF

The Marriage of   / Die Hochzeit von

Matthew Arnold Jefferson   Claudia Gottesschenk

'Typical that the German comes second,' he said and leant back.

Silence in the room. Telling and discussing the story had taken nearly an hour; the night had deepened and grown quiet.

'Do you understand what I'm saying?' he asked.

'Maybe.' She stretched her legs from the bedside. 'I need to think about it. Don't you wish we were smoking right now?'

'Still off them, I'm afraid,' he said.

'I wish we had music then. Leonard Cohen.'

'That he feeds you tea and oranges?'

'That come all the way from China. Or maybe - the sisters of mercy, they are not departed or gone...'

'They were waiting for you, when you had the strength to go on...'

'I love that song,' she said. 'Love. It.'

They had sung it together, but now he spoke again, asking 'You know what he wrote it about?'

'Mmm?' she was back on her feet now. 'Wasn't it about a

threesome?'

He laughed. 'Check you out with the knowledge! Shame we can't recreate it.'

'Well, it was your call. We're short on numbers anyway. Listen – Dave - maybe I should go to bed.'

'No –' he said, very firmly. 'Please stay. This might be the last night we ever spend together.'

She turned to him, pulling down her dress, and moving a step towards him. 'Yes – you might be right.'

'Well,' she said, looking across to where he sat in quiet contemplation, standing up to stretch her legs, 'I guess I should tell a story as well. I've never been much of a storyteller to be honest. But I did hear something that I really liked recently. Remember my friend Carly?'

'I do. She was very attractive.'

'Oh, it's all coming out now, isn't it? Anyway – she was telling me a story about her Dad, Peter. He grew up on a farm in Texas. Real heavy Southern Baptist atmosphere. Carly's not religious at all, as you know. She's more a Bacardi and blow jobs kind of girl.

Anyway, religion doesn't seem to have done anyone in that family much good. Or at least their variety of it. They used to beat him with a hard black boot, and lock him out the house in his briefs.'

'Why?'

'There's a kind of sadism that gets into people in the middle of nowhere. Far from all the checks and balances. And they abused each other too. Peter said one time his Mom was sitting at the table and his dad entered, spat at her and walked out. Really, just like that.

Peter saw all this and one day, looking out across the plains with wind churning the dust, resolved that he would never have a family of his own. He resolved that he would never bring someone into the suffering of this world, to be beaten and kicked and spat on at will or, even worse, then be hugged and kissed when neighbours visited.'

'His parents were sociopaths,' he said.

'All parents are sociopaths. Wanting to become a parent is inherently crazy. We agree on this.'

'But you still want kids.'

'Yes I do.'

'Well, how do you square that?'

'I don't. Anyway, back to the story. Eventually Peter got away – he got a job working near Austin. He was a notary at a law firm, and at night studied for his legal exams. In those days, there were still decent stipends, and just as many lawyer jokes.

It was one day at that legal firm that he met Marigold –'

'Carly's mother.'

'Right. She was wearing a floral print dress – Marigold said she wore it just because she had seen him before and thought he was so cute – and had her blond hair done up in a bun. The light was coming through the window of the legal office, and Peter said the world stopped when he saw Marigold.

This was in the mid-70s and Austin was still quite cool. They bathed in springs, drank cheap beer, went for Sunday drives. They fell in love – there'd been no prohibition in Peter's vow of that, remember. But already it was becoming clear that Marigold and he were getting close, 'already becoming a family' as Obama writes in one of his books.

One day over a big brunch at her place she asked him whether he wanted children. Peter went white as a sheet! He equivocated, said that it was a difficult question which she would have seen, if she had known him better, was already a step toward her. She said he'd make a wonderful father and, he, if he had understood the jerks she'd dated before, would have known what a compliment that was too.'

'You told me I'd make a good father,' he said.

'You *would*,' she said, and resumed; 'But Peter couldn't deal with it. He went very pale and said, quaking, that he presumed she wanted kids.

'Of course I do. And with you,' said Marigold.

'So, time passes. Things are left, you know, to bubble under. They take a lot of road trips. And the way Peter tells the story – I'm not a storyteller, remember – is that she was out of town one day. He went to meet her at the airport and was waiting outside in the car, when after an hour she still hadn't come through. So he went into the lounge and saw her flight was delayed. He sat down at the bench, looking up at the arrivals board. According to the information she would be through soon.

'There was an old man there. "Waiting for someone?"

"My girlfriend, sir."

"Where's she from?"

"Dallas."

"She pretty?"

"Yes, sir, very."

"You should get married," said the old man. "I miss my wife every damn day. Miss my kids too – but they're okay. It's my wife that I miss."

"She's passed, sir?"

"Two years ago. Heart. I'm waiting for my son here, he's coming from California."

"From LA?"

"Yeah, he's trying to make it as an actor. God knows he's good-looking enough. Gets it from his mother. You got kids?"

"No, sir."

"Planning to?"

"I – " Peter paused and then looked at the man directly. "I don't know." You know how sometimes you get open with a stranger. Particularly in the U.S.

The old man goes on, "Take it from me, kids are the most fun you're gonna have. I lost a million dollars once. All wiped out. Know what? I didn't give a damn, because that week my oldest brought home a science prize. Nothing can hurt you if it don't hurt them."

"What if they get hurt?"

426

"Yeah, that's bad. But you can only do your best. And you get freedom – because 99% of things aren't gonna bug you no more."

Peter had gone quiet.

"Listen buddy, take it from me," said the old man. "I've made a lot of mistakes in my life. I busted up a guy's face in a *taqueria* in Houston real bad; when I was twelve I stole a car. But the one thing I did real good was to have kids. You sit that nice little lady of yours down and quit thinking about what you gotta do and do it. I can see it in you – you're one of those professor types. Just quit worrying so damn much."

At this point a tall, young man could be seen crossing the airport foyer in cream slacks with one hand raised. The old man stood, beaming, and waved. He checked before he exited, and said: "Follow your dick and your heart and you'll be alright."

A couple of hours later Marigold came through customs, and he kissed her like a man holding his coat to himself in a storm.'

'So they got married,' he said.

'They got married, and Carly was born six months later.'

'Ha!' he said. 'He didn't have a choice anyway.'

'Oh, he had a choice – he had to learn to actively love his fate. And they're so good, Dave, they're just so good; I've never seen such a happy family. They're just a team.'

'It's a nice story,' he said. 'Reminds me of Mr. Johnnie Walker.'

'Who?' she asked and yawned. 'Oh yes, the guy we saw today.'

'Do you think that was his real name?'

'I don't know. Listen, I'm sleepy; I should...'

'No – please stay just a while more. I'll wake you.'

Now was the time to tell her the things he needed to, what he had thought about the year previously, the deep insights of his heart in the few remaining hours. (It was now two in the morning). He wanted above all to acknowledge the sadness, to say that it was not right what had happened to them, as to so many of their generation, where people met and formed the most amazing bonds, came close to the most incredible people, and then lost them forever like some precious deleted file. He wondered if he would ever love someone so much again.

But when he turned she was fast asleep. He went to the side of the bed and pulled the blanket over her legs. She gawped a little. Her mouth was slightly open, face in its normal slumbering repose, chest sighing gently up and down. He stared at her and listened to her breathing, integrated with the deep quiet of night. For a few minutes he sat next to her watching her, moving through trusted sequences of thought, before he himself fell into a doze on the chair, a light sleep dominated by dreams of the person who slept before him.

But before he fell asleep he did one little thing. He went to his bag and took out the chocolate he had forgotten about, and very quietly placed it into the pocket of her shawl.

They were woken a few hours later by the beeping of her phone alarm. She inhaled and sounded a series of ws – 'Wa – wah – uu – oh, righty.'

'Hey,' he said, still seated, bleary.

'Shit! My train is in an hour and a half.'

'Go and pack. I'll come with you to the station.'

'Sure?'

'Just go and pack.'

She got up, pulling her dress down to her legs. 'I can't believe I fell asleep,' she said.

He quickly showered and changed his underwear. Downstairs he asked the receptionist to call a taxi. Outside, it was turning light.

She emerged, packed and neater, her hair brushed back to its new fringe again. 'Did you -?'

'Yes,' he said. *'Danke für die Unterkunft,'* he said to the receptionist, who gave a slight unimpressed nod.

The taxi was waiting round the corner. He helped her carry her bag. The driver dropped it in the boot with a satisfying clunk and they drove to the train station.

'So you're picking up the flight at Brussels?'

'Did I not tell you? I'm going to London to see Carly on the Eurostar.'

He smiled. 'I didn't even know she was in London.'

The streets were quiet; Luxembourg, never wild, was not inclined to Sunday morning haste. Old baroque houses, large gardens and blackened sandstone gargoyles could be seen; the whole city slept in beauty.

'How long will you stay for?' he asked.

'Just four days, then back to Chicago,' she said.

'Surprised you got so much time off,' he said. There was no answer.

The taxi driver had put on the radio and it was John Lennon, a solo record, singing 'I'm just sitting here watching the wheels go round and round...'

They disembarked at the station; he asked to pay but in the end she insisted. 'Merci,' she said, and they began their walk towards the station entrance.

'Platform seven,' he said. 'Plenty of time.'

They ascended a flight of stairs, he helping her carry the carry-on. 'What do you keep in this thing?'

'Books, mainly,' she said.

They passed a small bakery, and she went back to pick up a croissant and coffee – there had been no time at the hotel. He smiled as she waited. Then they went up to the final elevator to platform seven.

'Ten minutes.'

'On time,' she said quietly.

They waited.

'You know,' he said, 'In one sense I'm happy.'

'What?' she said.

'When I first met you, my ambition was not to break up with you at an airport. And here we are at a train station. Of course we're already broken up. But still – this is where it ends, at a train station.'

She nodded, saying, 'A very beautiful one too.'

'What else do we live in Europe for but beauty?'

'I do miss the way it looks.'

'When will the wedding be?'

'Summer.'

'Am I invited?'

'Do you want to come?'

'No. Although I'm sure there'll be lots of cute girls there.'

'Yeah – there will be. Some of them looking for husbands.'

'I wish them well in their search. Are you excited?'

'Of course...'

The train was coming, curving and sliding round the track in the distance.

'So.'

'So.'

'Seat number?'

'Oh, I'll find it.'

'We should have lined ourselves up.'

'Well – something to do on board isn't it?'

'Yeah – keep yourself busy.'

She smiled. 'I guess this is goodbye.'

'That's exactly what it is.'

'Will I see you again?'

'I don't know. Where?'

'Yeah. Exactly.'

'Can I do anything for you?'

There was a pause. The train was now there.

'You've already done a lot. Thank you.'

'No problem. Any time.'

'Are you going to stay in Berlin?'

'I don't know.'

'OK, then – I'll write you a postcard.'

'Do it.'

She was crying quite a lot now, and he would have if he could. They embraced; it didn't seem right not to. He held her body very close for a while and then she ducked out of it. He looked at her hard; her little button nose, her thin, red-tinted hair. He saw her as an older woman – that was what came next.

'Thank you,' she said, a tear falling down.

'Your carriage awaits!'

She backed off and began to walk away from him. He stayed there on the train platform as she moved towards a central door. There was a porter standing there. As she reached the porter she turned and waved and, brushing her hand over her lips, blew him a little kiss. It headed towards him and, after a couple of seconds, a suitable time, he acted as if it had struck him hard. She saw this – it was the last thing she saw – and gave a big smile. The train doors closed and the porter blew their whistle.

He stood very still on the platform for a while, the train still standing in front of him. He decided against going forward, turned and headed out of the train station and to the exit floor. He found a relevant bus, stepped on and rode on before disembarking at the hotel, where he walked up to his room and, hearing the bells strike for eight o'clock, fell asleep on his made bed.

EPILOGUE

On a bright spring day several months later, Dave Benthorpe went for a coffee with Stuart Holmes meeting at Knöfi, a small Turkish café in *Bergmannstraße*. The two expatriate Englishman had become close over the last months, and also happened to live very near to each other, making it possible to squeeze in this last meeting. Stuart was hunched over a piece of paper writing when Dave arrived.

'Good to see you, mate,' said Stuart standing to shake his hand.

'We've got some time,' Dave said. 'My train is not until 12.40.'

Dave ordered and sat next to Stuart near the door. 'So –

excited?' asked Stuart.

'Pretty much,' Dave said. 'I mean – I don't have much there apart from friends.'

'You're going to be fine,' said Stuart. 'I sent you Luigi's number, right?'

'Yes, thanks.'

'I met him in Heidelberg last year, he's a good guy. He's running a whole chain of pubs over there now. You can do quite well with pub work in London. I mean, not that I ever did it.'

'I'll need to earn more than here, that's for sure.'

'Well, there are only four jobs in Berlin.'

Dave laughed, and Stuart asked him; 'Will you miss Berlin?'

'Sure, I miss it already.'

'Even though you're here?' Stuart smiled. 'In London you need money. Pieces of paper. Facts.'

'I do have a degree from LSE,' he said.

'I know, I know. You're ready.' Stuart tapped him on the arm. 'Berlin will miss you.'

'I'll miss it. My whole adult life here.'

'Adult life? *Das wurde bisher in Berlin nicht gefunden.*'

Which translated: adult life was not found in Berlin until now. They laughed at the joke.

'And Anna?'

'I haven't heard from her in a while, actually. Her wedding's coming up soon, I'm sure.'

'How you feeling about that then?'

'I've come to realize,' Dave said, 'that to love someone like that is a great source of strength.'

'Very poetic!' Stuart shook his head. 'And it's funny because Dave you know honestly – I tell you this as friend – I never really liked her.'

There was a pause. 'You know,' Dave said, 'I don't think that really makes any difference. Anyway – what are your plans?'

'Oh you know, same as always, keep gigging. I've got a tour of East Germany coming up; think it's Dresden, Chemnitz, Zwickau. And Leipzig. And I have a job interview for a secretarial role at a dentists. You know, typical Berlin.'

'No money, lots of freedom,' Dave said.

'Exactly. You know how it is.'

'I do. It's all I know.'

'I will miss you,' said Stuart. The Englishman looked across, melancholy in his green eyes. 'I kind of envy you going back you know. Maybe I will one day. Now excuse me, I need a shit.'

When Stuart emerged Dave was stood looking down Bergmannstraße, at its cafés and craft shops, looking contemplative. Stuart tapped him on the shoulder, pointing then to his small carry-on.

'You should sit on that thing.'

'What?'

'In Russia, before a journey, you sit on your luggage.'

'I didn't know that.'

'Well, go on then.'

'But I'm not Russian –'

'Neither am I!' Stuart replied. 'Come on, what'll it hurt?'

'OK.' Dave sat on the luggage, rising up pretty quickly. 'There, are –'

'No! Not like that! You have to sit down and contemplate your journey.'

'For how long?'

'Several days. I don't know! A minute?'

Dave gave a slight sigh, but only the sigh of the secret enjoyer. 'Alright – I get it.' So he perched down on the luggage again, the little handle jolting his rear. For a long moment he sat there, looking up at the city, thinking about things; he felt a tightness in his throat. Finally, 'That's alright,' he said.

'Great,' said Stuart, and leant forward to hug Dave. 'Take care buddy,' Stuart said.

'I will.'

They looked at each other; Dave smiled, nodded, and began walking.

'Is that all your stuff?' Stuart asked.

Dave looked back, saying, 'I put the rest in storage,' before continuing.

'Take care! Do it well!' called Stuart.

He walked along *Riemannstraße* to the U-Bahn. The snow season was drying off, and the buildings had that worn but chipper quality he had loved so much when arriving all those years ago. Arriving here, in this very area, this little square to which his world had been boiled down. He could see pedestrians and dog-walkers further down the street, parked bicycles and open windows in the grand North European townhouses. He stopped and enjoyed the view before him, thinking about all which had brought him here before, dragging his little carry-on, he wheeled straight down the street to move through the underground and leave the city of Berlin.

Berlin/London 2012 – 2022

ACKNOWLEDGEMENTS

I worked on this book for so long that I've almost certainly forgotten some of the people who helped me with it. To those people, my thanks, and please don't view it as a slight that the flood of experience has swept your contributions from easy recall.

First of all, I'd like to thank two of the people who were most assiduous in helping me edit the manuscript, Dr Richard Bates and Dr Jenny Chamarette, both of whom read multiple drafts. Both of you improved the text immensely, which is what you want from your editors really.

Thanks of course to all in the Berlin English language comedy scene, the sauce in which this book stewed. There are too many people who supported me in that time, but Paul Salamone, David Deery, Caroline Clifford, Perry Filippeos, Neil Numb and Dharmander Singh are all worthy of particular thanks. *Mulțumesc* too to Cristina Katana, who provided some of the material for the love letters in the second section. And special mention to Chris Davis, who may well recognize something of himself in one of the characters here – well, who definitely did - but who, in the true Berlin spirit, wasn't bothered about it at all.

Thanks to my London supporters too, Paula Varjack, Jonathan Nassim, Alan Cunningham, Philip Womack for the read and of course, Chris Hogg, who has gone above and beyond in his support for my work. And a big thanks to Ariane Sherine, for both designing the cover, proofreading the manuscript and encouraging me to go down the self-publishing route.

Infinite thanks are of course due to my parents, whose financial support in my early youth enabled me to live my German dreams. They have brought me so much.

And finally thanks to Ke Zuo, the illustrator who provided the images for this book and who also happens to be my wife. This book waited a long time to come into the world, and now we can all see why; it was waiting for her pictures to make it complete.

ABOUT THE AUTHOR

Ke Zuo

Ke Zuo was born in Guilin, China, in 1991. She lives in London and is active in a range of visual media.

ABOUT THE AUTHOR

James Harris

James Harris is a writer and comedian from Nottingham, England. He Tweets @JamesHarrisNow, and writes a weekly Substack newsletter called Stiff Upper Quip.

Printed in Great Britain
by Amazon